# CONFEDERADO DO NORTE

## LINDA BENNETT PENNELL

SOUL MATE PUBLISHING

New York

CONFEDERADO DO NORTE

Copyright©2014

LINDA BENNETT PENNELL

Cover Design by Fiona Jayde

This book is a work of fiction. The names, characters, places, and incidents are the products of the author's imagination or are used fictitiously. Any resemblance to actual events, business establishments, locales, or persons, living or dead, is entirely coincidental.

All rights reserved. No part of this publication may be reproduced, stored in a retrieval system, or transmitted in any form or by any means (electronic, mechanical, photocopying, recording, or otherwise) without the prior written permission of both the copyright owner and the publisher. The only exception is brief quotations in printed reviews.

The scanning, uploading, and distribution of this book via the Internet or via any other means without the permission of the publisher is illegal and punishable by law. Please purchase only authorized electronic editions, and do not participate in or encourage electronic piracy of copyrighted materials.

Your support of the author's rights is appreciated.

Published in the United States of America by
Soul Mate Publishing
P.O. Box 24
Macedon, New York, 14502

ISBN: 978-1-61935-811-9

ebook ISBN: 978-1-61935-500-2

www.SoulMatePublishing.com

The publisher does not have any control over and does not assume any responsibility for author or third-party websites or their content.

## Acknowledgements

I am the most fortunate of women. The support and encouragement received from family, friends, my editor, and my critique partner has been tremendous. My gratitude is greater than words are adequate to express. In addition, the camaraderie among the Soul Mate Publishing family and the northwest Houston writing community is phenomenal. One may hear that authors are a jealous, envious, cantankerous bunch, but this has not been my experience. It has been quite the opposite, in fact. I have found the writing community to be among the most supportive and generous I have ever experienced. And so to friends, family, and colleagues, I want to say thank you from the bottom of my heart. You have created the joy in my writing journey.

## Chapter 1

I dreamt the dream again last night. In the small hours, I awoke in a tumble of bedclothes and bathed in perspiration despite the howling snowstorm blanketing the city. I rearranged quilts and plumped pillows, but sleep remained elusive. My mind refused to be quiet.

As often happens after such a night, I felt unable to rise at my usual hour and remained abed long after the maids cleared breakfast from the morning room. My daughter-in-law, bless her heart, meant well. I told her it was ridiculous to bring the doctor out on such a frigid day, but apparently the very old, like the very young, are not to be trusted in matters of judgment. After the doctor listened to my chest, a studied sympathy filled his eyes and he gently suggested that perhaps I should get my affairs in order. No doubt he wondered at my smile for he couldn't have known I have no affairs other than my memories and the emotions they engender.

Unlike most elderly persons, I don't revel in slogging through the past. It isn't wrapped in pretty ribbons or surrounded by a golden aura. Instead, its voices haunt my dreams, demanding and accusatory. Until recently, I've resisted their intrusion into my waking life, but I now believe the past can no longer remain buried in nocturnal visions. It must be brought out into the light of day. From its earliest moments onward, the past's substance must be gouged out, pulled apart, and examined bit by bit until its truth is exposed. While total objectivity may not be possible,

I have concluded that committing the past to paper is my best hope for sorting facts from imaginings. Perhaps then I will achieve the peace that has so long hidden its face from me.

You see, when I was quite young—only a girl really—I killed four people. Two were dearly beloved, one was a hated enemy, and the last was a dangerous criminal.

## Chapter 2

My story begins at the end of a terrible war, one that destroyed many lives and much property. But for that war and a handful of newspaper editorials and advertisements, my life would have turned out quite differently. Sometimes it seems no time at all has passed since I was a nine-year-old child standing on the deck of a ship watching home disappear over the horizon.

Warm Gulf breezes tugged at the brim of my bonnet, setting its ribbons dancing. Leaning over the *Alyssa Jane's* railing, I stared back in the direction of Mobile Bay and pretended I could see the dock where my beloved Bess stood, probably still waving. Mama, her pretty features marred by a furrowed brow and down turned mouth, paced beside me.

"Mary Catherine MacDonald! Get down before you fall overboard. All we need right now is another crisis. And stop wiping your nose on your sleeve."

Mama didn't seem to understand anything anymore. Before we left home, she was calm and kind. Afterward, she snapped at the least little thing. I threw her a hateful glance, but she had already turned away, so I stubbornly leaned a little farther out over the railing. The wake trailing behind the *Alyssa Jane* looked like a blue-green path lined on either side by mounds of ginned cotton, a path pushing me away from the only life I had ever known. Only my sniveling broke the silence of that October morning.

A swish of crinolines brought Mama beside me. She grabbed my arm and whispered through clenched teeth,

"Mary C., I told you to get off that railing. Go below and stay there until you can do as you're told!"

I stomped across the deck, pausing once beside the mainmast to scowl over my shoulder. It was all so unfair. I hadn't asked to be dragged along on this blasted trip. I wanted Bess. I wanted to go home, no matter how damaged it was, no matter who ran the stupid government. I wanted to be anywhere but here. But Mama turned away from me. She wasn't even going to watch to see that I did what she said. Her indifference was like a slap in the face.

As I jumped through the open hatch leading below deck, the pungent odor of pine tar mixed with burning kerosene assailed my senses. I hated the smell. Besides making me slightly queasy, it reminded me of how final my losses were. Nothing at home smelled like the interior of that old tub. I hit the steps at a near run with plans to fling myself into my hammock and stay there forever. It would serve them right if I just upped and died. I bowled along toward the sleeping area blinded by tears and the sudden gloom of the narrow passageway.

Without warning, I crashed headlong into a pair of wool-encased legs. The trousers' owner and I struggled momentarily in an awkward dance. With a standoff in the making, he harrumphed once, picked me up by my arms, deposited me on the other side of him, and stepped toward the hatch.

Tears forgotten, I tugged on his retreating coattails, ready to let him see my displeasure. Hooded eyes with ink black irises stared down in return. He didn't look particularly angry, but authority hung about him like a mantle.

I swallowed, choked back what I intended to say, and instead muttered, "I'm sorry for running into you."

He gazed at me for a moment and then simply nodded before turning away. The Reverend Jonas Williams might be a man of God, but his unsmiling countenance raised the hair at the nape of my neck as though someone stepped on my grave. Mama often fussed that Bess planted too many of her superstitions in my fertile imagination. I was now old enough to understand that some of what Mama said was true. But the Reverend Brother Williams still affected me like a haint. A slight shudder slithered down my spine, as though my body was trying to rid itself of his effect. I turned and fled down the hallway toward our sleeping quarters. Many months later, I would come to see this encounter as an omen, a foreshadowing of all that came afterward.

We passengers, immigrants one and all fleeing the defeated South, slept in a large open area that most likely was used as a cargo hold in the *Alyssa Jane's* younger, more prosperous days. Most of the canvas partitions separating the fifteen or so families from one another had been drawn back in hope of allowing fresh sea breezes from the few portholes to circulate. Unfortunately, the plan wasn't meeting with much success for the air remained stale and fetid with the odors of sweat and bodily functions.

I slumped on the edge of my hammock and kicked at the floorboards, allowing tears to drip from my chin unabated. Life wasn't at all how it was supposed to be. It hadn't been since the day Papa rode away to war. He looked so handsome in his gray captain's uniform. He sat on his favorite stallion at the head of his unit and rode toward a conflict that everybody said would be over by Christmas. Everybody had been terribly wrong.

My ruminations, while sad and haunted, didn't last long, for my mind turned to more immediate indignities and irritations. I hated staying below deck. I hated the stench. I hated the isolation. I hated the boredom. When I figured enough time had elapsed that it was safe to go above again, I bolted back into the fresh air. Mama now leaned on the stern railing, her gaze fixed on the faint line where the sky's lighter blue met the Gulf of Mexico's deep azure. She sniffed once as I approached and turned unusually bright eyes on me.

"Are you feeling better, child?"

When I nodded, she gripped the railing and resumed her observation of the horizon slipping away behind the *Alyssa Jane*. I eyed her for a moment, before sidling up beside her.

"Mama, why couldn't Bess come with us?"

Her arm slipped around my shoulders and gave a little squeeze. "Why, darlin', you've been told at least a thousand times. Bess has got to stay in Georgia."

I jerked away from Mama's grasp. "That's not fair! She's part of our family."

A pained expression filled her eyes and her lips parted, but no words escaped. Her head lifted slightly and her gaze locked onto the space behind me.

"Mary Catherine MacDonald, you will not raise your voice to your mother." Mama drew a quick breath as Papa strode to her and took her hand. His attention then returned to me. "No slave has ever been part of our family. It's unthinkable! Furthermore, Brazil doesn't allow slaves to be imported anymore." The more he spoke, the harder his voice sounded and the more clouded his face became. He concluded with sharper words than I had ever heard him use before. "So stop whining about that nigger mammy of yours and learn to live without her."

Surprise made me momentarily mute, but my heart pounded and the sun was suddenly much hotter on my upturned face. I drew a couple of rapid breaths so hard that my cheeks puffed in and out. "Bess is too part of our family. I love her and she loves me. You love her too, don't you Mama?"

A rosy flush crept over Mama's face and her gaze darted around at the other people on deck. I ignored the warning in her eyes. "Bess took care of me all my life. That makes her part of our family." Heady with righteous indignation, my eyes narrowed and I delivered my coup de grace. Jabbing an index finger in Papa's direction, I yelled, "And besides, Bess isn't a slave anymore and you damn well know it."

My words rang across a suddenly silent deck. People turned from their own conversations, shook their heads and stared at us. The only sound I could hear was the blood thumping against my eardrums.

Papa's face blanched. He stooped down until his eyes were level with mine and gripped my upper arms, nearly lifting me from the deck. My head snapped back and forth while he hissed, "You will not speak to anyone, most especially your mother or me, in that manner. Do you understand?" My hands went numb as his grasp tightened. "Now, stop your crying or I'll give you something to cry about."

Only when he stopped speaking did I notice tears streamed down my cheeks.

As we swayed in silence on the *Alyssa Jane's* deck, Papa's grip slackened and the fire in his eyes burned less brightly. "Besides, your aunts need Bess to cook and clean their house in town. At least that's one thing that escaped Sherman's destruction."

Papa got a far off look in his eyes. His hands released me and dropped to his side as he straightened to his full height.

I knew better than to speak again. Spying a cargo box lashed to a railing on the main deck, I slunk down the steps and made my way to it. I wanted to stay up top rather than breathe the stale air below decks, but I also couldn't bear being near my parents at that moment.

Papa's present personality still caught me off guard. Before the war, he rarely raised his voice or hand to me. In truth, I was rather spoiled and cosseted. I begged for pretty dresses and china faced dolls by the dozens. Sometimes, I actually got them too. Now, we were on a ship bound for a place where they didn't even speak English just because some stupid newspaper advertisements promised defeated Southerners free land. All I wanted was to go home, to have life the way it used to be.

Home. The way it used to be before Papa and Nathan decided they would not endure Yankees and carpetbaggers, our former enemies, being in charge of everything.

I was only five when the War Between the States began. Our old way of life now seemed like a gauzy dream—pleasant upon waking, but dissipating when you reached out to grasp it. Afraid of losing the last tenuous hold on that dream, I invented a little ritual, hoping it would glue fading images to the pages of my memory. Now that Papa and my mother's only surviving brother were dragging us away from Georgia never to return, the ritual's importance had taken on the stature of an obsession. I closed my eyes and once again conjured up my earliest memories.

In my mind's eye, I looked down on the Oconee River from the deep porch of an unpainted dogtrot farmhouse. Cotton fields that came right up to the house stretched out as far as I could see in every direction on our side of the river. The house and the farm wouldn't have been terribly grand by most people's lights, but it was home and, therefore, my whole world. The clapboard house and outbuildings existed only in shadowy visions after the war. While I retained only a few hazy memories of the farm, one stands out clearly. It is of Mama's favorite rose bush to which I did some considerable damage one spring by picking off all the buds before they even broke color and for which I received the first spanking of my life.

A few other people lived on the farm in tiny houses out back of the barn. They were the colored slaves, most of whom worked in the fields, but of their faces, it was only Bess's that mattered to me. My Bess, who lived in the house, and who took care of me, and whom I loved as much as I did my mother.

My clearest memories of my parents before the war were that Papa spent his days with the field hands and that Mama loved music. Beautiful music filled the house when she played her pianoforte. Sometimes when Bess brought me into the parlor to say goodnight, Papa would be sitting beside Mama, kissing her neck as she played and she would be smiling at him in the special way she reserved only for him. I think they must have been very happy. They laughed a lot back then. Then, the war came. Nobody and nothing was ever the same again.

Papa had come back from the war haunted by what he had seen and the losses he had endured. For a time, we thought he had permanently lost his mind. These days, it didn't take much to rile him. Mama said not to mind, that he just had so many worries it made him harder to live with than before. Even so, I still couldn't understand why he spoke so cruelly about Bess of whom he'd always been so fond. My papa's sunny nature was the most important thing destroyed by the war.

As the days under sail passed into weeks and America became nothing but a memory, Papa's disposition evolved. To everyone's relief he seemed more like his old prewar self. The farther we traveled, the more his mood lifted so by the time we docked in Jamaica to take on supplies, his good days outnumbered the bad. I even saw him and Mama kissing under the stars one night when they thought no one else was on deck.

The *Alyssa Jane* was an old clipper fallen on hard times, reduced to ferrying passengers and commodities along the trade routes extending from ports in the southern United States to destinations in the other Americas. Its confined space provided limited opportunities for me to get into trouble, so I was allowed unaccustomed freedom. The morning we sailed toward Kingston Harbor, I hung over the portside railing from the moment the city's outline came into view.

Footsteps running up behind caused me to turn and I lost my balance. Papa grabbed a handful of my skirts. "Mary Catherine, you're going to topple into the water if you keep this up. Get off that railing and put your feet squarely on the deck or you can go below and stay there."

Instant compliance and a sweet smile seemed to go a long way these days, so I did as I was told. I didn't want this new/old version of my papa to disappear again.

We passed through Kingston Harbor's narrow mouth with sails snapping, pushed along by Caribbean breezes. In the distance, I could make out the familiar marks of human habitation trailing along the waterfront, but nothing in my experience had prepared me for Jamaica. Low emerald mountains surrounded an oval bowl of aquamarine water that rolled gently forward to kiss sand the color of cotton just breaking from the bole. Within minutes of entering the harbor, the city's buildings became distinct and grew in size. A little thrill swept through me as the old clipper bumped against the dock and the sights and smells of Kingston spread out before us like a feast awaiting revelers.

"Papa, please, why cain't I go with y'all?"

His mouth became a thin line. "Because Kingston isn't particularly safe." Then he placed his arm around my shoulders and pointed to the opposite side of the harbor. "Did you know that a wicked pirate city used to be right over there? An earthquake destroyed Port Royal. The whole city simply fell into the sea." Papa grinned and his eyes grew big. "Why, I've heard you can see pirate ghosts rising from the water when the moonlight is just right."

This was my old Papa, the one I hadn't seen since war was declared. I slipped my arms around his waist. "Oh, Papa, you're just so silly sometimes. Everybody knows there's no such thing as ghosts."

Papa smiled and picked me up, swinging me around like he used to when I was little. When he placed me on the deck again, I pressed my advantage.

"Please cain't I go? Please?"

"You're cutting me in half." Papa pulled my arms away from his middle and smiled. "If it means that much to you, I guess it won't hurt for you to go into town. But you absolutely must stay by your mama's side. When she says it's time to return to the boat, there will be no arguments. Understand?"

As I stretched up to plant a kiss on his cheek, angry shouts and the percussive report of a pistol rang across the harbor.

# Chapter 3

I whirled around and stared, my heart racing at the all too familiar wartime sound of gunfire. Farther along the dock, a small group of armed men peered into the water, shouting and gesturing toward a form flailing in the water. They seemed to argue for a moment and then one of them tossed a net. It floated in the air momentarily before settling over the thrashing form, which struggled to free itself before it was dragged under. Puffing and straining, the men hauled their catch onto the dock where it landed hard with a very human groan. The group's leader strode over as the trapped man attempted to rise. In one swift motion, a pistol butt crashed down on the captive's head and he fell in a heap back onto the dock. Every member of the group then pummeled him with their rifle butts.

"Why are they hitting him? Papa, he can't get away. Why are they doing that?"

Papa didn't answer, just shook his head and put his finger to his lips. He then grabbed my hand and marched off, practically lifting me from the ground as he dragged me along. His eyes were dark and hard, but I wasn't sure why. I mentally reviewed my own actions, wondering if I was in any way responsible for his mood shift, but could find nothing to account for it.

We drew up in the passageway beside a cabin and Papa pounded on the door until it flew open. The ship's captain filled the empty jamb.

"What the hell is it now? You bastards better not—" Captain Peterson's face reddened as he choked on his words.

He took a long breath and adjusted his features. "I beg your pardon, Captain MacDonald. I thought you were one of the crew. What can I do for you?"

"You can tell me exactly how what we just observed taking place on the dock in any way conforms with your promise that our voyage would be interrupted only by stopping at safe ports." Papa raised his arm and pointed in the direction from which we had come. "Is a white man being assaulted in broad daylight your idea of safety? Kingston, as I predicted when we discussed the terms of transport, has already lived up to its reputation and we haven't been in port for fifteen minutes."

Captain Peterson's eyes narrowed and his jaw clenched. "I'm assured by the harbormaster that the recent troubles here are under control and that passengers will be safe if they wish to go ashore to visit the town. Now, if you will excuse—" He gripped the doorknob and gave it a jerk, his final words cut off by the slamming door.

"Arrogant ass. He's going to bring me to violence before this trip is finished." Papa squeezed my hand as he again dragged me along the corridor.

"Ouch, Papa. That hurts."

He looked down at me in confusion and his grip softened. It was as though he had forgotten my presence. "Mary C., I'm . . ." He shook his head and resumed walking down the dark, stuffy passageway.

Papa had every intention of canceling the excursion into the city, but after Mama's pleas, his resolve wavered. In any event, he acknowledged we all needed a break from the tedium of life aboard ship and so my parents, my mother's brother, and I departed the *Alyssa Jane* shortly before noon on a bright November morning, glad to place our feet on terra firma again. As instructed, I clung to Mama's hand and listened with interest as she chatted animatedly about what we might find.

Market stalls lining the street leading us away from the docks were piled with a variety of shapes and colors, none of which looked familiar to me. I gaped in amazement at the wonders spread out in all directions.

Forgetting my manners, I pointed at several colorful mounds. "Mama, what are those yellow finger looking things and those orange balls? Are they good to eat?"

"Yes, Mary C., they're delicious and you'll have plenty of those pretty fruits to eat once we're in Brazil. The fingers are bananas. They're sweet and soft on the inside. The orange balls are oranges." She laughed and winked, giving my hand a little squeeze. "Not very original, but they're wonderful all the same. So sweet and juicy. They were one of my favorites before the war. How I've missed fruit!"

Kingston's spice laden air stirred long ago memories of cakes and pies, making me wish I'd eaten more breakfast, but I had been much too excited. I fairly bounced beside Mama as we chattered, lifting our skirts and stepping carefully to avoid the dirt and refuse that lined our path. Papa and my mother's brother, Nathan led the way and urged us females not to dawdle for they were hungry and wanted their dinner before we started any shopping.

I was beginning to feel overheated, not only from all the excitement, but also from the increasing temperatures. The strong sun made the buildings' white walls brilliant, and in turn, they reflected the heat onto all who passed. Sweat popped out on my upper lip and forehead. Bess would have said this was unladylike and would have immediately begun mopping at me with a handkerchief, but Mama didn't seem to notice, so I just used the sleeve of my dress to wipe at the offending moisture.

Our surroundings improved in both design and appearance the farther we got from the docks until we suddenly found ourselves in a lovely open square lined on one side by commercial establishments. A small hotel with a sign hanging from its eaves advertised food available within. We crossed the hotel's wide veranda and passed through its open front door.

The cooler air of the hotel's interior helped to stanch the flow of perspiration again threatening to run in an undignified stream from my upper lip. Feet aching from walking on cobblestones, I cast about for somewhere to sit. Low slung chairs with caned bottoms and backs seemed the perfect solution. Turning from my parents, I made a beeline for the closest one.

"Mary Catherine, just where do you think you're going? Get back over here." Papa's scowling face brought me to his side.

"I only wanted to sit down."

"You'll be sitting in a moment. Don't make us regret allowing you to accompany us into town."

"No, sir." I knew better than to continue arguing or whining. I'd heard the warning edge in Papa's voice.

We moved into a bright room with open French windows all round. Nathan and Mama sat down at a table near the veranda and fanned themselves while Papa insisted that I tag along to the bar where he placed our food requests.

"Will that be all, sir?"

Papa hesitated and then said to the barman, "I wonder if I might ask your advice."

"Certainly. Always happy to be of help."

"We noticed an unfortunate incident on the dock this morning and I'm concerned about the ladies' safety as they take the air this afternoon. Do you know the white man who was attacked?"

"Weren't no white man, sir. He's a mulatto named Joe who's been on the run since the rebellion was put down over at Morant Bay last year. Hang for certain just like the others before him. If I was you, I'd stick to the square here. Don't go wandering into the shantytowns. The coloreds are all riled up and there's a recent outbreak of sickness there."

"Thank you for the warning. We'll certainly heed it."

As we walked back to Mama and Nathan, Papa looked down at me. "Mary Catherine, did you hear what the man said?" I nodded in silence. "Do not under any circumstances stray from your mother's side."

We left the hotel feeling less animated than when we arrived. The barman's advice had cast a pall over our little group, I suppose, because it reminded us of our own recent experiences and of the reasons we had chosen to desert our home.

As we walked through the few small shops along the square, the adults became involved in boring conversations, oohing and aahing over the number of British items for sale. We had lived for so long cut off from the wider world that even a few trinkets and cheap objects d'art in the shabby little shops of a colonial backwater seemed like high living.

We were in a shop where a blue and white china tea set had pride of place when Mama dropped my hand and lifted the teapot to admire its Chinese pattern. Bored and still angry about being unfairly reprimanded, I sidestepped a pace or two from the adults. No one noticed. I took another three steps. The stupid tea set seemed all Mama and Papa cared about.

I slipped to the door, completely ignoring my promise not to leave Mama's side. The most beautiful doll I had ever seen graced the window of a corner shop only two doors back. I would just die if I couldn't at least see her close up. I peered over my shoulder. My parents ignored me in favor of the tea set, and so I took my chance to make for the doll's window. It was really only a few steps.

I sidled up to the window where she sat and pressed my nose and fingertips against the glass. Within seconds, the shop owner came out to the street. "Young lady, would you like to come in and hold her?"

My head bobbed up and down like a jack-in-the-box as he escorted me into the shop's interior. He reached into the window and placed the beautiful creation in my outstretched arms. Full red lips and rosy cheeks shone in the alabaster face of her painted porcelain head. She wore a yellow and blue striped dress of real silk and her shiny black hair made her white skin glow. I loved her instantly.

The floor creaked behind me and a throat cleared. "Does the young lady believe her father might purchase the doll for her? Is he nearby?"

The man's question jarred me from my rapture. A worm of fear crawled up from the pit of my stomach, slithering its way into my heart. How long had I been in this shop? I looked around trying to estimate, but I could only assume it had been long enough to be missed. I thrust the doll into the shop owner's arms. Rushing out the door, I looked toward the shop in which I had left my parents and Nathan. I saw no one on the street nor did I hear anyone calling my name. If I was lucky, I might be able to slip back without being noticed, so I ran in the direction from which I had come.

The shop proved to be an apothecary. As I poked my head through the door, the man behind the counter and his customer both stared at me and then returned to their business. The worm of fear I had felt in the doll's shop returned to the pit of my stomach and erupted into hundreds of moths all banging their wings against my insides. I started running. My churning legs slowed at the intersection of two unpaved, dusty streets. Sweeping my eyes up and down all four pathways and seeing nothing recognizable, I bolted forward into the intersection. A screaming horse made my head jerk to the right and my heart pound. The animal veered sideways as the wagon driver hauled on his reins and hurled curses at my fleeing back. The farther I ran, the more unfamiliar and shabby my surroundings became. Solid brick walls and tile roofs gave way to crumbing mud daub and palm thatch.

When my legs couldn't run another step, I stopped, panting in the sultry air. I was completely and utterly in the wrong place. An open square appeared at the end of the street, so I ran to it, praying I had perhaps gone in a circle.

A square filled with market stalls offering fruits and vegetables to people dressed in ragged work clothes told me how wrong I was. Uncertain what to do, I stood in the street looking for anything that was remotely familiar. I had done a bad thing in disobeying Papa and now I was being punished for it. My heart pounded like it was trying to escape its ribcage.

Several men lounging on the edge of a water well noticed me shifting from one foot to the other in the middle of street. They pointed in my direction and then turned to one another, talking and laughing among themselves. Within the moment, they moved as a body, advancing toward me wearing ingratiating smiles.

"Why, it's a little mistress." The spokesman's head bobbed above the group surrounding him as his deep voice resonated in the small square. His light colored clothes, though stained with sweat, had fewer holes than those worn by the others. "What you doin' here with us poor folks? Coming to see where ole Joe live? Maybe we take you to trade for him. Dey don't let him out and dey hang him, den we hang you." He looked around meaningfully at his companions, who nodded and laughed.

My stomach churned in rhythm with my pounding heart. I took a step back.

"What's matter? Cat got yo' tongue? Or you just tink you too good to talk to the likes of us?"

"I . . ." The words stuck in my parched throat. "I don't know what you mean."

"Why Joe, him what got caught today and put in de jail. Everybody knows 'bout Joe."

"I don't, unless you mean the man who was caught in the net at the docks." I realized my mistake as soon as the words left my mouth, but there was no way to snatch them back. The men's eyes widened and then filled with anger.

"What you know about dat?"

"Nothing. I just saw it from the ship. Those people who caught him were mean, bad men. They hit him after he gave up. It wasn't right."

"And just what you tink you know about what right and what ain't?"

Not knowing how to extricate myself, I simply shook my head and stared up at my interrogator, who stood so close that his shadow covered me. Tears began coursing down my cheeks.

"Girl, I ask you a question. You—"

But he never finished the sentence. A dark hand patted my shoulder and from the corner of my eye, I saw the hem of a gingham dress brushing the ground. Bess had come with us after all and had found me. I turned and wrapped my arms around her waist, burying my face in her skirts.

"Leave de child alone. She cain't hep Joe and you gonna bring de guards down on us all if you hurt her. Go on away!"

For some inexplicable reason, the men obeyed.

With both hands, she pulled me away from her and looked me up and down. "What a white child like you doing in dis part of Kingston? Dis ain't no place for de likes of you."

I wiped at my tears and looked up into a face that in no way resembled my beloved Bess. This face was so gaunt that the eyes were sunken far into the skull's black hollows.

Tears flowed harder. "I'm lost. My parents and I came on a ship and we're supposed to sail this afternoon. What if they leave without me?"

"I don't tink dey is gonna leave such as you behind. Dey'll come lookin'. You just sit wit me and we'll wait for dem. You'll see. Dey'll come." Suddenly, she was wracked by a fit of such hard coughing that she bent double and placed a cloth to her mouth. When she stood upright again, rusty droplets stained the cloth. This must be the sickness the barman had mentioned.

And so we sat and waited for most of that long afternoon. My new friend coughed often and seemed to have little energy for anything else, but she was very kind and shooed away the curious, who approached wanting to know why a little white girl was in their midst.

When the sun was almost level with the rooftops, I heard a blessedly familiar voice call, "There! There she is." I was quickly engulfed in Mama's skirts as she threw her arms around me and began to cry. "I thought someone had taken you. I was so afraid."

I began to cry too. "I'm so sorry Mama. I just wanted to look at the pretty doll and then I went out the wrong door and then I came here and my friend found me."

I looked over at my savior and realized I didn't know her name. Something in her eyes told me mentioning the threatening men would be unwise. And with Papa's mercurial nature, it was rarely a good idea to talk about bad or unpleasant things these days.

She looked at Mama. "Dis little one be very afraid for you to leave her behind when de ship goes."

Papa stepped in and pulled mama to her feet. "We want to thank you for finding our daughter and for protecting her. How much do I owe you?"

My friend's eyes narrowed. "I don't help de child for money. I help because I don't let little children wander around all alone and afraid in unfriendly places."

Papa's eyebrows rose in chastened surprise. "Will you allow me to give you a gift or to buy something you need?"

But before she could answer, the coughing came again. Papa hastily placed some money beside her and hustled all of us away. When the square was out of sight, Papa turned his attention to me.

"Mary Catherine, we've walked the length and breadth of this town searching in the most unlikely places, some of them containing people who would have just as soon slit our throats as look at us. To make matters worse, we've been coughed on at every turning. And what did that woman mean by unfriendly places? Did someone threaten you?"

"Oh, no, Papa. My friend didn't let anyone come near me." This was the first time I could ever remember lying to Papa.

Thoroughly chastened, I silently clung to Mama's hand as we located Nathan, who had searched the waterfront, and then we all headed for the ship. Captain Peterson paced the wheel deck and scowled up and down the dock as we rushed up the *Alyssa Jane's* gangway. Sailors unfurled the mainmast almost as soon as our feet touched the ship's boards and we departed Kingston as the sun dipped into the western Caribbean.

I was confined below for the duration of the voyage. After all the trouble I had caused, I deserved my punishment. Fortunately, there was a porthole near our hammocks, so I spent our remaining days under sail staring at the rolling sea and the occasional birds, whatever could be seen through this small opening. That activity took all of two minutes at any given point, so I voraciously read whatever books came my way. Papa said reading would help me in preparation for the almost forgotten obligation of regular lessons. Mama tried to keep up my education after the local schoolteacher was taken by an impressment gang for military service, but she was fluent in only a few areas. In music appreciation, French, spelling, and grammar, I was far ahead of my peers, but my math and sciences were woefully inadequate. Since I liked history, I had read everything in Papa's small collection by the time I turned eight, which was fortunate, because all of his books burned with the house. My education could be said to have been spotty at best.

One morning about three weeks after we departed Kingston, Mama came into the sleeping area. "Mary Catherine, you may go above for half an hour. I don't feel well and need to lie down." She gasped as though she was winded, but I was so elated to be set free I barely noticed when she started coughing. I flew into the hallway and made for the open air.

I found Papa near the bow, leaning against the railing. Since he didn't seem to be aware of my presence, I tiptoed up behind him and flung my arms around his waist, crying, "Guess who?"

Instead of laughing as I thought he would, he grabbed my arms and pushed me away. "Not now Mary C. Who gave you permission to come up here?"

I answered quietly, "Mama. She said she didn't feel well and wanted to rest."

Papa's face lost some of its color. "Sit over there out of the way while I see about your mother. And don't get into any mischief."

It may have been the unexpected edge in his voice or perhaps the renewal of the haunted expression in his eyes, but whatever the unspoken signal, I sensed it and was suddenly uneasy.

## Chapter 4

By the day Rio de Janeiro's green mountains appeared over the starboard railing, no one seemed to remember my punishment. The *Alyssa Jane's* sails snapped in gusty winds as she turned toward Guanabara Bay and the city's docks. The slightly choppy sea evolved from deep navy blue with tufts of white foam to rolling azure to a crystal clear aquamarine that became ever lighter the closer we got to shore. But as lovely as our surroundings were, I had a far more important occupation than admiring the scenery. I ran circuits around the main deck, slapping various riggings, and chanting Bess's old good luck rhyme: bat, bat, come under my hat. My legs ached and my palms became quite red, but I wouldn't let myself stop despite the infernal teasing of two brothers from Alabama. The irritating duo with their sandy red hair and Celtic blue eyes might have been deadly attractive had I been a little older, but as it was, their adolescent teasing just interfered with my very important mission. The years spent in Bess's care had left me with a few illogical, but deeply held superstitions, and we needed all the good luck I could conjure.

As I rounded the mainmast headed for the stern, all thoughts of bats and irritating boys disappeared. Mama emerged from below decks, leaning heavily on an older woman's shoulder. Every step looked to be an effort. At the top of the steps they halted because a coughing fit made Mama bend double. When she took the handkerchief from her mouth, rusty stains practically jumped from the snowy linen. Papa, who was conversing with the ship's captain, hurried to Mama's side and helped her to a closed hatch.

She slumped onto it as though her legs could carry her no farther and when she looked up, her face was the color of rain clouds.

"Mary Elizabeth, why didn't you wait? I told you I'd only be a few minutes?" Pain darkened Papa's eyes as he took Mama's hand.

She smiled weakly. "I know, Jonathan, but I just couldn't stand the dark and the foul air another moment. You know how things get when the ship isn't moving." Every word was a struggle and the last few left her coughing violently.

The older woman patted Mama's shoulder. "There my dear, you just rest here." She looked up and continued, "I'll stay right here beside her, Captain MacDonald. You go on back to what you were doing."

Papa hesitated for a moment and then looked at me. "Mary C., don't leave your mother's side. If she needs something, get it for her and be quick about it. I've got to finish our business with Captain Peterson."

I edged onto a corner of the hatch and slipped my hand into Mama's, which felt cold and clammy despite the mid-day heat. The rattling that accompanied each breath she took cast a pall over the excitement of making port and the novel prospect of celebrating Christmas during the Brazilian summer. My own throat tightened as she leaned over with renewed coughing.

Someone apparently summoned Dr. Pruitt, because he appeared, bustling and fussing his way around groups of passengers waiting to go ashore. As he approached, he mopped ineffectually at rivulets pouring down his beet red face. It seemed the calendar to which he was accustomed, not the climate, dictated his clothing for he wore his best winter suit.

"This heat will be the death of us all," he declared to no one in particular. He observed Mama for a moment and then took her wrist. "My dear, we must get you out of this sultry air. Your coloring is positively gray. Are y'all to stay at the immigrant hotel with the others of our colony?" Mama nodded. "I'm sending for a sedan chair. Mrs. MacDonald, you'll be carried straight to your bed."

"But, I couldn't let—"

A slicing motion from the doctor silenced her. "You can and you will. It's for your health and I will brook no refusals. Now, where is that confounded captain?"

The doctor released Mama's wrist and stormed away. As he passed a group of passengers, the words "galloping consumption" drifted in his wake.

Mama suddenly slumped against me and we might have toppled from the hatch, but the lady passenger grabbed Mama's arm and righted her.

"I'm sorry to be so much trouble. I just don't seem to have any strength today. I reckon it's the heat, don't you?"

The older woman's eyes were unusually bright as she patted Mama's hand. "I'm sure that's all it is, but you've got to do what the doctor says." She turned away quickly, looking for the men with the sedan chair I supposed.

The colored men summoned to carry Mama arrived with their strange looking contraption. They waited patiently at the end of the gangway until Mama descended and was settled in the conveyance. The chair itself was a curious affair with long poles sticking out from both ends, but it certainly made carrying a person easier.

We picked our way along dirty, unpaved streets surrounding the docks. Two months spent on rolling wooden decks made walking difficult at first, but I soon regained my balance. I was glad to be on solid earth again, even though I huffed and puffed from the steady incline we traversed. The men carrying mama's chair staggered occasionally on some of the steeper parts and my small satchel became a load of stones. When I feared I couldn't make another step, Rio's beauty suddenly enveloped us in a tropical bouquet.

Broad cobbled streets spread out toward the city center. White buildings with red tiled roofs and little iron balconies hanging from their upper floors clung to the hillsides just as I had imagined their European counterparts described in Papa's books of cultural and architectural history.

I trotted along beside Mama, peering upward until my neck ached. The farther into the city we went, the more fanciful my daydreams became. I envisioned an elegant black-haired lady appearing high on a balcony, her hand resting on its railing. Her dark eyes swept the grounds below. A handsome man, leaning against one of the tall palm trees below her window, began a romantic ballad as their eyes met. Scheherazade had left her stamp upon my imagination. She had also left me with notions beyond my years.

Bess's deep chesty harrumphing echoed through my memory when I imagined her reaction to my daydream and a smile played across my lips. She always said that stuffing my head full of fancies was a waste of time, but Mama understood and encouraged my imagination, especially since I inherited absolutely none of her musical ability. When the war came, I mentally escaped into make-believe where there was no fighting and no Yankees burning out families. It made survival bearable. I think Mama must have used her music in the same way, which the ever-practical Bess never understood.

How I missed Bess. She had anchored my world since my birth and now I would never see her again. My heart ached a little more with each step we took toward our new life, for the door was closing permanently on the only life I had ever known and locking my beloved Bess away forever.

A lump rose in my throat and I tried to staunch my tears by lagging behind just long enough to wipe a sleeve across either cheek. Running to catch up, I stumbled and would have lost my footing if one of the porters hadn't reached out his free hand to me.

As the road curved up a hillside, it widened into a broad avenue cobbled with white stones that were pretty to look at, but made walking difficult. When my feet felt as though they were turning to lead and my eyes started welling up again, the tears I was trying so hard to hide from Mama suddenly vanished. Just ahead of us lay immense iron gates.

We passed under heavily filigreed wrought iron arches and proceeded up a long gravel driveway lined with imperial palms. Fountains on either side of the path spewed water high into the air and vine-covered arbors shaded marble benches. My head swiveled from side to side as I gaped at masses of green, red, pink, yellow, any color one could name, all joined in a controlled riot that were the gardens surrounding the largest and most ornate structure I'd ever seen. Beyond the last shrubs sat a three-story edifice, whose large eyes, overarched by richly carved stone brows, looked down on our travel-stained, bedraggled selves with superiority and disdain. The great lady apparently had no choice other than to tolerate our presence, but as I gazed up at her, I felt *Casa de Saude* obliged grudgingly.

I tugged Mama's hand. "It's a good thing Emperor Dom Pedro wants us to stay here or they probably wouldn't let us in."

Mama smiled. "Yes, it's an even better thing that he wants us to settle here. Brazil needs . . ." She never finished the sentence because a coughing fit seized her with such force her face became quite inflamed. As red sputum soaked her handkerchief, her lips took on a bluish tinge and she wrapped her arms around her sides as though she was trying to keep them from exploding.

The manager rushed from the front door and led us to a ground floor room. I guess he must have been expecting us because he called Mama by name in heavily accented English and then explained that the room would be ours for as long as it was needed. After the porters and the manager left, I stood looking around at a room the size of our former dining room and parlor combined. Mama lay on an iron double bed with a green painted washstand next to it. These simple items were in marked contrast to the deep reds of the richly flocked paper covering the walls and the gilded plasterwork on the ceiling.

I crawled up onto the single bed tucked into a corner and watched Mama as her chest struggled to rise and then collapsed again as a light breath escaped. She was truly beyond going and certainly could not provide any company. She had fallen into a deep slumber almost the moment the manager left the room. I lay back and let my mind drift. I thought about what our life would be like when we moved inland to the land grant that Papa and Nathan were constantly discussing. I made comparisons between Kingston and Rio de Janeiro, deciding the Brazilian city was much more beautiful and far grander. I thought about anything and everything except home, Bess, and the life we had left behind.

With the sun slanting directly into our room, I went to the window and looked down the long driveway for familiar faces. Seeing none, I glanced over at Mama. Now that she had been asleep for a while, her breathing seemed less labored and she wasn't quite as gray. Boredom, my constant enemy, made its unwelcome appearance.

I cast another glance in Mama's direction. She slept soundly, and even though her breathing had a gurgling sound, it was even. I decided she couldn't possibly need me in the next few minutes, so I tiptoed toward the door.

For a building that seemed ancient, the floorboards, door hinges, and latches were remarkably quiet. I slipped into the hallway and was in the gardens within moments, wandering between well-manicured flowerbeds and along winding paths, feeling the hot sun on my pale arms. A sun hat protected my face, which popped out in a horde of freckles at the slightest encouragement due to my auburn hair, blue eyes, and fair

Scotch-Irish complexion. As I skipped over the gravel lanes, I felt pride in the heavy sausage curls dancing on my back. No fire-heated curling irons ever touched my hair because it spun into long natural spirals on its own account with only minimal help from tie-up rags at night.

It was unnaturally hot for December 23 to a child reared in the Northern Hemisphere, so when I spied a large cement pool with a fountain in its center, I went to it like a nail to a magnet. Water spilled from a cupid's mouth, sparkling like droplets falling from icicles melting in bright winter sun. It was completely irresistible. I sat down and removed my boots and stockings. After rolling up my pantaloons, I lifted my skirts and stepped in. Babies' lips began kissing my wiggling toes and when I looked down, I saw little shiny orange fish nibbling all around. I forgot everything that made me sad, including Mama. There is no telling how long I would have waded, but a man in work clothes, waving a rake and yelling in a language I didn't understand, interrupted my pleasure. Although his words were unintelligible, their meaning was not. I jumped from the pool, grabbed my belongings, and ran for the hotel with the gardener behind me shaking his rake and shouting until I was out of sight.

Entering the cooler, stone-floored lobby, I slipped onto a chair hidden from public view by a large potted palm. I replaced my boots and rearranged my clothing. If luck was with me, no one would know I had disobeyed and caused a minor international incident. Pretending I had simply been on a brief excursion to the lobby, I swished back toward our room, believing I could return undetected and that all would be well.

As I sashayed down the hall, I recognized a group of our fellow passengers gathered near the closed door to our room. Some of the women dabbed at their eyes with handkerchiefs. My feet slowed as my heart's beating increased. The adults saw me, but no one said a word.

Instead, the woman who had helped Mama on the boat came over and put her arm around me. "Come with me, darlin'. This is no place for a child right now."

I pulled away. "What's wrong? Why is everyone crying? I want to see my mama."

"You can't do that right now, Mary Catherine. Just come with me and we'll sit in the lobby until you're sent for." As my mother's friend drew me along the hallway, I looked back over my shoulder, eyes glued to the closed door.

It was probably less than twenty minutes, but it seemed an eternity before Dr. Pruitt stood beside my chair. He took my hand and said, "Come, Mary Catherine. Your mother wants to see you."

I wanted to see Mama, but at the same time, I dreaded it. Even though no one told me what the matter was, the sensitivity that came with being long accustomed to life's turbulence made my heart bump harder with each step. Dr. Pruitt led me to the room and opened the door. My heart stopped for a moment and then raced to the bursting point. Papa and Nathan were on their knees, one on each side of Mama's bed.

Mama held their hands and struggled to speak to Papa. "Jonathan, you must promise. You must swear before God that you will be strong for our child." Then she turned to her brother and spoke in a voice so weak it was nothing but a whisper. "Nathan, if Mary Catherine ever needs you, promise that you will take care of my little girl."

Papa and Nathan stared at each other for a moment with an expression I didn't understand.

Papa mumbled in a shaky voice, "Of course, my darling."

Nathan replied in a manner that seemed carefully devoid of emotion. "Mary Elizabeth, I'll do what needs to be done when the time comes."

She closed her eyes and I knew, without understanding how, what would happen next. I ran to the bed. "Mama, I love you so much. Please, don't die. Don't leave me. Please!"

With effort, she covered my hand with her trembling cold one. Her eyes remained closed and a rattling sound came from her chest as she spoke. "Mary C., be a good girl."

Tears slid down my cheeks as I held Mama's hand and heard her ragged breathing slow and then stop. She sighed once and then the rattling in her chest stopped forever.

Through a veil of tears, I saw a shadow move from the window toward the bed. It was the passenger who had manhandled me in the passageway aboard ship, Brother Williams, the preacher. His voice sent a chill through me as he intoned, "Let us pray."

We buried Mama on the afternoon of December 25, 1866. The day was hot and sunny with only a few high puffy white clouds, making the sky's blue more brilliant by contrast. It was hard to believe it was Christmas Day. I stood by the open grave clutching Papa's hand while Brother Williams's voice rolled over us. His tone sounded appropriately pious, but his words couldn't penetrate the fog that shrouded my mind and soul. I could concentrate only on what was most immediate. The borrowed black dress I wore was of some shiny stiff material that became itchier with every drop of sweat that ran down my body. Every time I absentmindedly raised my hand to pull at the waist, Nathan squeezed my shoulder until it hurt.

Staring into the grave where Mama's coffin lay compounded my misery a thousand fold. When I could bear it no longer, I distracted myself by looking up at the adults in attendance. All of the *Alyssa Jane's* passengers remaining in the city were there along with a few local people I had seen coming and going from the hotel. Each face wore an appropriately solemn expression and some of the ladies were dabbing at their eyes with their handkerchiefs.

My gaze settled on Papa's hollow cheeks where tears streamed unabated. He wasn't wiping them away or trying to hide them. Even in his despair after the war I hadn't actually seen him openly cry. This, coupled with the return of a vacant stare, sent an icy stab through my heart. That expression, the open yet unseeing eyes, brought on by his fragile mental state had haunted our lives for months after he returned in defeat. It had only lifted once the decision to immigrate had been made. That it should now return when I most needed for him to be strong stirred horrid memories.

When Papa came home from the war, he was much changed. His uniform, in which he had taken such pride as he was preparing to ride off to lead his unit, was tattered and hung on him as though he had borrowed clothes from a much larger man. His skin seemed to fold loosely over his tall frame and his eyes were so sunken his once handsome face had taken on the appearance of a death mask. But the thing that frightened me most was that he didn't speak to us, not even when Mama cried and begged him to tell her how she could help him. By day, he spent most of his time alone simply walking the fields that had once been so productive. He wept at night when I suppose he thought no one could hear him, but why he thought he couldn't be heard is beyond me, for all of us slept together in the only structure that escaped destruction, the freestanding kitchen house. Some nights nobody got much sleep because he cried out in his dreams so much. There came a time when he drifted into a phase of almost complete inertia, and for a while, we feared for his sanity. He refused to be roused from his bed despite all efforts. He just stared at Mama and got a strange look in his eyes when she pleaded with him. I wasn't supposed to know Mama and Bess thought he might completely lose his mind, but it didn't take medical training or age to see the vacant stares and hear him in the night. Slowly, he regained his senses and got a grip on himself, which was worse in some ways because of the rage that replaced the vacant expression in his eyes. He became a stranger. Head spinning with grief and despair, I now wondered if we were ever again to be free of those black moods.

Brother Williams's droning slowed to a halt. People began patting Papa's shoulder and shaking his and Nathan's hands. Mentally, I was snatched back to the graveside. Glancing around at the small congregation, I saw they were turning away. The service had ended. I didn't want to leave. We couldn't leave, not without Mama, but then unaccountably, we did. We turned away and left my Mama in the little Presbyterian Cemetery, the only Protestant burial ground available. I looked back as long as I could see the mound of dirt being shoveled by the gravediggers while Nathan dragged me along by my hand. He walked so fast he fairly lifted me from the ground as he strode from the cemetery. I don't know why it was he who held my hand. It should have been Papa.

Late that night, a presence beside my bed woke me. I thought Papa was going to kiss me goodnight, but instead, he just stood there looking at me with that strange, far-away expression in his eyes, as though he didn't really see me. After a moment, he turned and slipped through the door.

I pondered Papa's actions and wondered why he seemed so withdrawn. Didn't he understand that I suffered just as much as he did, that I needed him more than ever now? No desirable answer came. Invisible fingers gripped my heart as I felt for the first time that I might possibly be all alone in the world, despite the promises that had been made to my Mama.

## Chapter 5

The period immediately following Mama's funeral passed in a cloud of vaguely recognized activity. People came and went. Meals must have been served and eaten. The sun certainly rose and set. The world functioned in its pre-ordained pattern. The normalcy was unbearable. Somehow I got through those first weeks, but both time and I moved as though dragging lead balls. Nothing seemed important, not even my tenth birthday, which passed unnoticed on New Year's Day.

Papa slipped into a deep melancholia. He refused to leave our room except for the nocturnal ramblings that brought him to stand by my bed before he slipped through the door. He never spoke to me during these strange visitations and I somehow knew he would not welcome my waking self, so I peered at him through the fringe of my lashes and did not utter a sound nor make any movement. I'm not sure he ever slept for more than a few minutes at one time.

By day, he sat in an armchair with a bottle and glass never far from his hand. He kept the room as dark as it was possible to make it in a city of brilliant tropical light. The exterior shutters were closed, the Venetian blinds were down, and the drapes were drawn. The room was not only in semi-darkness, but hot and stuffy as well. Papa, however, was as oblivious to his surroundings as he was to me. He eluded all attempts to draw him from his sanctum, not with outright rebuffs, but by a simple refusal to exist in the world inhabited by the rest of humanity. He met entreaties from family and friends alike with stony silence or by simply turning away to stare at some distant image that no one else saw. When touched, there was no response. It was as though the person he had been no longer existed.

With determination, I chose to believe there was nothing unusual in Papa's behavior, especially since I had become so accustomed to his mood shifts. Since Papa provided no companionship or support, I spent my days wandering the grounds of Government House, waiting for life to begin again and greedily gathering whatever crumbs of adult attention fell my way. I shunned the company of other children because they didn't understand my sorrow and wanted to play silly games that no longer held any appeal. By night when sleep proved elusive, I hugged Mama's treasured small tintype of Papa in his uniform wrapped in her best rosewater scented handkerchief. I had secreted those precious items in my small grip not long after her funeral. Papa didn't miss them and they made it seem that at least a little bit of her was still with me. I left the valuable family pearls that were my inheritance from her in their silk lined case, however, because I was pretty sure he would notice their disappearance from her little tin trunk.

It was during this time that my mother's eldest and only living brother, Nathan, came to loom very large in my life. My mother's people were Jordans and they were very proud of it. They pronounced their name "Jerdin", which caused no end of confusion among those unaccustomed to this inexplicable southern tradition. Before the war, Grandfather Jordan was one of the wealthiest landowners in Oconee County and it was generally agreed Mama had married beneath her. Her brothers, led by Nathan, had been especially vocal on this point, but she was determined to have her way. As a late in life miracle baby and the only girl, she got whatever her heart desired and Papa was what she most wanted. After the war, Nathan was the only Jordan left and we were his only living relatives.

When I was small, I found Nathan's critical nature and perpetual frown forbidding and I hid in the kitchen with Bess whenever he came to visit. Although he was what some people thought handsome in a tall, thin, hawkish sort of way, I never found his beaked nose, gold flecked brown eyes, or sharply angular face anything other than intimidating. Mama used to say a broken heart caused his unhappiness, but then, she always did try to see the best in others, most especially in her beloved, trusted, much older brother Nathan.

Late on a sunny February afternoon, I returned from feeding the fish in the garden pond to hear Papa and Nathan arguing, or rather, Nathan yelling and Papa simply looking away while Nathan's harangue poured over him.

As I stood just outside the open door to our room, Nathan's voice rang out. "If it hadn't been for you and your brat, my sister would still be alive. Coming to Brazil was your idea and now we're stuck here. We missed our first chance for land because you wouldn't leave my sister's gravesite. Now instead of helping find another colony to join, you sit around feeling sorry for yourself."

Nathan stopped speaking for a moment. Through the crack between the door and its frame, I could see him move in front of Papa's chair, gripping its arms and lowering his thin hawk's face to within a few inches of Papa's, his coat stretched taut over his shoulders. "For God's sake man, get a grip on yourself and do something useful for a change. Or do you intend to make as complete a mess of this as you did of your infantry unit during the war?"

Nathan's words were mean and unfair. The already over-warm corridor suddenly became unbearably hot and I flew through the door. "You can't talk to my papa like that. He was brave and he fought hard in the war, which is more than you ever did. All you did was sell timber on the black market. I heard my aunts talking about you. You leave my papa alone!"

A deep red, as brilliant as a Brazilian sunset, crept up Nathan's neck and onto his face. His hands balled into fists so tight that his knuckles went white. Setting his sights on me, he said, "You! You, my dear girl, are the reason my sister is dead. She would still be alive if you hadn't disobeyed and wandered off into that pestilential hellhole where she contracted that dreadful disease. You killed your mother. It should have been you who died instead."

Nathan's words struck me as though he had used his fists. Nauseated and dizzy, I ran to Papa, threw my arms around his neck, and crawled onto his lap. I thought surely the horrible things Nathan said would rouse him, but he merely patted my shoulder in a feeble, absentminded manner.

The icy fingers of Nathan's words dug their way into my core. "Papa, I didn't mean for it to happen. Tell him. Please, Papa. I didn't want Mama to die."

For the first time since Mama's death, Papa looked directly into my eyes. He didn't smile nor did he look particularly angry. In fact, he didn't seem to be feeling any emotion at all. He simply met my gaze and then turned away. Whatever his intent or his feelings, he might as well have said that I killed Mama because his failure to defend me had the same effect. Bewildered and confused, I slipped off Papa's lap and ran from the room. I didn't return until most of the windows in Government House were dark.

After the confrontation with Nathan, I steered clear of him. His room was just down from ours, so I peeked around the doorframe before venturing into the hallway. If I saw him, I made sure he didn't see me. If by some failure in vigilance he came near, I bolted for the closest potted palm or armchair and crouched behind it until he was gone. I became a shadow.

Becoming anonymous had an unexpected effect. By creeping around unnoticed, I became the unintended witness to events that would prove to have a far-reaching impact on my life and how I viewed the world.

One day in late May while I hid in a dark corner under a table, something rather spectacular occurred. A wave of excitement rippled through the mansion's common areas followed by people rushing for the front door. Unaccountably, for it wasn't Sunday, they all wore their best clothes. I couldn't bear not knowing what created such a commotion, so I slipped from my hiding place and through one of the tall open windows, coming to light behind a large palm. The group on the lawn seemed to be holding its collective breath and staring toward the front gates. Coach wheels crunching on gravel elicited cheers and shouts. Shinnying up the palm's trunk, I peered at the driveway. Five men stepped down from a huge coach bearing a fancy insignia on its door. A short man in a black suit with a star on his left breast seemed to be the focus of everyone's attention. He wasn't handsome, but he possessed an air of natural authority and the others in his party stayed back, bowing slightly as he assumed the foreground.

An immigrant threw his hat into the air and others followed suit. Cries of "Viva, Dom Pedro Segundo!" rang through the courtyard.

This was my first glimpse of Dom Pedro II, Emperor of Brazil, our patron. Without his having subsidized our passage, we would still be in Georgia. I didn't know exactly how I felt about him, but he was a splendid sight.

With a great show of formality, the leader of a newly arrived party of colonists stepped forward, bowed, and then ushered Dom Pedro into the main reception area of Government House. I scurried back to my sanctum under the table.

The emperor made a circuit of the room, exchanging brief pleasantries through a translator. Before long, he stood directly beside my table. I could have touched him if I had wanted. Afraid of discovery, I started inching my way farther back into the shadows. Unfortunately, I didn't take into account the table's central leg and backed right into it, setting items on top rocking and clattering.

Dom Pedro bent down and peered. He blinked twice, then his mouth twitched and his hand beckoned. "What have we here? Is it a ghost? Why no, it's a little girl."

Apparently the emperor could speak English after all. Since I had no choice, I crawled between the table's legs, coming to rest at the royal feet. He reached down, took my hand, and lifted me to stand. "And why is it that little girls hide under furniture?"

My mouth was as dry as a Georgia cornfield in August. My tongue turned to lead. Dom Pedro laughed and patted my head. "You have nothing to fear, *meu pequena*. You will soon have your own home in a country that welcomes you. Brazil and I are glad that you are here."

"Thank you, Sir," I whispered. "I'm happy to be here." If Dom Pedro suspected my words were false, he was gracious enough not to acknowledge it. Instead, he winked at me before moving on.

From the corner of my eye I caught sight of Nathan. Cold hatred clouded his hawk's eyes. He started toward me, but a stranger waylaid him with a hand on his shoulder. Nathan glared at me for another second before turning to the man. I took this opportunity to dash back to my sanctuary, but I kept the men in sight through the space between the sofa back and table legs. Nathan and his companion moved forward as they talked, coming to rest so close by that the stranger placed his hat on my table.

The stranger put his hand on Nathan's arm. "Mr. Jordan, I'm returning to Igaupe on June 2 with the last of our colony. We can't delay because this will be the last free passage south for some time. And none of us should impose on Dom Pedro's hospitality longer than absolutely necessary."

I couldn't see Nathan's face, but I could hear the ice in his voice. "I see. Thank you for letting me know. And I'm greatly indebted to you for writing to Mr. McMullan on our behalf."

"Unfortunately, I haven't had a reply, but Frank McMullan's a good man and an intelligent leader. I'm sure he'll see the wisdom of adding two more able-bodied men to our colony." The stranger paused and then continued in a lower voice. "It won't make any difference either way to Mr. McMullan or the colony, but have you found a family to take the little girl? As you have said, sending for her later after you have your house built might make things easier."

"I'll redouble my efforts regarding the girl. Captain MacDonald and I will be ready to travel on the second." Nathan turned and headed toward the hall leading to our rooms. I sat frozen, stunned by his plans for me. Surely Papa wouldn't agree to leave me behind. I hurriedly crawled from under the table and followed my uncle at a distance.

Once again, I stood in the corridor and peeked through the crack in the doorway into the room Papa and I shared.

"Get yourself ready to go. Now!" Nathan swept Papa's bottle and tumbler from the table in one swift motion. The sound of breaking glass echoed down the hallway, bringing several people to their doors. They whispered among themselves and stared.

Lurking in the hall focused too much attention on me, so I slipped just inside the door. Papa and Nathan stared at one another in silence. Deciding the best defense against Nathan might be direct action, I called out in the sweetest voice I could manage, "Papa, would you like for me to start our packing?" Nathan swung around and glared.

Papa looked up in surprise, then smiled slightly and nodded. "You're a good girl, Mary Catherine."

It felt like the sun peeked momentarily from behind dark storm clouds, chasing away the cold. Papa didn't know about Nathan's plan to leave me behind. My mother's brother, my uncle, had lied to the stranger. My guilt about Mama weighed me down from the moment I awoke until sleep provided its brief refuge, but I didn't believe she would have wanted Papa and Nathan to desert me. After all, they had promised her they would take care of me. In my mind, Nathan's behavior turned family attachment on its head. I raced from beds to the chests of drawers, dragging out our two bags and filling them with possessions while trying to pretend my nemesis was invisible.

Nathan watched me with a calculating expression and then said to Papa, "You've got to send her back to Georgia. Leave her here in Rio with one of the families who've just arrived. Surely a captain can be found who'll take her on consignment. Your sisters can pay for her passage when the ship arrives. Without the burden of a motherless child, our chances of joining the McMullan colony will greatly increase. MacKay said as much this afternoon during the Emperor's reception. Why can't you see reason?"

My heart stopped. That wasn't what the man had said at all. In fact, he had said it was Nathan's idea I should be left behind in Rio. Icy fear gripped me as I realized I wasn't actually sure of Papa's answer. Nathan's lie coupled with Papa's withdrawal from life could be enough to seal my fate.

Papa looked over at me for a moment and then something akin to anger lit his eyes. He jabbed an index finger at Nathan. "We both promised Mary Elizabeth we would take care of Mary C."

"You always were a sentimental fool. Mark my words. No good can come of having that girl along. She's already caused one death." Nathan was shouting again. "Why risk any other unfortunate events?"

Papa rose from his chair and rocked unsteadily on his feet. His hand trembled as he placed it on the table that had held his glass and bottle. "Nathan, the answer was no the first time you asked and it remains no. I'm not going to abandon Mary C. to strangers. I intend to keep my promise to her mother to take care of our child."

Nathan scowled. "How ironic. You won't even get out of that chair. How do you propose to take care of anyone or anything?"

Papa's face went white. "Watch your tongue, Nathan, and hear this. I may not have been myself for a while, but from now on, I'll take care of me and mine."

The effort of resisting Nathan's bullying seemed to have drained Papa, for he slumped back into the chair where his head dropped onto the back. Disgust filled Nathan's face. He turned and stalked from the room.

I ran to Papa and threw my arms around his neck, hugging him tightly. "Oh, Papa, thank you. Don't ever give in to Nathan and leave me behind. Please!"

He didn't return my embrace, but patted my shoulder instead and then pushed me away. Profound confusion descended. What, exactly, did Papa feel and believe? Was it simply pride preventing his openly agreeing with Nathan that had I killed Mama? Would there come a time when he would regret not leaving me behind? Tears threatened, but I managed to hold them back. One of us had to be strong for the challenges that lay ahead and I was determined to demonstrate my worth. And really, what other choice did I have?

## Chapter 6

Mama's death was the most devastating blow that could have been dealt Papa and me, but when our date to depart Rio arrived, I started to feel something that had been absent for a long time—hope.

The steamship *Constancia* waited at the docks to transport us on the next leg of our journey to a new life. Unlike the *Alyssa Jane*, the *Constancia* was new and modern. Large paddlewheels, centered on both sides of her gleaming black metal hull, propelled her at record speeds. Instead of hammocks strung out in a cargo hold, passengers slept in individual cabins complete with built-in beds. Apparently, Dom Pedro wanted the best available to ease the transition from city to countryside for his protégés.

A little over five months after we arrived in Brazil, walking up a ship's gangway once again set my heart fluttering. For the first time since leaving Georgia and Bess, I found myself actually looking toward the future instead of back over my shoulder at what had been. Wandering alone around Government House and enduring Nathan's loathing produced at least one positive effect. I clearly understood that change was the only course open to Papa and me.

I stepped onto the *Constancia's* deck and went immediately to the bow, leaning on the rail, trying to see into the future, just as Mama had stood on the *Alyssa Jane's* stern trying to keep sight of the past. The sun shone in regal solitude from a lapis sky, the type that occurs when refreshing winds have blown the heat and humidity from the air. I tugged my light cotton shawl tighter around my shoulders because the breeze off the Atlantic was cooler than expected. I wished I had worn my heavier wrap, but it was stashed somewhere in *Constancia's* belly with our baggage and the farm implements that had traveled with us from Georgia. Thus far, the Brazilian winter seemed to share a greater similarity with late spring than what we thought of as winter.

Familiar footsteps sounded behind me. Papa took my hand and squeezed it twice, our long ago secret signal. My head snapped up in surprise.

"Mary Catherine, don't lean out so far. We'll be under way soon and then you'll have to come away from the railing. I'm going below to make sure our things are safely stowed."

"I'll be careful, Papa, I promise."

When he was gone, I resumed watching the activities in the harbor. Workers loaded bags with *café* painted on their sides into a commercial ship tied up farther down the dock. Smaller vessels out in the middle of the bay, their little white sails bulging, tacked to and fro as though they had no purpose other than playing in the wind. Seagulls wheeled above, eyes ever peeled for the main chance and screaming at one another over who had seen some favored morsel first. And I considered what my life might become now that I had dedicated myself to Brazil. How would Papa be? For the first time since Mama got sick, he actually seemed more like his old self. The thought that maybe everything was going to be all right warmed me as the steam engines rumbled to life.

Our passage down the coast to the small river town of Igaupe was interrupted only once, by a half-day layover in Santos where most of the immigrant families disembarked. Their destination was a colony near Santa Barbara, a small inland village northwest of Sao Paulo. During the trip from Rio, they talked continuously about how life as we had known it would one day flourish again, but as I watched the group disappear into Santos's center, I felt pretty sure they were going to be disappointed.

The small number of Confederados, as the Brazilians called us, remaining aboard the *Constancia* steamed on toward Igaupe. In our cabin each night, Papa and Nathan argued about what they might say to cast their application for a place with the new colony in the best light. When Nathan became particularly nasty, Papa used my bedtime as an excuse to move the conversation elsewhere. After they left, I tossed and turned unable to sleep until Papa returned to our cabin. I hated listening to them argue, but I was terrified of what Nathan might convince Papa to do in my absence. Sometimes, I could hear them shouting despite Nathan's cabin being two doors away from ours. I began to wonder if they actually hated one another. The familial camaraderie Papa and Nathan displayed before we sailed for Brazil seemed to be a permanent casualty of their grief and their ongoing disputes.

By the time we made port, Papa and Nathan were what Bess would've called jumpy as long-tailed cats in a room full of rockers. Papa and I were putting the last few things in our satchels when Nathan stormed into our cabin and slammed the door.

"Jonathan, you've got to see reason."

"Well, good afternoon to you, too, Nathan." Papa's words might have seemed welcoming to anyone unable to see his face. His frowned deepened. "I cannot and will not do what you ask."

"The interior is no place for a child without a mother. I'm sure Frank McMullan will tell you that. MacKay hinted rather pointedly that she might keep us from joining the colony." Nathan's voice was tinged with pleading. "This may be our final chance at a place with people of our own kind."

"If McMullan won't take us just because of Mary Catherine, he's not the kind of man I want to follow." Papa shook his head and then he laughed. "Besides, I can't just fob my child off on some family here and hope that she somehow gets back to Georgia. It's a ridiculous notion." There was a welcome note of determination in Papa's voice that had been missing for a long time.

I expected an angry rebuttal from Nathan, but all he said was, "I hope you don't live to regret your decision. Life will be very hard for all of us."

I couldn't keep quiet any longer. "Papa, I won't be any trouble. I'll work hard, I promise."

Both men looked down at me as though they had forgotten my presence. One face was filled with sympathy, the other with contempt.

At that point, the ship's bell sounded the first call to go ashore and I returned to our packing while Papa and Nathan went above in search of Mr. MacKay. As I snapped the satchels' latches shut, I thought about Nathan. He might be family, but he wasn't acting like it. No wonder his sweetheart had married somebody else. In a way, he was meaner than Sherman's soldiers back during the war. They had burned our house down and stolen from us, but at least they hadn't tried to hurt Mama, Bess, and me. Nathan, on the other hand, had said he wished me dead. Well, he could just go to the devil. I wasn't going to give him any excuse to persuade Papa to leave me behind.

When I came up on deck, Nathan and Papa were talking to the man I had seen with Nathan on the day of Dom Pedro's visit to Government House.

"McMullan's ill. Doctor's confined him to bed, so we'll need to go to him."

Papa extended his hand. "Thank you, Mr. MacKay, for arranging this." As the two men shook hands, Papa's voice sounded less sure. He put his arm around my shoulders. "I hope my daughter won't—"

"We're wasting time standing around talking." Nathan smiled broadly and stepped in front of Papa, placing his hand on our sponsor's shoulder. "We need to know McMullan's decision."

Papa scowled at Nathan and Mr. MacKay looked slightly startled, but they both started for the gangway without comment. As I trotted along behind the men, a shudder swept through me. If the colony leader didn't want us because of me, would Papa fall back into his troubled, ineffectual mode? It terrified me to think he might not be able to withstand a renewed onslaught of demands from Nathan.

Mr. MacKay led the way through Iguape, greeting and being greeted by the locals. It was a rather pretty place and bigger than I had been led to believe. We passed a large public garden with crumbling walls at its center. Mr. MacKay said a Jesuit monastery was to have been built there until the religious order was run out of the country. When we reached the town's center, a surprisingly beautiful church loomed before us, but what riveted my attention was an even more amazing sight descending its front steps. A lady dressed in a rich green velvet frock cinched at the waist to within an inch of her life strode toward us on elegant feet encased in fine embroidered kid boots. Her matching hat and parasol dipped in Mr. MacKay's direction when she drew abreast our party. I watched in fascination as he tipped his hat to the lady whose skin was the color of polished mahogany.

"We've found the people here to be very friendly and kind. I'm afraid my wife will miss her new friends when we leave."

Nathan cut his eyes at our sponsor. "That's one thing I'll never get used to. Why do the Portuguese allow some of these coloreds to wander around wherever they want? The way they act, you'd think they're the equal of whites."

A tight smile played across Mr. MacKay's lips. "I'm sure your time in Rio showed you that the well-connected free coloreds here are mostly the equals of whites."

"What fools. Don't they know a nigger can't be trusted any farther than you can throw him?" Several passersby turned to watch us, their attention no doubt attracted by

Nathan's stridency. It was probably fortunate they didn't understand the substance of his words.

"Mr. Jordan, this is Brazil. They have their own ideas and way of doing things here. I suggest you accommodate them or you may find these kind people less friendly. Until we establish our worth, we're only guests in this country."

Nathan's mouth became a thin line, but he fell silent, apparently deciding his cause was better served by discretion. If any of the adults had bothered looking my way, they would have observed a satisfied smirk. Seeing Nathan put in his place and forced to keep his opinions to himself was worth the discomfort of having to practically run to keep up with the three men. I decided I liked Mr. MacKay immensely.

We crossed the breadth of the town, our only stop being at a street market to purchase a little fresh food. Presently, a curious sight appeared. A house surrounded by tents rose up from the end of the street. Children ran about the yard, playing in any vacant spot. Women stood over cast iron pots of boiling laundry, pounding long handled dashers among the clothes and wiping at their streaming faces. As we got closer, we could see that packing crates lined the house's veranda. There didn't seem to be an inch of yard or porch that hadn't been pressed into service. I wondered why so many people lived together like this, but then I caught the sounds of American accents floating above the general din. Looking around at the barely controlled chaos, my heart sank. Was it really for this that we had traveled so far?

Behind the house at some distance, late afternoon sunlight glinted off the Ribeira de Igaupe, creating the effect of jewels sparkling on an inky velvet background. As Mr. MacKay guided us around sleeping quarters and outdoor kitchens, a couple of boys raced toward the river with cane poles on their shoulders. Suddenly, I wished I were among their carefree number instead of going to meet the man who would determine our fate.

The house's interior was even more crowded than its yard. Beds, cots, and pallets took up any floor space not already covered with piles of baggage. Mr. MacKay negotiated the maze with ease and we were soon standing in a small room at the back of the house. Lying on a narrow bed was a youngish looking man. He might have been quite handsome had it not been for the gray pallor emphasizing his sunken eyes and hollow cheeks. When he attempted to rise, a coughing fit took his breath, leaving him gasping and blue lipped. It was a condition I recognized immediately and I wondered how long he had left.

"Frank, don't get up." A flicker of concern furrowed Mr. MacKay's brow. "No one expects it."

It took only a few moments' conversation for Frank McMullan to agree that Papa and Nathan would be good additions to the colony. He was impressed by Papa's military service and by their collective agricultural knowledge. I could see relief in my father's eyes as he shook McMullan's hand.

"You won't regret this." Papa paused while he placed his arm around my shoulders and drew me to his side. "There's one condition, though. I simply can't leave my daughter, Mary Catherine, behind. She may be motherless, but I assure you she'll be no trouble."

Confusion filled Frank McMullan's eyes. "Captain MacDonald, I'd never expect a father to desert his child, especially one who's lost her mother." Mr. McMullan glanced at Mr. MacKay before continuing, "I can't imagine where you got such a notion."

Papa's face glowed crimson. "I beg your pardon. I certainly intended no offence." His voice took on a hard edge when he cut his eyes at Nathan. "I must've misunderstood something that was said."

Nathan held Papa's gaze without blinking. "It wouldn't be the first time you've made a mistake." He then turned and marched from the house.

I have no idea where Nathan went or what he did in a place where he knew no one. Papa and I were left to set up our tents and make camp on the only space left in the yard. The sun was hanging on the horizon as Papa made a ring of stones that were lying about. When he had a fire going, he rummaged through our gear and pulled a frying pan from the depths of our toolbox.

"Mary C., do you think you could scramble eggs while I see where Nathan has gotten himself to?"

I'd never prepared a meal much less handled a frying pan over an open fire in my life, but since I believed my being useful was vital, I answered with far more confidence than I felt. "Of course, Papa. I'd be happy to."

Papa handed over a basket containing eggs and a small portion of pork loin, patted my head, and left. By the time six eggs lay broken in the pan, I had a mess. The eggs on the bottom were burning. The eggs on the top were a glutinous mass. I poked at the mess with a spoon, but the pan wobbled hard and threatened to fall into the flames. I hoped moving the pan to the fire's edge would slow down the cooking process. I grabbed the handle and let out a yelp. Jerking my fingers away sent the pan flying upside down into the dirt. Supper was ruined and it was my fault. I stuck my damaged fingers into my mouth and sat down on the ground, burying my face in my skirts.

As I cried, a soft arm slipped around my heaving shoulders and a kind voice said, "There now, honey. Crying isn't going to help, but I tell you what will. How about we get that pan clean before anyone is the wiser." I looked up into a face with smile crinkles around the eyes and a halo of wispy hair going gray at the temples. While I wiped my eyes and sniffed, my new friend said with a wink, "By the by, I'm Mrs. MacKay."

The twinkle in her eyes made me smile. We set about scraping the ruined eggs with spoons. When only the blackened bottom layer was left, scrubbing with sand finished the job. Mrs. MacKay put her hands on her hips and admired our work.

"It isn't any worse for wear. Won't anybody know."

"Thank you so much, but what am I going to tell Papa about the eggs?"

"That you gave them to me for everybody's breakfast. When I saw y'all setting up, I thought to tell Mr. MacKay that we should share our meals. Two men and a little girl aren't likely to get much decent food prepared. And since our girls married, I can't get used to cooking for just two."

The men returned just as the meal of fried pork and hoecakes was ready. I'm not sure Papa believed the story about the eggs, but he gratefully accepted Mrs. MacKay's offer to cook for us and promised to keep her food box filled. Nathan sat down without saying a word to anyone. He remained taciturn throughout supper, giving one or two word answers to any question addressed to him. After Nathan rebuffed a final attempt to draw him out, Mr. MacKay glanced at his wife with a swift lift of his eyebrows and turned to Papa.

"Frank McMullan asked me why y'all thought this sweet little girl might be a problem. He was concerned someone had given you the wrong impression of him." Mr. MacKay frowned at Nathan. "I can't think of anything I might have said, but even so, I'm sorry if I gave you the wrong idea."

When Nathan failed to respond, Papa answered for him. "I'm quite sure the misunderstanding wasn't your doing. Please put it out of your mind." Mr. MacKay looked inquiringly at Nathan who stared straight ahead into the night, silent and stone-faced.

We went to bed shortly after the dishes were cleaned and the fire was tamped down. The ground's lumps and knots poked through my thin pallet, making me toss and turn, but exhaustion finally overcame discomfort and I drifted off. I don't know how long I had been asleep when I bolted upright, my heart pounding. Angry whispers from just outside the tent had broken into my dreams. I couldn't hear everything that was said, but at one point Papa's raised voice cut through the canvas.

"Don't threaten me, Nathan. You're not man enough to back it up. Liars like you rarely are."

Papa slipped through the tent flap and returned to his pallet while I feigned sleep. Pretending was all the sleep I got for the remainder of the night because I spent most of it wondering why I hadn't just told Papa what I'd overheard that day in Government House. I knew Mr. MacKay hadn't told Nathan that I would be a liability in applying to the colony. In fact, he had said it wouldn't make any difference to Frank McMullan. It was Nathan's idea, and his alone, that I should be left behind. Because I had been unsure of Papa's reaction, I had been afraid to accuse Nathan of lying. Months of Papa's distance and seeming coldness had confused me and killed my trust. Though I hated admitting it, I believed he too blamed me for killing Mama and it was only his pride that kept him from abandoning me.

## Chapter 7

The tension swirling around Papa and Nathan as we waited our turn for transport inland to our land grant was something that I couldn't control, but for which I felt responsible. My feelings of guilt over Mama's death had now grown to include responsibility for driving a wedge between what was left of my family. Papa and Nathan spent as little time in one another's company as possible and when they were together, they conversed only when necessary.

During suppers with the MacKays, they managed to be stiffly polite to one another. I couldn't decide what Mr. and Mrs. MacKay thought, but from time to time I saw Mrs. MacKay looking from Papa to Nathan with what seemed a speculative expression.

The river became a refuge from the adults in my life and my favorite haunt was a path running along the Ribeira de Igaupe between the town and a small dock upriver. Just before dusk on an early June evening, I plopped down on the sandy riverbank, seeking distraction from my troubles. The antics of little brown and white plovers sometimes did the trick. I often found their fussing with one another and their chasing about under the pampas grass amusing, but that evening they only served to remind me of the on-going battle of wills between my father and uncle. How much longer, I wondered, would we remain in Igaupe and would things get any better once we left?

Presently, mechanical chugging broke the silence and puffs of smoke appeared above the treetops. As the source of the disturbance wallowed toward the dock, I jumped up. If this was our steamer, I wanted to have a look at her. I felt little thrill of excitement at the thought of at last being on our way to our new home.

The slap-slap of my bare feet on the worn dirt path stopped abruptly as the vessel hove into full view. Paint that once must have been white appeared only in occasional patches scattered about the boat's wooden sides and railings. A single smoke stack, missing most of its decorative finial, looked as though a strong breeze might topple the remaining structure. I could actually see the sun's rays flashing through holes in its metal. Two men, occupied with tying off mooring ropes, stopped working and looked at me. They then made what I suppose was a joke at my expense because they pointed, exchanged a few words, and burst out laughing. My heart fell. If we were traveling on this broken down tub, it was hardly an auspicious beginning for the next leg of our journey.

By first light on the following morning, tents were down and crated, bags were packed, and we were standing in a chilly fog watching our possessions being loaded into the ancient *Esperanca's* hold. Colony contingents had been traveling inland every few days since our arrival, so there were only five families remaining for this final trip, but we still crowded the small steamboat to overflowing. Two Confederado men carrying a stretcher arrived as the last of the baggage disappeared into the steamer and Frank McMullan was taken straight way to one of the few cabins. Shortly before eight o'clock, the steamboat creaked and wheezed away from the dock and began the upstream struggle. With nothing else to do, we passengers lined the rails watching marshlands and sandbars slip by as the boat plodded along. Where Nathan had gotten himself to on the small vessel was unclear, but no one seemed to miss him.

In fact, I would have been thrilled if he stayed away from Papa and me until we reached the colony lands.

"The captain says we'll stop tonight at a place with sufficient shelter for at least the women and children." Mr. MacKay stood beside Papa with me between them. "I'm sure Mrs. MacKay won't mind watching over Mary Catherine."

"She's very kind." Papa raised an eyebrow. "I'm just hoping we make it that far."

Mr. MacKay chuckled. "This old tub may not look like much, but I'm assured she's watertight."

The *Esperanca* took that moment to groan and roll slightly onto her side. My feet scrambled while my hands flailed. Papa shot an arm around my shoulders and we both grabbed the railing. The boat then righted herself just as quickly as she had tried to throw us overboard. She must have brushed against a submerged log or unseen sandbar. When I looked up at Papa, I saw a shadow in his eyes.

He bit his lower lip and then spoke hesitantly. "Mr. MacKay, I'm at a loss for why I feel compelled to speak about this. I guess the war and my wife's death have left me feeling uncertain about the future." He looked uncomfortable and paused for a heartbeat then looked directly into the other man's eyes. "If Mary Catherine should ever need protection, will you and your wife look out for her? I can't bear thinking of her alone and friendless."

My head shot up and I stared at Papa. I couldn't remember ever hearing such a declaration from him, not even before the war when life was simpler. Papa just never spoke about his feelings, not ever. He assumed we knew he loved us so saw no need to say it aloud. I also had no memory of his ever having openly expressed fear, not even after the war when things were so uncertain. I slipped my hand into his and felt him squeeze it twice.

Mr. MacKay glanced sidelong at Papa and took his time in answering. "Captain MacDonald, while I'm certain the need will never arise, I assure you no child of our colony will ever be left to fend for itself. We look after our own."

Papa nodded, but didn't speak again. Instead, he leaned on the railing and stared at the low trees and pampas grass lining the riverbank.

The *Esperanca* was watertight as advertised, but she also had an uncommonly deep draft, which we discovered about six o'clock that evening. A sudden loud grinding followed by bone jarring shudders brought the steamer to a standstill mid-river. No matter how hard the little engine revved, a sandbar held *Esperanca* fast. Since the light was fading fast, we had no choice but to sleep on the boat that night. Our bedding was packed away in the hold, so after a cold supper of hardtack and dried meat called *charque*, I wrapped myself in my shawl and lay down on the deck, using my arm for a pillow. Any warmth from the day disappeared once it was completely dark. A cold mist formed on the river, the kind that seeps into your core and squats there. Shivering kept me from falling asleep, so I tossed and turned, occasionally kicking people who were bedded down around us. Papa eventually placed his arms around me and pulled me to his chest where I snuggled against his warmth and shortly dropped off. For the first time in a very long while, I actually felt safe.

"Wake up, Mary Catherine." Papa shook my shoulder. I opened my eyes and squinted into the rising sun. "Go to Mrs. MacKay and stay with her. Nathan and I are going to help get the boat off the sandbar."

A shadow moved and Nathan materialized, backlit by sunlight pouring over the treetops. "This is outrageous. The steamboat company knows this river and should've sent along enough men."

"That may be so, Nathan, but since we're traveling at Brazil's expense, I guess we beggars can't expect to be choosers, can we? Stop complaining and get your boots off."

Nathan's scowl and displeasure were nothing unusual, but Papa's ordering him about was something new. Could this be a sign? I crossed my fingers, muttered another of Bess's good luck incantations, and said a quick prayer. While Papa and Nathan took places by a burley black boatman at the stern, I went in search of Mrs. MacKay. I found her not too far along the deck lounging under a staircase leading to the upper deck. Mr. and Mrs. MacKay's only children, two married daughters, lived at home in Texas with their husbands and in-laws. I guess she really missed her daughters and grandchildren, because ever since we joined the colony, she made a fuss over me. I liked her an awful lot. When I sat down on the deck beside her, she took one look at me and declared that I was still tired. She insisted that I place my head in her lap, and even though I fought it, I soon drifted off again.

The sun was much higher in the sky when a sudden heaving sent those of us on the deck sliding toward the portside railing. We were next tossed back against the cabin wall. Mrs. MacKay grabbed a rope tied to the staircase banister and I held tightly to her skirts. With additional rocking from side to side, *Esperanca* inched her way off the sandbar and into deeper water. The captain steered against the current, keeping the boat relatively stationary, while the men in the water heaved and crawled their way back onto the deck.

Papa and Nathan dropped down beside me, putting on the socks and boots I had gathered up.

"That was certainly invigorating. Care for another dip, Nathan?" Papa winked at me.

"If I catch my death, it'll be on that blasted captain's head. The man's an incompetent imbecile." Although

Nathan's lips were blue and his teeth chattered, his childish complaining irked me no end.

Papa smirked at him for a moment and then laughed. "Well, I don't suppose we can all be as smart as you. Tell me truthfully. Do you consider everyone a fool? Or do you favor only the fortunate few?"

"I don't see anything funny about this, Jonathan. But you seem to have recovered the ridiculous sense of humor you were so famous for when we were boys." Nathan's eyes narrowed. "Of course, it's very cheap humor, the kind only low class people of limited means find amusing."

Papa's smile disappeared. Red flooded his face and his eyes flashed. "I suppose you would know. But as I recall, having class is a matter of honor, not merely inheriting wealth. Now, exactly what was it you did during the war?"

Nathan drew a sharp breath as though he had been slapped across the face. When he spoke, his voice had a slight tremor. "One day you'll go too far."

Papa grinned broadly. "But not today. No, not today." His accompanying laughter had a hard edge and his eyes glittered as he watched for a reaction.

Nathan puffed up like a wet hen and jumped to his feet, shouting over his shoulder as he stormed off, "I'm going to the boiler room where it's warm. Do me the favor of not following."

When Nathan was out of hearing, Mrs. MacKay cleared her throat. "Why, Captain MacDonald, if I didn't know better, for all the world I'd think that you and your brother-in-law are enemies."

Papa had the good grace to appear embarrassed. "Please accept my apologies. We shouldn't have made a kind lady uncomfortable with our petty disagreements. Mr. Jordan and I have just been together too long without anything to do. You know what they say about idle hands." Papa smiled, took Mrs. MacKay's hand, and bowed slightly as I had seen him do long ago when he and Mama had guests. "Now, if you'll excuse us. Mary Catherine, come. I need to dry off too."

I was overjoyed. Maybe the incantations and prayers were working! This was the confident, charming Papa who had ridden off to war all those years before.

*Esperanca* chugged upstream for another two days managing to avoid further entanglements with the numerous sandbars dotting Ribeira de Igaupe. With nothing else to do, I hung on the railing observing changes in the landscape through a veil of nonstop rain. The riverbanks became higher, the trees increased in height, and green parrots flapped and squawked at our passing. Occasionally, the palm-thatched roof of an isolated farmhouse could be seen through the mist, but nothing to indicate what might be considered civilization.

On the fourth evening, *Esperanca* pulled up to a small dock next to a clearing. We disembarked with all of our possessions because we had traveled as far as the old tub could take us. From now on, we would go by dugout canoe. In the gloom of a rain-soaked evening, Papa, Nathan, and Mr. MacKay started unpacking tents while Mrs. MacKay and I gathered firewood.

By the time tents were erected, the daylight was gone. We sat under a tarpaulin strung between trees eating another cold meal of hardtack and *charque*. Night as black as any I had ever experienced closed in, which wouldn't have been a problem by itself, but strange cries ringing from the forest sent chills down my spine. They were a cross between a woman's scream and the growl of a very large, angry cat. When the sounds approached the forest's edge accompanied by crashing in the undergrowth, I jerked hard enough to spill my supper into the dirt. The sight of my now inedible food produced a gush of tears and heaving shoulders.

Papa came over and put an arm around me. He then held out his hand. "Here, Mary C., you can have the rest of mine."

"I don't—want—your supper," I gasped between sobs. "I want my Mama and Bess. I wish we had never come here. I want to go home."

"But this is our home now. We're going to build a new life here."

"I don't want a new life. Maybe you should have just sent me back to Georgia like Nathan said. At least I would still have Bess."

Papa looked as though he had been punched in the gut. "Sending you back isn't an option. Besides, there's nothing to go back to."

"Yes there is." I was practically screaming now. "Bess is there and she's the only one who really ever took care of me. I want Bess! I want to go home!"

Papa looked into my angry eyes for a moment and then his mouth turned hard. He lifted me off the log on which I perched and then jerked me upright. I heard his belt buckle come undone and the snap of the leather as it swung around against my legs. My screams echoed through the black night. I don't know how many times Papa slammed the belt against my backside and thighs, but I saw Mr. MacKay's appalled expression when he stood before me.

"Captain MacDonald, that's enough. Spanking a child is one thing, but if you keep this up you're going to really hurt her." He grabbed Papa's arm. "Stop it now. She's just a little girl."

Papa looked at Mr. MacKay as though he didn't recognize him, but the hitting stopped. Papa shook his head like he was trying to clear his mind then he turned me around and looked into my eyes. I was terrified. Just as suddenly as it had come, the rage subsided and he released me. I swayed and would have fallen if he had not caught me. Papa picked me up like he had when I was little, and as he carried me toward our tent, my gaze met Nathan's. The self-satisfied gleam in his eyes told me just how much he was enjoying my misery. In that moment, the discomfort my mother's brother had always produced in me turned to hatred.

"Mary Catherine, I'm sorry I lost my temper." Papa knelt down and put me on my pallet, wrapping a blanket around me. "Go to sleep. Things will look better in the morning." Before he got up, he kissed my forehead and then pulled me into an embrace so tight that I had trouble breathing. "We've lost everything that matters. We mustn't lose each other."

Between renewed sobs, I gasped, "I'm sorry I said nobody can take care of me but Bess. Papa, we won't lose each other."

In the morning, I awoke to rain hammering on canvas and feeling I hadn't slept at all. Terrible dreams of lost children seeking dying parents had kept me tossing and turning most of the night. I dreaded seeing the adults, especially Nathan, but hunger won out over fear, so I got dressed and braved the torrent. I found Papa, Nathan, and the MacKays huddled under the tarpaulin. Mrs. MacKay hovered at the shelter's edge poking the contents of a pan set over a smoking fire.

"Between this weather and the wet wood, I'll be lucky to get this bacon fried before the fire dies out. Mr. MacKay, do you think you could fan those flames a little harder?" Mrs. MacKay coughed as smoke flew up into her face. "I swanee, for two cents I'd turn right around and go back to Texas, Yankee government or no. If we don't all drown first, the malaria or yellow fever will surely get us."

"Now, Mrs. MacKay, remember the child. She doesn't need to hear such talk." Mr. MacKay stopped fanning. "My dear, I'll watch that bacon and pour the drippings on the hardtack when it's finished. Why don't you go see about some dry clothes?"

Mrs. MacKay placed her hands on her hips and cocked an eyebrow at her husband. "As if I have anything dry. And no thank you. I remember what happened the last time you offered to watch food cooking. Watch was all you did until it turned black as molasses. This is the last of the bacon and I intend to enjoy it."

Mrs. MacKay wasn't the only traveler out of sorts. Coughing and groaning could be heard throughout the encampment. Everyone seemed in low spirits and several colonists complained of fever and tight chests. There was one exception to the general feelings of malaise and illness, however.

"Johnny, stop teasing that snake and get back over here this instant before you get bit," rang through camp. Five-year-old Johnny Mashburn, traveling with his parents, elderly grandparents, and spinster aunt, was still full of life and mischief.

Mrs. MacKay exchanged knowing glances with other adults. "My land, if that boy makes it to manhood, it'll be by the grace of God alone. Poor Miss Mashburn. Having to chase that little monster and tending to those old parents seems a hard bargain just to be allowed to come along into this jungle."

"I don't believe she really had a choice," Papa said. "Her brother sold the family farm and her sweetheart was killed in the war."

"I don't see why you think Miss Mashburn should be exempt from being useful," Nathan interjected. "What else does she have to offer? Spinsters and females in general are nothing but a burden for the most part. She should be grateful her brother didn't leave her behind in Texas."

Papa glared while the MacKays looked around in embarrassment to see who might have overheard. Nathan's implied reference to me didn't escape my notice, either.

I tried to shut out Nathan's presence by staring at the river's rain-chopped surface while I gnawed at the hardtack and washed it down with bitter boiled coffee. The best that could be said was the food and drink were hot. After a while the deluge eased, but was replaced by a dense mist limiting visibility to just a few yards. Without warning, six forms appeared out of the gloom. They seemed to hover above the river as they drifted toward us accompanied by the sound of rippling water and an almost imperceptible rhythmic thumping. The dugout canoes had arrived.

Each of the three long, thin canoes looked to have been carved whole from individual tree trunks. To see them was to wonder how all of us, not to mention our things, could possibly fit, but with a lot of heaving and pushing, the baggage and the tents were eventually crammed into the first, the women and girls into the second, and the men and boys into the third. After delivering us to the colony's outer most edge where a Colonel Bowen waited for us, the dugouts would return for the crates and farm implements and again ferry everything upriver.

From my seat in the stern, I turned to see what Papa was doing and caught sight of little Johnny hopping from one gentleman's lap to the next. He stamped on as many feet as possible before settling himself in the bow. He then proceeded to hang out over the river and slap at the water with both hands. With the upper half of him wiggling and splashing, the canoe started rocking pretty hard. The native boatmen on each end maintained their balance by sticking poles into the muddy river bottom and swaying on reliable sea legs like the experienced sailors they were. The passengers, on the other hand, grabbed at any handhold available. Several of the men scowled at Mr. Mashburn, but he seemed oblivious to his offspring's behavior.

"Johnny, get back in the boat and sit down. Now!" The timbre of Papa's voice resulted in compliance, but Johnny's protruding lower lip made me think a storm might be brewing. Johnny stomped his foot and I thought he was going to pitch a tantrum, but Papa lifted the boy by both arms and propelled him into his father's lap. "Mr. Mashburn, take charge of your boy before he dumps us all into the river."

Mr. Mashburn looked offended, but he nodded and remained silent.

I was mesmerized. I hadn't seen Papa muster that kind of authority since before the war. He really was getting better in some ways, although frightening anger still bubbled just under the surface. His moods were so unpredictable. He had rarely spanked, much less beaten me in the past, but the purple bruises on the backs of my thighs brought home to me again just how much he had changed. Would there ever be a balance between the old Papa and the stranger he had become? The question was one that I pondered for some time to come.

## Chapter 8

The dugouts carried us upriver for another six days amid increasingly rougher terrain. Cliffs rose on either side of the river, forcing it into a much narrower channel strewn with rocks and boulders. When sudden differences in elevation created waterfalls or the water churned into too many rapids, we were forced to put ashore, parcel out the baggage among the three canoes, and then portage everything until a suitable place farther upriver could be found to return to the water.

On the morning of the seventh day, the Ribeira de Igaupe played out at the confluence of two tributaries and we made a sharp right turn into the Ribeira Juquia. Shortly thereafter, we were forced to put ashore and begin a journey around several yards of impassible white water. The path we followed rose at a sharp incline, turning what might have been a walk of just a few minutes into a trip of more than two hours. I tied my shawl around my waist because just a few minutes exertion brought sweat rolling down my back. Papa and Nathan's long legs handled the climb in stride, but my short ones soon ached. When we were about halfway to the top, climbing around boulders and stumbling over tree roots, someone shoved me hard in the back and flew past, giggling and yelling, "Get out of the way, you girl."

"Johnny, slow down. Come back here right now." Poor Miss Mashburn struggled by me, going after her charge as best she could while her long skirts caught on sticks and rocks.

"For God's sake, boy, watch where you're going." The rear stretcher-bearer carrying Frank McMullan nearly lost his footing when Johnny bowled into the backs of his knees. The man couldn't look directly behind him at Johnny's parents, so he shouted over his shoulder, "Get that boy under control before he hurts somebody."

Johnny whirled by the stretcher, bumping it so hard Mr. McMullan groaned and gripped the sides while the bearers fairly danced a jig in order to keep from dropping their passenger. Johnny looked back at the scene he had created and howled with laughter.

I looked behind me at Johnny's parents and then ahead at a red-faced, panting Miss Mashburn who at last had a grip on her nephew. The woman practically lifted the chubby little body from the ground as she dragged Johnny back toward their family.

"Papa, why do they let him act like that?"

"That's a good question. If he keeps it up, I'm going to have an answer from his father."

For a change, Nathan and Papa were in agreement. "The boy's a positive menace. McMullan's got to do something about the brat."

Papa cut his eyes at Nathan. "You can't be serious."

"It's his job to keep order, sick or not."

Papa chose not to respond and simply shook his head in disgust. Anyone with eyes could see the colony leader was in no condition to deal with anything. We were headed as fast as we could go to Colonel Bowen's place at the edge of the land grant so that Mr. McMullan could have shelter and a real bed.

As I struggled up the steep path, lifting my skirts and praying not to twist an ankle, it occurred to me that Nathan Jordan and Johnny Mashburn had a lot in common. They had to be the two most self-centered people alive. Johnny might be forgiven due to his age and his parents' neglect, but there was no excuse I could see for Nathan.

We topped a steep incline and one of the boatmen pointed through the thick forest toward a path leading down to the river. A few minutes quick descent brought us to a small clearing. Stones and sand were again visible through the clear water, but roaring downstream told us a waterfall couldn't be far away. Glancing upstream, I saw that the river rushed through a narrow hollow with sheer cliffs on both sides. When the canoes went into the water, the swift current tugged on them so hard that I wondered if we would be able to use this place and might have to try again much farther upstream.

It was when the men and boys were loading into their canoe that screams rang across the water and bounced off the cliffs.

"Save my child! Over there!" Mr. Mashburn stood in the men's dugout, pointing at a spot in the river where Johnny flailed, carried downstream by the rushing current. "Please, someone save my son!"

The other Mashburns sat frozen in place in our canoes while mother, grandmother, and aunt screamed and pointed. I saw Papa look at Mr. Mashburn in stupefied wonder. Instead of going into the water after his own child, the man just rocked the dugout with his gesturing.

In an instant, Papa had his boots and coat off. He jumped from the dugout and yelped as the frigid water covered him to the shoulders then he started swimming toward the receding child. At this point, the boy must have been truly terrified because we could hear his screams and see his little arms struggling to keep his head above water. The current propelled Papa forward and with a few strokes, he swam up next to Johnny. Papa stretched out his hand to the child, who grabbed it and was at once in Papa's arms. Johnny chose to repay his savior by trying to literally climb onto Papa's head, plunging both of them underwater and sending them rushing toward the falls. Mama on her deathbed flashed before my eyes and I must have tried to launch myself from the canoe because Mrs. MacKay threw her arms around me, crushing me tightly against her. I scanned the river for any sign of Papa and Johnny, but they were nowhere in sight. The river rushed onward carrying them with it and I couldn't do anything but watch.

"There!" Frank McMullan extended a trembling hand toward a point on the opposite side, downstream but above the falls. My gaze flew to the place and there, clinging to a sapling that hung out into the current, were Papa and Johnny. The men jumped out of their canoe with the exception Frank McMullan, Mr. MacKay, and the natives manning the poles. The dugout edged into the current and washed swiftly downstream. When it came abreast the sapling, the boatmen struggled to ease the canoe within reach. Papa sank beneath the water, extending his arms into the air and thrusting Johnny into Mr. Mackay's outstretched grasp. The boy jumped onto Mr. MacKay and crawled up his chest like a monkey. When Johnny was level with Mr. MacKay's shoulder, the boy wrapped his arms around the man's head and commenced howling. It might have been funny if the whole situation hadn't been so terrifying.

The canoe rocked against the rippling water while my head snapped from side to side searching for Papa. There was no sign of him. With muscles bulging, the boatmen pushed the dugout away from the sapling and into the main current. It wobbled in place for a moment, then hurled backward toward the bank. Johnny's screams increased while the dugout maneuvered into the current again, tilting and rocking violently. Its occupants grabbed the upper side and leaned into it, righting the dugout and enabling the Brazilians to gain enough purchase on the river bottom to propel them back into the main current for a second try, but the bow slammed into a rock midstream, setting the dugout across the current and bouncing toward the falls. At this point, even the boatmen's eyes were wide with fright, and as hard as I searched, I still couldn't see Papa.

The men leaned into their poles until the wood began to bend.

From somewhere outside myself my voice floated over the water. "Papa? Where's my Papa?"

No one paid the least attention to my cries. All eyes were trained on the canoe wallowing in the rushing river. Straining until it looked like their muscles might burst, the boatmen gave one mighty heave and the dugout turned upstream. After several more forceful thrusts of the Brazilians' poles, the dugout shot bow first into place in front of the women's canoe, slamming into the riverbank, sending the sound of wood scraping on stones echoing through the narrow hollow.

I searched every inch of the dugout, but there was no sign of Papa. My brave papa had saved that horrible boy and those men had left him to drown. I struggled against Mrs. MacKay when she put her hands on my shoulders and began turning me toward our canoe's bow.

"Look, Mary C! Look."

As the pole men turned the dugout parallel to the bank, there clinging to its off side was Papa. Lightheaded with relief, I slumped against Mrs. MacKay.

Papa was out of the water and onto the shore in one beat of my heart. Within the next, he had Mr. Mashburn by the throat. Papa lifted the man until his toes brushed the ground, then slammed him into the mud and straddled him like he was no more than a log needing its bark peeled away. Mashburn covered his face with his arms in an attempt to ward off the blows raining down.

When Papa began banging Mashburn's head against the earth, Frank McMullan called out, "Jordan, pull your brother-in-law off."

Nathan looked like he was sucking on a lemon and actually seemed to shrink. He remained rooted in place.

"Did you hear me? Pull Captain MacDonald off before he kills that fool." McMullan then fell back into the canoe, covering his mouth with a cloth as coughing took control.

Two men closer to Papa than Nathan grabbed each of Papa's arms and pulled him backward, away from the whimpering Mashburn. Papa bucked and struggled against their grip but they held fast. As I watched, it occurred to me that the men who restrained Papa hadn't moved nearly as quickly as they might have. My guess was they, too, were more than a little tired of the Mashburn clan.

Once others had restored order, Nathan found his voice. "Frank, I hope you can overlook my brother-in-law's actions." He cleared his throat and turned toward Papa. "The balance of Captain MacDonald's mind has been somewhat disturbed since he returned from the war, but I promise to keep him under control in the future."

Papa pulled free of his captors with one vicious jerk and lunged. His eyes had the same expression as the stray dog that once attacked the hens back home. The mongrel ate one hen, then kept on killing, leaving feathers and broken carcasses strewn about the yard until Bess's shouts brought Papa with his rifle. When Nathan's throat was wrapped in a stranglehold from behind, I became truly afraid that Papa really would finish him off. Frank McMullan might overlook the beating of the unpopular Mashburn, but I doubted he would forgive outright murder.

I clambered out of the dugout into the sucking mud of the riverbank. My boots held fast, so I kicked out of them and ran barefoot to Papa, wrapping my arms around his waist. "Please stop. He's not worth it. Oh, Papa, please stop!"

Papa's chest heaved, but his grip on Nathan loosened as he grabbed my arm and slung me around in front of him. The wild expression in his eyes sent me struggling backwards. He looked down as though he didn't know me, ready to inflict a portion of his wrath on the individual trying to thwart him.

I think the terror in my eyes must have cut through his rage, because the hand held poised to strike dropped to his side and he released me.

After a moment, he pulled Nathan to his feet and shoved him aside. "Keep your mouth shut. Not another word, you understand?" Nathan's eyes burned, but he nodded and wobbled back to the edge of the group.

Papa pointed at Mashburn. "Keep your boy under control from now on." He sighed deeply and glanced around at the other colonists. "I reckon we ought to get started, if we're to make Bowen's place before dark." He then walked over to the men's canoe and got in beside Frank McMullan.

Our traveling companions looked at one another like they weren't quite sure what to think. The women, for the most part, looked frightened. They shook their heads and whispered among themselves. The men, appearing torn between wanting to congratulate Papa and being disturbed by his sudden violence, elected to quietly follow him into the canoe. Johnny, the scruff of his collar held in a firm grasp, frog marched beside his father to a seat as far away from Papa as they could get.

"I think I'll ride with the baggage where I can stretch my legs." Nathan, massaging his assaulted throat, turned on his heel toward the third canoe.

Between the rain that began again as soon as we pulled into the main current and Papa's actions, a pall descended and we were a subdued party that pulled up to Colonel Bowen's dock that evening. There was just enough daylight left to make out our surroundings, such as they were. The "Government House" built with limited Brazilian funds by Colonel Bowen was the first thing we sought. I looked at the structure and wondered how this place and Casa de Saude (Government House) in Rio could possibly share the same title. Instead of a converted mansion or even a normal house, we stared at a long, low building with no windows and slatted doors standing open on either end. I could see past a woman standing in the front door clear to the other end and out the back. There didn't seem to be any interior divisions at all. It was like we were returning to the *Alyssa Jane* with hammocks strung between posts and pallets on the floor. Palm leaves made the roof and palm slats set up picket style, three inches apart, comprised the walls. Several families who had traveled ahead of us already filled the place to capacity. Papa took one look and started searching for a spot in the yard to pitch our tents among those already lining the little open square surrounded by thick forest.

The only structure of any worth lay opposite the Government House. It looked a lot like the farmhouses built by people of middling means back in Georgia. In fact, except for being somewhat smaller, it looked like our former home. Colonel Bowen had been in Brazil for over a year, so he had been able to build himself a decent dwelling during that time. The stretcher-bearers carried Frank McMullan there. When they passed through Bowen's door for the second time, a familiar figure came out with them.

I slipped up by Papa and took his hand. "What's Brother Williams doing here? I thought he was going to Santa Barbara."

Papa glanced over at the Bowen porch, surveyed the group conversing there, and shrugged. "I have no idea."

When the preacher walked to the Government House and entered as though he lived there, I wondered what had made him change his mind about the colony he would serve. But Mrs. MacKay called to me for help with setting up her kitchen and I let Brother Williams slip from my mind.

An uneasy truce evolved between Papa and Nathan by unspoken agreement and no one mentioned what had transpired between them. The Mashburns stayed as far away from us as possible, which suited me just fine. I felt like I might commit violence on Johnny myself if he came near again. We continued taking our meals with the MacKays because Mrs. MacKay insisted it was easier to cook for five than two and that she needed my help. I sometimes wondered if she just felt sorry for us, especially me, because I knew next to nothing about cooking, but I was learning from her and trying very hard not to be underfoot and in the way.

We had been at Colonel Bowen's for about a week when Papa killed a deer and Mrs. MacKay chose a haunch to roast. After supper that evening, we sat around the fire with heads nodding in a half-dozing stupor produced by too much meat, a too warm front, and a too cool back. The sound of boots on hard packed earth brought me back to the waking world.

"Gentlemen, M'am, it doesn't look good. Most of the Texas folks don't have the heart to leave here before they know for sure what the outcome will be. MacKay, what're your plans?" Brother Williams had taken on the role of liaison between the sickbed and the rest of us in addition to being the colony's conscience and spiritual advisor.

"Mrs. MacKay and I could no more leave now than any of the others. We've known Frank McMullan since he was a boy." Mr. MacKay looked at Papa and Nathan. "This doesn't mean that y'all can't go on. Nobody'll take umbrage if y'all go on upriver to your parcel and get started."

Papa and Nathan looked at each other and then Papa said, "Since the plows and other things have arrived and the dugouts are still here, I guess it's best if we go now. It'll make one less family to have to deal with when everybody is ready to move on."

Brother Williams nodded. "I'll let the boatmen know."

"By the way, has anyone heard from the drovers bringing the mules and cows overland from Santa Barbara?"

"Nothing yet."

Mr. MacKay put his hand on Papa's arm. "Don't worry. I'll make sure your livestock gets to you once it arrives here."

The next morning we set out for our new home. Blessedly, the rain clouds of the last few days had dissipated overnight and we pulled away from the trees lining the bank into bright, clear sunlight sparkling on the river's rippling current. Every foot of land on the left bank from now on belonged to the McMullan colony. We were headed for the northern most corner where we were told we would find a small valley that was ours alone. Though it was as far from civilization as the McMullan lands could get, it was supposed to contain rich soil and plenty of water from a year round creek flowing through its heart. Papa said it sounded perfect. I thought it sounded too far away from other human beings, but I was determined to make the best of our new situation.

A morning's poling on the Juquia brought us to the valley, which was everything promised and then some. We pulled ashore where our creek poured into the river and walked inland a few yards to a natural glade where Papa and Nathan began making camp. The river men unloaded all of our goods, including a plow, a crate of tools, a two-man crosscut saw, three featherbeds, and a little potbellied stove brought from our kitchen back home. I looked around at the natural beauty crowding in on us and felt like throwing myself down and screaming. I would never see Bess or my real home again.

## Chapter 9

After weeks of camping in the tents, Papa and Nathan worked in the rain tying the last palm fronds to the exterior of our first home in Brazil. I stood in the open doorway, protected by long, low eaves, and surveyed the interior, trying to decide where Papa and I would sleep. A limp tarpaulin strung along the palm-thatched ceiling hung to the dirt floor in the middle of the hut creating two cramped rooms. It really didn't matter which one I chose. Neither offered any comfort beyond protection from the rain. Selecting one by the time-honored 'eeny, meeny, miny, moe' method worked as well as anything and I settled our things in the room on the west side. As the day edged toward evening, the downpour eased off and watery rays from the setting sun filtered through the palm slat walls where the fronds weren't completely tight. I wondered if the flimsy structure would be any protection from the *oncas*, the Brazilian name for jaguars, I could hear screaming at night. I sat down on a piece of log pressed into service as a stool and tried to understand why life was going so terribly wrong, wondering how much of it was my fault. If I hadn't disobeyed, if I hadn't wandered off, if Mama hadn't gotten sick, if she hadn't died, if, if, if . . . If Nathan was correct, my culpability was considerable.

Of all the changes so far, the lack of contact with other people looked to be the most depressing. Sometimes I wondered if I just had a perverse nature. In Rio and Igaupe, I had sought refuge from those around me by wandering alone, but now I craved the company of others. I especially missed

Mrs. MacKay, who had partially filled the holes left by Mama and Bess. Now she and Mr. MacKay were two hours downriver by dugout or even farther if we took the overland route back to Government House at Colonel Bowen's. Papa and Nathan spent all day manning the crosscut saw, and at first, the sound of falling timber echoed nearby. But as they worked deeper into the forest, the only sounds that broke the silence of my days were those of wildlife scurrying over the natural trails around our camp or flitting through the forest canopy above me. Papa taught me how to load and shoot his rifle in case any of the four-legged travelers ventured too close, but I still felt afraid when he and Nathan were no longer within calling distance.

It was fortunate, I suppose, that cooking the meat that the men killed and learning how to grind *mandioca*, a plant the native boatmen had shown us, into *farhina* for making bread provided considerable distraction. By trial and error, I learned to wash our clothes in the cast iron pot, but not before dropping Nathan's best shirt into the fire. He added this to his growing tally of my sins and general worthlessness.

As I looked around our thatched shelter, for it could hardly be called a house, I thought about how strange life had become. It was a mystery to me why Papa and Nathan continued to work together because the tension between them was palpable. But as much as I would have liked to ask the question, fear kept me quiet. I sensed there was more to their conflict than simply my presence and I wondered if the angry things they had said to one another during the trip inland about honor and class hinted at the underlying causes. They worked together all day clearing land and discussed only business in the evenings after supper. The evening of the day we moved into the hut proved to be no different.

"Jonathan, we've got to get the coffee plants in the ground before summer sets in if there's any hope for them to survive."

"And just what do you suggest we use for money to buy them?"

Nathan paused for a moment and then glanced at me before answering. "I think you're holding something we can barter. I know Mary Elizabeth saved our mother's pearls during the war by wearing them in a linen bag attached to her pantaloons. Where are they now?"

Tears filled my eyes as my head swiveled between Papa and Nathan. "Mama said those pearls would come to me. She said you were supposed to save them for when I'm grown up."

The words were out of my mouth before I could stop them, but what I said was true. Mama had lovingly shown me the double strand choker and told me the story often. Those pearls had passed from mother to first-born daughter ever since a Cavalier ancestor's wife had smuggled them out of Scotland on the run from Cromwell's troops. The necklace had provided a small sense of security for the generations of women who wore it and a feeling of connection to the next generation, something usually reserved only for men.

"Papa, please, you can't sell my pearls."

"They are not, nor have they ever been, your pearls. They belonged to my mother." Nathan hurled his words like a cobra spitting venom. "It's a stupid tradition anyway. Everyone knows women are incapable of rational thought. That's why they don't own property."

"Mary Catherine has every right to those pearls and you know it, Nathan. Why don't we let her decide what to do with them?" Papa turned and put an arm around me, pulling me to within a few inches of his face. "Mary C., I know the pearls are yours, but here is the problem. They are the only thing of value we have left. If we don't sell them or use them in trade, we won't be able to plant coffee. We don't know if the cottonseeds we brought will produce in this climate, but we've all seen how well coffee does here. We need the coffee trees to make a go of the farm."

Papa stopped talking and his eyes held mine until I couldn't stand it any longer. I loved my father desperately despite all that had happened. Other than a mere bit of lawn handkerchief, the pearls were all I had left of Mama, but Papa was still alive. It broke my heart, but I didn't really have a choice. I looked from Papa to Nathan and back, and then whispered, "I guess we should sell them."

I might have said more, but the sound of hoofs crashing through the forest sent Papa and Nathan for their rifles. We didn't get many visitors and certainly never at night. As I strained to listen, I thought it sounded like more than one animal approaching.

"MacDonald. Jordan. We've brought news and your livestock." Mr. MacKay rode into our camp followed by a young Brazilian leading two mules and a cow. Strapped across one mule's back was a chicken coop containing hens and a rooster. The other mule bore two wiggling, squealing sacks draped one on either side. The farmyard had arrived and there were no barns, sheds, henhouses, or pens to receive it, so we put the poultry and pigs in our shelter and tied the cow and mules to trees. The tents would have to be home for a while longer.

After the livestock was settled, we sat around the fire talking long into the night. I guess Papa and Nathan were as starved for other people's company as I was.

Mr. MacKay shared bits of news that had traveled upriver from the coast and then turned to the subject closer to home. "You may have heard that Frank McMullan was taken back to Igaupe because his health has deteriorated so much. He was sick before we ever left Texas, but some people live with consumption for years, so he thought to give Brazil a chance." Tears ran unfettered down Mr. MacKay's cheeks. "We got word last week that he's died. I'm not sure the colony is going to hold together without him. People are already talking about going home."

"What'll you do?" Papa asked.

A rueful smile played across Mr. MacKay's lips. "I guess we'll be going home to Texas. Mrs. MacKay misses our daughters and the grandchildren sorely. Says I was an old fool for thinking we could just up and start over at our age. I suppose there's something in what she says, but I'd like to have tried anyway."

"Do you know who's going to stay?"

"Mashburn's wife was begging to leave, but he's put an end to that. Preacher's staying. Says sinners need a shepherd to keep them within the fold." Mr. MacKay grinned despite his earlier tears. "With Frank gone, looks like he sees an opening he wants to fill. Well, good luck to him."

Depression descended as I realized how much Mrs. MacKay had come to mean to me. I closed my eyes and dropped my chin onto my fist. Who could I depend on now that she was leaving? And what about Mr. MacKay's promise to take care of me if the need ever arose? As much as I loved Papa, somewhere deep within me I knew he wasn't capable of being the rock I needed. Though Nathan's reasons were far from charitable, I wondered again if he was right that everyone would be better off if I was sent back to my aunts and Bess in Georgia. But since it didn't seem to be an option, the realization that I might have to be my own rock hit me like a bucket of cold water thrown in the face. As I pondered this completely new concept, Bess's loving face danced before my closed eyes. What would she do in my place? Her words and actions came back to me and slowly the answer was revealed. Although in bondage, Bess had always remained true to herself. She had never sacrificed who she really was or what she valued and she loved Mama and me despite the soul-crushing situation in which she lived. Granddaddy Jordan and then Papa might have owned her body, but her spirit had always been hers alone. Bess had remained quiet when it was prudent, but she had never doubted herself or denied what she believed in. She was just about the strongest person I had ever known. What I needed to know was whether I would have the strength to be like her, to be my own person in what was very much a man's world? The idea was so foreign to the way I had been brought up that I felt like I was contemplating something akin to treason.

Mr. MacKay and the livestock handler wanted an early start the following morning for their return to Colonel Bowen's. We gathered to bid them farewell in a damp mist that matched my mood. Despite my new resolution to be like Bess, I couldn't help myself. When Mr. MacKay moved toward his horse's flank, I flung my arms around his waist. "Please tell Mrs. MacKay how much I'm going to miss her. I don't want y'all to go."

"Well, there now." Mr. MacKay patted my shoulder rather awkwardly. "It'll be all right."

Papa gripped my shoulders and pulled me back. "Please forgive Mary C. She's grown quite fond of your wife, even in the short time we've known each other."

"Mrs. MacKay is easy to love. I should know after forty years of marriage." Mr. MacKay patted the top of my head. "Now, don't you worry little one. You're going to be just fine. You've got your father and uncle to look after you."

Kind Mr. MacKay meant well, but I feared he might be terribly wrong.

With Frank McMullan's death, the colony did begin to fall apart as predicted, but Papa and Nathan were tenacious in their refusal to return to what they saw as an untenable situation back in Georgia. My pearls must have been sold or bartered because within a month of Nathan making the demand, young coffee trees arrived and were planted in the cleared fields beside the creek. After six months living rough, Papa and Nathan completed a real four room house with the timber that came from clearing the land. It was in the traditional dogtrot design with a sitting room and kitchen on one side of the open central hallway and two bedrooms on the other. The clapboard structure was finished with a porch at the front and the back. The little wood-burning stove that had traveled with us from Georgia was placed in the kitchen and I began to really learn to cook.

Our first two years at Little Georgia, as we called our farm, passed without further loss or unhappiness. Papa and Nathan, resigned to the fact that they needed one another to survive, seemed to put aside their conflicts in favor of mutual cooperation. Life settled into a pattern that was beginning to feel normal: work six days, rest on Sunday, pole downriver Saturday afternoon once per month to Colonel Bowen's for Sunday church service with Brother Williams, stay overnight in Government House, and go home early Monday morning. As far as my education was concerned, Papa did the best he could with instruction at night after supper. He ordered a few books from New York and might have sent for more, but Nathan pitched a fit over the expense. Fortunately, the books filled in the gaps in my mathematics and science, so I by my twelfth birthday, I had acquired more education than most people ever got. My life was bearable, if not exactly happy, and I felt a sense of accomplishment with all I was learning. Things could have been much worse.

On warm evenings, I still found solace in wandering alone near water. My constant tread wore smooth paths along both river and creek. To my great annoyance, Nathan took to walking after supper also, saying he wanted to check on the coffee trees or check out a location for another new field. For some reason, he seemed to think I was interested in what he was doing because he warned me to not follow him every time he left the house. Why he thought I should find him fascinating enough to speak to, much less follow, was beyond me, but he was very persistent with his warnings. It was this odd behavior that piqued my interest one lovely October evening.

Nathan paused at the kitchen door after supper. "I'm going to walk downriver. I want to see if the ditches we dug are sufficient to drain the marshes. Jonathan, Mary Catherine, I don't need or want any company."

Rather than respond, I frowned at him for a moment and then returned to clearing the table. Papa glanced up and nodded absentmindedly before hunching over his farm accounts journal again. Boiling water for washing up and scraping plates and pots took another thirty minutes or so, but when the dishes were finally clean and stacked on their shelves, I walked out onto the back porch and down the steps, following the path that ran between the vegetable garden and the creek.

I had recently begun putting my waist-length hair up on top of my head, which Nathan roundly criticized as inappropriate for my twelve years, but it was so much more comfortable and safer than having it trailing down my back. I was almost thirteen, but I felt like I was closer to twenty-three. There were no more nighttime lessons because Papa considered my education complete and I ran our home with the efficiency of a grown woman. Why shouldn't I wear my hair the way I wanted?

Standing at the edge of our backyard, I considered whether I would use the steppingstones to cross the creek or stay on the house side where the path was easier to walk. A welcome light breeze blew down our valley from the west, lifting stray curls around my face, setting them dancing. The sun, hanging low over the distant hills, painted the surrounding forest's green canopy with golden light, sparkled on the creek's gentle water, kissed the wildflowers, and hid less lovely areas like the swamp near the river in long shadows. Seen like this, it was possible to believe that we were living in the paradise that had been advertised back in '66. The early summer warmth promised to linger into the darkness, so I chose the rougher, but more colorful path along the opposite creek bank.

After lifting my skirts and flitting from one steppingstone to the next, I followed the sun along the creek. I loved this meandering trail in spring and summer because flowers were everywhere. They hung in yellow and pink cascades from the trees. They sprouted in purple, white, red, and orange clumps scattered over the ground. When I looked beyond the hardships of the way we lived, Brazil's great natural beauty lifted my spirit and restored my soul.

I walked perhaps a third of a mile to where the path widened and the forest thinned until it played out altogether in a small meadow lining both sides of the creek. I usually stopped to dangle my feet in a shallow pool beside a fallen tree and I was looking forward to this break. If a parrot's squawking above my head hadn't drawn my gaze upward, I would have walked straight into the open. My feet stopped so suddenly that I grabbed a low hanging branch to keep from toppling over. Slipping behind the tree, I gazed mesmerized at the scene on the creek bank.

Nathan stood beside the water with a large metal pan in one hand and a small leather pouch in the other. The western sky held only a rosy glow and I knew I should have started home by now, but Nathan's behavior seemed so suspicious that I couldn't stop watching. He gazed at the water for another moment or two then he peered around in every direction. Seemingly satisfied, he next strode to a pile of boulders. There, he shoved the pan into a crevice and covered the opening with several rocks.

His covert task completed, he crossed the creek and took the easy path home. I couldn't wait any longer or I would have found myself caught out in the forest at night without a lantern. I waited long enough for Nathan to be out of sight and then I, too, crossed the creek, but I made a mental note to get a better look at that pan the next day when he and Papa were working near our southern boundary. Nathan had a secret and I was determined to find out what it was.

## Chapter 10

The next morning, I waited until Papa and Nathan were out of sight. If I was careful, I could get to the pool and back in time to take them their midday dinner without either of them knowing I'd left the house. Instead of meandering and admiring the scenery as I usually did, my feet flew over the worn earth. After fifteen minutes, I entered the meadow and raced to the pile of boulders where Nathan had hidden his pan. The rocks covering the secret hole were heavier than I anticipated and shoving with all my might didn't budge them. I thought back to Papa's lessons about levers and pulleys. What I needed was a long, sturdy stick. Since nothing suitable was immediately at hand, I went back into the forest. Much of the fallen wood was already rotting due to the humid climate, but with some searching, I found a branch I thought might work.

After the dimness of the forest, sunlight flashing off the creek blinded me for a moment. When I placed my hand over my eyes to shield them, my heart jumped into my throat. The sun was much higher in the sky than it should have been by my reckoning. I ran to the boulders and applied my branch to the biggest of the rocks. To my great relief, it quickly rolled away from the opening. My arm extended into the space up to the shoulder, but no matter where I patted the ground or waved my hand, I encountered nothing. Glancing nervously up at the sun, I realized I couldn't waste any more time searching what was obviously an empty hole.

As I scurried along, questions tumbled through my

mind. When, and more importantly why, had Nathan come back for his pan? I became even more determined to solve the mystery of what was in that bag.

As I closed our back gate, the sounds of male voices floated to me from somewhere near the river. Papa and Nathan weren't supposed to come back to the house until evening. Hitting the kitchen at a run, I reached the stove and jerked open the firebox door. Embers still glowed red-hot so the dry wood I shoved onto them flamed nicely within seconds. I lifted the cover on the stove's small water reservoir and scooped up a ladleful, dashing it onto the last of the previous summer's canned beans that I cooked last night. Lard dashed into cast iron skillets began melting as I grabbed the wooden bread bowl. I threw a couple of handfuls of *mandioca farinha* into its center and then ladled more warm water. Plantains were a mealtime staple, so I peeled a couple and started slicing. By the time footsteps echoed from the front porch, hot water bread and plantains were sizzling in the skillets and the beans were bubbling gently in their pot.

Lifting my hand to swipe at a little rivulet of sweat, I turned from the stove and smiled brightly as Papa and Nathan entered the kitchen. They removed their hats and threw them onto the pegs by the door, mopping their own sweaty faces with their kerchiefs.

"If you two had gotten here any later, you'd have missed your dinner because I would've already left for the field with it. Why are y'all back so early?"

"Nathan's got a bee in his bonnet. Thinks he's got to go to Colonel Bowen's this afternoon for the mail come hell or high water, leaving me to finish clearing the new field alone. I think he just wants to get out of work." Papa winked at me and then cut his eyes at Nathan.

Nathan, as usual, rose to the bait, his face flaming.

"We're expecting the coffee roaster from Rio and you know it. The blasted machine should've been here two weeks ago along with the book on processing the harvest. What good is planting all of these trees if we don't know what to do with the beans when they come in?"

"Mind now, I could be wrong, but I think we've probably got a little time to study the subject since the trees won't bear for another two or three years. Of course, you may feel you need that much time to read a single book and absorb its contents." Papa chuckled lightly.

"The book isn't just about processing. It's about cultivating, propagating." Nathan stopped speaking and stared angrily at Papa. "I'm not going to continue this insipid conversation." He grabbed his hat, and then glared at me. "What are you grinning at, girl? You think your father's so funny? Ask him what will happen to us if our coffee crop fails." With that, Nathan grabbed cold breakfast biscuits, crammed his hat on his head, and stomped off toward the little dock he and Papa had built on the riverbank just beyond our front porch. I'm sure he could hear Papa's laughter as he untied our dugout and set off for Colonel Bowen's.

Since Mama's death, I had accepted Nathan's rejection as my punishment for the disobedience that led to our tragedy, but I was also now old enough to begin questioning what I observed in my small world.

"Papa, why does Nathan stay here? He hates me and it seems like you enjoy taking every opportunity to make him angry."

"Beats me." Papa shook his head and turned to look out the kitchen window. "I've asked him that question a hundred times. I've offered to buy him out with what we have left from selling your mother's pearls. Then he could go anywhere he wanted. About six months ago, I thought he was going to take the offer, but now he acts like he's never considered leaving."

Papa stopped speaking for a moment, then turned back to look at me, a puzzled sadness shadowing his vibrant blue eyes. "Mary C., he's a man of contradictions and that's a fact. I know he's capable of deep affection. Look at how much he loved your mother. And we all thought he was going to go crazy when he was jilted two weeks before his wedding. But he can also harden his heart so that nothing will ever thaw the iceberg he creates in himself." He stopped speaking and put his hand on my shoulder. "You shouldn't take Nathan's words about your mother's death to heart. You know that, don't you?"

It was the first time he had said anything about my part in losing Mama. My lower lip trembled as I answered, "But Nathan says she wouldn't have died if I hadn't disobeyed and gotten lost. He says I killed Mama."

"She might have gotten sick even if we hadn't gone looking for you. There's just no way of knowing for sure."

He might as well have slapped me. I thought he was going to finally give me the reassurance I so desperately needed, but instead, he revealed his own ambivalence. Papa loved me, of that I was sure, but he, too, seemed to hold at least some belief that I caused Mama's death. Was I never to be free of the guilt? Perhaps if I solved the mystery of why Nathan changed his mind about leaving, Papa would forgive me. I felt pretty sure the creek had something to do with Nathan's resolve to stay.

Papa returned to work as soon as he finished his dinner and I was left alone to puzzle over Nathan's secret while I cleaned the kitchen. When the last plate was dried and placed on its shelf, I began looking for places big enough to hold his pan. In the house, there was only one room where he could possibly keep anything from us. Our living quarters were simply too close for much privacy. I went out onto the front porch and down the steps, walking quickly to the dock. There was no sign of Nathan returning from downriver.

In a flash, I was in his room, which contained only a couple of trunks, a cane bottom chair, and his bed. The trunk at the end of his bed was where I put the clean clothes after I washed and ironed them. Since there weren't that many clothes, I was already familiar with every square inch of its red and green paper lined interior, so I turned to the other trunk sitting beside the door. A packet of letters tied up in a ribbon, a picture, and some leather bound books were all it contained.

Intrigued by the picture and packet's pink satin ribbon, I struggled with temptation. Nathan certainly didn't seem to be the sentimental sort and his intense animosity made me curious about him. Although I knew it was wrong, I just couldn't go on until I peeked at those letters and studied the picture. I picked up the tintype and turned it over.

Centered within a frame gilded in what looked like real gold leaf was a formal portrait of a beautiful young woman. Her hair and gown were in the style worn by pre-war southern belles. Plump sausage curls were arranged to one side of her face so that they covered her bare collarbone and flowed onto her décolletage. The portrait's size made it difficult to see her dress's pattern details or type of material, but I thought a flower-sprigged muslin to be a pretty good guess. Since the tintype hadn't been hand tinted, as sometimes was done, the girl's coloring was indeterminate, but her eyes might have been bright blue. They fairly jumped out of the portrait just like Papa's did in the picture of him in his uniform. Her complexion appeared very fair. She looked familiar, though I knew I had never met her. I could only think of one girl who had ever been important to Nathan other than my mother. Would he really have kept a picture of her?

Next, I turned over the packet of the letters. The top

one bore a return address of The Dogwoods, Savannah Road, Toomsboro, Georgia. That was the plantation where Papa's maternal grandmother grew up. Why, I wondered, would Nathan be writing to someone there? I would have loved to read the letters, but feared Nathan would notice their binding ribbon had been tampered with, so I reluctantly returned them to their resting place in the trunk. Next to the letters lay a stack of four leather bound books. From the bottom, Holy Bible stamped in gold leaf shone on the largest volume's spine. This had to be the family Bible from which Grandmother Jordan had read to me and had taught me my mother's lineage. The two volumes in the middle of the stack were not as thick as the Bible. Their spines were broken and frayed at the edges. The volume on top appeared to be the newest. I lifted its cover and flyleaf, revealing the first page where Nathan's precise penmanship flowed from top to bottom.

*January 5, 1866*

*Jonathan has proposed that we pool our resources and follow the advice of the Oconee Tribune advertisement. I am reluctantly considering what I feel may be a fool's errand. If my brothers were still living, I would never consider it and I would do everything in my power to prevent it. But with the plantation and family gone to dust and ruin, I have little energy for such a struggle.*

*He is right in one respect. Our present situation is untenable with the local and state governments in the hands of scalawags and carpetbaggers; although, I truly believe that they cannot be in power forever.*

*The crux of the problem is this: I can hardly let that incompetent fool drag my only living blood relatives off into the jungle alone. They would all be killed by savages or disease in a fortnight. I cannot bear the thought of my beloved sister and niece so far from me, so I suppose he has really left me with no alternative but to accompany them to Godforsaken Brazil. Why did Mary Elizabeth insist on marrying beneath her? She could have had anyone. Damn that man! Damn that man and his whole lowbred family!!*

Beloved niece? If you had told me that men had sprouted wings and suddenly learned to fly, I would not have been more surprised than I was by Nathan's declaration of familial affection for me. I knew he doted on my mother, but I had no idea he had ever felt anything for me beyond a dutiful tolerance for his beloved baby sister's child. Papa was right about his being a puzzle.

I closed the trunk lid because I couldn't waste any more time poking into Nathan's business, fascinating as it was. I hadn't found anything remotely like the mystery pan and I still had the floors to sweep, some ironing to do, and supper to fix, all before the men returned. I stood up and glanced around the room. Since the house had a raised floor, it was possible there could be a secret hiding place under one of the floorboards, but I could find it better by crawling under the house, if it came to that. The only place left to look was the bed. I dropped to my knees and began running my hands around the edges of the featherbed, feeling for anything out of place. Several minutes of kneading the edges and then pounding the whole blasted thing from end to end resulted only in dust flying up my nose. In frustration, I lay down on my back and stared at the bedstead. It was of an old fashioned design, with rope used to support the mattress. The ropes on this bed were still tight because Nathan had replaced them soon after we arrived at our land grant.

For lack of anything else to do, I ran my hand along one of the ropes and then I wiggled under the bed. As my fingers groped along the last horizontal length of stretched hemp, they encountered a loose piece of cloth. I might have missed it since it wasn't even remotely close to what I was searching for. I tugged on the flap of cloth and a small leather bag fell down, landing on my nose. It stank of body odor. Nathan apparently carried it in rather private quarters when it was on his person.

I scooted out from under the bed and sat up. The bag's drawstring was tied with a very particular type of knot. I turned it over and back. I wasn't sure I could duplicate the knot, but if I was going to discover what was so important as to be hidden at all times I had no choice. I undid the string and turned the bag upside down. Five rocks about the size of quail eggs fell into my hand. They were a mixture of several colors, but the one that grabbed my attention and then held me mesmerized was bright yellow. I had never seen it in its natural state, but unless I was seriously mistaken, what I held were five gold nuggets. All thoughts of the mystery pan disappeared. No wonder Nathan no longer held any notion of leaving Little Georgia.

I pushed the bag back into its sanctum and rushed about completing my work. Supper was bubbling on the stove when Papa came in from the field toward dark. Nathan must have decided to stay overnight at Colonel Bowen's since there had been no sign of him.

After we ate, I asked casually while I cleared the table, "Papa, has anyone ever said anything about gold being found around here?"

Papa glanced up from his farm journal with a slightly surprised expression. "There were rumors in Igaupe that gold might be lurking in these hills, but rumor is all it is. Why do you ask?"

"Nathan has a bag hidden under his bed and I think it contains gold."

"What were you doing under Nathan's bed?" Papa's eyes narrowed and his brow creased with a frown.

I thought for a moment before I answered. "I was

cleaning and couldn't get all the dust with the broom, so I used a rag. I had to crawl under the bed to wipe everywhere." This was the second time that I remember lying to Papa, but I didn't think he would approve of my spying on Nathan and then setting out to discover his secret.

"What makes you think it's gold?"

"Let me get it and you can see for yourself."

I brought the bag and dropped it into Papa's hand. He stared at it like he didn't really want to know what it contained before he slowly slipped the knot apart and turned the bag over into his open palm. The five little rocks tumbled out. He picked one up and held it so that the kerosene lamp's flame set it glowing. After turning it on all sides, he put it between his teeth and bit down.

"Mary Catherine, you're right. It's gold." Papa slipped the bag in his pants pocket. When he looked up at me, his vivid blue eyes were dark with anger. "It appears your uncle has been hiding a rather important discovery from us. I wonder how long he thought he could keep it secret?"

The question kept me tossing and turning that night. I had wanted to show Nathan in the worst possible light and I had succeeded, but now I feared the consequences. Papa had said little after seeing the bag's contents, which indicated how very angry he really was. I hated Nathan as much as he hated me, but I didn't want Papa to do something he might regret. Even though his disposition had improved with the passage of time, his moods could turn on a dime and a tightly controlled violence bubbled just under the surface much of the time. Years ago, I had accepted that he would never again be the man I had known before the war, but I feared the violent stranger who sometimes took control of him.

I awoke the next morning with a fuzzy head and a

sense of dread I couldn't explain until I remembered the gold and Papa. We were just finishing breakfast when the sound of a dugout scraping on the riverbank announced Nathan's return. He stepped onto the porch and entered the house in the same manner in which he had left, his feet stomping angrily across the floorboards.

He threw his hat onto a peg by the kitchen door and growled, "Get me some breakfast and be quick about it." The sound of his hand crashing against the table made me nearly jump out of my skin. "Did you hear me, girl?"

Papa was on his feet so fast that his chair flew back and hit the wall behind him. "Do not ever speak to my child like that again. Do you hear me?" Papa's slowly measured words echoed through the open door and bounced off the opposite wall across the breezeway. His fist was within an inch of Nathan's nose.

Nathan grabbed Papa's wrist and stood up so their eyes were level. Through clenched teeth he responded. "Your child, need I remind you, killed your wife. Why do you care how I speak to her?"

Papa opened his mouth, but only a strange strangled sound came out. His face flamed as his unfettered hand flew up, snatching up the front of Nathan's shirt. Papa propelled his captive backward until Nathan's head slammed into the wall.

"You aren't worthy to speak to Mary Catherine, much less order her about. She does the work of two grown women without complaint. She is a good, kind, honest girl."

Papa shook his arm free of Nathan's grasp and jerked the gold bag from his pocket. "And speaking of honesty, just when were you planning to tell me about your little discovery?"

Nathan's face turned ashen. "I—how—that's mine.

Give it to me!"

"Not until you show me where you found this. If it was on our land, then half of it belongs to me. If it was on someone else's land, then it doesn't belong to either one of us."

A fist slammed into Papa's head, stunning him momentarily. His head rolled from side to side and then he pounced on Nathan as though he had been waiting for this opportunity for a long time. Papa's fists pounded Nathan, who tried vainly to fend off the blows. Papa's fury seemed to grow with each assault and I became afraid for a second time that he might actually kill Nathan. As much as I hated my mother's brother, I couldn't bear for my father to become a murderer. I flew to Papa and wrapped my arms around his neck.

"Papa, please. Stop." I must have started crying because salty tears rolled into my open mouth. Hanging onto Papa was like riding a bucking horse, but slowly my weight on his back registered with him and he shook me off. He stood up then, his fury spent, looking around like he wasn't quite sure what had just happened.

He ran his hand over his face and then turned back to Nathan, speaking in an even, quiet tone that was more frightening than shouting would have been. "When I encouraged you to come with us to Brazil, it was because Mary Elizabeth wished it. She couldn't bear being separated from you and she worried about what would become of you since the war destroyed your family's wealth." Papa's eyes darkened and his mouth became a grim line. "It was never, mark you, never my desire for you to accompany us. You've always lorded it over other people, thinking yourself so superior, but it was Dom Pedro and my sisters' money that got us here. You didn't contribute a single dime to this venture. Get your things and get out. Take the dugout. Your never ending deceitfulness has demolished any obligation I've ever felt toward you."

Nathan's eyes were wide, like a child caught stealing sweets. "You can't make me leave. This place is half mine. My name is on the land grant and I intend to stay." His gaze shifted to the bag dangling from Papa's fingers. "There's enough gold to share."

"Too late. If you found the gold, so can I. Now, begin packing before I finish what I started."

"You will regret this. I promise you!" Nathan wiped at the blood dripping from his nose and stormed to the door. As I watched his retreating back, it dawned on me that he was actually afraid of Papa. Nathan's being afraid was a satisfying concept. A door slammed and the sound of a trunk being dragged across the floor came from the other side of the house, followed by what sounded like a board being torn from its support frame. My guess was that Nathan had hidden more gold somewhere beneath the floor.

I slipped my hand into Papa's and said quietly, "I know where he found the gold. I can show you tomorrow."

He looked down at me and gave me a hard hug. "Mary C., until we know exactly what we have here, it might be best not tell anyone about Nathan's discovery. It may amount to nothing, but if word were to get around that even a little gold was found here, we'll be overrun with trespassers and hooligans of the worst sort, just like Sutter's Mill, California back in '49."

I nodded and then leaned my head against Papa's chest. As I stood in the security and warmth of my papa's embrace, it occurred to me there had been no sign or mention of the coffee roaster or book Nathan had gone for yesterday and I wondered what he had done while he was away, but it was a mystery no longer of any consequence.

Nathan didn't come out of his room again before we went to bed. Papa occupied the other bedroom beside Nathan's and I slept in the sitting room on a small bed beside the fireplace. I lay awake for a long time listening to the forest's night sounds and thinking about how much better my life would be with Nathan gone. Although Papa's actions had frightened me out of my wits, his words demonstrated a real love for me. Even if he harbored the belief that I played a part in Mama's death, he cared enough to take my side against Nathan. I found comfort in focusing on the love and eventually drifted into an exhausted sleep.

During the night, Papa's boots thudding on the front steps brought me near the surface of consciousness. He still wandered about sometimes when he couldn't sleep, so there was no need to awaken fully. I returned to deep sleep in an instant. When Nathan's door opened, I was momentarily roused again, but late night calls of nature were nothing new for him. Grumpy and irritated at having noises disturb my rest, I rolled onto my side and fell back into oblivion. I needed sleep, even if Papa and Nathan didn't.

## Chapter 11

I sat up, rubbing my eyes and squinting into the sunlight pouring through the window above my bed. The house was unnaturally quiet. Papa usually woke me before dawn so I could fix breakfast for him and Nathan because they wanted every ray of daylight for work, but today the morning was clearly already advanced. I leapt out of bed and threw on my boots and everyday frock, then rushed to the washstand out on the front porch. As I dipped my hands into the tin washbasin's cool water, a figure at the corner of my vision startled me and I whirled around.

"Nathan, what are you doing just sitting here on the porch? Where's Papa?"

He didn't answer immediately. Instead, he studied me with such a bland expression that it became chilling in its lack of emotion. "I have no idea where your father is. I haven't seen him this morning."

The bitter taste of fear filled my mouth as I rushed to Papa's room. The door was closed, so I knocked and waited. I knocked a second time, but no answer came from the other side. Pressing down on the latch, I swung the door open and stepped into the room. The bedcovers were tossed back as though he had gotten up quickly, but expected to return to bed. I glanced at the ladder back chair beside the bed and saw Papa's work trousers laid over the back and his shirt folded neatly on the cane seat, ready for him to put on when he awoke for the day. With trembling hands, I closed the door and returned to the porch.

"Papa's not in his room." The words tumbled out in a high-pitched cry.

Nathan simply nodded in reply.

"Don't you think we should look for him?"

Nathan remained silent and turned his gaze toward the river.

"Nathan, help me look for him. Please!" My words had a frantic edge.

That man, my mother's beloved brother, refused to answer or look at me. He tilted his chair back against the wall and crossed his arms over his chest, continuing to stare at the river, as though he was waiting for something or someone.

"Please, Nathan, he may be hurt. Get up and help me search!" I stepped over to him and touched his shoulder.

He turned eyes on me that were filled with disgust and he grabbed me by both shoulders. Shaking me until my head snapped back and forth, he shouted, "Do not ever touch me again, you sniveling, murderous brat. If your dear father has chosen to desert you because he can't stand the sight of you anymore, then you'll just have to accept it." He pushed me away and continued, "Now, do something useful. Fix my breakfast."

I stumbled backward, staring at Nathan because I couldn't believe I had heard him correctly. It just didn't make any sense. During the argument with Nathan the previous evening, Papa had made it clear he loved me despite my awful mistake. I stared into Nathan's golden hawk's eyes and saw the truth. He was a conniving liar, and worse yet, he appeared to be enjoying the fear that must be radiating from my every pore. What, I wondered, could make family, and a close blood relative at that, so hateful, so hell-bent on inflicting as much emotional pain as possible? As I stood watching him, I felt my hatred for Nathan evolve into an intense loathing, but one tinged with fear. The sounds of two doors opening and two sets of footsteps echoed in my memory. Was it a dream or had it really happened? Although I couldn't answer the question with complete confidence, one thing was clear to me. It seemed there might be no end to what my mother's brother was capable of. I turned away and fled to the kitchen, a familiar, comforting place that now took on the mantle of refuge.

Dizziness overcame me and I grabbed the edge of the kitchen table with both hands. The wood's grain swayed and jumped before my eyes and my breath came in short gasps. Fearing I would fall, I drew up the nearest chair and dropped down onto it before my legs betrayed me. My elbows found the table and my head settled into my upturned palms. I couldn't understand why Papa would leave without telling me. In fact, I was quite sure he would not. If my papa hadn't yielded to Nathan's pressure and left me behind all those times before, he wouldn't just up and abandon me now, especially not to Nathan's tender mercy. Something was dreadfully wrong. As my heart hammered, I made a decision driven as much by rage as by fear. To hell with Nathan and his damned breakfast. I removed my boots and padded through the kitchen door without a sound, slipping onto the porch and down the back steps, pausing only long enough to replace the boots before fleeing through the back gate.

The sun wasn't directly overhead, but it was well above the forested mountaintops that were the shoulders of our valley. I judged that it must be mid-morning at least, giving me sufficient time before dark to walk the possible locations where Papa might have gone. Although our land grant was large, almost 1,000 acres, only the areas along the creek and river had been cleared. I prayed he had not gone into the forest, because the thick trees and undergrowth would make searching alone almost impossible.

I followed the creek for a short distance to the beginning of the coffee fields. Row upon row of carefully spaced young trees marched through the valley, paralleling the creek as far as I could see. It was a daunting task, but there seemed no other choice other than to walk each and every one of those rows from end to end.

Once the fields were searched with no result, I followed the creek to where it ended at Nathan's pool, the name I had given the place since the day I saw him panning for gold. The sun momentarily blinded me as I left the dimness of the forest and I shaded my eyes, praying for any sign that Papa was or had been there, but all was quiet and still. No freshly trampled grass, no indentations left by his boots in the damp earth, no stones disturbed by his tread, nothing to indicate he had been there. In despair, I turned to follow the path back to the house. Hunger was making me lightheaded and I knew I must eat something before continuing my search along the river. The sun's position showed it was three quarters through its daily journey and I hadn't eaten since supper the night before.

The back gate stuck a little, swollen as it was with the humidity, and my dress was wet all round the neck, under my arms, and down my back. Sweat ran from my forehead into my eyes and when I wiped it away, my hand came back grubby from the dirt that must have accumulated on my face. All I wanted was a quick wash and a cold biscuit so I would have the energy to finish my search along the riverbank.

The porch's deep dogtrot was a cool respite from the bright day's heat and I paused there, leaning against the kitchen wall. I became lost in my own ruminations until male voices penetrated my consciousness. I practically jumped out of my skin because I was almost always alone during this part of the day. A broad smile spread across my face and I started to race toward the voices until I realized with a shock that Papa's wasn't among them. A deep bass, punctuated by Nathan's tenor at its most unctuous, resonated from somewhere near our small dock. It could only be Brother Williams talking to Nathan, for no one else's voice had that particular timbre. Crestfallen, I crept to the edge of the front wall, hoping its shadow would keep me concealed long enough to eavesdrop on my uncle and the preacher. Something in the rhythm of their speech was beginning to send chilly fingers playing along my spine.

"What could have been the cause, Brother Jordan?"

"I have no idea. Yesterday was no different from any other. Nothing out of the ordinary happened. We all went to bed after supper as usual." My growing loathing for Nathan may have influenced my perception, but his voice seemed to ring with the particular tone it took on when he was lying. After years of experience, I was expert in identifying his prevarications. "I must say, however, that the balance of my brother-in-law's mind has been affected for some time. Surely none of you has forgotten the incident over the Mashburn boy. He never recovered from the war or my sister's unnecessary death."

"I pray your view is inaccurate. That would endanger his immortal—"

"Let's leave the matter to the Almighty, shall we? It doesn't alter our earthly concerns." Colonel Bowen's voice, colored with impatience and irritation, interrupted the preacher. "Where's the child? The situation affects her most."

"She isn't here. Of course, wandering off is nothing new for her."

Silence followed Nathan's response and then Colonel Bowen spoke slowly. "I see. Has something unfortunate happened to your niece, as well?"

"I'm sure I have no idea. She didn't confide her plans to me before she sneaked off this morning." Tension brought out an unattractive whine in Nathan's voice.

My head swam and my vision blurred. I don't really remember running from the porch to where the men stood. One minute my feet were firmly planted on wooden boards, the next I was standing trembling beside Colonel Bowen. When I looked around, I was surprised to see six men, all of whom were looking at me with eyes clouded with emotion.

"What do you mean by unfortunate? Where's my papa?" My shrill words filled the otherwise silent yard.

The men looked from Colonel Bowen to Brother Williams and back. The colonel sighed and placed his hand on my shoulder. "Mary Catherine, there is no way to make this any easier. I wish I knew a way, but I don't. We aren't sure exactly how it happened. You've got to be brave, child."

I wanted to scream. I couldn't bear the protracted politeness and platitudes, but I also prayed for time to stop.

"Around daylight, one of the colonists saw a large piece of white cloth caught in river brush. When he went to investigate, I'm afraid he found Captain MacDonald in his nightshirt, floating in the water. In the night, he must have fallen in and drowned, then the current brought him as far as Government House. I'm very sorry, my dear."

A numbing cold began in my mid-section and crept outward in all directions, filling my mouth with a strange metallic taste. The yard tilted strangely on its side and then someone snuffed out the sun.

When my eyes opened, they gazed up through the porch's support beams at the roof's wooden shakes. The pattern of overlapping wood slices was comforting and homey in its molted shades of brown and tan, reminding me of our porch at home in Georgia. Colonel Bowen wiped my face with a wet cloth and murmured, "There, now, child. It's just the shock."

I looked toward the river where four of the men were lifting a long, white form from one of the two dugouts pulled up on the bank. Each man held a corner of what was obviously a bed sheet, their feet sliding in the mud as they struggled up the riverbank's gentle slope. I watched them as though as I was the casual observer of some inconsequential event, assessing their progress, judging how many times they might stumble before they made it all the way to the porch. Papa didn't have an ounce of fat on him, but he was tall and muscular. He must have been a heavy burden in the ankle deep mud and I wondered if the men would drop him. It's strange the way absurdly normal thoughts sometimes appear unbidden when one's world is about to end.

They brought the sheet up onto the porch and laid it down next to the wall. I sat up slowly, dreading what would come next. As the cloth fell away, Papa's head was uncovered. It lolled oddly to one side, marred by an ugly gash that split the skin starting at the temple, extending beyond his hairline. The skin around the wound was pale and puckered from so many hours in the water and something white shone through his hair. Where pronounced lethargy had been a moment before, rage now stormed. I jumped up and flew at Nathan.

"You killed Papa! Murderer!" Fists pounded against his chest.

Nathan grabbed my wrists and pushed me back without easing his grip. "How dare you accuse me? I slept soundly last night. I had no need to leave my bed." He then glanced around the group while I kicked at his legs and ankles. "You can see for yourselves what she's like."

A restraining hand dropped onto my shoulder. "Mary Catherine, no one believes this was anything other than a tragic accident. You are understandably distraught and I'm sure you already regret accusing your uncle." Brother Williams stepped forward, placed his other hand on Nathan's arm, and fixed him with an unreadable glare.

Nathan's eyes were first to break away. He looked across the yard toward the river as though he suddenly needed to search for some lost or forgotten object and thought it might be floating by. Gradually his grip on my wrists slackened and I pulled free.

Brother Williams next turned his hooded black eyes on me. "What possible reason could Mr. Jordan have for wanting to harm Captain MacDonald? Young lady, you owe your uncle an apology."

I returned his steely gaze with one of my own. No power in heaven or earth could have made me apologize. "Look at Nathan's face! You can see the marks of where they fought after supper last night. Then I heard both of them walking on the porch just before I fell asleep."

Nathan sighed heavily and shook his head. "Are you now adding lying to your character defects? I suppose I shouldn't be surprised." His voice grew louder and more emphatic. "The damage to my face was done by a glancing blow from a tree that fell the wrong way due to Jonathan's incompetence. I was lucky not to be killed."

"You're a liar. You've lied for years! First about how Mr. McMullan wouldn't let y'all in the colony because of me and now you're lying about what happened to Papa. You killed him and I know it!"

"What I know is that you killed your mother through your willful disobedience and your father has now run true to his low breeding as a suicide." Nathan looked around at the other men, who seemed shocked by my outburst, and a self-satisfied gleam filled his eyes. "No one believes your lies and I have no intention of being saddled with a child who accuses me of such a foul deed. Have your bag packed because we are leaving for Igaupe as soon as we get your father in the ground. You'll be on the first boat bound for North America."

An uncomfortable quiet fell over the group. Our visitors wore embarrassed expressions and seemed to be trying to distance themselves from the whole ugly scene by slowly edging toward the steps. The preacher actually turned his back and moved to the opposite end of the porch.

After exchanging perplexed glances with the other colonists, Colonel Bowen said, "Mr. Jordan, regardless of the circumstances, you can't possibly expect this child to travel all the way back to Georgia unaccompanied."

"What else would you propose? Perhaps you and your wife might take her? She is fairly useful around the house."

Colonel Bowen's face flamed, but he didn't respond. I felt the preacher stirring before I heard him speak. He had been leaning against a post, watching butterflies flit among wildflowers at the edge of the yard, acting as though he had lost interest in the drama regarding my future. He shifted his weight and strode over to rejoin the group.

"Brother Jordan, are you forgetting the promise you made?"

Nathan's eyes widened. "I'm sure Mary Elizabeth never envisioned a situation such as this when she extracted that promise, and besides, she was verging on delirium. She didn't know what she was saying."

"You forget I was less than four feet from the bed when she spoke. She was weak, yes, and she knew she was dying, but she gave every appearance of having all of her mental faculties intact."

Nathan looked from man to man and then replied, "I will not give a home to the person responsible for my sister's death and who now accuses me of murder."

"You swore to that same dying sister you would take care of her little girl. Moreover, half of this land grant is hers, inherited from her father. You are family, and as such, yours is not only a legal, but more importantly, it is a moral obligation to provide for her until she marries."

"He murdered my father. I don't want to live with him and I don't care about this land." I searched each face, my neck aching from the strain of looking up. "Why won't you listen to me? I want to go home."

Brother Williams looked down at me. A small sympathetic smile played across his lips and crept up into his eyes. "Mary Catherine, I know you don't mean what you're saying. You know in your heart that your uncle, someone of your own blood, couldn't have killed your father. I fear grief and exhaustion have affected your thinking. You are simply overwhelmed. It's understandable given the circumstances." He stooped down so that his eyes were level with mine. "As much as you may want to go back, there is no one to travel with you, my dear, and you can't go alone. It's unthinkable and unsafe. You and your uncle have no choice." Brother Williams's eyes lifted, meeting and holding Nathan's gaze like a snake mesmerizing a small animal just before it strikes. "That is, unless he intends to shirk his moral duty and fails to keep his promise to his dying sister. Of course, the rest of the colony would probably take a very dim view of such negligence. They might not want such a man living among them."

The burning black eyes continued to challenge Nathan, who met their gaze as long as he could before he lowered his head and spoke without any of his usual hubris. "Perhaps it is what Mary Elizabeth would want."

Brother Williams turned back to me. I looked into those eyes and was struck dumb. I wanted to protest. I wanted to shout that I would never tolerate such a plan, but the words wouldn't form on my tongue, which felt as though it was glued to the roof of my mouth. For a second time, the preacher's natural authority enveloped me in its mantle as it had in the *Alyssa Jane's* dark passageway, but on this occasion the hooded eyes fixed me as though they could penetrate my flesh to the very core of my being. Given my age, I was no match for such a force. And so I accepted that I was to remain in the loving bosom of the only family I had left in Brazil.

Papa's funeral, if it could be called such, took place the same afternoon. We all recited the 23$^{rd}$ Psalm, then Brother Williams read from the Book of Revelations, said a prayer, and that was it. I sat on the ground next to the grave until the sun's last rays disappeared, wondering why no one believed me about Nathan. Why did adults never listen to children? Did they think I was so stupid that I couldn't see my mother's brother for what he was or did they think I was lying like he said? I also wondered if I should have told them about the gold as proof of my indictment against Nathan, but the last thing Papa had said to me was to keep it a secret. I put my arms on my knees and rested my forehead on them while silent tears rushed to water the earth in which Papa lay. I was so alone and so confused.

Nathan returned to the grave when the twilight was fading. He grabbed my arm and jerked me to my feet without a word. For the second time in three years, he marched me away from a parent's grave without allowing me to pause for a final look back. The six visitors stayed the night and departed at first light the following morning, leaving me completely alone with the one person in the world who detested me. The emotion, you can be assured, was returned a thousand-fold.

## Chapter 12

Nathan and I stood on our dock the morning after Papa's burial watching the six men from Government House load into their dugouts and push off. When they were out of sight around the first bend in the river, Nathan turned on his heel and walked to the house without saying a single word. Instead of stopping on the porch or going into the kitchen, he went straight to his room where he stayed for about ten minutes and then returned with his small valise in his hand.

"Where are you going? Am I going too?" My heart beat a little faster as Nathan brushed past me in stony silence.

"Do you want a lunch pail packed? What would you like for supper?" Again there was no reply. Nathan was now on the dock, untying the mooring line of our dugout.

"Nathan, please tell me where you're going and when you'll be back." My voice now had a high-pitched pleading tone.

When he was seated in the canoe, he deigned to speak. "Where I'm going is none of your business. Time will tell whether I return or not. I suggest that you learn to make do on your own until I've made my decision."

"Nathan, you can't leave me here by myself! We ate the last of the meat this morning and the garden vegetables aren't ready yet. Please! How will I get help if something bad happens?"

Nathan gave me a look that chilled my very soul and then his lips curled into a small sneer. "I think you should be able to ride the plow mule over to Government House, don't you?"

"But that's a day's ride over the mountains and the saddle is too heavy for me to lift."

"Well then, you'll just have to walk, won't you?" And with that, he too shoved off into the current and began paddling away to the south.

"Nathan, please come back. I'll be good, I promise!" My shrill words echoed from the high riverbank on the opposite side.

Soft laughter drifted back over Nathan's shoulder, but it contained no merriment.

My knees shook as I walked back to the porch. How could he just leave me alone and unprotected? I don't think I really understood how little he cared what happened to me until all sight of him disappeared around the river's bend. I sat on Papa's porch chair and stared out at the river. It wasn't even mid-morning, but the day was already hot and sweat gathered on my upper lip despite the porch's shade. Even after three years in Brazil, the reversal of the seasons was still difficult, especially in December. I leaned back so that my head rested on the sitting room's exterior wall and let the tears roll down my face, onto my neck, and into my ears. Sobs came so rapidly they shook my whole body. It was hard to believe that Christmas was only a week away, even more so that my once happy and secure life had come to this: I was left an orphan and abandoned to survive as best I could in a dangerous place that barely tolerated my existence.

That night as darkness fell, I couldn't decide whether to use the oil lamp or not, so I lifted the tin that held the oil supply to see how much I had left. It felt much too light for comfort. When I shook it, the liquid inside sloshed around as though it was only perhaps a quarter full. With nothing else to do, I dropped down onto my bed and tried to go to sleep, but an *onca* growling somewhere in the forest outside my window sent chills down my spine. Crashing in the forest undergrowth followed by the terrified death screams of some small animal chased all possibility of sleep away and I tossed and turned for what felt like hours. Realizing I might never get to sleep if I didn't get control of my fear, I got out of bed and tiptoed to the sitting room door. Why I felt the need to creep so silently was a mystery since there was no one around to hear me for many miles.

When I reached the door, I stood dumbly before its wooden planks, wondering what to do to make my refuge safer. Finally, I grabbed a ladder back chair and shoved it under the latch to prevent the door from being opened from the outside. I removed Papa's tintype and Mama's handkerchief from their hiding place behind a loose rock in the chimney and carried them to my bed where I climbed under the sheet, pulling it over my head. The picture pressed into my cheek where it lay with the handkerchief on my pillow. The faint fragrance of Mama's scent still wafted from the delicate lawn fabric. Or, perhaps it was just that my desire for it was so intense. Since my pearls had been sold, these were literally the last remnants of my parents I possessed.

Only then did the tears begin again. They started as a trickle, but were soon a flood so great that my sobs shook the bed. A question kept rolling over and over through my mind: was the fight for survival worth the effort? I have no memory of actually falling asleep. One moment my pillow was soaked with my misery and the next I was peering at bright sunlight through itchy swollen eyes.

The only thing good that can be said to have come from Nathan's desertion is that the answer to my first night's question came to me rather quickly, and consequently, I learned something important about myself. When my thirteenth birthday arrived on January 1, 1870 and I found myself somewhat malnourished but still very much alive, stubbornness rose in me. It hardened me and drove me on, preventing total despair. Sheer determination to deny Nathan the pleasure of burying me kept me toiling to get enough food. I was sure by now he would eventually return, if only for more gold.

At night, Bess's face, not Mama or Papa's, came to me in my dreams, speaking words of encouragement and comfort. Her smile flashed in my waking memory. Her courage and common sense had kept Mama sane and me safe during the war years and I made up my mind to heed her words only. I loved Mama and Papa desperately, but I needed strength, not gentility. Bess had been my rock when I was little and memory of her provided the example I needed for survival now. From that time forward, nothing Nathan said or did would matter as much as surviving. I would live to spite him.

My recent diet, consisting mainly of native *mandioca farinha* bread, milk, and eggs, had taken a toll on my digestive track, but the tomatoes, beans, okra, potatoes, and cabbage were now ready for harvest. A pattern developed that wasn't exactly soothing, but the exhaustion it created left me little time to feel sorry for myself. My grief, deep though it was, became a tangible thing that could be packed away when necessary. Although I missed Papa terribly, the struggle for survival shoved my grief into a box and kept the lid firmly closed until it was allowed to creep out into the shadows as I ate my meager supper in each day's fading twilight. I crawled into bed as soon as darkness descended because I wanted to save the little remaining lamp oil for emergencies. As long as there was any light in the sky, I worked. Gathering vegetables in the morning, eating my main meal of the day at noon, and preparing the produce for drying or pickling in the afternoon filled my days. I thank the Good Lord for my years spent with Bess in the garden and kitchen. At her elbow, I had learned by observation how to clean the crock jars used for pickling beans, corn, and kraut.

From my second mother, I knew how long to leave okra and corn spread out in the sun on their clean white sheets. Selecting tender young beans and then using a stout needle and thread to string them so they could be hung on a shady outside wall and turned into leather britches in the warm summer air had been a wonderful game played with her on long hot afternoons. She taught me how to milk the cow and then churn butter to an old chant.

*Come butter come*
*Come butter come*
*Peter standing at the gate*
*Waiting for a butter cake*
*Come butter come*

Tending the young sweet potato plants would ensure food for the fall. I even knew the basics of salt curing meat, but not how long it needed to hang before it could be eaten. Of course, meat was beside the point since I couldn't shoot Papa's rifle well enough to kill game and I had no idea how to go about butchering an animal even if I had managed to kill one. Very importantly, though, I knew how to select, dry, and store seeds for future crops. Working kept my mind occupied during the day and exhaustion sent me into instant oblivion the moment my head touched my pillow at night.

On the Wednesday of my fourth week alone, I awoke when the sun had climbed high enough to peep over the treetops outside Papa's bedroom window. Even though I had moved into it a week after Nathan left, I still thought of the room as belonging to Papa. Another important change was that I now slept from dusk to full daylight because it sustained sufficient energy to keep me going.

Standing before the pegs on which I hung my clothes, I put my nose to both of my everyday dresses. The odor emanating from the worn muslin was rather foul in both garments. Washing clothes had fallen by the wayside in favor of more pressing needs, so I grabbed the least offensive and put it on. As I buttoned up the bodice, I noticed it was getting tight across my chest and hung about my waist as though it belonged to a chubbier child. And glancing down where we weren't supposed to look when I sponge bathed the night before last, I saw hair sprouting in a place that I wasn't sure it should be growing.

If I had had the time to ponder the situation, I might have been frightened by the mysteries of my body, but there was too much work for me to waste energy on questions to which I had no answers. At least three pecks of beans needing to be strung for leather britches waited for me. I removed the chair that I used to block the door latch at night. At first sight of me on the back porch, the hogs grunted accusingly from their lot, demanding that the kitchen slop bucket be emptied into their trough without further delay. The milk cow bawled from her shed that her udders were painful and she needed immediate relief. After attending to the animals' needs and throwing out a few handfuls of dried corn for the hens, I settled myself in the shadiest part of the front porch. Working my needle and thread through the tender green flesh of the beans, though a mindless activity, was soothing once I established a rhythm.

The bean pile had diminished by half when ripples going against the river's current flashed in the afternoon sun. Soon, the nose of a dugout edged around the bend, creating a flurry of excitement. Maybe someone from Government House was coming to check on me. I would tell them what Nathan had done and how he had left me alone for all this time. They would take my side, drive him from the colony, and find a safe home for me until I married. My imagination galloped on. I dropped my needle and started running for our dock, practically dancing at the thought of human contact, of rescue. Then Nathan's sour visage appeared and my heart plummeted to the soles of my bare feet.

A few swift paddle strokes brought the canoe to the dock. I stood frozen in the middle of the yard, waiting for what I wasn't quite sure. How would he act? Was he home to stay or would he gather gold and be off again to God only knew where? But most important, I wanted to know how he would treat me. Fear juxtaposed with my determination to survive set my mind whirling and my heart thumping.

Since it felt like being the first to speak would cast me in the weaker position, I gathered my flagging courage and glared at my uncle as he strode across the yard to where I stood. He paused when he reached my side, looked me up and down, then smirked.

"Well, I see you've managed all right." That was all he said before heading straight for the kitchen. When I followed, I found him lifting pot lids and dipping my meager vegetable supper onto a plate. "Don't you have any meat? Oh, I suppose not. I'll go hunting after I eat."

Amazement hardly describes how I felt watching Nathan just walk back into my life as casually as though nothing out of the ordinary had happened during the last four weeks.

"Not going to speak to your uncle? Have it your way then, but be ready to cook me a decent supper when I return." He glanced at me before continuing, "Don't worry. I'll bring enough meat for two." After eating everything in both pots, he took Papa's rifle from the wall and left.

It took a moment, but when my situation eventually sank in, my screams filled the dogtrot and the thudding from my fists pounding against the walls echoed from the dense forest surrounding the house. Up until now, the fight for survival had consumed my mind and time, but now I realized just how trapped I was. I had nowhere to go and no way to get there even if a place was found. Nathan controlled the farm, all means of transportation, all finances, and by default, he controlled me.

Thus became the pattern for the next year. Nathan came and went from the farm at will, expecting me to keep it going in his absence and doing little more than watching the coffee grow and presumably looking for gold during the days when he was home. He stayed away from the house from dawn 'til dusk, returning only for meals that were eaten in silence. When he had been around for two or three weeks, he would load the canoe and paddle off again, but where he went and what he did while there remained a mystery because he communicated nothing and I refused to speak to him anymore than was absolutely necessary. Wherever it was he went, though, someone did his laundry because he only added to my wash load after he had been home for a week or so. I also noticed a few new garments on the pegs in his room when I went in to sweep and dust. A new suit of fine wool and two new gaily patterned waistcoats and silk neckties hung among the older things. The item of greatest interest, however, was something that I knew could not possibly belong to my uncle.

Just after my fourteenth birthday, Nathan returned from one of his extended absences and dropped a pile of dirty clothes in the middle of the kitchen floor. He had been absent for a longer period than usual. This fact, coupled with the dirty laundry, made me wonder if he was traveling to some new location where they were less inclined to do his washing for him. After separating the garments destined for the wash pot from those that would simply get a good brushing, airing, and pressing, I began turning out the contents of the pants pockets. He rarely left anything, but Bess had always turned out pockets, so I kept up the ritual as a way of keeping my tenuous connection to her alive as much as to avoid any potential complaint from Nathan. When I stuck my hand into the pocket of his good suit coat, it fell upon a swatch of soft fabric I recognized instantly as the type of fine lawn used to make ladies' handkerchiefs.

I tugged it from Nathan's pocket and opened my hand. Pure white fabric unfolded and draped across my palm. Someone had gone to great trouble and expense in embroidering a complicated wildflower motif in shades of pink, lavender, and green silk on one corner. Exquisite handmade white lace edged the fabric all round. The original owner was certainly no peasant. And to have willingly let this treasure go, the owner probably had others of equal or greater value. Of course, Nathan could have stolen this one. I wouldn't put anything past him, not with what I knew about him. Hearing his footstep on the dogtrot's floorboards, I hastily folded the handkerchief and returned it to its sanctum, hoping he wouldn't realize it had been disturbed.

Where on earth had it come from? And who would have willingly given him such a token? It was very difficult for me to see Nathan as anything other than my hideous persecutor and Papa's murderer, but I also recalled that ladies had often turned to watch him pass during our travels together. Perhaps there was one who had caught his fancy?

Nathan paused in the open kitchen doorway, his valise dangling from his hand. "I'll be gone overnight. Have a good dinner prepared when I return. Make sure we have a meat dish that's edible."

How like Nathan to want a good dinner with a meat course when there was no meat and he hadn't stayed home long enough to kill any. Well, fish would have to do because I was not prepared to kill a hen. Their eggs kept me strong when Nathan disappeared for weeks on end and the meat ran out.

The next morning, I took my fishing pole to the end of our dock and before too long a big corvine was sitting beside me. By necessity I had become quite an accomplished fisherman. While I was scaling and cleaning the fish to fry for dinner, the dugout's nose appeared around the river's bend, but it bore two passengers and one of them was clearly female. I squinted for a better look at the woman and was astonished to see Miss Mashburn, little Johnny's spinster aunt, sitting primly in the bow of the canoe. Surely this wasn't the owner of the handkerchief. The Mashburns had come from Texas with little more than the clothes on their backs and I doubted that their time in Brazil had produced enough income to allow for such frivolous expenditures.

The dugout bumped against our dock and Nathan tied it off, then he offered his hand to Miss Mashburn, assisting her moderately graceful assent from transport to dock. Once she was steady on her feet, she looked down into Nathan's eyes with an expression that could only be described as adoration.

Good Lord, I knew she wasn't the smartest person I'd ever met, but I hadn't realized she was stupid enough to be charmed by my uncle. Perhaps spinsterhood had made her desperate. This surprising turn of events still didn't explain the expensive handkerchief, however.

"Hello, Mary Catherine. Is dinner ready, my dear?" Nathan's voice sounded as though he was speaking to a cherished loved one. Shocked doesn't begin to describe how I felt.

"You remember Miss Mashburn, of course. She will be staying with us for a while. I'm sure you won't mind moving back into the sitting room?"

A dumbfounded expression surely spread over my face because I had to consciously close my mouth. The situation was just too bizarre to be fully grasped.

"Mary Catherine, I see you have a very nice fish cleaned. May I help you in the kitchen?" Butter wouldn't have melted in Miss Mashburn's mouth. She placed her hand on my arm and continued, "Come, my dear. Let's finish preparing dinner, shall we?"

I looked from Nathan to Miss Mashburn and back, then nodded and followed them into the house. Whatever these two were up to, seemingly willing compliance would go a lot farther in uncovering the plot than obstinacy.

Dinner was prepared, served, and eaten floating on a calm sea of polite adult conversation, but beneath the surface, a torrent of emotions raged. The tension between Nathan and Miss Mashburn was palpable as they focused their attention on me.

"My dear, I hope the surprise of my coming here hasn't been too much for you. You haven't said a word since we arrived." Miss Mashburn's features were arranged into an expression of urgent compassion. Her eyes looked directly into mine and her smile was achingly broad.

I could no longer avoid speaking, so I answered, "I'm sure that having you here will be a pleasure. Do we know how long we expect to enjoy your company?" Now where, I wondered, had those artificial words come from? They sounded stiff and out of character for someone my age. I guess I must have heard Mama or Grandmother say them at some time or other when they were less than pleased with the arrival of unexpected guests. Miss Mashburn seemed happy with my response, but Nathan glared. I suspect he detected the truth hidden behind formality's veil.

"Oh, how kind! We can begin your instruction in the morning."

"Instruction?" I couldn't help shouting.

"You must not know yet." Her gaze flew to Nathan. The adoration shining in her eyes turned my stomach. A brilliant smile spread across her rather plain features as she continued, "Nathan, Mr. Jordan, has brought me here to give you instruction in the social graces and ways of being a lady. This is going to work out so well for all of us!"

I looked into Nathan's golden hawk's eyes and tried desperately to determine what lay behind this sudden and inexplicable altruism, but the shades were drawn too tightly, allowing not a single glimmer of truth to escape.

## Chapter 13

"The first thing we're going to do is get rid of those horrid freckles! No more running around out-of-doors unprotected for you, young lady." Miss Mashburn stood beside me as I washed the breakfast dishes, fanning herself against the summer morning's heat, and swept her eyes over me from head to toe. "And when your uncle returns from Igaupe, there will be no more household chores. We've got to get those hands softened and manicured."

"Igaupe?"

"Why, yes. He's packing for the journey as we speak. He shouldn't be gone for more than two weeks at most." She paused and smiled brightly. "You needn't worry, my dear. Your uncle would never leave you all alone in such a wild place. In his absence, we will begin our etiquette lessons and burn that disgracefully tatty garment. Why on earth do you wear such?"

I stared at her dumbfounded and then looked down at my dress. It was on the verge of falling to rags. Despite having let out the bodice and lengthening the hem until there was no selvage left, it was still too tight, too short, and had too many patches. The woman clearly had no idea, or was choosing to ignore, how I'd been living over the past two years. Moreover, she was seriously deluded if she thought Nathan was ever going to take on the housework and gardening, and somehow, I knew Miss Mashburn had no intention of doing either. If we were to eat and have a livable house, then there wasn't anyone left but me to do the work. And my freckles had been part of me for so long that I couldn't begin to imagine how she thought they could be eliminated. As I tried to sort through all of the contradictions, laughter threatened to disrupt the surface calm I was trying so hard to maintain. The situation would have been howlingly funny if it hadn't also been so disquieting.

Good to Miss Mashburn's word, Nathan returned two weeks later, but he wasn't alone. A man and woman accompanied him. When the dugout pulled alongside our dock, the man crawled onto the dock. His heavy muscles rippled under skin so dark it shone with purple undertones in the bright sun. An ankle shackle attached to a strong chain impeded his progress. He struggled to stand and then bent over to pull a heavy iron weight from the canoe. He then began tying off the mooring lines, while the woman, nearly as dark as her companion, began lifting baggage, several canvas wrapped parcels, and a small wooden crate onto the dock. The woman repeated the man's struggle to gain an upright position on the dock. This must have been what Miss Mashburn, or Miss Ida as she now insisted I call her, meant by no more work.

When everyone was on the porch, I put out my hand to the new woman, who reminded me very slightly of Bess. "Hello. I'm Mary Catherine." The woman's frightened eyes briefly met mine and then darted away. She stood stone still.

A quick intake of breath accompanied Ida's slapping my hand as she hissed, "One does not greet slaves as though they are honored guests. I thought you would have remembered at least that much from before the war."

"But, we aren't supposed to have slaves anymore because of the war."

"Don't be foolish. This is Brazil. Slaves are still bought and sold here, thank goodness." Ida turned to the new arrivals. "Place Mr. Jordan's bag in the second room on the left. You do know left from right?"

The man and woman both looked at her uncomprehendingly while Nathan chuckled. "They only speak Portuguese. Perhaps you can teach them basic household English while you're refining my niece's manners?"

Ida looked at Nathan as though he had just uttered the vilest obscenity, but replied, "Of course, whatever is needed."

She motioned to the slaves and through signs and gestures made clear their orders of the moment. Lifting the heavy iron weights that prevented any hope of escape, they began shuffling as best they could.

When Nathan's valise and the parcels were stored away, only the little wooden crate remained. Nathan stooped down beside it and began pulling off the top slats. "This is a gift for you and Miss Mashburn, Mary Catherine. Would you like to see what's inside?" My thoughts must have been written on my face because he laughed and continued, "Well, come on and see. It's not full of snakes."

Ida cast a quick glance in my direction and then gave me a little push. "Go on, don't keep your uncle waiting. Lack of gratitude is both rude and ungracious. A lady always exhibits a gracious spirit."

I took a few steps toward the box as Nathan removed the last slat, revealing a jumble of straw and old wadded newspapers. He beckoned for me to join him on the floor. I sat down beside the box as he pushed back the packing material and lifted out the crate's contents tightly wrapped in paper. He put several objects into my lap. The first one was the largest and felt solid enough. When I had a hole torn in the paper, I could see a shiny blue and white surface. Tearing the paper completely away revealed a china teapot, much like the one Mama had admired in Kingston. The remaining parcels contained a creamer, sugar bowl, four cups and saucers, a silver sugar shell, and four silver teaspoons.

"China service for twelve and the rest of the silverware had to be ordered, but they should arrive within a few months, then we can have a dinner party."

The world shifted on its axis.

"We only have four chairs that fit under the table. How are we supposed to have a party?" I sounded stupid, but I couldn't help it. This 180-degree turn in Nathan had me reeling.

"Aren't you going to thank your uncle?" Ida's sharp tone demanded a reply.

"Thank you, Nathan."

"Young ladies do not address their elders using their Christian names unless the names are preceded by titles indicating a close relationship. In the future, you will address Mr. Jordan as Uncle Nathan."

"I'm sure she'll learn under your excellent tutelage, Miss Mashburn. Let's take all of this to the kitchen and see if the woman can be gotten to prepare a meal for us."

My stupefaction was so profound that I had completely forgotten the two Negroes standing a little distance from our group. "What are their names? And where on earth are they going to sleep?"

"I believe Fatima and Henrique is what the trader called them." That must have been correct because two pairs of black eyes turned toward Nathan expectantly. "We'll call them Tina and Henry. Easier to pronounce. They'll sleep here in the dogtrot until Henry gets a real barn built for the mules, then he and the woman will sleep in the shed. After the barn, he'll start the new house."

"New house?" I decided my hearing was playing tricks.

"I've ordered glass for windows from a supplier in Igaupe and Henry is a skilled carpenter. That's why I bought him. It's time we returned to our previously finer way of living, don't you think?"

I didn't answer. What could I possibly have said in response to such a question? I rose and gestured for Tina to follow me. Ida followed as well and among the three of us, we managed to get supper together.

As we ate, I glanced at Nathan and commented as casually as I was able. "You know, Tina would be able to work a lot faster if her shackle was removed. She can hardly get around. I think you'll get more work for your money if she's freer to move about. Don't you agree, Miss Ida?"

Ida's fork paused mid-air as she glanced at Nathan and then beamed at me. "I believe you might have the makings of a chatelaine after all, my dear. Of course the girl will be worth more if she is able to work faster."

"That chain is there for a reason." Nathan's glare took in all present. "There's been a lot of unrest lately. There's even talk of slave revolts, stirred up by those damned fool abolitionists, no doubt. It's John Brown and Harriet Beecher Stowe all over again, only in Portuguese. Those shackles stay right where they are until I see no further need for them."

Thinking of Bess and how she must once have been in chains, I couldn't keep from glancing sidelong at the two unfortunates who waited silently by the kitchen door, chains and weights at their feet, but surprise made my eyes linger on the male. It was probably my imagination, but there seemed to be comprehension in his expression. His gaze dropped to meet mine for the briefest moment, and then darted back up to stare straight ahead as though he had never looked at me.

"Niece, what are you gawking at? Finish your supper and leave the management of slaves to me."

Not wanting to make trouble for the newest members of our household or myself, I looked back to my plate, but not before I saw another flash of understanding in Henry's eyes.

After all of the kitchen work had been completed, Tina and Henry were permitted to eat our supper scraps on the porch and then bed down for the night with thin blankets that Miss Ida had declared too ragged for use in the house anymore. The rest of us went to bed shortly afterward.

I tossed and turned in my corner of the sitting room far into the night. My mind was afire with such a conglomeration of emotions that I wasn't sure I would ever sleep again. I had no idea Nathan was such a good actor, but apparently he could have competed with the Booth brothers for center stage had the situation required. Of all the emotions racing through my mind, fear was the strongest. It would take more than a pretty teapot to convince me that Nathan had suddenly remembered we were family, that we shared the same blood and memories of earlier, happier days.

Since my eyes refused to stay closed for more than a few minutes at a time, I eased from bed and went to the chimney where my fingers slipped under the loose rock and pulled my dearest treasures from their hiding place. As usual when sleep refused to envelope me in its sweet oblivion, I carried the little scrap of canvas containing Papa's portrait and Mama's handkerchief back to my bed. Moonlight pouring through the open window above illuminated my papa's handsome, young face. The excellent cut of his new military uniform made him a dashing figure astride his war stallion. As young as I had been, I still noticed how women's eyes followed him as his unit paraded down the county seat's main street on its way to war. I ran a finger over his tintype face and asked myself for the thousandth time exactly what had happened the night he died. I had been drifting toward sleep that night when I thought I heard a second set of footsteps on the porch. Had I dreamt them? Imagined them afterward? Simply made them up because in my grief and anger I wanted Nathan to be guilty?

I placed the portrait on my blanket and picked up Mama's handkerchief, removing it from its protective rag wrapper. The fine lawn was still snowy white. I didn't ever want to wash it because then her scent would be gone. It was all I had left of my beautiful mother, whose exact features were beginning to fade with the passing years. These two objects were my talismans against Nathan's emotional assaults, his attempts to destroy my spirit, and I returned them to their sanctuary to rest in secret until I took them out again.

Sleep still hid itself, so I decided a trip to the outhouse might help pass some of the interminable night. Padding across the cool floorboards in my bare feet gave me a delicious sense of rebellion because Miss Ida insisted that ladies never went without shoes, not ever. When I had outgrown my old boots, I simply went without until Nathan brought back a pair of someone's cast-offs, but by then, I had found I liked going barefoot. Besides, the used boots were much too big and were hard to keep on even with rags stuffed into the toes. Now, however, I pushed my feet into those blasted boots every day.

It was only a few familiar short strides to the door, but when I swung it halfway back, it bumped into something and wouldn't go any farther. It was then I remembered the unopened parcels lying next to the wall. Curiosity extinguished all thoughts of going to the outhouse. The teapot and silver spoons were so out of character that I wondered if the parcels might provide some clue as to Nathan's motives for his sudden change. I carried them back to my bed. If I were careful with the twine and rewrapping, no one would be the wiser about my unauthorized inspection. The twine's knots were difficult, but when I finally got them untied, the canvas proved to be only one layer and fell open easily.

Fabric that could only have been blue silk shone dully, its color faded by the moonlight. I lifted the material and it fell into the shape of a formal gown, similar to the ones Mama had worn for dinner parties. The second parcel revealed two muslin day dresses, one sprigged with deep green fern fronds and the other with pink rosebuds, both trimmed with lace and matching velvet ribbons. Whatever Nathan was up to, it seemed I might actually benefit. The dresses couldn't be for Ida because she was at least a head taller than the intended wearer and would certainly be too plump to fit the small waists, but they would be just about right for me. Under the day dresses lay a pair of soft cream colored leather slippers. When I tried them on, they fit nearly perfectly. Did my uncle really mean to change toward me? We were the only family either of us had left. Perhaps that and Miss Ida's influence had softened his heart. If so, I would gladly welcome her to stay forever, which I had begun to suspect was her own heart's desire.

The forest's noises drifted through the open window, reminding me that we were never really alone in this place. Bushes rustled, feet crunched on debris, and an *onca* screamed, sending chills down my spine. As I rewrapped the parcels, another sound added itself to the night's cacophony. I returned the parcels to their place by the wall and pressed my ear against the door. The sounds of human misery came from the porch.

I had been focused on my own unhappiness and fight for survival for so long, I guess I had forgotten others could suffer too. Feeling ashamed that three dresses and a pair of shoes had sent such a thrill through me, I eased the door open and went out onto the dogtrot. The porch between our two sets of rooms was much dimmer without direct moonlight, but I could still make out Tina's form leaning against the kitchen wall, her shoulders shaking with the force of her sobs.

"Tina?" Large black eyes looked up at me. "What's wrong?"

She continued to stare, but said nothing. I stepped closer and she withdrew against the wall until her back pressed flat against the logs. "I'm not going to hurt you." I knew she didn't understand, but I hoped my tone would communicate that I was trying to help. "Please just tell me what's wrong. Are you sick?"

From the other side of the dogtrot a bass whisper came out of the darkness. "She has no English. Would you like for me to translate?"

"I thought you didn't speak English either!"

Henry chuckled softly and replied, "I speak many languages, but only when it serves my purpose."

"Yes, please. Ask her."

"*Que e o problema?*"

"*Eu sou amendrontado pelo onca.*"

I recognized one of the few Portuguese words that I knew and her tone made the rest clear. "She's afraid of the jaguar, isn't she?"

"That she is."

"Are you?"

"I am able to defend myself when I have need."

I went to Tina and held out my hand. At first she refused to move, but eventually she placed her hand in mine and I helped her to stand. When I bent over to pick up her blanket, she snatched it up as though she thought I was trying to steal it. I tugged on her hand, but she hesitated and pulled back until I motioned toward the sitting room door. When she understood my offer, she lifted the weight attached to her ankle and stumbled after me as quietly as she could. Once we were standing next to my bed, I held out my hand for her blanket, but she shook her head and spread it on the floor herself. Just before sleep descended, I slipped my hand into her cold work calloused one as I had once done with Bess, who had slept on a trundle beside my bed back home in Georgia.

"What the hell is that nigger doing sleeping in the front room?" Nathan's shout could have woken the dead.

I bolted upright, my heart thumping like it would jump clean out of my chest. Tina leaned against the bedstead, grabbing the edge of the frame. "I . . . she . . . Tina was afraid of the *onca* that came near the house last night. I just brought her in here so she could sleep."

"She isn't going to smell up this room by sleeping here again. Do you understand?"

A movement at the door drew my gaze. Miss Ida stood halfway into the room wearing a scandalized expression. "Mary Catherine, young ladies do not fraternize with hired help, much less with slaves. How could you?"

Hot anger shot though me. "If she can't sleep at night because she's afraid out there on the porch unprotected then she won't be able to work as hard as you might want, but I don't suppose y'all have considered that, have you? It seems to me an intelligent slave owner would at least let Tina sleep in the kitchen."

Nathan's face turned bright red and his fists balled, but instead of striking out at Tina or me, he turned on his heel, shouting over his shoulder as he left the room, "She can sleep by the stove from now on."

At last I had won a small victory in a face-to-face confrontation with my uncle.

Miss Ida grabbed my upper arm and dug her fingernails into the soft flesh on its underside. "Young lady, take that ungracious smirk off of your face and help me open these windows to let a little fresh air into this room. The very idea you would speak to your uncle like that over something such as this."

I looked over at Tina who stood with her back against the wall looking confused and scared. Any similarity I thought I had seen between her and Bess disappeared when I realized how vulnerable she was and how precarious life for her must be. Then it struck me. Bess had surely once been just as vulnerable, her life certainly just as sad. Hadn't Papa Jordan sold her husband and child? Yet she managed to rise above the pain, cruelty, and harshness of her reality in order to love Mama and me. This gave me something to think about for a long time afterward and I did what I could to make Tina's life easier, to shield her from Nathan's wrath and Miss Ida's imperious expectations.

Life at Little Georgia took on a strange new pattern with Tina gradually taking on all of the house and garden work and Henry tending the coffee fields, which left Nathan free for even more time away from the farm than in the past. Every day for four months Miss Ida and I practiced deportment, posture, and the graceful feminine arts. Daily applications of buttermilk to my hands, arms, and face gradually faded my freckles until my skin returned to its natural fair state. By the time cooler weather arrived in June, I could pour tea without spilling a single drop and carry on inane conversations with skill and aplomb.

With Miss Ida's advent, I also became a regular churchgoer again. Nathan joined us when he was at home. Because Brother Williams pastored two widespread small Confederado congregations, services at Colonel Bowen's were held only once per month. We resumed our former habit of traveling downriver on Saturday afternoon with Henry at the rudder of the canoe. We stayed overnight in the new two-story wood frame Government House that had replaced the old one made of sticks and palm fronds. This new structure's first floor now served as community center, and its second as a travelers' hotel for the little village that had grown up, named McMullanville for the colony's deceased leader. After Sunday Service, we dined with one of several families with whom Miss Ida was close, most often with her brother, and then made the two hour journey back home. Oddly, colony life for those families who had chosen to remain in Brazil was beginning to bear a limited similarity to what we had once known.

On a cool rainy Sunday morning in the middle of July, Miss Ida turned from the wash bowl and looked me over, adjusting the side seams of my new winter frock that had been brought back from another of Nathan's trips. "My, but you are certainly becoming a woman. Since your monthlies have started, you've just blossomed."

I was too embarrassed by this line of conversation to reply, so she just chattered on. "I wonder if any of the other families from outlying farms will be here today. The weather may keep them away. I've heard the colony has a newly bereaved gentleman lately arrived from Alabama. His wife died in childbirth aboard ship. So sad, don't you think?"

Unmarried gentlemen featured prominently in Miss Ida's conversation when it was just us females. I found these confidences both embarrassing and amusing. It seemed to me she had decided to cast her net in a wider circle, broadening the focus of her husband hunt beyond Nathan to any available man. Part of me felt sorry for her because she really had no life other than that which she lived vicariously through others. Her brother's wife seemed delighted to have her out from underfoot now that Ida was no longer needed as a child minder for the rambunctious Johnny or caregiver for the elderly parents, who went to their reward within a month of one another shortly before she came to be my keeper. I looked at her and feared I might one day find myself in similar circumstances since there were only two options open to women: wife or spinster, neither of which was particularly appealing to me at age fourteen. But the extreme alteration in my own situation and the changes in my maturing body didn't allow my attention to focus on Miss Ida for more than a few moments at a time. I was young and far more interested in the present, especially in other young people.

## Chapter 14

Meeting Sundays became my favorite days of the month. My childhood had been a lonely one, but now I had developed a small circle of friends who attended services at Brother Williams's First Missionary Baptist Church of Sao Paulo. Church had always been the center of social life for Southern families and had become so again under Brother Williams's leadership.

Miss Ida stood before the washstand in our Government House room, adjusting her bonnet as she watched me in the mirror's reflection. "Hurry up, Mary Catherine. A lady must time her arrival just so. One doesn't want to be too early for fear of seeming socially anxious, but tardiness is rude and a sign of selfishness." She looked over at Tina, who was repacking our little overnight bags, and pointed at the floor. "Tina, stay." Tina nodded. Her English was still very limited, but at least Nathan believed she wouldn't try to run away and had removed the ankle chain and weight. The chain dragging on the floor as she did housework and served meals got on his nerves. Sadly, the same could not be said for Henry, who still endured his shackle in all weather as he worked in the fields or on the new house.

From the front window, I observed the arrival of several families at the little church across the village square from Government House, but I didn't see the one that really mattered. My heart sank at the thought that they might not be in attendance today. I took one last look at my reflection in the washstand mirror, tucked an errant curl under my own bonnet, and followed Ida obediently. As we descended the building's exterior staircase, the object of my particular interest emerged from the parsonage and my mood soared.

When we reached the bottom step, Ida pointed to a spot by Henry's feet where the iron weight stood. "Henry, stay. No leave." She always spoke to him and Tina as though they were idiot children, but then, Henry still had not revealed his facility with languages to anyone except me and I felt I couldn't betray his confidence by coming to his defense. As I passed him, our eyes met and a conspiratorial smile crossed his lips.

I tripped along behind Ida thinking how it never ceased to amaze me that the colony's ardent believers could espouse such devotion to love thy neighbor and when thou hast done it unto one of the least of these during church services and then exclude anyone of color from those very services. No one else seemed to see any contradiction, so I guessed the lessons of racial acceptance learned in Rio and Igaupe had lost their effectiveness once we became isolated among our own kind. The greatest dichotomy to my way of thinking, however, lay in the fact that people who considered themselves good Christians in all other ways participated in the cruelties connected with slavery. I knew the institution was pure evil, especially when I thought of Bess, Tina, and Henry.

Ida hurried ahead of me, her head swiveling from side to side as her eyes swept over the little groups socializing and waiting for the steeple bell that would call worshipers to obedience. The closer we got to the church, the more self-conscious I became until my heart beat a tattoo against my corset. When we reached the other side of the village square, the voice I had hoped to hear murmured, "May I offer you my arm, Miss Mary Catherine?"

I smiled up at him from under my lashes and placed my hand into the crook of his elbow. "It's good to see you this morning, Jacob." My heart did a little flip, sending a thrill radiating out in all directions.

Jacob Williams, Brother Williams's recently arrived nephew, fell into step beside me and my happiness was complete. Jacob was seventeen and very mature, unlike the other colony boys who were still pimply-faced children. His manners were impeccable, but he could be a lot of fun, too, when the adults were out of earshot.

Miss Ida turned back toward me, her duty as shepherdess always uppermost in her mind. When she spied my hand on Jacob's arm, a frown contorted her plain features into what I'm sure she thought an authoritative expression, but which actually gave her a rather comical appearance. I dropped my eyes, hoping she wouldn't notice the smile that I couldn't suppress.

"Mary Catherine, come along and leave young Mr. Williams to his family. We must not monopolize his time and there are others to whom we must speak."

I glanced up at Jacob and silently mouthed, *I'm sorry*.

He nodded, his eyes soft with what I hoped was regret.

Ida grabbed my hand and pulled me in the direction of two middle-aged ladies, both of whom I knew to be widows. A tall male figure who I didn't recognize had their faces turned upward in rapt attention. He held a bundle in his arms, presenting an incongruous sight considering his gender.

"We must speak to Mr. Dooley. He's a widower, you know."

No, I didn't know and I couldn't have cared less about his marital status.

Around the periphery of the little group raced a dozen or so boys ranging in age from toddlers to young teens. The dust from their trampling feet drifted up, causing the ladies to discreetly cover their coughs with pristine handkerchiefs. Wailing from the bundle suddenly interrupted the buzz of conversation, and both ladies held out their arms while cooing sounds rose in volume equal to that of the infant's cries. Mr. Dooley seemed only too happy to unload his offspring into the nearest outstretched arms.

Miss Ida used this lull in the conversation to advantage. "Good morning, Mr. Dooley. How lovely to see you and your family here for the service. Did you have a pleasant journey from your farm?"

Mr. Dooley looked down on Ida with a quizzical expression. "Tolerable, Mrs. . . . ."

"Oh, it's Miss. Miss Mashburn. You may have met my brother?" Without breaking stride, she yanked my hand, forcing me to stumble forward. "You have not met my charge, Miss Mary Catherine MacDonald, but I'm sure you know her uncle, Mr. Nathan Jordan?"

Although we had never met, a look of recognition entered Mr. Dooley's eyes as he turned to me and bowed slightly. "My pleasure, Miss MacDonald. I had hoped to visit with your uncle. Is he with you today?"

Unaccustomed to being treated by adults as anything other than a burdensome child, I stuttered, "No, he doesn't attend—" Ida's fingernails dug into my hand. "I mean he is away on business."

"That's too bad. Perhaps I might call on him when he returns?"

Ida looked as though the sun was rising in her face. "Oh, please do on Sunday next. You may not be aware, but I am staying at the Jordan farm as governess to Miss MacDonald. We would be most happy to have you come for dinner."

Governess? Sunday next? Who was she kidding? Her formality made our situation sound as gentile as that of English aristocrats. I saw smirks on the other ladies' faces edged by anger at having been bested by what they must see as a rival for Mr. Dooley, one of the few single males in the colony. All of the time I thought Ida had her cap set for Nathan, but perhaps she was finding him a more difficult quarry than anticipated. I glanced around at the tribe of boys and wondered how many of them were Mr. Dooley's. Well, good luck to her. The faster she was settled elsewhere, the faster I would regain my independence and could pursue my own dreams. As hard as the two years struggling for survival virtually alone had been, returning to suffocating domination chaffed more than I ever thought possible.

"Sunday next" arrived in a tangle of nerves and agitation. Ida flitted from mirror to window to door and then began her circuit all over again. "Mary Catherine, how many times have I told you to change into your best? Mr. Dooley will arrive at any moment and we must make a good impression."

You, I thought, might want to make a good impression, I, however, couldn't care less. Aloud, I responded, "Will he be alone or will the wild Indians come along as well? I don't think Tina has prepared enough dinner for the entire tribe. I doubt there's enough food on the place for that voracious mob."

"Mary Catherine! Those are precious, motherless children. How can you be so unkind? He will, however, be alone. He has found a native woman to act as temporary nursemaid and housekeeper until his situation changes."

"Situation changes? Just what does he think is going to happen? A miracle?"

"Why, I do believe he intends to marry again in the near future," Ida replied, a coy smile brightening her thin lips and small, close set eyes.

It was all I could do not to laugh aloud. Ida wore her excitement at the prospect of being released from spinsterhood like a fine new Parisian bonnet. "Well, I wish his bride great joy."

"Oh, I'm sure she'll be the luckiest of young ladies."

Young lady? The extent of her self-deception was amazing. If Miss Ida was young, then I was a lap-baby. She had to be at least twenty-eight.

Nathan's voice coming from the porch steps cut through our little tête-à-tête. "Joshua, take this chair. How about a restorative libation before dinner? This is the best Henry's made so far." The sound of chairs scraping on porch floorboards just outside my door accompanied his shout. "Tina, *dios pingas, rapidamente!*"

"Glad to hear your sugarcane's growing well, but I thought you were growing coffee."

"Coffee is the cash crop, but my small plot of sugarcane provides for the spirit." Male laughter drifted through the open front room window.

A brief silence followed Tina's soft steps from the kitchen and then Mr. Dooley picked up the conversation again. "I see you've begun the new house. When do you think it'll be ready?" Mr. Dooley seemed to know about the new house without ever having been here and I wondered how he and Nathan had come to know one another so well.

"I'm afraid it'll take longer than I hoped. The rains have held up the work, but I assure you this won't affect our agreement."

"I'm relieved to hear that. I need to have my situation settled as quickly as possible." Again, the widower's situation entered a conversation.

I glanced over at Ida. A broad smile lit her face and I wondered how Nathan's new house and her marriage to Mr. Dooley were related, but Nathan's call ended speculation. "Ladies, will you ever be ready? We're waiting for y'all so that we can eat."

Ida grabbed my cheeks and started pinching while hissing, "Run your teeth over your lips several times to bring out the color. Like this." I rolled my eyes, but followed her example.

Dinner was uneventful and filled with polite conversation among the adults focusing on such thrilling topics as the weather and the progress of crops. For anyone in a more prosperous household, I believe we would have presented a rather comical picture. The new china and silverware had arrived and graced the rough hand-sawn boards of our kitchen table, swathing it in a glow of greens, yellows, gold, and silver. The china dishes had stamps on their backs declaring Haviland, Limoges, France. The silver flatware was marked sterling.

It boggled the mind to think what Nathan must have spent to purchase then haul these beautiful items cross an ocean and into the Brazilian hinterland. He must keep his gold supply hidden well away from the house because I had searched high and low in every conceivable place during the periods when I was alone but to no avail. When Ida arrived, my searching ended, but with each purchase he made, my animosity grew. It was for this that I suspected he had murdered my father and was now controlling my inheritance. No amount of feigned affection or amount of pretty dresses from him could wipe out the memory of the past three years.

Nathan's voice cut into my musings. "Mary Catherine! Mr. Dooley addressed a question to you."

I looked up to see three pairs of eyes focused on me. "I beg your pardon. I was admiring Uncle Nathan's taste in the table service and I'm afraid I was so dazzled that my attention was completely absorbed. What was it you wished?" My contrived smile felt tight, but my words were at least partially true. Though my newly developed talent for delivering ironic, double-edged comments with such guiltless ease sometimes still surprised me.

"Miss Mary Catherine, I was wondering if you had ever acted as hostess for your uncle?"

Surprise kept me silent for a moment before I stammered, "No . . . I've . . . never done that."

"Well, perhaps when I return in two weeks' time, you might do the honor?"

I stared at him for so long that Ida interjected, "Of course, Mr. Dooley. Miss MacDonald will be pleased to perform her debut as hostess when you return. It will be a festive occasion and we will all have reason for celebration, I assure you."

"We'll see about that in two weeks' time."

Two weeks passed before I knew it, filled with lessons and correction at the least mistake. Even so, I wished the days would slow their pace. It is one of life's paradoxes that time moves most quickly when you wish it to stand still. I didn't want to be Nathan's hostess or anybody else's, for that matter. I loved daydreaming about one day sitting opposite Jacob while we entertained our guests, but that was in the distant, hazy future, after we were both adults and ready for the responsibilities of marriage and a family. At present, the only thing I wanted was to get this interminable tutoring over with. Miss Ida revisited previous instruction on table etiquette until I think I could have held a dinner party in my sleep. We spent hours practicing polite conversation, dull though the topics were. And any territory which she felt had thus far been neglected kept the oil lamp burning late into the evenings. It was exhausting and boring, except for one rather halting discussion not long before the dreaded Sunday.

We were practicing laying the table for at least the hundredth time, when out of the blue Ida said, "Mary Catherine, it's time you learned about relations between men and women. Do you understand?"

"Do you mean when you fall in love?"

"Well, I would not use that vulgar term and a lady does not refer to herself or others in the second person with the personal pronoun you. But, yes, I mean when one forms an attachment. Have you given the subject any consideration?"

I guessed my feelings for Jacob Williams were plain for all to see. I was surprised and pleased at Miss Ida's concern.

Jacob's handsome face hovered in my mind as I answered, "I've given it a great deal of thought lately."

"And do you know what it entails, to what it leads?"

"Well, I suppose that one day it may lead to marriage."

"Quite. And do you understand what marriage means?"

I wasn't sure what she expected me to say. "That one lives as husband and wife?"

Ida's face flamed and she cast her eyes toward the window. "Exactly. I'm glad we have the subject settled. We'll speak of it no more."

The nearer the day drew, the more excited and jumpy Ida became. Although I would never want to take on the job of raising twelve boys, it seemed to be what Ida wanted and I was glad to see her find some happiness at last. Even though I found her mannerisms amusing in a less than charitable way, I still felt compassion for her situation. After she lost her fiancée in the war, her family had treated her like an unpaid servant and her brother had expected gratitude in return. Her life had been a sad one thus far. Everyone deserved some happiness, especially those who had so little control over their own lives.

When the appointed Sunday at last arrived, the atmosphere positively crackled with Ida's nerves. "Wash that buttermilk off your face and get your dress on this instant. Mr. Dooley will arrive at any moment and we must be on the porch to greet him," Ida snapped. "Oh do come on, will you? Why do you always take such pleasure in trying my patience?"

I wasn't aware I took pleasure in aggravating Ida, but maybe she had felt my silent laughter at her expense from time to time. Feeling a little ashamed of myself, I hurried to do as she asked. She wouldn't be with me much longer, so it wouldn't hurt me to try to please her. But all the rushing around had been needless because we sat on the porch, enduring unusual heat for the time of year and slapping at insects, for about an hour before the nose of Mr. Dooley's canoe appeared at the river's bend.

"We'll stay on the porch, Mary Catherine, while your uncle goes to the dock. A lady must never appear too anxious for a gentleman's attention." She snatched my hand that dabbed with a handkerchief at the sweat on my upper lip and forced it into my lap. "Put your hand down. Mr. Dooley must not think we await him in agitation. Furthermore, ladies do not perspire. How many times must I tell you?"

I glanced at her, apparently with my own irritation showing, for she continued, "And remove that disagreeable expression from your face. Gentlemen dislike sullenness. They expect only graciousness and gentility in their ladies, not displays of temper."

Caught off guard by her words, I wondered briefly why she was so concerned that I make a good impression on the man for whom she had set her cap. The only gentleman whom I wished to impress, Jacob Williams, wasn't even to be present. Perhaps through me she hoped to demonstrate the excellence of her maternal skills. That must be it. It was the only logical explanation. Although I dreaded the evening, I decided to do my best not to embarrass Ida as my engagement gift to her.

Since it was already half past one when Mr. Dooley finally stood beside us on the porch, we wasted no time in going to the table. Once we were all seated, Ida looked at me, nodding encouragingly.

I glanced up hopefully at Tina and Henry, who avoided my gaze, expressions blank, ready to do as they were bid. For once, Henry's shackle had been removed. Nathan thought the sound of chain being dragged around the table would detract from the occasion. How like my uncle to be so considerate!

I swallowed hard and said quietly, "*Sira o alimento agora, por favor.*"

Five faces snapped in my direction, two of which wore disgruntled expressions. Henry and Tina's smiles showed only in their eyes, however, as they began serving the food, the white cotton gloves that Ida had ordered looking ridiculous on their work-roughened hands.

"You speak Portuguese, Miss Mary Catherine?" Mr. Dooley sounded surprise.

"Only a little. Tina and Henry have been helping me."

Across the table, Nathan's eyes became hard and they darted to Ida and then back, but his voice was as smooth as velvet. "My niece has always been a quick study. And she will do whatever is needed to make the household run smoothly. Isn't that right, my dear?"

"Yes, Uncle Nathan. And since we live in Brazil, being able to communicate with the natives makes running the house easier." If glances were daggers, I would have died in that instant.

"I certainly admire your initiative, Miss Mary Catherine. Some might find that an unattractive quality in a woman, but I believe it well suits the unfortunate situation in which we find ourselves since being driven from our homes and nation by scoundrels and scalawags." Mr. Dooley smiled brightly as he watched for my reaction to his compliment.

"Thank you." My reply had a hollow ring. I couldn't decide whether he was being genuine or ironic, but either way, I felt very uncomfortable. He should be complimenting and paying attention to Miss Ida, not to me. "Mr. Dooley, did you know that Miss Mashburn is an excellent cook? She has taught Tina everything about preparing our kind of food."

For some reason, Ida looked distressed by my effort on her behalf. She frowned and looked at Nathan. "As you can see, my niece is both accomplished and generous of spirit. Will you have more plantains?"

The conversation moved on, but I had the uncomfortable feeling that Mr. Dooley's eyes were on me for much of the meal. I couldn't be sure, though, because I avoided his gaze as much as was politely possible.

As dinner crawled to conclusion, Mr. Dooley again addressed me directly. "May I seek your opinion of children, Miss Mary Catherine?"

I couldn't hide my surprise. In addition, it felt as though the tension around the table had just multiplied tenfold. According to Ida, such personal questions were singularly unsuitable for so limited an acquaintance. "I don't suppose I've really given it much thought, but like all of my gender, I hope I will one day have children of my own."

A broad smile lit his face. He turned toward Nathan and said, "I believe she'll do, Mr. Jordan. Yes, I just believe she'll do. How soon can the matter be settled?"

"Why, Mr. Dooley!" Ida's voice held a sharp edge of reproof. "Is that any way to propose? Remember a lady's tender feelings."

"As you wish," he replied curtly. I could see he didn't like being admonished and it seemed the height of foolishness for her to risk offending him. "Miss Mary Catherine, would next Sunday suit? It's a meeting day."

"Suit for what, Mr. Dooley?"

"For the wedding, of course."

"Oh, congratulations! I'm so happy for y'all, but you don't need my approval. I'm quite able to dispense with a governess, especially now that Miss Ida has an opportunity for a home of her own. I would never stand in the way of her happiness."

Nathan's fist slamming against the table made everyone seated at it and everything placed upon it jump. "You stupid girl! You are going to be married to Mr. Dooley." The silence that followed echoed throughout the room.

"Me? I'm too young to get married. I don't want to get married, not even to Jacob. You can't mean me."

Time crawled. It moved so slowly that I felt like I stood outside myself, watching things that were happening to someone else. A silly smile clung to my lips as my mind worked to wrap itself around what was occurring.

"Don't be a fool. Who else at this table would he marry? Now give him the answer both he and I expect!"

"That's right, my dear. Give Mr. Dooley the answer he deserves." I hadn't known Ida was intelligent enough to be capable of irony. Clearly, I had underestimated her.

My smile faded as the full force of what these three had intended all along hit me. How could I have been so stupid? My heart felt like it would explode if I remained in their presence for another moment. I jumped to my feet so quickly that my chair toppled backward, crashing against the kitchen wall. I stared around the table at three pairs of eyes, all focused on me and filled with expectation.

"No! Never in a million years!" My words echoed behind me as I ran from the room, down the back steps, and away from the house.

## Chapter 15

When the sun disappeared behind the mountains, I had no choice but to return to the house. Only someone with a death wish trudged about unprotected in a night forest filled with predators who could rip a grown man apart with little effort. After climbing over the back garden gate to avoid swinging it open on its squeaky hinges, I removed my shoes and crept up the back steps. An elongated pool of light shone across the porch floorboards through the open kitchen door. I stopped in the dogtrot's shadows and pressed myself against the wall, straining to hear what Nathan might be planning to do now. The clatter of cutlery against plates signaled that supper was in progress.

"She'll be back soon. She's not stupid enough to stay out after dark." Nathan's voice, filled with contempt, rolled through the open door and bounced off the opposite wall.

"Do you think Mr. Dooley will still have her after such a display? He seemed so surprised by her refusal and left in such a huff."

"He'll have her, all right. What other girl will agree to marry a widower with twelve boys? He needs a strong, young wife to raise those children and to keep his house. Even though he's not paying the native woman very much, it's an expense he can ill afford."

"Oh, I do so hope you're right, Nathan. This affects all of our futures."

Ida's simpering tone turned my stomach. To think that I had felt sorry for her and was so happy when I thought she had at last found a suitor. Rage and despair born of betrayal created a hurricane. How could she? She knew what it was to be at the mercy of others, males who determined where she lived, what she did, controlled every aspect of her life. The answer had been there all along, dancing and laughing like a jester playing the fool. I had just been too stupid, too blind to see that I was the one being mocked. She wanted Nathan after all and was willing to do whatever it took to gain a permanent place in his life. How I hated them both! But some of my anger was reserved for myself. I had been duped by my own naiveté and now I faced a life of servitude, chained to a man I hardly knew, much less loved. All at once, I felt much older and sadly wiser than my fourteen years.

I was trying to decide how to pass the kitchen unnoticed when Tina and Henry came through the door. Henry's arms were filled with soiled laundry for tomorrow's wash pot and Tina carried a pail of what would be their supper. When she caught sight of me, her eyes widened but she didn't utter a sound. She moved toward the back steps and the shed where they now slept, turning to mouth, *nos nao diremos*, as she passed.

A shirt slipped from Henry's grasp and floated to the porch floor. He bent to retrieve it, whispering, "We won't tell."

He pointed toward the back steps and made a circling gesture with his hand.

I slipped down the steps, around the house, and into the sitting room where I slept. Although I moved across the hand-hewn floorboards as silently as a ghost, Nathan's form darkened the doorway within a moment, as though he had a sixth sense where I was concerned.

"Well, well. Look who's returned." His voice drifted lazily across the room. "Come into the kitchen, dear niece. We have an issue to settle."

When I was seated at the table with Nathan and Ida on either end, he said, "Mary Catherine, I really don't see that you have a choice. You will marry Mr. Dooley or you will face the consequences."

I stared at my uncle. What I saw in his golden hawk's eyes chilled me to my very core. "Why do you hate me so much? I've never done anything bad to you." I knew my mistake the moment the words were out of my mouth, but once spoken, they couldn't be snatched back.

Nathan's eyes narrowed as he cocked his head to one side. "Do you really believe that? You killed my only remaining blood relative, the baby sister whom I adored, the only person who ever really loved me unconditionally and you say you haven't done anything to me?" With each sentence, his voice rose in volume. He stood up, placing his fists on the table, and leaned forward until he loomed over me. "Did you know I was once betrothed to your father's cousin? She claimed to love me, but deserted me for another. Did you know when your father was a boy, he took every opportunity to torment me simply because he enjoyed playing practical jokes and I was a convenient target? Are you aware that you are the spitting image of your father's treacherous cousin?" Nathan's face was so close to mine that I could smell the remains of his supper on his breath. "Now I will be rid of you because I cannot stand the sight of you. Next Sunday you will put on your best dress and you will marry Joshua Dooley. Do you understand?"

From deep within me a scream formed. It rose until it reached my lips. "No, I don't understand. I don't understand why someone who promised his dying sister, who he claims he loved so much, that he would take care of her little girl and then would try to force that girl into a marriage she doesn't want. I don't understand what looking like a MacDonald cousin I've even never met has to do with anything. And I certainly don't understand what the consequences of refusing to marry could be unless you intend to murder me like you did my father."

Nathan's fist slammed into my face sending blood from my burst lips spraying through the air. I felt myself falling from the chair as everything went dark. When I regained consciousness, I was lying on my bed and Ida was dabbing at my mouth with a damp cloth.

"Mary Catherine, my dear, what your uncle asks may seem difficult, but you must accept it. You see, he wishes to marry and it simply won't do to have two grown women in the same house. You and I would contradict one another and things would become too confused. And those poor children need a mother and Mr. Dooley needs a wife. It's best for everyone."

I leaned up on one elbow, but fell back down immediately. As the room's spinning slowed, I wanted to shout, but only managed to whisper, "Except me."

Nathan's voice came from the doorway. "Leave her. She'll stay in this room and will have no food until she sees reason."

"But Mr. Jordan, what if she continues to refuse?"

"Then I guess she'll starve."

Ida looked scandalized. "Oh, Nathan, you can't mean . . ."

The coldness in Nathan's eyes silenced her before he turned on his heel and walked away. Ida glanced at me with a pained expression and then dropped her gaze. She fled from the room, closing the door after her.

Full darkness came quickly, but not sleep. Although my head ached and I was drowsy, my eyes refused to stay closed for more than a few minutes at a time. Despite my accusation that he had killed Papa, a very small part of me had clung to the hope that I was wrong. After all, I was still young and he was the only family I had left. But when Nathan told Ida to let me starve, something deep within me burst and then shriveled until it lay like a dead thing, putrid and rotting. I saw that there was something missing in Nathan. He had failed to develop the trait that allowed a person to put himself in another's place, to be able to see the world as another saw it, to feel what another person might be feeling. He only understood his own pain, his own desires. With this realization came the death of hope, like a weight dragging me under in a riptide of despair. Much worse, however, was the dark pit that opened when the last spark of family attachment was snuffed out. Into the void flooded venomous rage.

I lay on my bed far into the night, studying my choices, such as they were. It seemed to me that Ida would not literally let me starve, but I visualized a horrible scene come the following Sunday. I saw myself being manhandled into the dugout and being forcibly transported to Government House where Brother Williams would have no difficulty in ignoring my protests. I would be chained to a man I hardly knew who would expect me to share his bed, to raise his children, and to work in his house with little or no consideration for what I wanted.

I thought about some of the marriages I had observed among our colonists. They were a form of bondage for the women, who were haggard and old by the time they were thirty from hard work and constant childbearing. Perhaps death might be preferable.

I must have drifted off because Bess was suddenly beside me, holding my hand and swabbing my forehead with a cool cloth. My head rolled to one side so that my eyes could meet hers.

"Is this how I raised you? To just give up and die when things get hard? You ain't my girl no more if this be how you gonna act. Now you just get up outta that bed and stop feeling all sorry for yo'self. You hear?"

"But what can I do? How can I stop Nathan?"

Bess cocked her head to one side and then after a moment said, "That Henry, he seem like he pretty smart. You thought to ax him?"

"But he's just—" I stopped before I uttered the hurtful words.

"Yeah, he's like me, he just a slave, but if I wanted help, it'd be him I'd go to."

Her face began to fade and I reached out to grab her so that she wouldn't leave me. I tried to call out, but no sound came. I awoke in a flood of tears. Strangely, I could still feel the weight and warmth of Bess's hand against mine.

I lay for a while thinking about my dream. It didn't seem like Henry could help me. He couldn't even help himself. But what harm could it do to talk to him?

I got up and held onto the bedpost until I was steady on my feet, then crept as quietly as I could to the door, taking my cloak from its peg. Nathan had not jammed the latch from the outside. Since mountains and many miles of untamed forest separated us from other *fazendas*, or farms, he probably thought barring my escape unnecessary.

A bright full moon cast its cool blue light over the garden, forest, and outbuildings, creating areas of ghostly shapes and deep shadows. The chill night air sent a shiver down my spine as I picked my way toward Henry and Tina's shed. It had originally been built to stable the plow mules and the milk cow, so its floor was hard packed earth and the exterior wallboards had gaps that let in breezes, but also all manner of biting, stinging insects. The animals now had an American style barn, solid and sturdy, while the dark skinned people lived in a hovel. How like Nathan to equate black skin with being subhuman, and therefore, unworthy of a proper abode. He also wasn't much of a businessman since he seemed oblivious to any need to protect the health of his investments, as he called Henry and Tina.

"Henry," I whispered through the space where the door didn't quite meet the jamb. My burst lips began bleeding again. "Open the door."

He must have been awake because the door flew back immediately. Watching me dab at the trickle of blood running down my chin, he said, "What are you doing out here in the middle of the night? Go back in the house where you belong."

"No!" I grabbed the handle as he tried to close the door. "Please. I need your help."

"What could I possibly do for you?"

The answer presented itself as though it was the simplest and most straightforward of plans. "I'm leaving. Tonight. You and Tina will come with me."

He was quiet as his eyes held mine for several heartbeats. "And where do you think two runaway slaves and a white girl could go?"

"I thought you would know. You know so many things."

A smiled played across his lips, but failed to reach his eyes. "Your faith is misplaced. I have no special knowledge."

"Please Henry, I can't stay here any longer. I've got to get away."

"I cannot help you."

Tina appeared behind Henry, drawn no doubt by the tone of our voices. Her eyes were huge as she slipped one hand into his and clung to his shoulder with the other. He turned slightly and whispered something that only Tina heard. Her eyes grew even wider. She shook her head violently and pulled on Henry, as if trying to drag him back into the shadows.

Henry sighed deeply. "It is late. We should all go to sleep. There's much work to be done tomorrow."

"You can go to sleep, but I'm leaving. I won't stay here another day."

"And where do you hope to go? I doubt any of the white people will take you in. They will think your uncle should determine your fate."

The last thing he said sent a river of fire coursing through me. "I will never marry that old man. I will not! I'm leaving this farm and I'm never coming back, whether you go with me or not."

Henry's eyes looked searchingly into mine. After a few seconds, he said, "I believe you are in earnest."

"I will never, understand, never marry that man. The only way to prevent it is escape and I'm leaving tonight, but I need help."

"Then you best come inside. Do you have the slightest idea of where you might go?"

I shook my head, feeling despair attempting to push its way into my heart, and stepped over the threshold.

Again Henry whispered to Tina and she disappeared into the dark interior. When we were seated on the floor beside a pallet on which Tina huddled, Henry continued. "There is a place upriver, hidden well back in the forest where no white man ever goes. It is difficult to locate and dangerous once found, but it offers a refuge to all who wish to escape their bondage. The journey is not easy."

"I don't care. Just tell me how to get there."

"You will need a map. The way is complicated. Tear off a piece of cloth from the skirt of your undergarment."

I was taken aback to be asked to expose my ankles and legs, but I did what he asked. When the white cloth was spread out on the floor, he lit a stub of candle. In the faint glow of the small flame, he began to draw using purple berry juice and a sharpened stick.

When he finished explaining the route, he asked, "Now that you know the way, how will you get upriver? There is no path beyond this *fazenda*."

The answer seemed improbable, but there was no other way. "I'll take the dugout."

"You have never handled a canoe, have you?"

"No, but I've watched you."

"Poling upriver is not easy and the river can be dangerous. It takes more strength and skill than you have."

"I'm plenty strong. I did most of the work that you and Tina do before you came here. I'll handle the dugout because I don't have another choice."

I snatched up the map and rose to go, but Henry gripped my wrist. "At least listen to some instruction before you dash away to your likely death."

He explained about currents and how to use the pole to ensure that the dugout canoe stayed upright and true in direction. With the lesson completed, he pressed a small figure hung on a length of leather into my hand. "If you manage to get to the sanctuary, tell the leader I sent you and show him this token as a sign that you are speaking truth. It is a symbol of our struggle. Wear it around your neck. You will need it for safe passage among our people."

I did as he bid and then looked at the little form as I fingered its curves and ridges. An *onca*, muscles tightly bunched and ready for a leaping strike, wore a heavy collar and chain around its neck. The figure's wood was smooth and shiny from the caresses of those who undoubtedly cherished it. It was a fitting symbol of rebellion, no doubt intended to inspire courage in the face of the terrible cruelty of slavery.

"Thank you, Henry. But how do you know about this place?"

"That is something I will not tell, for your protection, as well as mine." Then he turned to Tina. "*De-lhe o alimento.*"

Tina rose and crept farther back into the darkness. When she emerged, she carried a small parcel wrapped in a piece of torn canvas that she placed in my hands.

"Food you will need for your journey. It is preserved. It will not spoil."

"Why do you have this?"

"For the day that I would leave, but I cannot go now."

"Why on earth not? For the love of God, what's keeping you here?"

"It isn't the love of God that keeps me here, but love for another person. Tina is with child. I have begged her to escape with me. It would be so easy, but she is afraid of the journey and the wild animals in the forest. Until I can convince her to leave, I will stay to protect her and our child."

"Tina's a very lucky girl."

How could I have said that? Tina was a slave who could be sold away from the man she loved at Nathan's whim. And yet I thought her lucky, even felt a little envious. Jacob Williams's handsome face appeared in my mind's eye and I wondered if he would ever have loved me enough to make the kind of sacrifice Henry was making for Tina. Somehow I didn't think so. As I looked at them, I realized their love was a palpable thing, a bond between them that could be touched if I only extended my hand.

Hesitating at the door, I turned back and said, "Well, I guess I'd better go if I'm going to put distance between me and this place before daylight. Wish me luck, as I wish it for y'all and the baby." A sudden thought brought unexpected laughter or perhaps I was simply near hysterics. "With me gone, Nathan and Ida can marry now without any encumbrances on their joy."

Henry looked incredulous. "Is that what you think? That your uncle will marry the ugly spinster woman?"

"That's why they want to marry me off, to get me out of their way so they can have the *fazenda* all to themselves. Didn't you know?"

"She may believe he will marry her, but I assure you it will never come to pass. Your uncle has more exalted notions. Did you not ever wonder where he went on his travels?"

I shook my head. "I guess I was too busy staying alive." Then I remembered the lovely embroidered handkerchief of finest lawn fabric that I found in his pocket all those months ago. The unfinished new house, the fine china, the sterling, the beautiful linens that had recently arrived, all of it was being bought to impress someone who was decidedly not Joshua Dooley.

"He's been visiting a woman, hasn't he?"

"Not just a woman, but a lady. Her father owns the big coffee *fazenda* where your uncle bought the trees planted here. That is also where he purchased us. The only impediment to the marriage is the family's objection to your uncle's religion. They are devout Catholics. So devout in fact, they have built a church on their *fazenda* and have brought in a priest who lives in a house built especially for him. They attend daily mass in their own church whose windows would put the great cathedral of Rio to shame."

I clapped my hand over my mouth to prevent a fit of hysterics from ringing all the way to Igaupe and back. After the uncontrolled laughter, sobs sent a flood of tears rushing down my cheeks, shaking my body until Tina's arms went around me. She held me until the wave of shock driven emotion passed, then stepped back into the shadows.

I looked up into Henry's pained expression. "What a lovely triangle Nathan's created. Well, I wish him joy of it. I hope that conniving schemer Ida scratches his eyes out when she discovers the truth. But they will never get the chance to marry me off to the wretched Widower Dooley because I'm leaving."

Henry grabbed my arm and spoke to Tina in Portuguese. She drew back from him and shook her head. Then she came over and wrapped her arms around me again. "*Nao! Por favor nao va.*"

"Tina, I have to go. I have no choice. Henry, please explain to her."

"She knows why you are leaving. She is simply afraid for you."

I returned Tina's embrace and then stepped out of her arms. "Goodbye. I won't forget you."

I stopped just beyond the door and looked back into two pairs of black eyes following me with care and concern. There was one more thing I wanted to know.

"Henry, how did you learn so many languages?"

A look of surprise crossed his face. He drew a long breath before he answered. "A man who once owned my mother forced her into his bed because he had no woman. Of course, he didn't plan on growing to love her so deeply. When she asked, I moved into the big house with them and he taught me many things. She died in childbirth when I was twelve and he no longer had a reason to care what happened to me, so he sold me to the first bidder."

"Why didn't you ever try to escape?"

"Do you remember when I first came here I wore chains all the time?" I nodded. "My previous masters kept me in leg shackles attached to a metal collar that encircled my neck. It had a long lock at the back that extended from my shoulders to the top of my head. It made movement difficult and escape impossible. It was put on me because I ran away many times. After my final escape, a metal mask that made seeing and breathing difficult was added as punishment. I was sold to your uncle because I was considered too great a liability."

I looked at Tina. The quickening in her middle was obvious, if one only stopped to really look. Fragments of a discussion overheard at Sunday meeting earlier in the year came to mind. The colonists had been aghast and made dire predictions.

"Did you know your baby will be freeborn? Parliament has passed a law saying that all children born to slaves are free at age eight."

"Yes, we have heard. The *Ventre Livre*, the Law of the Free Womb. A father's dream of a better life for his children will be realized simply with the birth of our child. It gives us hope."

"Goodbye and good luck, Tina, Henry."

"Henrique."

"What?"

"My name is Henrique. She is Fatima."

"Of course. I'm sorry, Henrique."

With nothing left to say, I hugged Fatima again, shook Henrique's hand, and then fled into the night.

## Chapter 16

The instant my feet touched down in the dugout's stern, the thing came to life, trying to throw me into the river. It rocked hard from side to side, steadying only when I sat down. Precious time was being wasted and too much noise was being created by my inexperience. Consciously trying to control my panic and visualizing Henry standing in the canoe on past trips, I cautiously rose and positioned my feet on either side of the stern, bending my knees and swaying until I synchronized my timing to the dugout's rhythm. Henry's words echoed in my mind while I untied the mooring ropes from the dock. The long pole, worn smooth from handling, made my muscles complain when lifted. Its ungainly weight tilted me off balance again until I slammed it against the river bottom.

Slowly, trying very hard to emulate Henry's every movement, I pushed off and the dugout slid away from the dock, out into the current. The river flowed dark and swift beside our land on its rush to escape the mountains' maternal embrace, but was blessedly without dangerous churning white water. Henry had warned me to keep the bow aligned with the current in order to move upstream against it, but this proved more difficult than I had thought possible. Without warning the bow swung out away from the main flow and the dugout turned across the current, setting it spinning like an out of control dervish. Pure fear driven instinct made me drop to my knees, drag the pole into the canoe, and then grab the short paddle lying in the bottom. Using the paddle as a rudder sent the canoe nose-first back into alignment with the current. The spinning stopped so suddenly that I lurched to the side, nearly flying overboard into the inky water. As I straightened myself and sat on my haunches, it occurred to me that all of this might have been funny, if it weren't so desperately frightening. It also hit me like a punch in the midsection that I had left my most treasured possessions behind in my rush to flee Little Georgia. Papa's portrait and Mama's handkerchief were still in their hiding place in the chimney. All I had left now were my memories.

My trip upriver began with the moon's slender crescent floating high above the trees lining the steep riverbanks. It progressed with difficulty, but without major incident, until the stars were twinkling their farewells to a murky red morning sky. A rhyme learned from the sailors during our days aboard the *Alyssa Jane* came to mind, bringing with it the fear that I might be in for stormy weather. The seasons of inland Sao Paulo State were similar to the middle Georgia climate of my childhood, only in reverse on the calendar. Summers were hot and winters were mild with the occasional cold snap, whose arrival would be announced with high winds followed by rain and cold air that blew in from the east and slammed against the coastal mountains lining the edge of the Brazilian Plateau.

The forest canopy on the eastern bank began swaying and whirling at full daylight. The wind whipped my cloak around, creating a billowing sail that threatened to pull me from the dugout, which was now harder to keep in line with the current despite its low draft. The wind howled its way west and disappeared, which felt like a blessing until the frigid torrent began. I was drenched to the skin and my clothes felt like they gained fifty pounds in a small space of time. Another gust from the east sent rain sliding sideways, chopping the river into whitecaps that splashed into the dugout and rocked it so violently that I squatted down in order to not be thrown overboard.

Within minutes, the canoe jerked hard as it banged into a half-submerged log. The jolt sent the pole flying from my hands into the water where the current swept it out of sight. Without the pole to use as a rudder and for balance, the paddle was my only hope, but it was no match for the raging goliath that the river had become. The dugout spun, rocked, and crashed its way downstream. I held onto the sides for dear life and prayed, but could see no way to stop the dugout's headlong rush.

When the canoe straightened into the current, it picked up speed. It raced out of control until it failed to make a bend in the river and slammed into a large boulder. Cold river water enveloped me. My clothes became lead weights pulling me under until I was completely submerged and being pushed downstream without hope of gaining footing. I felt myself lifted up over rocks and then down into a crashing, tumbling white foam where the water's crush kept me rolling over and over. The world was going black when my body went limp. Like a rag doll with no will of its own, the churning river spit me up and away from the waterfall toward the opposite bank. My arms weighed a ton each, but their feeble flailing brought me to the water's edge where a tiny rocky beach welcomed me with bruises and abrasions. I pulled myself onto land panting and shivering in the cold wind. I managed to sit up, but my head fell onto my knees. I surveyed my surroundings from a cockeyed angle until my neck yelled in protest. It was odd that this place was flat while all up and down the river for several miles the banks rose sharply. Then I remembered the small island I had passed and hearing a waterfall on its opposite side. I had been swept a long way back downstream and was now stranded in the middle of a wilderness.

By what must have been mid-morning, I was shaking violently and my eyes felt so heavy that I lay down on the rocky beach to avoid falling over. Strange animals, half *onca* and half bear, floated in the air around me and then disappeared like puffs of smoke. Mama and Bess sat by a roaring fire in our house in Georgia, but they seemed unable to see me. I remember calling their names and wondering why they didn't come to help me. There were weird occasions when I drifted above the earth and saw my body on the ground below. It reached up and clutched my hand, its mouth in a caricature of a smile. At other times, my mind was a complete blank and I couldn't remember who I was or where I was supposed to be. It was a strange, unsettling period with voices that mumbled incomprehensible words. Occasionally, I thought I heard Henry and Tina speaking in their lilting Portuguese, but their words had lost the spice of African undertones they inherited from their people. When I struggled to speak to them, my lips refused to form the words.

"*Esta acordada?*" Tina's new voice asked softly.

Yes, I wanted to answer, I'm awake, but my voice refused to utter a sound.

"*Nao ainda,*" Henry answered.

Sunlight painted my world glowing red as my eyelids fluttered. When they opened fully, I looked up into two pairs of dark eyes, but they were set in tan faces rather than the ebony ones I expected. Where I expected to see Tina and Henry, two strangers stood. Where I expected rocks and water, a soft featherbed, pillow, and blanket surrounded me instead. The woman was short and round with the wrinkled, gentle face of a kindly grandmother. The man was equally as wrinkled, but darker in complexion and wore a worried expression.

When he spoke, his words were difficult to follow. His Portuguese was heavily accented and mine was still new and untried in a world that knew no English. I watched the couple for a moment as they smiled and nodded at me.

Finally, I asked in halting Portuguese, "Where am I?"

They looked puzzled for a moment and then the man smiled and replied slowly and distinctly, "You are in my house, near the *Fazenda Oliveira*. I am Ricardo Dias and she is my wife Adriana. You have been very ill. Your family must be very worried. We must get you to them without delay."

Memory flooded my foggy brain and sent a knife stabbing into my heart. I struggled toward the wall against which the bed sat. The woman's face filled with concern.

"Leave her be for now, Ricardo. She has had a bad time and you don't need to add to it."

"But she was a white girl alone on the river. How can that be? If her family finds her here, they may blame us."

"Why would they think we put her onto the river? Let her rest. When you have gone to the fields, she may be more willing to talk. Come to the kitchen for your breakfast."

The bedroom in which I found myself was small, furnished simply with an iron bedstead and a simple cane bottomed chair. The walls had no decoration other than a simple wooden crucifix hung above the bed. A minimal veil of whitewash allowed tan patches of wattle and daub, *pau-a-pique* in Portuguese, to show through. Through the room's single deeply-silled window, I glimpsed a yard with outbuildings and a vegetable garden lying fallow, ready for spring planting. Beyond the yard, the land rolled with trees occasionally dotting the hillsides where cattle and horses grazed belly deep in winter-browned grasses. In the far distance, the tops of what looked like coffee trees fluttered in the breeze. The thick forests of the riverbanks were nowhere to be seen.

How was it Senhor Dias had come to be on the river and what caused him to notice me on the island? Pondering possible answers made my head ache. When I tried to rise from the bed, the room began to spin and the weakness of a newborn kitten descended. I fell onto the pillow where I drifted back into another profound sleep.

Bizarre scenes appeared in which people drifted around in a murky haze, merging with one another until I could no longer tell one from the other. Bess and Tina and Senhora Dias all blended into a woman who felt as though she might be kind, but whom I didn't fully recognize so I hid from her. Henry and Senhor Dias became one body with two heads, both of which spoke to me in Portuguese so rapid and heavily accented that what they said was lost in a jumble of foreign syllables. Only Papa and Nathan stood out as separate individuals, but each of them displayed the darker side of his nature by shouting at the other. They became so enraged that they tumbled into an extended fistfight with no clear outcome. Oddly, Mama didn't appear at all. Perhaps it was because my memory of her face had begun to fade despite my desperate efforts to keep it clear.

When I awoke for the second time, instead of the fogginess I had felt before, my mind was clear with no sign of the debilitating headache that had so sapped my energy. I lay staring at the view from the window for some minutes. The treetops and pasture grasses were completely still. The sun shone in a cloudless sky of deepest blue. A beautiful winter day waited just outside my compact little bedroom, if only I had the strength to rise from the bed. I sat up, testing my energy. The room remained still, and while I felt weak, I was steady enough to swing my feet to the floor. Holding the bedstead for support, I stood and waited. No dizziness descended to cloud my progress. I took a tentative step, wobbled, and then stepped again with more confidence. Hunger announced itself with a loud growl from my stomach, prompting a laugh from the bedroom doorway. Senhora Dias stood watching me and smiling broadly.

"You are awake and walking. That is very good. Come to the kitchen." She spoke slowly and carefully so I could understand. As I neared the door, she held out her hand. After encouraging nods, I placed my hand into her strong, reassuring grip.

The little kitchen leaned against the house's back wall, probably added on after the main construction was completed. It was much like its sister space at Little Georgia with a small cast iron stove, a counter on which a dishpan sat, and a small table with two chairs. On the wall opposite the counter, rough board shelves stretched from the floor to the ceiling, stacked with cooking pots, crocks of preserved food, sugar, salt, flour, and other staples of a well-supplied larder. Everything was tidy, clean, and serviceable, but lacked any trace of decoration or finery. Senhora Dias motioned for me to sit and then went about setting a plate with cheese, cold meat, and bread before me. Next a cup of coffee, turned light tan with milk and very sweet with unrefined sugar, joined the food. Until I took the first bite, I hadn't realized I was ravenous. I forgot my manners, gobbling every crumb without looking up or speaking. The food restored more than just my energy. It also quieted some of my fear.

Sated and calmer, I asked my hostess in halting Portuguese, "Senhora, how did I come to be here?"

"Ricardo, my husband, found you on his way back from Igaupe where he sold our coffee crop. You were on an island in the middle of the river where he stopped. If it hadn't been for a call of nature, he would never have seen you."

It struck me that my prayers had been answered because what other explanation could there be for Senhor Dias's personal needs to coincide with my crawling onto that island other than divine intervention?

"I'll never be able to thank him enough. You are both so kind. How long have I been here?"

"Oh, for many days. You burned with fever and we thought you might die, but my special medicine cured you like it always does."

"Special medicine?"

"I make medicine from a secret recipe given to me by my mother and her mother before her. I use certain herbs and wild plants. The local people come to me when they need healing."

"You're a doctor?"

"Me? No, I'm a healer and midwife. Doctors are for rich people like the Oliveiras up at the big *fazenda*."

"Oh. Are we close to the *fazenda*?"

Senhora Dias laughed and pointed toward the front of the house. "Did you see the pastures and coffee fields from your bedroom window?" I nodded. "All you saw and much more belongs to the Oliveiras. Our little farm is just a few acres sitting beside a giant. I am laundress and sometimes seamstress to the Oliveira family." The last statement was delivered with an expression that I could not interpret. Perhaps there was more to her story than she was willing to tell or perhaps my muddled imagination was simply looking for an excuse to run wild after my recent dreams. At any rate, my headache was returning, so I thought no more about her relationship with the powerful family that seemed to control everything for miles around.

We were silent for a while as Senhora Dias cleaned her kitchen. She started to speak twice, but something held her back. When she at last sat down at the little kitchen table opposite me, I understood why. She looked into my eyes with compassion, but also with determination.

"Who are you, little one? What is your name and where do you come from?" Then she held up my *onca* amulet and placed it in my hand.

My eyes wandered to the kitchen window while I tried to decide how much to tell. Across the narrow strip of earth that passed for the back garden stood a corral with a fence in need of repair. Its only inhabitant was an elderly donkey munching hay in a slow, bored manner. These people didn't have much and yet they willingly shared their meager portion with a complete stranger. They deserved the truth and yet, I hardly knew them. Telling Senhora Dias everything could send me packing back to Nathan. I just couldn't bring myself to do it.

"I think you have a secret you are not ready to tell. Why else would a young lady like you be alone on the river? For now, you may keep your secret, but at least tell me what to call you."

"Maria."

"Maria? Not Mary?" She took my hand and turned it palm up. "This hand has not seen heavy work. There are no calluses, only the remains of blisters. You know only a little Portuguese and when you speak, it is with the accent and phrasing of black slaves. Is that where you learned? From your lady's maid?"

I shook my head and tried to think of what to say next. "If you let me stay with you, I promise to work for my keep. I won't be a burden. I know how to work without complaining. Just please don't ask me to tell you anymore. Please!" The longer I spoke, the faster my words came and the more frantic my voice sounded. Tears rolled down my cheeks, dripping, along with my newfound energy, onto the borrowed nightgown I wore. My eyes felt very heavy and I leaned my forehead on my hands.

"I won't ask again for now, but if you are going to stay here, we must know everything. We are simple people who live under the eye of a very powerful family. We cannot be put in danger because you are hiding from the wrong people."

"I promise you no one has any interest in me," I replied in words so soft they were almost a whisper.

"We'll see. For now, you have had enough time out of bed. You must sleep more and regain your strength. When you are well, we will talk again. At that time, I expect the truth." With that, she stood up and offered her hand, which I took. She led me back to the little room I already thought of as a sanctuary against the world.

For two weeks I spent my time between sleeping, eating, and gradually walking a little farther each day. At first, I shuffled around the house's small rooms. There was a second bedroom next to the one I slept in, a sitting room that ran the length of the other side, and the lean-to kitchen. On sunny days, Senhora Dias wrapped me in shawls and took a chair out into the front garden. I spent those days walking, sitting, and doing simple tasks that didn't require too much energy. I felt cared for in a manner I had not known since we left Bess behind in Georgia. The Diases were kind and concerned without being fussy. We ate simple food at the kitchen table where they talked about news from the far-flung community.

During these meals, I learned that my hosts had little family left. Senhor Dias's ancestors were from the rain forests of the north, from a little village along the Amazon, not too far from the coast. They had migrated or been brought out of the forest as slaves, he didn't know which, to the port city of Fortaleza long ago, but he had lost all contact with anyone there once his parents and all but one of his siblings had died in a smallpox epidemic. His only remaining brother had long ago emigrated far away and they had lost contact as well. Senhor Dias had become a wanderer, an itinerate farm worker, roaming Brazil from one end to the other until he had fallen in love with his Adriana during the winter that he worked for her father helping to harvest coffee. They married in the spring and he traveled no more. Their babies, born many years ago, had all died in infancy or childhood. As for Senhora Dias, she was all that was left of a large extended family of siblings, cousins, aunts, and uncles who once lived all around the countryside. Times in this part of the Brazilian Plateau had been hard and epidemics had taken a terrible toll. For me, however, being in their simple home was a time of rest, recuperation, and the first real security I had known for a very long time.

On a day that was too cold for anything other than

staying inside, I sat mending a pair of Senhor Dias's socks when he turned to me from his chair by the fireplace and asked the question I had been dreading since shortly after regaining my senses. "Maria, the time has come for you to tell us who you are."

My eyes flew up from the darning and met his quiet, expectant gaze. As much as I feared revealing who I was, I couldn't bring myself to refuse him. I owed him and Senhora Dias my life, and therefore, my honesty. I nodded and searched for exactly what to say.

While I was thinking, Senhor Dias called to the kitchen, "Adriana, come. Maria is going to tell us her story."

When she was seated next to me, I began. "My name is Mary Catherine MacDonald and I'm an orphan. My parents died after we arrived in Brazil from the state of Georgia in the Confederate, I mean, the United States of America."

"So, you are one of the Confederados do Norte. That explains much. We have heard there is a colony of your people near Santa Barbara."

I told them about the war and the decision to leave our home rather than endure Yankee rule. I talked about our time in Rio where Mama died and how Papa had established our farm, then that he had died in an accident. I even told them about a bad man who was trying to make me marry against my will. What I told them was the truth, just not all of it. Not once did I mention that Nathan was the bad man or that he was my uncle. I felt ashamed of not being completely forthcoming with people who had been so kind to me, but I left them with the impression that I had no remaining family and that Papa's creditors had taken the farm. Fear can be a powerful motivator. I finished with another partial truth. "I was traveling to live with friends when I lost control of the canoe and fell into the river."

I'm not sure whether they believed everything, but they did not accuse me of outright lying. Instead, Adriana asked,

"And what will these friends do now that you have failed to arrive?"

"They didn't know I was coming. I left in a hurry and couldn't get word to them."

"Perhaps we should take you to them now," Ricardo said while holding my gaze with an expression that told me he expected the truth.

I couldn't meet his eyes any longer. "I don't really want to go there. They may not want me. Is there any way I could stay with you? I'll work for my room and board. I'll do whatever you need. I know how to work in the house and the fields because I've done it before."

Ricardo started to respond, but Adriana cut him off. "My husband, she has nowhere to go. Can you not see that? We have no children. God has provided one. She may not be of our blood, but she will be a comfort to us. She already is. And besides, Santa Barbara is a long way from here."

"Has your mind left you? How on earth will anyone believe this auburn haired girl with bright blue eyes and pale skin is our relative, much less our child? Is she to simply spring half-grown from the ground?"

Adriana smiled and took my hand. "I have thought of that. You once had a brother who went to those British islands down south to work in the shipyards, didn't you?"

And in that moment, Mary Catherine MacDonald became Maria Dias, who hailed from the Falklands, who spoke Portuguese rather poorly but English very well, and whose fair complexion and dark golden red hair could be explained by two generations of intermarriage.

## Chapter 17

My assimilation into the community surrounding the small village of Terra Oliveira began with Ricardo and Adriana's announcement that an orphaned great-niece from far away had arrived unexpectedly. The story they put about told of a young girl who was ill and traumatized by experiences surrounding her parents' deaths, thus rendering her unable to leave the house or speak of her pain. To further complicate matters, the girl spoke only English and a little French. Ricardo's brother, the girl's grandfather, had died before she was born and all knowledge of Portuguese had passed out of the family. It was a miracle that Maria, named for her great-grandmother, discovered the existence of relatives living near Terra Oliveira. Old letters, stuffed into her grandfather's traveling box and forgotten, provided the clues that led her to Ricardo and Adriana, who were thrilled to offer her a home. Her ignorance of the true religion shocked and embarrassed them, but the local priest would soon correct that with weekly visits for instruction in theology, dogma, and Portuguese. They hoped Maria would make her first communion as soon as her health allowed. At present her condition was too delicate to permit social calls.

The story was as close to the truth as Ricardo and Adrianna could make it and explained many of my oddities. Any raised eyebrows or untoward comments regarding its veracity were quickly squelched by a full frontal assault from Adriana. Those wishing her skill as a healer didn't dare incur her wrath.

Terra Oliveira had another relative newcomer. The village became an unexpected beneficiary when the scholarly, liberal leaning Father Paulo so offended Rio's ecclesiastical powers that he was banished to the remote location. The particulars of his crime remained a mystery, and therefore, a source of great curiosity. It was generally believed the big house knew his story since it would have been imprudent for the church hierarchy to offend the Oliveiras. They were generous benefactors who donated the land and then built the village church and rectory, but why they accepted the renegade was an even greater mystery than the priest's offences that got him evicted from the monsignor's presence.

My first meeting with him came three weeks after my arrival at the Dias farm. When we sat opposite one another at Adriana's kitchen table, I hid my trembling hands in my lap and prayed that the lies regarding my origins wouldn't be uncovered. Unlike our simple neighbors, this priest was educated and a man of the world.

"*Bonjour, Mademoiselle. Comment ca va?*" Father Paulo smiled kindly while Adriana bustled around us pretending not to listen as she prepared bed sheets for the wash pot.

"*Bonjour, Pere Paulo. Tres bien, merci. Et vous?*" Although Father Paulo spoke some English, he preferred French, so poor as mine had become with lack of practice, it would have to suffice as our common language until my Portuguese improved.

"Let's begin with the most basic practice, making the sign of the cross." His right hand moved to his forehead, then to his heart and from shoulder to shoulder, simple enough to follow, a few practices of the pattern made it feel natural and automatic. "And now for the Latin. *In nominee Patris, et Filii, et Spiritu Sancti.* Amen."

I stumbled through the recitation several times before the Latin began to feel comfortable on my tongue. "*Muito bem*! Can you translate it?"

His use of Portuguese caught me off guard and I answered before I thought. "*Sim*, Padre. In the name of the Father, and the Son, and the Holy Spirit."

"I was told you did not speak Portuguese. Your accent is unexpected. From whom did you learn?"

Adriana's head snapped around. "She learned only a little from the black maid who cared for her. Where the woman learned our language is anyone's guess, but I suspect she must have been a runaway slave from Brazil. The British have abolished slavery even in their colonies, you know."

"So, you had a maid on your English speaking island, did you?" I couldn't meet Father Paulo's eyes and simply nodded.

During the ensuing silence, the priest's eyes never left my face, making seconds drag like hours. Finally he drew an audible breath and said as he rose from the table, "*Tres bien*. I think that's enough for today. Maria, do you know the *Pater Noster*?"

I made a quick guess and replied in French, "The Lord's Prayer?"

"*Oui*." He dropped a leaflet onto the table. "Here it is in Latin. Have this memorized by our next lesson along with the Ave Maria and the Credo. Do what you are able to translate all three into French and Portuguese. I will baptize you at that time since Adriana insists you are still too weak to attend Mass."

I knew my Baptist ancestors, anti-papists one and all, were probably rolling over in their graves at the thought of my being baptized into the Roman Church, but they weren't around to help me and the Diases were. There was no way I was going to bring suspicion or criticism down on them. Since I had little else to occupy my mind, my indoctrination into the Catholic faith moved rapidly, as did my grasp of French and Portuguese. I could carry on simple conversations in each language by the time I made my first appearance at Mass in late September.

The first month of the Brazilian spring arrived on the coattails of a final winter storm, warming the air and painting the earth in bright greens. New calves nestled in tall grass beside fat cows, bags heavy with milk. Foals ran and played in the pastures under the indulgent eyes of grazing mares. Adriana's front garden became a lush artist's palette with hundreds of flowers turning their intensely colored faces to the sun. She had many beautiful specimens, but my favorite was a simple pink cabbage head rose similar to the one Mama had loved so much. I kept a fresh stem in an old jar on my windowsill and felt as though Mama was watching over me from her place beside the saints in heaven.

Surprisingly, I really liked praying to Mary and to female saints, a new idea since we Baptists didn't believe in such, but I'm afraid I adulterated the practice by turning it to my own purpose. In my mind, Mama sat right beside Jesus on a golden throne surrounded by angels. The fact that she couldn't be credited with a single miracle, much less three, made no difference. She became my personal saint to whom I offered a prayer every night after reciting the Hail Mary and Our Father.

On the last Sunday of the month, Ricardo, Adriana, and I set out to walk to the village for mass in a flurry of anxiety. Word had reached Ricardo that Constancia, the Oliveira matriarch, had learned of the new Dias girl and had become curious about her origins, especially why she needed private religious instruction and by her lack of Portuguese. When Adriana told me the Oliveira lady's name, giggling erupted and escalated until I bent double hiccupping with howls of laughter. It was the same name as the boat we took from Rio to Igaupe and for some inexplicable reason that struck me as hilarious.

"What are you laughing at, Maria?" Adriana stopped and turned back to watch me in alarm. "It won't be so funny if she takes a dislike to you or becomes suspicious of you. Although she is the grandmother, she rules Terra Oliveira with an iron hand." She and Ricardo hurried on because tardiness to mass wasn't tolerated.

When my hysterics subsided, I ran after them and grabbed Adriana's hand. "I'm sorry. I guess I'm just nervous."

"For all of our sakes, do not draw undue attention to yourself," she replied in a harsh whisper, then her stern expression softened and she squeezed my hand. "Don't be frightened. You're my smart girl. You'll do well." She was so like Bess in that moment that I wanted to dissolve in sobs and throw her arms around her neck.

The church was dark and cool after our walk in the brilliant morning sunshine. Once my eyes adjusted to the dimness, I stared in awe. It wasn't a large sanctuary, but the interior appointments left no doubt large amounts of Oliveira capital had been lavished upon it. Sunlight shining through jewel toned stained glass windows scattered rich patterns on floors, walls, and furnishings. Banks of candles burned in every corner, setting the highly polished dark wooden pews aglow and illuminating the generous applications of gold leaf on the icons that filled numerous niches. The altar cross and tabernacle were entirely covered in gold and set with semiprecious gemstones. The gold chalice and paten sat on a snowy lace trimmed altar cloth laid over an ornately carved table. The unfamiliar fragrance of incense hung in the air like a living, but invisible, presence. The sanctuary's beauty took my breath away. A sharp nudge in the back reminded me to genuflect and make the sign of the cross.

Like small communities in Georgia, the local parishioners had long ago settled the order of precedence regarding pew occupation. The Oliveiras sat in splendid isolation just below the altar in a family enclosure offset to the right of the center aisle. The *fazenda* managers and their families filled the front pews on both sides to about halfway back, leaving the rear pews to the lowly *vaqueiros* and peasants.

Ricardo guided me to a pew near the middle of the rear section. Once we were seated, I glanced around at the congregation. There wasn't an empty place anywhere save one.

"Where are the Oliveiras?" I whispered.

Adriana frowned and whispered so softly that I had to strain to hear. "They are always the last to enter, just before the priest and acolytes. Now be quiet and concentrate on the Mass."

The sound of boots on stone and the rustle of crinolines at the church door announced the family's arrival. A flash of aubergine silk interrupted my prayerful attitude, drawing my gaze toward an elegant lady passing down the aisle on the arm of a distinguished gentleman. An ebony cane topped by an ornate silver handle clicked softly on the stone floor as it aided the lady's stiff, straight-backed progress. Wings of white spread from the man's temples in an otherwise dark, full head of hair. The expensive cut of his suit marked him as a man of substance. A much younger man and another lady, probably old enough to be his mother, followed the aristocratic pair. The second lady wore a fashionable silk dress of sky blue while the young man was dressed like his older counterpart. They paused long enough to make their obedience to the altar and then opened the short door to their box. This must have signaled that Mass could commence because two acolytes in black cassocks and white surplices were halfway up the aisle by the time the Oliveiras' box door clicked softly shut.

"Stop gawking. They don't like it." Despite her reassurances to me, Adriana was nervous, but her nerves had not shown until the Oliveiras' appearance. I took one more speculative glance at them before focusing on the priest kneeling before the altar. During Mass, I concentrated on repeating the congregational portions of the Latin liturgy, trying to remember when to kneel, stand, and cross myself. Finally it was our turn to receive Holy Communion. As I knelt at the rail waiting for Father Paulo to place the Host on my tongue, my eyes drifted toward the Oliveiras. Constancia, the grandmother, must have been a great beauty in her youth. A fine patrician bone structure and glossy hair that was still dark complemented long lashed brown eyes set in a face whose creamy complexion was remarkably free of lines. The aubergine silk set her coloring to advantage.

Her features and coloring were stamped upon the faces of both men. The middle-aged woman was faired-haired and attractive, pretty even, but she was a drab little mouse next to her glossy thoroughbred family. While I was observing the Oliveiras, I felt someone's gaze on me. It was the young man and he stared straight at me. When my eyes met his, he grinned and winked, sending flames into my cheeks and a shudder through my mid-section. The dimple in his handsome right cheek was startlingly attractive. Father Paulo was on the verge of saying "the body of Christ" for a second time when I tore my eyes and attention away from young Senhor Oliveira.

Mass ended and parishioners filed out in reverse order from which they had entered the church. Only Father Paulo and the acolytes preceded the Oliveiras. As the family passed our pew, I stole another sideways glance at the grandson who, to my great surprise, was staring at me also. He again winked and grinned which somehow felt disrespectful despite my forwardness in seeking another glimpse of him. I felt confused and embarrassed. Heat flooded my face when I heard his soft chuckle. The young man clearly had a high opinion of himself and his expected effect on females. Unfortunately, his self-evaluation wasn't too far off the mark, which made me furious with myself. Why he should have such a strong effect on me was something of a mystery since we hadn't met and certainly weren't likely to. When Ricardo urged us toward the church door, I was in a fair huff.

"Maria, congratulations on your first communion. I'm sure Ricardo and Adriana are proud of you." Father Paulo paused expectantly.

My attention, which still lingered on that chuckle, joined the conversation where it belonged. "Thank you, Father. I really couldn't have done it without you." How stupid I sounded. Of course I couldn't have made my first communion without the priest's instruction nor would I be speaking Portuguese so fluently.

"Well, yes, I suppose that's true. It was my pleasure to instruct such a quick pupil. What are your plans now that you have fully recovered from your ordeal?"

What were my plans indeed? I had none because I had refused to think that far into the future. "I guess I'll find work to help Ricardo and Adriana. They're so kind to me. I just don't know where to start."

"Of course we are kind. You're family," Ricardo interjected. I suppose he felt the need to cover for me since I didn't seem able to make sensible conversation.

"Employment may not be as difficult as it might seem. I believe you noticed the Oliveira family?" I nodded miserably while my face flamed as though I had been caught doing something inappropriate. "Senhora Constancia recently mentioned their need of a new parlor maid. I could speak to her on your behalf, if you wish."

"She can't!" Adriana's abrupt response took everyone by surprise.

"I don't see any other work available at the moment. What other choice does she have?"

"That other girl was . . . you know very well why she was sent away, Father Paulo. A beautiful young girl shouldn't work at the big house."

I'm not sure which surprised me more—Adriana's outburst or being called beautiful. It was a word people had often used when referring to Mama, but I looked nothing like her.

"That is no longer an issue," Father Paulo replied. "Gustavo is leaving to study and travel abroad at the end of the week. He will be gone for at least five years."

Adriana glared. "Maria is innocent and unspoiled. She shouldn't be exposed to the goings-on up at the big house. Besides, they have no respect for anyone who isn't of their class."

"Adriana, be quiet before someone hears you!" Ricardo's face had gone white. "You can't talk about them that way. Please, Father, I beg you, do not repeat what she said."

"I'll treat her words as though they were spoken in the confessional." He took Adriana's hand and looked directly into her eyes. "I wouldn't suggest something that I thought might bring harm to Maria. I hope you know me well enough by now to understand that. She needs employment and you need the extra income. It's a good solution for everyone." Adriana nodded, but the expression in her eyes said very clearly that her fears were not allayed.

My interview with Senhora Constancia Oliveira came two weeks later. On a damp October morning, I waited twitching with nerves while Ricardo brought the donkey cart. Adriana was still expressing her fears in no uncertain terms, going so far as to tell me exactly why the last girl was dismissed. When her condition became apparent, she had been summarily evicted from the *fazenda*. Shortly thereafter, she disappeared from Terra Oliveira and no one knew her present whereabouts. Adriana hinted darkly that she had probably come to a tragic end, either by her own hand or one hired by others. Her final words on the subject were issued while we walked out to the cart sitting by the front gate.

"Do not let yourself be alone with any of the men up there. They cannot be trusted. Do not walk home at the end of the day. Wait for Ricardo to come fetch you in the cart. If they ask you to live in the servants' quarters, say you must be home every night or quit. Do nothing to anger Senhora Constancia or any of the others. They do not tolerate incompetence. Keep your eyes lowered whenever any of them enters the room where you are. Do not speak to them unless they speak directly to you. Move silently and make yourself as invisible as possible. Do not draw attention to yourself."

She would have gone on, but Ricardo interrupted. "For goodness sake, Wife, you are going to have Maria so frightened that she won't make a good impression." To me, he said, "Despite what Adriana says, the Oliveiras are not monsters and you have nothing to fear as long as you do your job well. And if anything happens to make you uncomfortable, you will quit and we will continue as before. It will be well, I promise."

I climbed up onto the cart seat beside Ricardo and he flipped the reins on the donkey's rump. The animal looked around over its shoulder as though to ascertain the extent of his master's determination to move forward. Finding Ricardo's hands halfway towards another flick of the leather, it sighed heavily and shuffled into a snail's pace slog down the rutted dirt path that connected us to the village and the main road through the valley beyond. I could hardly blame the little beast for wanting to return to the relative comfort of its paddock because the path was wet from last night's rain, turning pulling the cart into a mud bath. I gathered my skirts into my lap and prayed that none of the mud splattered as high as the cart seat. We set off under a glowering sky that threatened to drench us before our journey's end.

After about twenty minutes, Ricardo turned the cart off the main road onto a one-lane path. Its wheels crunched softly on crushed stone as we wound up the side of a promontory. Lining one side of the driveway was a mown grass verge planted with flowering shrubs and tall arching trees behind which a plateau rose sharply. The other side of the path was open to the countryside below except for an echoing line of trees that formed the canopy under which visitors traveled. The open side of the path allowed travelers a vista that stretched for miles over the pastures and fields below. The farther up we traveled, the more lush the plantings became until the vista ended abruptly and we passed between borders of banked plants flowering in full spring glory. When we reached the hilltop, the single path gave way to a broad circular driveway with a large fountain in its center. A pedestal, richly carved in a flora and fauna motif, spewed water high into the air before it fell into a large pool. Behind the circle's far curve of stood a house that reminded me very much in size and ornamentation of Government House in Rio de Janeiro where Emperor Dom Pedro had allowed us to stay. Once again I had a feeling of being observed and found wanting by an aristocratic dowager forced to tolerate the intrusion of lesser beings.

When we pulled up to the back entrance of the house, the threatened rain descended. It blew so hard I could only call a quick goodbye to Ricardo as I lifted my skirts and splashed across a little courtyard toward the deep veranda leading to the kitchens. The phrase *looks like a drowned rat* came to mind as I shook water from my clothing. After knocking, I waited, shifting from one foot to the other for what seemed an eternity. I had begun to wonder if Ricardo had misunderstood at which door I was to present myself when it finally opened.

A small plump form stood in the shadows and barked, "You're late. Senhora doesn't tolerate tardiness. Wipe your feet well because I don't tolerate dirt or those who track it into my kitchen."

I did as I was commanded, taking special care with the edges of my boots, which had become caked with mud in my leap from the cart onto the driveway's edge. When they were as clean as I could make them, I looked up awaiting further instruction.

"Well don't just stand there. Come in and close the door."

Once inside, I saw a large food preparation area furnished with long tables, a large wood burning cast iron range, and a fireplace big enough for a grown man to stand in. A small army of dark skinned maids was busy chopping, basting, washing, or stirring what must be the makings of luncheon. All this food and all those maids preparing it for how many diners? There could only be four by my accounting.

A hazy scene, made vague by distance in both time and geography, flitted though my memory. It was of a similar kitchen in which slaves labored to provide sumptuous meals for the hordes of relatives and friends who consistently put their feet under Grandpapa and Grandmama Jordan's expansive dining room table. Holiday celebrations at their home were some of my earliest memories. I wondered if the girls working here were free or slaves like almost all of the black people in Georgia were before the war. Bess had started as a kitchen slave when she was only eight years old, long before she became Mama's nursemaid.

"Follow me and keep up," the cook snapped. "You have already kept the senhora waiting. That is never wise." She turned on her heel, headed for a dark passage leading deeper into the house. I hurried after her waddling backside. It might have been a humorous sight if I hadn't been so apprehensive about my impending interrogation.

After what seemed a mile of dark tunnel, the hallway suddenly ended in an explosion of light. My guide turned and barked, "Stay here and do not touch anything." She then hustled to a tall door on our left. Just before she disappeared behind its mahogany panels, I glimpsed floor to ceiling bookcases filled with volumes.

The expansive entry hall contained matching ornate mahogany sideboards topped by gold-leaf framed mirrors and its ceiling rose seemingly out of sight. A grand staircase rose from the center of the hall's marble floor to a gallery above that appeared to be the size of a small ballroom. Filigreed wrought iron held a mahogany banister aloft on either side of a rich red stair carpet. Over both the hall and gallery hung crystal chandeliers with so many arms each that I couldn't count them all. The foyer's walls were covered in heavy red damask mounted with finely carved moldings painted white with gold leaf accents. Although I had never seen Brazil's imperial palace, I couldn't imagine it would be any finer.

My heart jumped slightly when the library door clicked softly and my guide reappeared, stating in a suddenly more refined voice, "She will see you now."

## Chapter 18

The cook, housekeeper, or whatever she was left the library door ajar and disappeared into the dark tunnel from which we had come without uttering another word. I glanced at my reflection in the mirror over the nearest sideboard. I saw a girl with a halo of unruly curls drawn from their hairpins by the recent dash through the rain. Dark blotches made an unattractive pattern over her dress from neck to hem. I sighed and ran a hand down my skirt to smooth out wrinkles, tucked an errant curl behind my ear, and stepped into the room.

Senhora Constancia Oliveira sat beside a huge fireplace fronted by a marble surround and mantle. Her chair would have been suitable for Emperor Dom Pedro. I waited with a thumping heart to be summoned into the presence.

"Don't just stand there, girl. Come here and present yourself." Her cultured accent was unlike the Portuguese I understood best, but an imperious wave of her hand made clear what she wanted.

I traversed what felt like a mile of dark hardwood floor, my boots echoing with every step until the tap-tap of their tread disappeared into the pile of a thick, richly patterned carpet.

"My goodness! Do you not own an umbrella?"

Of all the questions she might have asked, this was not one I expected. "I . . . no . . . I'm afraid I do not. I'm sorry."

A silence ensued during which she bored holes into my meager efforts at making myself presentable.

*"Je comprends que vous parlez francais?"*

*"Oui, Madame. Je parle du francais."*

*"Votre accent, c'est terrible."*

*"Oui, Madame."*

"I am told you also speak English, that it is actually your first language?"

Her change into my native tongue caught me off guard. "Yes, Ma'am. It's my best language." My words drawled toward her as though they were molasses pouring from the syrup pitcher on a winter morning.

"Once again, your accent is very odd. Where were you born?"

"In the Falklands, Ma'am. The islands are under British control."

"Don't be impertinent. I know what the islands are. Your English is unlike any I have heard. Can you explain?"

"I'm not sure. Other children teased me about my accent. I guess it's because our people originally came from Brazil." The interview had descended into a quagmire of lies so quickly I feared that afterward I wouldn't remember what I had said.

Senhora Constancia remained silent, a shadow drifting across her patrician features. *"Voce fala o portugues?"*

Once again, she changed languages without warning. *"Sim, Senhora. Eu fala um pouco portugues."* At least this was the truth. I did speak a little Portuguese.

"Do you have no accent that is presentable? You speak Portuguese as though you are a black slave. Explain." She spoke rapidly, making her cultured, educated use of Portuguese difficult to follow.

"I learned enough to communicate with servants."

"You had servants?" Her nostrils flared as her eyebrows rose.

"Just one. She helped in the house. She was a runaway slave from Brazil."

"And you now want to come down in the world by becoming a housemaid?"

"*Sim*, Senhora. My great uncle and aunt need the income. I know how to work and I'm not afraid of getting my hands dirty."

"I see. If you meet with my approval, getting your hands particularly dirty will not be required."

Her gaze swept over me again, the silent scrutiny making me feel like an insect pinned to a specimen board. After what felt an eternity, she spoke. "You may begin tomorrow on a trial basis. You will improve yourself, especially your Portuguese, while performing the duties of parlor maid. Take care to adopt the accents you hear in this house. Even the servants here speak with more cultured accents than yours. Adriana will find a uniform for you when she comes to tend to the laundry tomorrow. Accompany her and learn about your duties from Senhora Perez, the housekeeper whom you have already met."

"Thank you, Senhora. I will work hard to please you."

"Yes, you will," she said rather pointedly and then her eyes dropped to the book lying in her lap. Unsure whether I had been dismissed or not, I waited. Directly, her head flew up and her eyes blazed. "At what are you gawking? Leave. Do not intrude again unless you are summoned. And remember to curtsy in the presence of family members and our guests."

I lifted my skirt, bent one knee, and then walked from the room as silently as the wooden floor allowed. When I pulled the door closed behind me, I was able to breathe again.

My induction into *Fazenda Oliveira* moved quickly, once I learned what was expected of the parlor maid. Senhora Perez, while not particularly friendly, did what was necessary to ensure a smooth transition. My duties included, but were not limited to, dusting and sweeping the formal common rooms, polishing furniture with lemon oil and beeswax, polishing the silver service and flatware, answering the door to admit callers, and serving at table. It made me smile to think what Bess's reaction would have been if she could have seen me in my black and white uniform. I felt sure she would have called it trying to be 'big britches', her own special descriptive invention. One of the things she liked best about moving from The Dogwoods with Mama after she married Papa was getting rid of the uniforms required for serving downstairs.

I learned there were three classes of people living on or working at the *fazenda*—the exalted Oliveira family, the free peasants who tended to various tasks both within and outside the house, and the slaves who did the heavy outdoor labor and who rarely came near the house. Being a peasant worker on *Fazenda Oliveira* was certainly better than being a slave, but everyone, free or not, walked in fear of Senhora Constancia, whose wrath could be quick and unpredictable.

My life as an Oliveira servant and as the Diases' great-niece settled into a busy, but comfortable pattern, where I found stability in the former and family in the latter. Some nights just before I drifted off to sleep, I pondered all that had happened since my arrival in Brazil. It awed and amazed me that I had discovered unconditional love with complete strangers, who gave me what my real remaining family, Nathan, refused. When I thought of my uncle, I boiled with rage. My hatred of him had not lessened with the passage of time or my new circumstances. It burned as furiously now as it had the day Brother Williams and Colonel Bowen returned Papa's body to Little Georgia. If anything, Adriana and Ricardo's loving compassion juxtaposed with Nathan's terrible words and actions only served to increase my hatred. I occasionally allowed my imagination to wander to visions filled with acts of revenge, but that only made me feel frustrated and impotent because Nathan would always be beyond my grasp. Since vengeance eluded me, I determined to refrain from thinking about my uncle and my lost inheritance at Little Georgia. Self-discipline and hard work would become my armor against the pain of remembrance.

When one works in a great house, it is not unusual for one's employers' lives to seem far more interesting than one's own and so it was at *Fazenda Oliveira*. The servants discussed the family's words and actions in minute detail when they thought Senhora Perez was out of earshot. This was how I learned something of the relationships among the family. One afternoon while I was cleaning the silver coffee service, I went to the kitchen for more soda and came upon two maids with their heads close together. When they heard the door open, they looked up guiltily.

A look of relief crossed their faces and the closest one commented, "Pay her no heed. She hardly speaks Portuguese. Now what happened?"

The other girl gave me one more glance and then continued. "I was tending to the chamber pots in the family apartments when it started. I'm surprised you didn't hear it down here in the kitchen. Senhora Constancia was that angry. The old harpy yelled that as long as she lived, things would remain as they had always been and that Senhora Marguerite needn't complain to her husband because Senhor Eduardo agreed with his mother."

The two maids exchanged meaningful looks before the first girl spoke again. "Well, if you ask me, Marguerite should develop some gumption and tell the old biddy where to go. Our lives would be easier for sure if they traded places."

"As if that's going to happen in this lifetime. My guess is Marguerite picks her battles very carefully." The second girl stopped speaking and scowled at me as I stood at the kitchen door with the soda in my hand. "What are you looking at, you little sneak. Understand more than you let on? You better not tell or you'll be sorry."

Heat flooded my face. "I won't say anything. I promise."

I hurried back to the dining room. The second girl, Celina, resented me because she wanted out of the kitchen and the parlor maid position seemed her ticket until I came along.

She was pretty enough, but she spoke only Portuguese. Since foreign visitors were not uncommon at *Fazenda Oliveira*, it soon became apparent why I was chosen instead of Celina.

My life consisted of six full days of work, with half days after Mass on Sundays, and nights at home with Adriana and Ricardo. Ricardo came for me in the cart every evening after the Oliveira's supper was over and I was finally free to return home for a quick meal before I fell into bed.

While I can't say I enjoyed every task assigned me in the big house, some were pleasant enough. My favorite was dusting the library. I loved it because I could run my hand along the spines of hundreds of books, many of whose titles I recognized. One of the things I missed most from my childhood in Georgia was having lots of books at my disposal to read whenever I wished. Sadly, I hadn't completed all of Papa's books before the Yankees burned our house and his library with it. I saw some of the volumes I had not read sitting on the Oliveira's shelves. While I didn't have the nerve to ask permission to borrow any of them, I took pleasure in merely being in their presence.

On a cold July afternoon in my seventeenth year, I paused, as I often did, before a shelf containing a volume of Moliere. My cloth swished back and forth over wood and leather, raising poignant memories along with the dust. Not long before Sherman's visit, Mama had begun reading *Le medicen malgre lui* (The Doctor In Spite of Himself) to me as part of my French instruction. How we had laughed at the playwright's sharp wit. Sadly, we didn't get to finish the satire. I longed now to slip the anthology of plays from its place and curl up with it in a quiet corner.

As I wiped its top and spine for the third time, a voice coming from a tall-backed chair next to the fireplace startled me out of my reverie. "You may borrow a volume if you wish, my dear."

My heart dropped as the speaker rose and turned to face me.

Senhor Eduardo moved around the chair and came to my side. "You seem mesmerized by our French collection. And as you are fluent in the language . . ."

The way he leaned closer and let his words simply drift away set my teeth on edge. His tone was mellow and low. He took another step closer, forcing me to move back against the shelves.

His gaze swept over me from head to toe twice and he then chuckled. "It's merely an offer. I don't bite, despite what you may have heard."

When his fingers brushed a nonexistent dust mote from my shoulder, I drew back reflexively. At that moment, the sound of a throat being cleared reached us from across the room. Neither Senhor Eduardo nor I had heard the library door click open.

Senhor Eduardo took two steps back and adjusted his expression. "My dear, you have need of me?"

Marguerite spoke from the doorway, her voice tight. "No, I am looking for Maria. I have made a decision regarding her position in the house."

"Have you consulted my mother?"

"No and I do not intend to. I have made up my mind."

My heart flew to my throat as my gaze dropped to the floor.

"You know as well as I that it is never wise to cross Mama, but do as you wish." Eduardo turned away, his interest in the fate of a lowly servant flagging.

Before turning on her heel, Marguerite said to me, "Come to my sitting room immediately."

My skirts brushed the floor as I replied, "*Sim, senhora.*"

Enraged, I hurried up the servants' staircase. I had done nothing wrong, but this woman, who had everything, was going to dismiss me because of what she thought she had seen. In recent months, I had become increasingly uncomfortable in Senhor Eduardo's presence. His gaze haunted my movements, whether I was serving at table or cleaning the formal rooms. The attention had not escaped his wife's or his mother's notice either, for I had glimpsed their expressions as his eyes wandered up and down my body. I only received a pittance for my twelve-hour days, but it had already helped Ricardo purchase a mule so that the little donkey could retire from fieldwork. He and the mule were planting another acre of coffee at this very moment. Now, it seemed all of my hard work was to come to naught.

Eduardo and Marguerite occupied a suite of rooms that incorporated the entire east wing of the second floor. Their joint and individual sitting room windows commanded views out over the front lawns and the valley below. Other than Constancia's suite in the west wing, these were the most luxurious apartments in the house, but they were not where the couple should have slept. It was a topic of great speculation among the servants that the dowager managed to retain the grand master apartment that should have gone to Eduardo as his father's only male heir. The maids even snickered about how Marguerite trembled when her mother-in-law reproached her for some perceived failing. I knocked on Marguerite's sitting room door and waited with trembling of my own. Those who are persecuted can sometimes become persecutors in short order when the opportunity presents itself.

"Enter."

Senhora Marguerite sat at the end of a long room made gloomy by dreary weather, her back to tall windows, her pale face hidden in shadow. In all of my time at *Fazenda Oliveira*, we might have spoken a handful of times and only briefly at that. Supervision of my work fell to Senhora Perez, the housekeeper cum cook, and on rare occasions, to Senhora Constancia. Marguerite's reputation among the servants was that of a benign spirit who wandered the house, but never left any trace of her habitation. It was said that even the decoration of her personal rooms was determined long before she married into the Oliveira family and her mother-in-law would not countenance changes.

"Come."

I walked the length of the room, coming to rest at the edge of a small Louis XV desk. A pool of light from an oil lamp illuminated its parquetry top and gilt bronze ornamentation, but did not reach beyond the pearl broach at the neckline of Marguerite's navy wool dress.

"Have you been happy in your time with us?" Her voice was quiet.

"*Sim, senhora*. Very happy."

"Is the work to your liking?"

I prayed she could not see my hands shaking. "*Sim*, it is very pleasant work."

"Do you understand how it is with Senhor Eduardo?"

She surely must be setting a trap for me. "I'm not sure what you are asking."

"Oh, come girl. You can't be that naïve." Her voice rose slightly, becoming taut. "Have you not seen him watching you?"

My face flamed as I searched for the words that would proclaim my innocence. "Senhora Marguerite, I have done nothing to encourage attention from anyone. Please believe that I want only to do my work well."

"Perhaps." Her voice dropped so low I had to strain to hear. "You are Adriana and Ricardo Dias's niece, are you not?"

"*Sim*, I am their great-niece. They are the only family I have. We are very grateful for our work at the *fazenda*." The tremor in my voice couldn't have escaped her notice.

"I'm sure you are. Times are hard and there are many who would be happy to replace you and Adriana here." Her voice was soft, devoid of emotion.

I alternated between fear and anger. Marguerite toyed with me like a cat tormenting a mouse. Because I knew nothing that would make my situation better, I remained silent and watched as her fingers moved in slow circles over the glossy desktop.

After what seemed an eternity, she sighed. "Would you consider another position within the household? One that would require that you live here?"

Surprise kept me quiet while I thought of how Adriana would react to the proposal.

Marguerite filled the void. "You must understand it is either this or dismissal. I can see no other option."

I tried to keep the indignity of desperation from my voice. "Senhora, I work hard to please you and your family. Please tell me what I have done wrong and I will correct it immediately."

At this point, she leaned into the lamplight. Her eyes were soft with empathy, but darker emotions dwelt there as well. "Maria, the only thing you are guilty of is beauty and youth. Here is my proposal. As you know, my personal maid has left to care for her elderly parents and I need to replace her. You and Adriana need continued employment. Are you willing to take the position as lady's maid? I must point out that the Dias's long relationship with my family is the only reason I make this offer since you will have to be trained. I will ask Senhora Constancia's maid to teach you what is required. Well?"

"But what will Senhora Constancia say?"

"She will consent. I will make it clear this is my wish." Her voice held a steely edge.

While I doubted she could muster that kind of influence with Constancia, I decided that there was only one thing I could say at present. "Thank you, Senhora Marguerite. When would you like for me to begin?"

"Immediately. You will confine yourself to my apartments and my needs unless I request otherwise. You will sleep at the foot of my bed every night. You will have Sunday morning to attend Mass and dine with your aunt and uncle, but you will return to the *fazenda* no later than four o'clock in the afternoon. Go now and make your arrangements with your relatives."

Clearly, there might be more to Senhora Marguerite than met the eye. I wondered what hold she could possibly have over Constancia that could inspire such unexpected confidence. As I walked home to get my few possessions, it came to me that the source of Marguerite's trembling when challenged by Constancia might be rage, not fear. I decided I would need to tread very lightly where those two were concerned. The uncertain nature of their relationship might seriously complicate my life.

"What do you mean you are going to live at the *fazenda*?" Adriana's shout brought Ricardo running in from the vegetable garden.

"I have no choice. It is either become Marguerite's maid or lose my job. We need the money."

"Not at any price would I allow this." I couldn't decide if it was fear or anger glittering in Adriana's eyes. "You have no idea what those people are capable of. You must not return. I will make an excuse when I go to do the laundry tomorrow."

"But that's just it. If I don't take this job, neither of us will have work. Marguerite said as much."

Adriana placed her hands on her hips as her expression hardened. "She doesn't have that kind of power. It is Constancia who makes the decisions and she promised I would always have work."

Ricardo, who had silently observed our exchange from the kitchen door, placed his hand of Adriana's arm. "I think you are forgetting that Marguerite got her way once before when she really wanted something."

Adriana's eyes narrowed in speculation or remembrance, I couldn't be sure which, and she became quiet. After several seconds contemplation, she cocked her head to one side and asked, "But why would she want Maria as her maid badly enough to risk a confrontation with Constancia?"

My face flamed. When I described the scene in the library and my interview with Marguerite, Adriana declared, "You see? I told you it was unsafe for Maria in that house."

Ricardo thought for a moment and then said, "I think Marguerite may be keeping Eduardo away from Maria by keeping her close by. It would be difficult for him to have his way right under his wife's nose. And it is said he no longer goes to her at night."

"Husband, do not speak of such in front of the child."

"But you forget." I put my arms around Adrianna and looked into her eyes. "I'm not a child and I've decided to accept Marguerite's offer. Please understand that I'm doing what I think is best for all of us."

And so my life became even more entwined with that of *Fazenda Oliveira*. As Ricardo predicted, I saw little of Eduardo. Whatever it might once have been, the Oliveira's marriage was now one in name only.

## Chapter 19

"So, what do you know about serving a great lady?" Constancia's maid tilted her gray head and cocked a wrinkled brow in my direction. When I shook my head, she sighed and continued, "As I thought. You know nothing and I am expected to teach an ignorant girl in two weeks what it has taken me a lifetime in service to learn." She groaned softly and limped down the hall leading to Eduardo and Marguerite's apartments. "Follow me, do not speak unless addressed, watch everything that I do, touch nothing until directed, and above all, learn quickly. I have no intention of showing you anything more than once. My feet have all they can do to care for my lady Constancia."

Despite her gruff exterior, the old woman was an excellent teacher. I did exactly as she said and was soon attending Marguerite on my own. Although the hours were long, I really enjoyed many of my duties. I found that I loved the look and feel of beautiful things, even if they adorned another woman. Caring for Marguerite's clothing and jewelry gave me a sense of fashion and style I hadn't known since watching Mama dress for her dinner parties before the war. Eduardo made up for the niggardly affection shown his wife by lavishing upon her whatever was the latest or most expensive since appearances were of the utmost importance to him. For her part, Marguerite appeared to accept the exquisite things as her due. I suppose it was a kind of compensation for her arranged marriage to a man with a roving eye and a harridan of a mother.

But despite all she possessed, I found myself pitying Marguerite, an emotion I never expected to associate with an Oliveira. In addition to being ignored by her husband and dominated by her mother-in-law, she suffered ill health. There were days when she was unable to rise from her bed. When the trouble descended, she ordered the curtains closed to block out the light and the clock's hands stopped, for even its soft ticking increased her pain. At those times, I kept a basin by her bed into which she often vomited what little she ate. The only thing that seemed to bring any relief, but only a little, was a cold cloth pressed against her temples and forehead. I sometimes sat for hours mopping her brow until the pain would at last begin to diminish.

After one particularly bad episode, Marguerite was so weakened she remained in bed for some days afterward. I knew she was recovering somewhat when she turned to me and asked, "Maria, can you read?"

"*Sim, senhora.*"

"Are you literate in either Portuguese or French?"

"Well, I can read both, but French is my better language."

"Perhaps you might select something amusing from the library to read to me. I don't feel well enough to rise, but it's becoming very dull just lying here with only my own thoughts for entertainment."

I practically skipped to the library because I knew exactly which volume I would choose. I had waited long enough to learn the accidental doctor's fate. I left the library with the Moliere anthology tucked under one arm, and would have gone directly to the grand staircase, but bright light pouring through the open double front doors blinded me momentarily. When my eyes adjusted, I saw a dark haired man of middling height passing into the foyer. Behind him, slaves heaved trunks and other baggage from a carriage.

I couldn't help myself. My feet refused to move. My breath stopped. My heart flipped over. He was more handsome than I remembered, much more. I stood mesmerized as he glanced over his shoulder, issuing orders for the delivery of his baggage before walking to the center of the foyer where he paused. His eyes wandered over the large reception area as though he appeared to seek reassurance that nothing had changed in his absence. When he caught me staring at him, his eyes widened a little and he looked as though he were going to say something. My face flushed crimson as I curtsied and fled. To my mortification, he started chuckling as I ascended to the second floor. Within moments boots thudded on the stairs, taking them two at a time. Gustavo strode past me to his mother's suite and flung the bedroom door wide.

"Oh my darling boy, you're home at last," echoed down the hall.

I stopped in the doorway when I reached Marguerite's room. Gustavo sat on the edge of the bed with his arms around his mother. Joy lit her face for the first time since I had served as her maid.

"I've missed you so much. Was Europe all you hoped?"

"It was. Now tell me why you're abed at this hour of the afternoon."

Not wanting to intrude on their reunion, I stepped back, but the movement caught Marguerite's attention and then Gustavo's.

"Oh, it's you. You weren't at the *fazenda* before I went away, but I feel like we've met before."

Marguerite's eyes snapped back to her son's face, which she searched before saying, "You will remember Adriana, the laundress? This is her niece. Maria, prepare my bath and lay out my new gown. I'll dine with the family this evening." She placed her hand on Gustavo's face and turned it toward her. "Now tell me everything. What did you enjoy the most?"

Gustavo's return had already created considerable excitement in the servants' domain. Senhora Perez's voice rang down the back passage that led to the kitchen where

I headed to get hot water for the bathtub. "You girls get upstairs and make up Senhor Gus's bed immediately and take water for his bath. He'll want to wash before dinner."

Celina and the new kitchen maid passed me giggling conspiratorially. "I'd like to join him in his bath, wouldn't you?" Celina asked. The other girl put her finger to her lips, nodding in my direction, but Celina wouldn't be silenced. "What's she going to do? Tell her mistress? Not if she knows what's good for her."

Even though she had at last gotten out of the kitchen when I became Marguerite's maid, Celina had never forgiven me for taking the parlor maid job first. She not only disliked me, she did whatever she could to make me a pariah among the other servants. I avoided her whenever possible.

That evening as I buttoned Marguerite into her blue silk, Gustavo returned to his mother's chamber.

Marguerite glowed as her eyes swept over her son. "Oh my, I'm sure you set the European ladies' hearts aflutter!"

I kept my eyes glued to the buttons. He was absolutely the most handsome man I had ever laid eyes on and I didn't want a recurrence of the scene in the foyer.

Still not looking in his direction, I set the last button in place and said, "Unless there is something else you wish me to do, Senhora, the gown you want to wear for the celebration ball needs attention. The hem has come undone in several places."

"Yes, that should be attended to. And it may need alteration as well since I believe I've lost weight recently. With the ball only a month off, all of my best garments may need attention. We'll start on that tomorrow."

I curtsied, keeping my eyes down, and made for the door to the clothes room.

"Wait. I have a few things that need attending. Mother, would you mind?"

"Well, I don't think . . ." The hesitation in Marguerite's

voice was unmistakable. Several seconds elapsed and she then sighed. "Oh, I suppose she may help with the things you will need for the next day or two, but we must find a suitable man to serve you as valet in the near future."

"Maria, come to my room now and I can show you what needs doing."

"Gustavo! That will not do. Leave your things out in your room and Maria will collect them while we dine."

"But Mama, really."

"Really, indeed! Familiarity with female servants is not allowed in this house, as you know all too well. Did your years in Europe teach you to defy the wishes of your family?"

"No, of course not. Please excuse my presumption."

"Maria, you are dismissed."

I didn't look at I either of them, but curtsied again and fled to the safety of Marguerite's little clothes room where her dresses and gowns hung from every available space.

In the month separating his return and the ball planned in his honor, Senhor Gustavo reentered the life of *Fazenda Oliveira* with all the ease and confidence of one born to its great privilege. Everyone from his grandmother to the lowliest field slave seemed determined to emulate the prodigal son's father by showering Gustavo with fawning attention, but I had as little contact with him as possible. Adriana's dire warnings and reminders of my predecessor's fate rode with me every Sunday afternoon when Ricardo drove me back to the *fazenda*. My plan to avoid Gustavo succeeded fairly well until his mother was again brought low by her trouble.

Marguerite's pain subsided in a couple of days, but she was weak from the vomiting and bowel disturbance that was so often part of the illness that plagued her. After eating a little from the tray I brought up to her, she pushed it away.

"Enough. Read to me from Hugo. Fantine and little Cosette have been much on my mind."

Gustavo bought the very popular *Les Miserables* in Paris as a gift for his grandmother, but she found the premise offensive and refused to read it. I was delighted Marguerite didn't possess her mother-in-law's distaste for being reminded of how the lower classes survived. In fact, she seemed to find some strange connection to the story.

I had just completed the chapter where Fantine leaves her child, Cosette, with the odious Thenardiers and was about to ask if I should continue with the next, when Marguerite focused on some distant point that only she could see and said, "I once knew a girl like Fantine. She too was young and foolish. She loved too soon and too deeply and paid dearly for her error."

"Did she have a child also?" I was intrigued. Since one might say that we lived together, she and I, Marguerite occasionally let slip tidbits of information, but a revelation of this nature was something entirely new.

Marguerite looked at me as though she had momentarily forgotten to whom she spoke. I could see Fantine and Cosette's plight touched her in some significant way beyond Hugo's complicated plot. The story was real and personal to her.

"She had . . . Yes. She had a child."

"What became of them?" My curiosity still sometimes set caution to the wind.

The moment passed and her eyes resumed their usual guarded state. "It's of no consequence to you. Read a few more pages and then I'll retire for the night."

Gustavo's voice called from the doorway, "Read a few more pages of what? May I join you? I haven't been read to since I was little." And then he winked at me. I turned away quickly because I didn't want to encourage his impertinence or give him a glimpse of the effect he had on me.

A frown told me Marguerite had seen the wink and was reluctant to consent, but she couldn't resist having her only child with her whenever possible, and so began the nightly ritual of our reading in Marguerite's room. Gustavo and I read chapters in turn. Of course his accent, having been formed in Paris, was much better than mine, a fact he enjoyed teasing me about. The teasing irritated both his mother and me, albeit for very different reasons.

Eduardo and Constancia never joined us. Constancia retired to her apartment not long after dinner each night and Eduardo spent his evenings in the library. I assume he read also, but I have no idea which books caught his fancy. The family followed this pattern until shortly before Gustavo's welcome home ball.

By the flurry of activity and mounting anxiety among the household, one would have thought Emperor Dom Pedro was the honoree. Constancia whipped everyone, including her daughter-in-law, into such a state that I feared Marguerite would be confined to her bed when the great day arrived. Crates of champagne arrived, having been brought as far upriver as possible before being carried overland by porters. Fruits, vegetables, and meats were stock piled in underground cellars. When the final week of preparations arrived, tension swirled about the house like the tornado that had carried off our smokehouse one spring back in Georgia. There was an unforeseen benefit for me, however. As Marguerite predicted, her clothes needed taking in and as a consequence, Adriana came to the big house every day. When she wasn't doing laundry, she joined me in Marguerite's clothes room to work on the alterations. Two days before the overnight guests were to begin arriving, she made sure we were alone and then spoke her mind.

"I don't like it. Why would he want to read to his mother? He never paid her that much attention before," Adriana whispered around a mouthful of pins. "He's nothing but a spoiled, selfish boy who's already ruined one girl. You remember that and keep clear of him."

I couldn't help smiling. Adriana reminded me so much of Bess sometimes. "Well, I can hardly bar my lady's son from her room, now can I? And I can't refuse to share the book with him either." I glanced at Adriana and put my arm around her shoulders. "I know people say he was sent away because that girl disappeared, but let's acknowledge a person can change. He hasn't done anything that's made me uncomfortable. In fact, he's rather good company."

"That's exactly why I don't want you near him." Adriana turned to face me, her needle suspended midair. "Oh, he's a charmer all right. How do you think he got into the other girl's knickers so fast? She only worked here for three months. Handsome, charming, wealthy, and powerful. Hardly a healthy combination for the likes of us."

I didn't respond because anything I might have said would only have led to an argument. My mind, however, was anything but quiet. Now why, I wondered, did I feel a burning need to defend Gustavo? He did quite well without my help. I let my gaze drift to the open window that looked out over the eastern hills. He might be everything Adriana said, but my experience of him didn't jibe with the picture she painted. Shaking my head slightly to clear my thoughts, I returned to my attention to stitching a new lace collar onto one of last year's dresses.

As the week drew to a close, the driveway's gravel crunched constantly under the wheels of arriving carriages. Even though the house had many bedrooms, I wondered how we would accommodate everyone. People were coming from all over Sao Paulo State, some from as far away as Rio. Those who traveled the greatest distance would stay on after the grand ball.

At exactly ten o'clock on Saturday night, the strains of a waltz filled the house sending a sea of beautiful gowns and white tie attire swirling across the ballroom floor under the glow of crystal chandeliers lit with so many candles it was impossible to count them. The evening possessed a special magic that made even the plainest female guest pretty and every gentleman distinguished. All of us servants were pressed into service in one capacity or another. My assignment was seeing that no one was without champagne. Although the tray of crystal glasses was heavy, passing from room to room among the guests allowed me to feel a little like I was part of the excitement.

The only fly in the ointment of that lovely evening was my contrary attention. It sought out Gustavo in every room, no matter how much I concentrated on serving the guests. Shortly before midnight, however, it seemed as though he had disappeared.

"Maria!" Constancia's voice rang above the music. "Father Paulo has arrived and is in need of refreshment."

She, Father Paulo, and Gustavo were seated in a small alcove near the head of the room. "Grandson, how many times have you danced with the Du Bois girl? Her father did not desert his duties at the French consulate in Rio and travel all the way here to have his daughter ignored."

Instead of answering his grandmother, Gustavo's eyes met mine.

"Gustavo, I asked a question!"

He turned his attention to his grandmother, but not quickly enough. I was appalled to see a speculative expression in the priest's eyes as they drifted from Gustavo to me and back.

"Grandmamma, I've done my duty by every young lady here tonight, I assure you."

"That's not good enough. Have you forgotten the conditions of your return?"

"Of course not. I just haven't seen anything in particular to tempt me."

"How very like you!" I believe she would have said more, but the priest intervened.

"I believe what Gustavo means is he has not had time to become sufficiently acquainted with any of the young ladies to form an opinion."

"Thank you, Father Paulo. As always, you speak far more eloquently than I." A quick glance passed between the two men. I couldn't be sure if it was one of animosity or of grudging respect.

"Girl, why are you still standing here? See to my guests."

Sometimes the inconsistency of Constancia's imperious commands was almost beyond endurance. My arms were trembling from holding out a full tray from which no one had taken a glass. I turned away quickly before my tongue let loose the cutting retort she so richly deserved. I heard Gustavo draw breath as though to speak, but he remained silent. Fury renewed my energy for the remainder of the period before supper was announced. What surprised me, though, was the dawning realization that Gustavo actually didn't seem to be singling out any particular young lady for special attention and that his eyes seemed to follow me whenever I passed near.

The supper gong sounded at midnight, giving the dancers a welcome excuse to get off their feet. They crowded around the groaning buffet and then sat in clusters around linen covered tables. Lively conversation filled the supper room and poured out into the ballroom for the next half hour or so. This was the most demanding part of the evening for me, so I lost track of Gustavo completely. When the string quartet began tuning their instruments signaling supper was drawing to a close, I headed toward the kitchen to refill my empty tray.

"Maria!" floated from beneath the service stairs.

"Senhor Gustavo!" He caught me completely off guard.

"Come over here."

"Is there something I may do for you? Are you ill?"

"Yes, I'm sick."

"Then what are you doing here? Let me get the doctor. I saw him in the supper room just now."

"I don't need the doctor. I'm just sick of the crowd and with remorse for the way Grandmamma spoke to you. She can be difficult at times."

"Thank you, but you have nothing for which to apologize. None of us can control someone else's words."

He sighed and then continued, "However that may be, I couldn't bear the thought that she hurt you. You're really the only friend I have here tonight."

My surprise couldn't have been greater if he'd told me men were walking on the moon. "That's not true. Everyone here is your friend. Why else would so many have traveled so far?"

A cynical smile played across his lips. "Because everyone has 'expectations' and they're making me sick with boredom. Stay here and talk to me. And it's Gus to my friends, just plain Gus."

"Well, just plain Gus, I have work to do. Now if you will excuse me . . ."

I turned to go, but he placed his hand on my arm. "Maria, I meant what I said. You really are my only friend. Please won't you stay for just a minute or two?"

Against my better judgment I stopped and turned back to him. I couldn't resist the pleading in his voice, which made me furious with myself. "Senhor Gus, I can't lose my job. Senhora Constancia will fire me on the spot if she sees us."

"Ah yes, my grandmother! Did you know she expects me to choose a bride from among the young ladies here tonight, someone who will produce the next generation of Oliveiras?"

I shook my head because I couldn't form any words. For some reason the idea of his marrying felt like a blow to my midsection.

"The problem is, I can't abide any of these silly creatures."

The thumping of a cane on the steps above our heads silenced him.

"Gustavo! Are you down there?"

He placed a finger to his lips and pulled me farther back under the staircase.

"Gustavo? Upon my word, the boy will be the death of me!" Constancia's cane thumped again as she ascended the stairs once more.

Gus's silent laughter became contagious. We both shook until our eyes streamed.

He drew out a snowy handkerchief, wiped his eyes, and then passed it to me. "See, you are my friend." His grin faded and his face became solemn. "Maria, you are beautiful under the ballroom's chandeliers. Would you believe me if I told you that I've closed my eyes and pretended you were in my arms tonight with every dance?"

Just then the melody of another waltz floated down from the ballroom. "Come. Dance with me."

"What? Here?"

"Yes. Right here under the stairs."

"I can't. I don't know how. And besides, I'll be missed."

"They can wait for their champagne." Gus took the tray from my hands and placed it on a nearby table. "I intend to enjoy at least one dance tonight!"

I should have refused. I should have run to the kitchen where he wouldn't have dared follow. I should have done anything other than allow him to take me in his arms. But once we began swaying to the lilting notes from the strings, it just felt so right as though our bodies were meant for one another and the music. We moved from under the stairs into the corridor, twirling in the dim light of a single candle set in a wall sconce.

Gus bent closer and breathed into my ear, "I believe you're a natural dancer. Or were you just being modest? I've suspected for some time there is more to you than meets the eye. A literate servant is amazing in itself, but one who reads three languages? Tell me, Maria, tell me your secrets."

A knife-edge of fear ripped through me. I pulled myself free, retrieved my tray, and turned to go, but Gustavo grabbed my arm and stepped in front of me, a look of surprised anger distorting his handsome features. "What's upsetting you so? Tell me and I'll make it right."

"You can do nothing. Now let me go!" I fled for the safety of the kitchen with angry tears threatening to roll down my cheeks. How could I have let myself be drawn into such a compromising position?

For the remainder of the ball, I ensured that he and I were never closer than a tray full of crystal would allow. Each time he called for more champagne, I could feel him staring at me, but I refused to meet his eyes. One of us had to be sensible enough to end the foolishness before others noticed. By the close of the ball, I believe Gustavo was quite drunk and I wanted to flee to the safety Marguerite's bedroom away from chance notice and speculation.

## Chapter 20

The last of the local guests left the ball just before dawn on Sunday and we servants were finally allowed to collapse into our beds for a few hours before the onslaught of clearing up and feeding the guests in residence began. Because I couldn't bear to pass up time at home with Adriana and Ricardo, Father Paulo ferried me pillion on his little brown mare all the way to our front gate. The sun peeked over the mountains when Adriana greeted me at the door and insisted that I go to bed immediately. It seemed only minutes had passed when she laid her hand on my shoulder and shook it gently.

"If you are going to eat before you return to the *fazenda*, you must get up now, little one. It's almost two o'clock."

"I didn't mean to sleep so long." I yawned broadly and stretched my aching muscles.

"You have been up all night. Even the young need their rest. Come to the table when you are dressed. I've made your favorites."

Adriana and I were washing the dishes when Ricardo rose from the table to answer a knock at the front door.

"What an honor. Please come in." Tension made his voice higher pitched than normal. "Oh no, take this chair instead. It is the most comfortable. Would you like coffee?"

"Thank you. It would be most welcome. I take it black." My heart thumped and turned over. The visitor's voice was unmistakable.

"Adriana, bring coffee for Senhor Gustavo."

Adriana raised an eyebrow. In response, I could only shrug my shoulders and shake my head.

She poured the coffee into her best cup and hissed, "Stay here," before leaving the kitchen.

For the next ten minutes, conversation jerked and stalled in the front room. Gustavo did his best to put Adriana and Ricardo at ease by asking questions about the farm, but he finally gave up and said, "Forgive me for intruding on your day of rest. It's really Maria I've come to see. I just happened to be riding near here when it occurred to me she might need a ride back to the *fazenda*."

Thunderous silence ensued.

Ricardo coughed and then finally replied, "We could never trouble you with such. I will take Maria in the cart as always."

"But I can save you the trip."

"That would not be proper!" Adriana's voice was sharp. "It would cause gossip if the two of you were seen together."

"Forgive me, but I believe we Oliveiras determine what is proper and what is not in this community. I insist."

He sounded so much like his grandmother that I actually hated him. Fearing Adriana would say something that would bring trouble down all our heads, I rushed into the front room. "*Ola*, Senhor Gustavo. Thank you for the offer. I accept."

"But . . ."

I squeezed Adriana's shoulder. "If Senhor Oliveira says it is proper, then I'm sure he is right." As hard as I tried, though, I couldn't keep the anger from my voice.

When we were far enough from the house that I knew Adriana and Ricardo couldn't hear, I no longer contained my displeasure. I leaned forward from my place behind the saddle so that my mouth was close to his ear and said, "How could you? You've put the two people I love most in the world in a terrible position. We can no more refuse the lord of the manor than we can fly."

"Lord of the manor? Oh, yes, an English expression, I believe. Well lordship has its privileges." He laughed so hard I thought we might fall off his big bay stallion.

In retaliation, I squeezed his midsection as hard as I could, hoping he might choke, but all my effort produced was a tap with the crop on the horse's shoulder, urging it into an all-out gallop. Of course I had no choice but to hold on for dear life. We flew through the village past wide-eyed peasants, nearly running down Father Paulo as we skidded around the corner of the church. An angry shout at our flying backs was all he mustered before we were gone. When we turned onto the long drive leading uphill to the *fazenda*, Gustavo finally took pity on the sweating beast and pulled back to a sedate walk.

"Apparently you have no more consideration for your animals than you do for your servants. It's a wonder the horse hasn't collapsed beneath us." My anger rose in rhythm with the stallion's heaving sides.

Gustavo didn't reply, but at the top of the plateau he pulled on the reins and guided our mount to a secluded spot under the trees. He turned sideways so that his eyes met mine. "You're right. I'm sorry. I've been selfish and thoughtless. But since half the village and the priest have already seen us, your getting down and walking would be a waste of time and energy. The choice is yours, however."

As much as I hated to admit he was right and as much as I disliked myself for agreeing, I stayed where I was. There was nothing to be gained from walking to the house but sore feet. I looked up when we passed under Marguerite's east windows and saw her turning away. Since I had no idea how long she had been there, I couldn't be sure whether she had seen us or not.

Later that evening after Marguerite bid the guests goodnight and retired to her bedroom, I learned the answer.

"Shall I read to you for a while before you sleep?"

"That would be pleasant. One gets so tired meeting the demands of entertaining."

"Should we wait for Senhor Gustavo?"

"He will not be joining us now or in the future." Her direct eye contact said as much as her words. "And Maria, do not mistake his attention for anything more than the flirtation of a bored young man who is trying to accustom himself to *fazenda* life again after the excitement of Europe."

My face flamed. Although I knew her words were probably true, it didn't keep them from worming their way to my heart and leaving a hole there. To drive home her point, I was no longer asked to serve at table when the house was shorthanded as it had been during the ball week. Furthermore, Marguerite required that my movements were confined primarily to her rooms and that I was to use only the servants' stairs when I left them. I no longer enjoyed freedom of the library either because she now selected the books that I read to her. I believe she would have dispensed with my services altogether if it hadn't been for Adriana. The basis of their connection was still a mystery, but its bindings were clearly very strong.

Despite all of Marguerite's precautions, she failed to take into account her son's ingenuity or determination. He appeared when I descended the stairs, while I sat in the kitchen courtyard taking the air, when I waited beside the back gate for Ricardo on Sunday mornings. He never stayed long or said anything of great importance. He was simply ever-present. At mass, his eyes followed me when I went to the altar for communion as they had on the Sunday of my first outing and communion five years ago. Of course, I knew his eyes sought me out because I watched him as well. I couldn't help it, which made me angry with both of us. My greatest fear was that others would notice.

On a Sunday about two months after the ball, Ricardo and I were bumping along the road leading out of the village when a single rider approached from the opposite direction.

"Good afternoon, Ricardo. Maria." Gustavo tipped his hat and pulled his mount around so that they walked beside me. "May I accompany you?"

The man's lack of consideration for potential gossip annoyed me no end. "Suit yourself. You usually do."

Ricardo's face turned so red I thought he might be having a stroke. "What my niece means, Senhor Gustavo, is that you are most welcome to join us."

"Thank you. I'm glad at least one of you is my friend."

His arrogance really was insufferable. "Of course, Senhor, there are none for miles and miles who would dare be otherwise. But I'm curious. How can you be sure that the friendship is bona fide and not merely a product of the instinct for survival?"

"Maria!" was all Ricardo could manage before a coughing fit overtook him.

Gustavo laughed softly and then his expression became serious. "That's the rub, of course. And even more difficult is convincing others that my offer of friendship is sincere and carries with it only the most honorable intentions."

I opened my mouth to issue a pointed retort, but he silenced me by placing a hand on my shoulder. "They really are, you know. Honorable, I mean."

I glanced up at him and then over at Ricardo. Both men stared straight ahead as though this was the most common of topics and most casual of conversations. For my part, confusion reigned. I was angry with Gustavo for his presumption, with myself for having to put up with it, but also angry at the thrill that passed through me with the simple touch of his hand. The man was truly infuriating and the situation was quickly becoming intolerable. I brushed his hand from my person. We rode on in silence until the long driveway leading up to the *fazenda* came into view.

"This is where I must leave you, but Senhor Dias, may I

call upon you and Senhora Dias at eleven o'clock tomorrow morning? There is something of importance I must discuss with you."

Ricardo's head snapped around toward Gustavo. His eyes swept over the younger man and then he nodded. Gustavo touched his riding crop to the brim of his hat and turned away down a sidetrack that led around the plateau toward the Oliveira coffee fields.

"Oh, Ricardo! What can he want with you and Adriana? If he causes you harm, I'll kill him. I mean it!"

"Hush! Don't say such things, even in jest." Ricardo sucked on his lower lip as he often did when deep in thought. "I'm not sure what to think. If he were any other man, I would say he intends to ask permission to court you. What would you think of that?"

"That's impossible and you know it. All I can say is he better not cause trouble."

"But if he does want to see you, what are your wishes?"

"I . . . I have no idea."

Gustavo's physical beauty made my breath catch each time I saw him, but his reputation was frightening and his casual disregard for the needs and rights of others was insufferable. He wouldn't be interested in me for anything other than a casual dalliance. Yet, how could I refuse the attentions of the man who would one day rule Terra Oliveira as his own private fiefdom?

"Yes or no, Maria. I need to know."

How could I give him an answer I myself didn't know? No matter what I decided, trouble was the only possible outcome for the people I loved and for me.

We rode in silence until the cart came to rest at the kitchen courtyard gate. "Maria, you've got to give me an answer. We must be prepared."

"I guess . . . the answer is yes." I spoke so quietly that Ricardo turned to see if he had heard correctly, my own fear and confusion reflected in his eyes.

I slipped my hand into his and pressed gently. "You tell me. Do we really have any other choice?"

He answered with a single shake of his head.

And so, the Sunday afternoon visits began. Shortly after the midday meal, there would be a knock at the front door. When Ricardo opened it, there Gustavo stood with his hat in his hand, as meek and polite a gentleman caller as any girl could wish. Ricardo would invite him into the front room where the four of us sat in a stiff and uncomfortable caricature of courting couple with chaperones. It might have been comical if it hadn't been so disquieting.

Adriana issued dire warnings whenever she and I were alone. Her lack of graciousness when Gus appeared bordered on the inhospitable, but eventually she accepted that our powerful neighbor wouldn't be dissuaded from his course of unwelcome attention. And to my horror, I found within myself a growing inability to resist what I knew was a dangerous relationship that could only lead to tragedy and ruination.

At the end of the first month of Sunday visitations, a pattern emerged in which the first half hour was devoted to conversation in the parlor and then Gus asked permission for the two of us to walk out alone. I felt sure Adriana or Ricardo would refuse the first time the request was made, but to my surprise they murmured meek acquiescence.

Even though we were quite isolated, I refused the cart track for fear of being seen. Instead, we followed a path through the forest that descended to a rushing creek. A little glade at the path's end provided a shady refuge from which to admire an abundance of Brazilian flora. For three months, we walked and talked with Gustavo doing nothing more daring than offering his arm. His conduct was so exemplary that I began to wonder if the rumors about him were simply vicious gossip based on jealousy and envy.

On a particularly beautiful day, Gustavo took my hand

as we entered the little glade and pulled me toward a flat-topped boulder. "Let's sit. I don't want to go back yet."

When I was settled on the rock's cool surface, he broke a large red blossom from a nearby shrub and tucked it behind my ear. His hand lingered, creating a cascade of curls as he let my hair run through his fingers. "You're so beautiful with your hair flowing down your back. I've often dreamt of it spread across the pillow next to mine."

A cold hand gripped my heart. Here it was, the request that I had dreaded. Senhor Gustavo Oliveira was finally going to show his true colors and my greatest fear was I would not have the will to refuse him. How can one loathe what a man is and yet be drawn to him with a passion that felt like fire in one's veins? At that moment, I hated both of us.

"What a singularly inappropriate comment. Don't think because I'm a servant, I go weak at the knees at the sight of you and will drop into your bed at the slightest provocation. I have no intention of being another of your conquests."

I rose and would have fled, but he grabbed my arm and spun me around to face him. "What do you mean, another of my conquests? If I have done anything other than treat you with respect, pray tell me."

My fear and confusion boiled over. "Respect? Yes, you are a very good actor indeed—calling Adriana and Ricardo senhor and senhora, sitting in our parlor like a humble suitor, only offering your arm when we are alone. But I know why you were sent away and I will not take that girl's place."

"I doubt it." Anger glittered in his eyes.

"Doubt what?" I spat back at him.

"Doubt you know what really happened before I left for Europe."

"I know the parlor maid before me fell to your charms, got into trouble, and then disappeared. I will not be your next victim."

"Victim? Is that what you think? The girl was only too

happy to drop her knickers and she gladly accepted the rather large sum that was settled on her and the child. Fortunately for her the baby died, but she lives on in style enjoying the fruits of her brief labor at *Fazenda Oliveira*. I believe Rio is her current place of residence."

I forgot all about caution at this point and screamed at him, "How can you be so calloused about your own child?" To my disgust, tears flowed in little rivers down my overheated cheeks.

The fire went out in Gustavo's eyes. He withdrew a snowy handkerchief from his breast pocket and tried to wipe the tears from my face. He spoke calmly, almost dispassionately. "It wasn't my child."

"But everyone says . . ."

"Everyone is wrong because only three people know the truth. The child was an Oliveira bastard, it's true, but he wasn't mine. I tell you this because I want you, of all people, to think well of me and to trust me. I vowed to take the truth to my grave to save dear ones pain, but I will not let the lie destroy us."

"I didn't realize there was an *us*." If he thought he would be let off the hook so easily, he was mistaken. I wasn't a fool.

"There will be if you will have me." He paused and took both of my hands in his. "Maria, I love you and want you to be my wife. Please believe me. I may not be all you could wish, but I am not the man the gossips make me out to be."

Had Gus just asked me to become his wife or had my mind been tricked into hearing what my heart secretly wanted? It took a moment for his meaning to sink in. As I considered Gustavo's revelations, the scene in the library with Eduardo and Marguerite came back, as did her question later that day regarding her husband. She had asked if I knew about Senhor Eduardo. Had Gus spent years away from home to protect her from a secret she already knew? It now seemed very likely.

"Well, what is your answer? Will you become my wife? Father Paulo is waiting for us at the church if you will only say yes."

## Chapter 21

My heart hammered as though it was determined to be free of a chest no longer large enough to contain it. I needed time to think and to regain control. I had to find the courage to resist the most alluring offer that was ever likely to come my way.

"Father Paulo? Why would he marry us? I thought he was your grandmother's confidant and protégé."

Gustavo's finger lightly traced the contour of my cheek. He lifted my chin until his eyes looked into mine and he laughed softly. "Paulo is both, but he's also my first cousin and her favorite grandchild."

I stared at Gustavo in wonder.

"I suppose I should explain." A mischievous gleam I didn't quite like filled his eyes. "My cousin has great compassion for star-crossed lovers and with good reason. It's common knowledge that the ground in this area is fairly littered with Oliveira bastards and our local priest is chief among them. He's the son of my father's deceased sister, Bella. She loved unwisely, gave birth to Paulo in secret, and then died posthaste. Grandmamma strictly maintains the myth that Bella died in a cholera epidemic in Venice while on grand tour with Portuguese relatives. Poor Aunt Bella. She's rarely mentioned."

I was fascinated. I felt ashamed to be so engrossed in someone else's misery, but I couldn't help myself. "If it's such a great secret, how do you know so much?"

"Because I've listened at doorways and eavesdropped from under furniture since I was a small boy. After hearing the name Paulo whispered many times, I confronted my mother demanding to know the identity of the person who commanded so much of my grandmother's concern. Mother told me he was a secret and warned me not to ever mention him again, but over the years, I put the story together for myself."

"Does Paulo know who he is?"

"Priests can be such self-righteous prigs and Paulo's no exception. He severely chastised me about the parlor maid's condition and I blamed him for my being sent away. I got drunk the night before I left for Europe and told him what I knew about his birth. His reaction wasn't what I expected. He simply asked that I speak to no one about his background and saw to it that I got home safely."

He stepped closer and his expression shifted as his arms closed around me. He pulled me to him until our bodies crushed against one another. His hand lifted my chin until solemn eyes looked directly into mine. "Enough about my cousin. Give me your answer. I think I deserve at least that courtesy. Will you marry me?"

Flames raced from the core of my being, covering every inch of my body and consuming common sense. The words flew from my mouth before my brain realized they had been formed. "Yes. Yes, I'll marry you."

Strong arms swept me from the ground and warm lips covered mine, raising a passion I had only experienced in my dreams. My arms went around Gustavo's broad shoulders and I hugged him to me greedily. He was the one to break the embrace.

"We should go now and make our vows before God. If we stay here any longer, I will break my promise to never emulate my father."

We were married at the altar where both Gustavo and I had made our first communions. It somehow seemed very right, even though Father Paulo's housekeeper and gardener were our only witnesses. After the ceremony, Father Paulo went with us to tell Adriana and Ricardo. Gustavo might not have needed his support, but I did. We found my foster parents in the front room. Adriana only stopped pacing when Ricardo took her arm and guided her to a chair. He remained standing, resting one hand lightly on his wife's shoulder.

"Have you completely lost your minds? When you were gone for so long, we searched for you. We feared something bad had happened, but never this!" Adriana's voice must have carried all the way to the village. "I have prayed constantly this was just a passing flirtation. I thought that any day your attention, Senhor Gustavo, would fall on a girl of your own class. Your parents and grandmother will never stand for this. At the very least, Maria, Ricardo, and I will be driven from our farm."

She then turned accusing eyes on Father Paulo. "How could you? They are just foolish children, but you are our priest. You know better. Something terrible is going to happen and it will be on your head. People who displease the Oliveiras are always punished."

Father Paulo took Adriana's hand and held it in both of his. "You must not fear. Gustavo and I will see that our grandmother is kept under control."

Adriana's face paled and little beads of perspiration formed on her upper lip. "How did you find out?"

"One of the advantages of being the monsignor's senior secretary was a certain level of power. I used my position. In the orphanage, I was among a small number of children who had secret benefactors. It took pressure applied in the right places, but I eventually learned Constancia Oliveira had been mine. She really isn't the monster you make her out to be."

After some minutes of silence, Adriana recovered her voice. "And do you know who your parents were?"

"Yes, my source enlightened me there, as well. My

mother was Constancia's favorite child. My father was a rapist never brought to justice. A heritage anyone would be proud of, don't you think?"

"That isn't even close to the truth. If you knew everything, you would understand why I fear the Oliveiras."

"Then tell me. It would be a kindness. I promise you will not suffer for revealing what you know."

Adriana looked at Ricardo, who held her gaze for a moment and then slowly nodded.

"Your father was a vaquero who worked on the *fazenda*. He was handsome and kind, a truly good man who loved your mother with all his heart. On the night he disappeared, Senhora Marguerite overheard Senhor Eduardo and old Senhor Oliveira threatening your father. He was determined to marry your mother, but the Oliveira men would have none of it. After that argument, your father was never seen or heard from again. Senhora Marguerite believes her husband and father-in-law had the young man killed."

"How do you know that?" Gustavo said quietly. "My mother doesn't reveal her secrets to me, much less to casual servants."

It spoke volumes that Gustavo didn't protest his father and grandfather's innocence of possible complicity in murder. What kind of family had I so impulsively married into?

We waited in uncomfortable silence while Adriana considered her reply. Her answer came slowly and hesitantly at first. "I know because I was with Bella when Paulo was born. I'm a mid-wife and the great Oliveiras could never let it be known they had a fallen daughter, so they sent the two of us to their summerhouse in the mountains for Bella's confinement. No one was allowed near the place except Ricardo who brought supplies. But your mother, Gustavo, sneaked away to visit Bella as often as she could. Marguerite was a lonely young bride and Bella was the only Oliveira who had shown her any kindness. Those two unhappy girls became closer than sisters."

Paulo's gaze drifted to the open window and then he asked, "What actually killed my mother? My source didn't seem to know."

"It was a difficult birth. The blood just never stopped coming."

"Did she live long enough to say anything about me?"

"She begged Marguerite to be the one to take you to the orphanage. After Bella heard about your father's disappearance, she didn't trust anyone else. She loved you desperately, Paulo, and she knew she was dying."

"Did Marguerite do as she was asked?"

Adriana nodded and looked at Ricardo, who continued the story. "I traveled with Senhora Marguerite to Rio where we delivered you to the orphanage Senhora Constancia had chosen. For once, Senhora Marguerite was determined to have her way and she got it."

Lines formed between Gustavo's brows. "How do you suppose she managed it? Mamma never goes against Grandmamma's wishes."

Adriana glanced from my husband to his cousin and back. "I believe she threatened to reveal the whole story, especially her suspicions of murder."

Paulo's face filled with sorrow. "I've always believed people must be free to determine their own destinies. It was my abolitionist activities that got me ejected from the monsignor's service. How incredibly sad my parents never experienced the freedom to choose."

As we traversed the miles between farm and *fazenda*, I thought about what I had learned. Bella's story explained the mystery of Adriana and Marguerite's bond, but it also demonstrated the extent of Oliveira power. I silently prayed Marguerite might defy Constancia again and support Gustavo and me. Otherwise, Adriana might have good reason to be afraid, despite Father Paulo's assurances.

We found the three senior Oliveiras gathered together in the library when we entered the big house at dusk. All three focused sharply on Gustavo and I wondered if some villager had come running with the tale of our visit to the church. Constancia rose from her chair and steadied herself with her cane. Her gaze was glacial.

"Why are you accompanied by your mother's maid and the priest, Gustavo?"

Gustavo took my hand and drew a long, slow breath before he answered. "Grandmamma, Father, Mamma, I wish to present my wife, Maria Oliveira. Please welcome her to the family."

Constancia swayed slightly as her gaze fixed on Father Paulo. "How dare you betray me? My influence can break you!"

"Yes, that is certainly true. But do you really wish to destroy your grandson as you did your daughter? As you did my mother and father?"

Constancia's eyes widened and she sagged into her chair as though Paulo's words were a pin puncturing a balloon. All of the potions and unguents she used to keep the years at bay failed her in that instant for her face aged twenty years. She lifted glittering eyes to Paulo, her lips forming a thin line.

"You know nothing! I would have done anything for my daughter, but she chose a drifter, a worthless nobody over her family. Once she made that decision, she left me no choice. I did what I could for you because you are her son." Constancia's breathing became labored and she leaned heavily against the chair back. "How did you find out?"

"It is of no importance. What is important is what you decide to do next. You have an opportunity to learn from the past and to see that history is not repeated. You will feel better about your life if you do something kind now."

Constancia's mouth twisted into a bitter smile. "What would you know about my feelings? I have no feelings. My situation has never permitted me the luxury. It is my strength and control that have made *Fazenda Oliveira* the great establishment you see today. My dowry saved her from the ruin brought on by my father-in-law's mismanagement and gambling debts. My youth and energy were spent rebuilding her, saddled with an incompetent fool of a husband as I was." Nervous tapping from the other side of the fireplace caused her to glance at Marguerite momentarily, but then she focused on my husband. "The only thing Oliveira men have ever been capable of is marrying well. But you, Gustavo, haven't even managed to do that. This marriage will be annulled at once. The girl and her relatives will be allowed to leave Terra Oliveira without retribution as long as they remain quiet."

Paulo's eyes had remained fixed on his grandmother. It was impossible to tell exactly what he was feeling. "In order for that to happen, you will need my assistance and I will not give it. Please accept that for once your power has limits. It is for the best."

"Best? For whom?" Constancia's voice was as close to an anguished cry as I suppose it had ever come. "My idiot grandson and the conniving little *puta*? Or for you, my pious, self-righteous, forever cleaving to your principles priest? I used my influence to place you on the path to greatness. You were destined for a position in Rome. And the return on my investment? You threw my help on the ground and walked on it as though it was garbage."

"Constancia, it's true. You did for me all you've said and I have always been grateful. But in what was most important you failed. An orphanage and a career are poor seconds to knowing one's true name and having loving parents."

"But I love you above all others despite everything. I saw you were cared for and educated, that you had a position of respect with a glorious future when I could have turned my back. You could have one day been a cardinal. Why isn't it enough?"

"Your love is returned, please believe me. But love that must be hidden as a shameful secret leaves the beloved feeling less than whole. You robbed me of family and a home. You robbed my parents of each other. I'm determined Gustavo and Maria do not suffer the same fate."

"Then you are a fool who knows nothing of the real world and how society functions." Constancia's voice regained its steely edge. "Gustavo, the servants will have your things packed and waiting at the kitchen gate by dawn. Please see you remove them with as little disturbance as possible. Perhaps your new family will give you a bed. *Fazenda Oliveira* is no longer your home and you are no longer part of this family."

I had almost forgotten that anyone other than Constancia, Gustavo, Paulo, and I were in the room, but a flash of rustling taffeta near the fireplace caused my head to snap around. Marguerite strode toward Constancia with the fury of a charging lioness. When she came to rest, her whole body trembled. She wrapped her arms about herself and howled a single word. "No!"

She placed her hands on the arms of Constancia's chair and bent down until her face loomed only inches above her mother-in-law's. "No, you will not turn my son from this house or this family. I have endured your bullying and domination for my entire adult life, but no more! Harm my child and I will ruin the mighty Oliveiras."

"And ruin yourself in the process? I doubt it. You are nothing without us."

"Without my son, I am ruined. It is only when I'm with you and my husband that I am nothing. You will accept Gustavo and his bride or face the sordid past being made very, very public."

Eduardo finally bestirred himself. Placing his ever-present glass of *pinga* on the table beside him, he rose and grabbed his chair's back to steady himself.

"Marguerite! Remember to whom you are speaking."

Blazing eyes turned on Eduardo. "Shut up and go back to your alcohol! You've always been ineffectual. Why change now?" She then turned her fury back on her mother-in-law.

A thousand tiny needles pricked my skin so palpable was the tension in the room. Marguerite and Constancia's eyes remained locked. Neither spoke nor moved. Each woman's body looked as though it would shatter with the lightest touch. After an eternity, the fire died in Constancia's eyes.

"I believe you would actually be foolish enough to follow through with your threats. Very well, Marguerite. Have your way in this, but do not imagine you have attained a position of authority. You aren't equal to the task."

## Chapter 22

Marguerite removed her hands from the arms of Constancia's chair and for several beats stared at her mother-in-law with glittering eyes, then turned on her heel and floated across the great expanse of carpet and parquet toward the door. Watching her dignified retreat brought an odd realization. In a single, but very important way, she reminded me so much of Bess. No two women could ever have been more different, but they shared something I would never have considered before observing the confrontation with Constancia. Bess and Marguerite had so little control over their own lives and choices, but each woman fought like a tiger when someone she loved was threatened. Bess once went after a bear with a garden hoe when the animal unexpectedly wandered near the smokehouse steps where I was playing. She jumped between me and the hulking mass of teeth and claws, waving her hoe and shouting that no ole bear was gonna hurt her baby. I'm not sure who was more frightened, Bess or the bear. Marguerite had faced down the most powerful entity in her world and had protected her baby just as surely as Bess had protected me. Respect bloomed where I had once only felt patronizing pity.

After the library door clicked shut, Constancia rose from her chair. "I shall retire now. Maria, tell the cook to send up a tray. I will dine alone in my apartment."

I could hear Gustavo's breath quicken. "Grandmamma, my wife is no longer your servant. Do not order her about as such."

"Gustavo, please," I whispered as I slipped a hand onto his arm, then I spoke so that everyone could hear. "It's my pleasure to see that Senhora Constancia's wishes are carried out." There had been enough discord for one evening.

Constancia looked toward the door as though neither Gustavo nor I had spoken. "Eduardo, give me your arm. The stairs have been difficult today. Paulo, you must leave as there will be no dinner served here tonight."

Instead of my following Constancia's commands, Gustavo went to the kitchen after he had me ensconced on the divan in his sitting room. He seemed determined to defy his grandmother's wishes and I didn't feel an argument on our wedding night was the best way to begin our life together. Not long after he departed, a maid arrived and laid out things for a meal.

We had our wedding supper at a small linen covered table placed before Gustavo's sitting room fireplace. Champagne bubbles rose in crystal glasses set aglow by gently flickering flames. Their golden light kissed the pale liquid and then danced across sterling flatware and porcelain china. I never knew being in love could make simple cold chicken and salad taste so wonderful. After the tray of empty dishes was placed outside the door, we retired to his bedroom. I didn't yet think of it as our bedroom because it was the first time I had entered that private chamber. The bed, to my great relief, was large enough for two and piled with pillows. The silk counterpane had been turned down so that soft wool blankets and fine linen sheets beckoned invitingly.

Gus put his arms around me and pulled me close. My head nestled against his shoulder. His lips brushed the top of my head and then he said, "I've asked that the little room beyond the door there be equipped with a hipbath and other necessary things until something better can be arranged for your convenience. I believe the hot water has just been brought up. I heard the door on its other side close. Would you like to bathe before we retire for the night?"

When I looked up into his dark eyes, they were shining with a smile I had seen a lifetime ago, that which my parents exchanged in the evenings when they sat together on Mama's piano bench. Finally, I understood what they had laughed about and I knew they must have been very happy indeed. The memory was so poignant, but it was happy as well. I had an unexpected connection with Mama and Papa.

The image of Papa kissing Mama's neck while she played her pianoforte floated with the soap bubbles while I soaked. So this, I thought, is what it is like to be in love.

When the water cooled, I wrapped myself in the warm robe that lay on the room's only chair and then sat down, unsure what to do next. Gustavo was being so thoughtful and patient with his inexperienced girl of a wife. Should I put on my dress again? There had been so much confusion and emotions were running so high it hadn't occurred to me to pack a satchel before we left Adriana and Ricardo. I had no nightgown and nothing clean to put on in the morning. The robe seemed the better choice for a night's rest. Of course, I knew from talks with Adriana that there would be other activities before sleep. She, unlike Nathan's hired keeper Ida Mashburn, had not used polite unedifying euphemisms for what occurred in the marriage bed.

I opened the door and peeked into the bedroom. Gustavo had removed all of his clothes. His thick longish hair looked damp and a towel draped about his tawny muscled waist covered only the most intimate part of him. The dancing flames put his compact perfectly-formed body into shadowy relief. To my mind, he had to be the most beautiful man who ever existed. Just the sight of his bare chest with its delicious patch of dark hair and his broad golden shoulders sent a warm tingle rushing from my core outward to every other part of my body. I wondered if he would feel the same about me. Suddenly shy, I hesitated.

Gus must have felt me staring because he looked up. "You'll catch your death if you continue standing in that drafty doorway. Come over here with me by the fire."

He loosened the robe's sash and the fabric fell away, exposing my naked torso beneath. Gus's breath quickened until it was audible.

"You are more beautiful than I ever imagined."

His hands and lips began exploring my mouth and breasts gently at first, but soon we were lost in an overwhelming tide. He lifted me as though I were a feather and carried me to the bed. That night, I learned what it was to burn from within and to have that burning gloriously consummated. Gustavo aroused an intensity of passion I hadn't known was possible.

The clock chimed one when we finally lay quietly in each other's arms. His fingers lightly brushed my hair back from my face and he whispered sleepily, "Thank God you aren't the cold fish English girls are said to be. Now that you're my wife, you'll have to tell me all of your secrets. Remember you promised to obey."

Fear placed its clammy hand around my heart, but outwardly I laughed. "Don't be silly. I have no secrets so there's nothing to tell. Now go to sleep. I need rest even if you don't." I had no intention of ever disabusing anyone in Terra Oliveira of the belief that I was half English and hailed from the Falklands.

We awoke late the following morning. I dressed in the only garment I had and accompanied my husband, how I loved using the word, to the dining room where breakfast was laid out every morning on the sideboard. Strong coffee, cream to turn the brew tawny, cold meats, cheeses, breads, butter, sweet cakes, and fruits filled bowls and platters that always covered the highly polished mahogany surface.

When we entered, only Marguerite sat at the table. She stopped mid-sip and returned her cup to its saucer. Her face looked tired and pale in the bright sunshine flooding through the tall windows.

"Serve yourselves quickly. We must talk."

When we were seated, my new mother-in-law put the orange she was peeling on her plate and crossed her arms over her mid-section.

Her eyes shifted from her son to me and back for several seconds until Gus asked, "Well, Mother, are you going to say something or just stare holes in us?"

"Rudeness does not become you, Gustavo. It is also against your best interest. I stood between you and your grandmother last night because you are my son, but I can only play that card so often. What is your plan for returning to Constancia's good graces before she settles everything on Paulo?"

Gustavo looked at his mother as though she was an idiot child. "Don't be ridiculous. Father will leave *Fazenda Oliveira* to me as it has always been, father to son."

"Your father? Eduardo owns nothing." Contempt colored each word.

"What do you mean? Father owns the *fazenda*."

"No, he doesn't. Why do you think he never disagrees with Constancia? She controls everything—the land, the house, the slaves, the money."

Confusion stilled Gus's tongue until his eyes hardened. "Why have you never told me any of this?"

"Until now, you've had no need to know and Constancia wished it for the sake of appearances."

"I don't understand. Whoever heard of a woman inheriting her husband's property? Mother, you must be mistaken." The ring of condescension in Gus's voice made me want to rush to Marguerite's defense, but it wasn't my fight, at least not yet.

"Your grandmother is a sly woman. One night when your grandfather was drunker than usual, she presented him with papers to sign for the sale of some cattle. Sandwiched among the sale documents was a will, already witnessed by a maid and a vaquero. The will left Constancia in total control of *Fazenda Oliveira* and what money was left, relegating your father to the level of dependent in the home that should have been his alone."

"But what did Grandfather say when he sobered up? He couldn't have approved!"

"He probably would have destroyed the will and your grandmother too, but he was never completely sober by that point in his life. He died shortly afterward anyway."

"But why did she do it to Father?"

"From an early age, Eduardo was your grandfather's drinking companion, among other things. She didn't trust her son any more than she did her husband."

A range of emotions passed over Gustavo's face and he became thoughtful.

"You said a vaquero witnessed the will. Could he have been Paulo's father?"

"I don't know. I was never shown the actual document."

A speculative gleam entered Gustavo's eyes. "So, who do you really think had him killed? Grandfather, Father, Grandmamma, or all three? If Grandmamma was involved, then the knowledge can be used to advantage."

I didn't like the turn the conversation was taking. It brought home to me just how little I really knew my husband and the family into which I had so precipitously married. How could family members plot against one another like this? But then, why was I surprised considering Nathan's treatment of me?

"Gustavo, you must never speak of this to your grandmother, father, or anyone! The only reason I have ever been able to influence events is that they believe no one outside the three of us knows the truth. It is the only leverage I have and if you love your mother, you will not destroy it."

Gustavo took his mother's hand and raised it to his lips. "Of course. Shock has made me thoughtless."

Adriana's warnings played over and over in my mind as I listened to my husband and mother-in-law almost casually discussing murder, lies, and deceit. It chilled me, but living with Papa had taught me that a person can love his family and still possess unattractive qualities. Gustavo had married me rather than trying to force an illicit relationship. I desperately needed to believe that my husband loved me as much as Papa had loved Mama. For my part, I was prepared to love Gustavo with my whole heart and to turn a blind eye to his faults just as I hoped he would overlook mine.

I remained quiet while my husband and mother-in-law continued discussing the complicated nuances of Oliveira relationships, which struck an unexpected cord and stirred my memory. My mind wandered over ground that I had tread at least a million times. Was Nathan right? Was I to blame for Mama's death? Had Papa killed himself or had my mother's brother murdered him? Would I ever know the truth? The questions chased one another in endless circles like the swirls I created in my coffee cup.

"Maria, do stop that interminable clattering! Put the spoon down and drink your coffee or leave the table." The edge in Marguerite's voice was by now a familiar omen. It would not be long before she took to her bed with blinding pain.

"Of course. I'm sorry, Senhora Marguerite."

"Maria, you are a member of the family now." Gus's tone matched that of his mother's. "Do not address Mamma as though you were still a servant."

"She *is* a servant, Gustavo. Marriage above her station does not change her background. Were you blind as well as deaf to your grandmother's and father's reactions?"

"She is my wife and everyone had better adjust themselves to the fact."

"Gus, please don't argue with your mother! I will do whatever she wants."

"If you are so willing to please, my girl, why did you marry my son behind my back and cause all of this turmoil?" Marguerite spat at me before turning to her son. "Is she pregnant? Is that why you married her? You should have known there are other ways to resolve such difficulties. "

"Mother, must I remind you it is my wife of whom you speak so disrespectfully? Whom I marry is my choice, not yours."

"Do not speak to me of disrespect and choices! If you are so interested in respect, why marry in secret? If your choice in a wife is so respectable, why not announce your intentions to both families and then celebrate the marriage before all? Gustavo, in some ways, you are a bigger fool than your father. He, at least, has never placed himself in danger of being cut off from the *fazenda* and the family. How could you be so stupid?"

"Mother, I thought you would surely understand. You certainly didn't seem to object to Bella's liaison. At least Maria and I haven't committed any sins."

"There is absolutely no comparison! Bella was not in line to inherit everything and she was so young!" Marguerite's pained expression faded back into one of anger. "I thought that surely you would have learned a lesson from your exile. You really don't see the problem, do you? You ignorant boy!"

"Enough! I will not tolerate more insults. Accept my wife or be estranged from your son. The choice is yours, Mother. And as for Grandmamma, leave her to me."

Gustavo grabbed my hand and yanked me to my feet. I stumbled after him as he stormed across the dining room. Looking back over my shoulder, I saw Marguerite's head now rested on her upturned palms. The bright sunlight painting the room an exuberant lemon yellow created a sharp contrast against her chalky gray coloring.

When we were alone in our apartment, I put my arms around my husband and held him close. "Gus, they need time. Please don't make it harder for everyone by forcing the issue. They will come around eventually. I've been with the family long enough to understand them."

"But that's just it. You don't really understand anything. If you did, you would know the issue, as you politely call it, must be dealt with now or things will become intolerable. Only a full frontal attack will stop Oliveiras on the hunt."

"Please don't say that. You make me sound like some sort of prey."

A cynical smile curled Gus's lips. "But prey is exactly what you are. My mother will come around. She always does. But Grandmamma and Father will hound you and tear at you until you either run or turn and fight."

I pressed my cheek against Gus's shoulder so that he couldn't see how unsettled I was. My husband painted an ugly picture of his relatives, a portrait of ruthless power determined to perpetuate a calcified social order. If I'd considered it thoroughly, I might have seen that I'd already observed firsthand what Constancia and Eduardo's kind of order could bring about, but events in Georgia were all so long ago and I was so young when they occurred I didn't see the similarities until much later. What I saw instead was my husband's family, and therefore, my family. I would do my utmost to blend in and be the wife Gustavo needed. I had survived Nathan. I would survive becoming an Oliveira.

## Chapter 23

In the months following my marriage, I experienced changes on an order of magnitude of those brought about by the South's losing the war. My life turned 180 degrees, from poverty and servitude to riches and being waited upon. I traded my maid's uniform for lace trimmed day dresses and silk or velvet gowns. My once busy twelve-hour days devoted to caring for Marguerite were replaced with hours of idleness and boredom. Since I neither played the pianoforte nor painted, reading and attempts at decorative handwork filled my days. I wasn't allowed to participate in the running of the house, and except my husband, no one really wished to talk with me other than to point out my shortcomings as an Oliveira bride.

My only form of usefulness occurred during Marguerite's attacks. At those times, she wanted me at her side even though Celina had become her personal maid. Celina was not one to let go of grudges or perceived slights and our strained relationship came to a head one dreary afternoon three months after my wedding.

"She wants you. The silly cow's taken to her bed again." Celina's lack of sympathy, not to mention caution, was appalling.

"She really does suffer, you know. Surely even you can see that." I had lost all patience with this sour-tempered girl who walked in my shadow and had benefited each time my position at the *fazenda* changed. "Please bring a basin of cold water to her room."

"Well, aren't you the high and mighty madam! Giving orders just like you were one of them."

I couldn't keep the anger from my voice. "Celina, I am one of them. See to the water without delay."

The girl emitted an ugly laugh and cocked her head to one side. "Just because you tricked the young master into marriage, you think you have suddenly become a lady? Think again! You're no better than me. You never have been, although you liked to give yourself airs and flounce around like you were."

"I've never thought anything of the kind. I was given the parlor maid job because I could communicate with the foreign guests."

"Speaks three languages, Senhora Constancia said. You'll have to wait, she said. You took the job she promised to me!"

"That was hardly my fault. And this is the last time we will ever speak of it."

"Or what? You'll tell Grandmamma? She can't stand you anymore than I can. She'll do nothing you ask."

"Perhaps, but I don't think you can afford to offend Senhora Marguerite or Senhor Gustavo. Now why don't you get that water before the senhora thinks you've forgotten? It was she who sent you on the errand, after all." My nemesis sneered, but she did as she was told.

I found my mother-in-law prostrate on her bed in a room so dark that I paused at the door to let my eyes adjust before entering. Marguerite's lashes fluttered slightly.

"Is it you, Maria?"

"*Sim*, Senhora Marguerite."

"Come sit beside me."

When I was seated, she placed her over mine. "Thank you for coming. You're the only person who knows how to help."

"Senhora, I would do anything to ease your pain."

"I know you would. You're a good girl." She closed her eyes and sighed. "We've been rather hard on you, haven't we?"

Her question caught me off guard and I hesitated a beat too long before answering, "No, not really."

A small smile curled her lips as she replied, "You aren't a very convincing liar. I know from experience how difficult it is to marry into this family. I was Eduardo's social equal, actually his superior in ancestry, and coming here nearly broke my heart. I can only imagine how much harder it has been for you."

I didn't want to respond so I remained silent. I guess I inherited some of Papa's pride because I couldn't bring myself to openly admit that my new life and marriage were anything but wonderful and that I was anything but gloriously happy. It was almost the truth anyway.

"You don't have to comment. I watch Constancia and Eduardo treat you as though you don't exist. I also see that you make my son very happy. You actually seem to have a calming effect. I never thought he would be so domestic for this long."

"Gustavo is a wonderful husband. I couldn't be happier."

"You're very young and inexperienced in the ways of men. We'll see how wonderful he is once the bloom is off the connubial rose. I love my son, but I know his faults."

"Everyone has strengths and weaknesses, Senhora. Gustavo and I overlook one another's shortcomings because we love each other."

"That may be true now, but what will you do if there should come the day when a shortcoming can't be overlooked? What will you do then?"

"I . . . I don't know. I can't see it ever happening."

"Well, my girl, you have a lot to learn about life and marriage. And since we are alone, here is a lesson for you. Let me be very clear. As long as you make my son happy and fulfill his needs, then you will have an ally in me. Fail him and you will find yourself with three Oliveira enemies, not just two. Do you understand?"

"*Sim*, Senhora. I'll do everything in my power to make Gustavo happy."

"Yes, I believe that you will. Now do stop calling me senhora. You are my daughter-in-law, and as such, people will expect you to address me as Mother or Mamma. You should also address Eduardo and Constancia by the names Gustavo uses."

"Thank you. I'll do as you say, but I'm afraid Senhora Constancia and Senhor Eduardo will object. I don't want to be the cause of any more trouble."

"Leave my husband and mother-in-law to me. Appearances are very important to them. They will accept what they are led to see as being in their best interest." A groan escaped the tight line formed by Marguerite's lips. "Where is that blasted girl? My head will explode if she takes much longer."

Within a few minutes Celina stood beside Marguerite's bed handing me a basin of icy water from the well in the kitchen courtyard. I immediately began bathing Marguerite's temples.

"May I relieve Maria, Senhora? I'm sure she has other things she wishes to do."

Marguerite opened her eyes and pushed my hand away. "Celina, go to the kitchen. See if Senhora Perez can find some employment for you. And in future, you will refer to my daughter-in-law as either Senhora Maria or Senhora Oliveira."

If looks had been daggers, then Celina would have killed me on the spot. She turned on her heel and left the room in a huff.

Within a few days, Marguerite's illness passed and I returned to my daily round of meaningless occupations. I was struggling with tearing out embroidery thread for the second time when Constancia happened upon me sitting in a library window trying to get the most from late afternoon sunlight.

"My daughter-in-law informs me you wish to address me as Grandmamma. That will never do. You are not of my blood, thank goodness. She is correct, however, that we must put the best possible face on Gustavo's marriage. You may address me as Grandmother Oliveira in the future."

"Thank you, Senhora Constancia. I will do my best to bring no further shame to the family." I was really quite good by now at employing the double entendre.

Constancia paused for a moment and searched my face before saying, "See that you keep your word." She turned as though she would leave and then spied the fabric lying in my lap, now grubby from too much picking and handling. "I see you have no talent for delicate handwork. I must say that other than menial labor and languages, you are the least accomplished creature I have ever known. Put that away and find something useful to do. Have you seen Father Paulo? He is overdue."

The sound of a throat being cleared intruded upon our little tête-à-tête.

"I've just arrived and I believe I am right on time. Is dinner on offer as my reward for bringing the confessional to you rather than you traveling to it?" Paulo grinned at us from the library door. Neither Constancia nor I had heard the priest arrive.

"Such common humor is unbecoming in a priest, but yes, you may stay for dinner." An indulgent smile lit Constancia's face but quickly disappeared when she returned to me. "Maria, you may offer your confession after Father Paulo hears mine. He tells me you are lax in performing this obligation. Correct your error. Confession is crucial to our faith."

It was true that I didn't go to confession with any regularity. Since I hadn't grown up with the tradition, I didn't really see why it was so important. After about a half hour, Paulo reappeared in the library doorway and strode to the fireplace.

He dropped into the chair opposite mine and said, "Maria, I will hear your confession now."

"Thank you, Father Paulo." I felt embarrassed to be airing my faults before my husband's cousin, no doubt a holdover from my Baptist upbringing. I hesitated, trying to decide exactly how many of my unkind thoughts and actions had to be confessed.

Paulo reached over and took my hand. "Just say what is in your heart. Remember only you, your confessor, and God will ever know what is spoken. Confession is how we cleanse our souls and renew our spirits."

To my embarrassment, I felt my lower lip trembling and my eyes filling. "Oh, Paulo. I'm unhappy and I'm ashamed. I have everything a person could want, but I can't seem to be satisfied. I love my husband desperately, but he's gone all day on *fazenda* business. What's wrong with me?"

"There is nothing wrong with you, my dear. You gained worldly possessions with your marriage, but perhaps you have not yet found your purpose as Gus's wife. A child would change that and enhance your position in the family. Have you considered this?"

"We hope for a baby every month, but so far we have had no luck. I think much of my problem is that I'm so unaccustomed to being idle. I need occupation. I need to be useful."

Paulo looked into my eyes as though he was looking into my soul. After a moment, he said, "Perhaps there is something you could do. There are many in need and not enough hands to provide for them. Would you consider charitable work among our poor?"

Our conversation hardly counted as a traditional confession, but it provided a resolution to the problem weighing most heavily on me. That night while we dressed for dinner, I helped Gustavo with his cravat. When the knot was completed, I lightly traced his cheek with my fingertips.

"If I ask for something I desperately want, will you say yes?"

"What could you possibly need that you don't already have?"

"It isn't a possession. There is something I want to do. What would you think if I were to help Paulo with the parish charity work?"

"I would say no. Whatever put such a notion into your head? Oliveiras do not wander among the diseased and criminal element."

"Gus, how can you say that? Just because someone is poor doesn't mean they're dishonest."

Gus's eyes narrowed. "Paulo's been working on your sympathy, hasn't he?"

"Not exactly. I asked if I might help in some way. He only mentioned it afterward." I felt this slight prevarication would serve my purpose better than the truth. The relationship between my husband and his cousin was complicated. I never knew exactly how Gustavo felt about what he might justly see as an interloper. When I didn't get a response, I continued, "Darling, I love you more than my own life, but I'm not used to having to seek ways to fill my time. You're gone all day. I'm lonely and I have nothing meaningful to do. I need to feel useful. Please don't deny me this small request."

After a long sigh, Gus traced my cheek with his finger and replied, "When you look at me like that, I can deny you nothing and you know it. Go ahead and do your good works, but do not let them interfere with your duties as my wife.

And I don't want you going unaccompanied into homes of the destitute. They do not live as we do."

As much as I loved him, my husband's arrogance and snobbery grated on my sense of what was right and fair. I was preparing a suitable retort when a better idea presented itself.

"I'm sure Adriana or Ricardo will go with me if the need arises. It would be perfect because Adriana is midwife to most of the families. Would that be suitable?"

After raising an eyebrow, Gus commented, "Why do I feel as though you had the details already worked out before you ever began this conversation?" He lifted my chin and kissed me lightly. "Very well. Since they are relatives, I suppose it may be all right. Just remember who you are now and do nothing to embarrass the family."

It sometimes felt that appearances mattered more to my new family than anything else, but being able to call on my adopted parents whenever I wanted was a great relief. Constancia forbade me to help or even sit with Adriana when she came to do the laundry and mending. Such unseemly behavior would lose Adriana her job, so I contented myself with waving to her from the window above the kitchen courtyard or with finding an excuse to be taking the air when she arrived once a week. Since my presence was demanded at the *fazenda* during Sunday afternoons when visitors might call, my visits to the farm were also sharply curtailed. Constancia's grip on my life chaffed just as much as Nathan's had. Those two were really very alike in some ways and this fact alone may have accounted for some of the choices I made, choices that ultimately had serious unintended consequences.

## Chapter 24

"So, you are already bored with your new life?" Adriana was her usual curt self when confronted with the unexpected. "Did I not tell you the Oliveiras were not for the likes of us?"

I put an arm around my adopted mother's shoulders. "I'm not unhappy. Gus is wonderful. I just need something to do and Father Paulo wants my help."

Adriana turned her head away so her eyes could not meet mine.

"Please, Adriana. You know people need help."

Finally, she muttered, "I guess if the priest wishes this, it is not my place to say no. Exactly what are you going to do?"

"Collect clothes and blankets for the poor. Take food to the sick and shut-ins. Nothing very original or difficult."

My good works, as Gus teasingly called them, took us into the poorest homes in Terra Oliveira. It was disheartening to see how wretchedly the people lived, but it gave me a sense of accomplishment and purpose when Adriana and I were able to offer them some comfort, however small it might have been. If Gus and I had been blessed with a child, I probably would not have felt driven to become so deeply involved. I also would not have ventured from the *fazenda* early one foggy morning.

The air swirling on the valley floor below *Fazenda Oliveira's* plateau was so thick that one of the stable boys drove me to the church in a buggy instead of my riding sidesaddle on my little bay mare. When we arrived in the village, the square was empty and no light shone from the windows of the rectory. The air's damp chill sent me hurrying up the church's front steps.

A few votives glowing before a statue of the Holy Mother provided meager illumination in the otherwise dark sanctuary. The stone floor's chill quickly penetrated my boots, so I didn't tarry before the altar after making the sign of the cross. High windows in the sacristy shed pale light over the center of the room, but it was not bright enough to chase the shadows from the pile of garments awaiting me in the far corner. After bruising a shin while searching for matches, I lit a kerosene lamp and placed it on a high shelf. I didn't fancy tripping and spraining an ankle or worse. Turning from the tall bookcase, I paused and glanced around the room. It seemed something was out of place, but I couldn't put my finger on exactly what it was. I shivered involuntarily. Pulling my shawl tighter about my shoulders, I stepped over to the mound of clothes and dropped down onto a low stool.

I'm not sure whether it was a whisper of sound or a slight movement stirring the air, but suddenly I knew I wasn't alone in the little room.

"Paulo? Is that you?"

Silence.

I rose from the stool and turned around. My heart stopped. Paused mid-stride was a colored man taller than anyone I had ever seen. He would have to duck down in order to pass through the door.

We stared at one another. "What are you doing here?"

The stranger remained mute and wide-eyed, as though he was frozen in time and space. Both of us jumped when the sanctuary's front door banged against a wall. Neither of us moved as boots hurried across the stone floor. The new arrival yanked the sacristy door open.

"Maria, why are you here so early?" Paulo's voice was hard and tight. He turned to the other man. "Go through the back and to the garden shed behind the rectory. Stay there until I come for you."

When the man slipped through the back door, Paulo said, "I beg you. Do not speak of what you've seen, not even to Adriana and Ricardo."

"Is he a runaway slave?"

"Of course, why else would he be so afraid of being seen?" There was anger in Paulo's voice as he placed a hand on my shoulder. "Will you keep our secret?"

"Does anyone at the *fazenda* know?" A rising note of panic colored my voice.

Paulo grabbed both of my shoulders. "Maria! Will you keep my secret?"

Beloved faces swirled before my mind's eye. My husband's was contorted in anger. Bess and Fatima's were solemn with pleading. I was torn. There was no perfect answer, so I gave the one that would lie easiest on my conscience. "I won't tell, but you must promise that Gustavo will never know. I can't become involved even by implication."

Paulo visibly relaxed, but his voice held a note of contempt. "Only six months married and you have taken on Oliveira prejudices? How sad. I always believed you were someone rather unique. Ah well, I guess it's too much to expect that you could resist their influence for long."

I suddenly felt very angry. "You know exactly why I must be careful! I can't betray Gustavo or his family." The plight of the Oliveira slaves was something I had made a conscience effort not to think about since I felt powerless to change it. But why had I used the verb "'can't'" instead of won't or shouldn't? Had my short time as an Oliveira changed me so much that I felt I was no longer in control of my own decisions? Even under Nathan's thumb, I had determined my own fate. The conversation with Paulo had shown me things about myself that I didn't particularly like.

He must have seen I was really upset, because his eyes softened. "I'm sorry. Of course you must not offend them. They control everything and everyone for many miles. Much depends on your discretion, however. You *must* keep your promise."

"And you yours, Father Paulo. I honor my commitments. How about you?"

"You needn't worry, Maria. I think by now you know enough about priests in general, and me in particular, to know the answer to your question. I have already kept one of your secrets."

"What could you possibly know about me that everyone else doesn't?"

"I know you do not come from the Falklands, for instance. More likely, you hail from somewhere in the southern United States. Why the deception, Maria?"

"I don't know what you're talking about." A slight tremble in my hands belied the confident defiance in my voice.

"Oh come now, have you forgotten I lived in Rio for many years? It is your accent that gives you away. Confederados who were also Catholic found their way to the monsignor's office on occasion and I enjoyed practicing my poor English on them."

"As you have said, your English is rather poor. I assure you that you are mistaken about mine."

"Have it your way. Someday, maybe you'll trust me with your secrets. For now, I must trust you with mine. Speaking of which, I really must see to him. I'm sure he's scared out of his wits."

Paulo left by the back door, leaving me as frightened as the runaway must have been. For some insane reason, it had never occurred to me that anyone in Terra Oliveira would ever come into contact with, much less connect me to, other Confederados. Our isolation lulled me into a false security, but I failed to take into account that the world came to us even if we didn't venture out to it. For all my self-determination and survival skills, I really was just a young, rather unsophisticated girl. One who desperately loved a man she didn't always like, but who was intent on making him happy.

Keeping Paulo's secret was not easy. My first concern was the Oliveiras, but since I was of next to no importance to any of them except Gus, and on occasion Marguerite, they did not turn out to be the main problem. Unanticipated difficulties arose, however, with Adriana. As she drove us in Ricardo's cart on our usual rounds one morning not long after my encounter with the runaway, she spoke her mind.

"Maria, it is time for you to end this and concentrate on your husband. You might have more luck becoming pregnant if you weren't constantly gone from home on your do-good missions."

Adriana's bluntness caught me off guard. "But the work we do is important. Who will do it if we don't?"

"People survived before you entered their lives and they will survive after you leave."

"Why this sudden change of heart? What's happened?"

"Nothing has happened, but you are tempting fate by being around so much unhappiness and sorrow. It is affecting your fertility. I am speaking to you as a midwife."

"I'm perfectly healthy and I don't let the sadness get next to me. You worry too much." I patted Adriana's hand and laughed, hoping she would at least smile, but her mouth remained a thin unhappy line. I couldn't understand why she was suddenly so adamant in her opposition to my helping the needy. She, of all people, knew how much work there was to do. I decided to ignore her objections as silly superstitions.

I thought no more about Adriana's demand until Paulo came to dinner a week later. We had just finished the main course and were being served desert when Paulo turned to me.

"Maria, I've had a visit from Adriana. She is concerned about all the work you are doing in the parish and the effect it is having on your health. She said she advised you to stop and I quite concur. You have done enough. I'll find someone else."

Gustavo's head whipped around, leaving his grandmother's last comment unanswered. "Maria, are you ill? You have said nothing. What's the problem?"

"Nothing is wrong. My aunt is just being overly cautious."

Paulo spoke to the entire table. "Adriana believes that all the work Maria is doing is affecting her chances at motherhood. Adriana is very experienced in these matters and I think Maria should listen to her."

"That settles it." Constancia's voice rolled like thunder from the end of the table. "You will cease at once. You will stay at home and fulfill your matrimonial duties. Since past mistakes can't be changed, you must take care for the future."

"I won't quit! I don't want to." I hated the childish whine in my voice. I hated that I was actually afraid of my husband's grandmother and it made me very determined to have my own way.

"Gustavo, is this how you control your wife? If so, you aren't equipped for the *fazenda's* challenges. Take care of the situation. I do not wish to hear any more about it." The ice in Constancia's voice chilled the entire room. Gustavo's eyes turned from me to his grandmother and back.

"Maria, you will cease as your aunt advises. It is my wish. Do you understand?"

It really wasn't a question so much as a directive. My time with Nathan had taught me to pick the time and place of my battles carefully. "Yes, I understand." I turned angry eyes on the priest. "Father Paulo, I left a few things in the sacristy that I wish to collect when I next ride into the village. Will tomorrow morning be convenient?"

"Of course."

Gustavo took the hand lying in my lap and squeezed it hard. "My dear, did you or did not you just promise to end all of this?"

I flinched involuntarily. "Yes, I promised." As my husband squeezed my hand, my anger answered his pressure. "But surely I am not to be denied a favored pastime. Am I to be held prisoner in our quest for a child?"

Gus looked chastened and released my hand. "No, of course not. Ride out whenever you wish. I'm sure that even your aunt won't find fault with fresh air."

"Thank you, Gus. You are very good to me." At that moment, I'm not sure which one of us I disliked more, my husband or myself.

The following morning, I stormed into the rectory without knocking. "Where are you, Paulo? I have a bone to pick with you."

The priest's voice drifted from the back of the house. "Good morning, Maria. Join me here in the kitchen."

When I stood beside the table, he continued, "When you said morning, I didn't realize you meant the crack of dawn. Join me for breakfast?"

"I've eaten, but I'll take coffee. Thank you."

Paulo got a second cup and poured from the pot of the stove. When the steaming brew was on the table, he returned to his chair. "Please sit down. I prefer being scolded at eye level. Now what particular bone have you brought with you this morning?"

"This isn't funny and I am not amused."

"My goodness, the Oliveiras really are rubbing off on you, aren't they? If I closed my eyes, it might be my grandmother speaking." Paulo's grin was infuriating. "Oh, don't be so angry. Sit down and drink your coffee."

"Paulo, how could you undermine me like that with the family? My life is restricted enough without your seeing to it that I can't even go out now without someone commenting."

"Maria, your work in the parish has helped many and it is appreciated. I'm sorry you believe I have betrayed you. It isn't what I intended."

"That wasn't how it appeared at dinner. Now I'm back where I started. Nothing useful to do except handwork at which I am woefully inadequate, and keeping my husband entertained. Of course, Gus is out all day, which limits that commission."

"Perhaps it may seem you have nothing of value to do, but that is not necessarily true."

"Really? Last night Gus demanded that I account to him for my movements in the future. I feel like I've been given a jail sentence and it's pretty much your fault."

"Surely you realized Constancia wouldn't have tolerated your charity work for much longer. She had already demanded that I put an end to it some weeks ago. I agreed because I couldn't allow attention to be drawn to the church and the sub rosa activities carried out there. And because I have a more important task for you."

"Pray do tell me, what could possibly be more important to the church than helping those in need?" I fairly spat my words at the priest.

Paulo had lowered his voice so much that I didn't understand his reply.

"What?"

"I said, helping those like the man you met last week in the sacristy."

It took a moment for his meaning to sink in. "Help runaway slaves? Is that what you're asking me to do? Do you have any idea how the family would react?"

He smiled and deliberately misconstrued my meaning. "Adriana would be aghast, but she could hardly complain considering her own involvement."

I was stunned into silence. I hadn't been thinking of Adriana and Ricardo at all. It never occurred to me they would be taking such chances for people they didn't even know. Of course, they had taken a chance with me, but nothing compared to what would happen if they were discovered helping runaway slaves. I was suddenly very afraid for them.

"How involved are my aunt and uncle?"

"Only in providing occasional transportation from the river to the sacristy. Ricardo's trips to sell his coffee and to get supplies are the perfect cover. Adriana provides medical care and food when they are needed. She was appalled when I told her of your meeting with one of my guests."

"And why do they risk so much for strangers?"

"You mean like they did for you? They are people of high principle and it is the right thing to do. No more; no less."

I found myself chewing on a thumbnail, a new and not particularly attractive habit that appeared when I was feeling my life was out of control. "And what is it you want of me?"

"Nothing difficult. In fact, it will require very little. Only that you take the air by riding out at least once a week when the weather permits. You would become a creature of habit by following the same route and making the same stops. The first stop would be under a certain tree on a hilltop from which you will admire the scenery below, the second would be at the church for prayers and a donation placed in the poor box."

"And why would I take this route and make these stops?"

"So that you could collect and deliver messages for me. The rich, especially the Oliveiras, are given to eccentric behavior as everyone knows, so your taking up a new ritual will not be commented upon."

"And why should I risk everything for strangers?"

"Because you know it is the right thing to do. Have you changed so much that the names Fatima and Henrique no longer hold meaning for you?"

"How do you know about them?" My heart pounded and I could feel a vein throbbing at my temple.

"They are well and send their best wishes for your marriage."

"You didn't answer my question. How do you know them?" I found myself on my feet, leaning over the table, the priest's shirtfront clutched in my fists.

Paulo reached up and gently removed my hands from his clothing. "You have nothing to fear from them or me. How I know them should be obvious, but since you may understandably need reassurance, look at this." Paulo reached inside his shirt and produced a familiar object suspended from a leather thong. "I believe that you own one of these as well, unless you discarded it when you moved into the *fazenda*."

He returned the *onca* amulet to its hiding place and looked at me expectantly.

"How much do Adriana and Ricardo know?"

"Only that you were in desperate need of protection when Ricardo stumbled upon you on the river island. Your necklace told them as much. I have kept your secret. I told them nothing of the story Henrique shared. Nothing about the abusive uncle or his attempt to force you into an unsuitable marriage. Your uncle, by the way, has himself married and become unaccountably rich. Henrique says he cares little about the coffee and leaves its cultivation to the slaves."

"How are they, Fatima, Henrique, and the child?"

"They are well. Henrique is now your uncle's trusted overseer. Their lives are reasonably well for those still in bondage. And there are three children, a boy and two girls. The elder girl has an unusual name for a Brazilian slave's child. They call her Mary Catherine."

When I reached up to push a curl away, I found my cheek was wet. "Will you continue to keep my secret?"

"I'm not sure why you think it is so important at this point. You're married. Your uncle no longer has any claims on you."

"As you have said to me, it should be obvious. Gus is a proud man. He would be very angry to find that I've lied to him. You must not tell."

My head swam with the sudden revelations. "Will Adriana and Ricardo know if I agree to become your courier?"

"No one in our organization is told more than is absolutely necessary. They have no need to know our business."

"Tell me truly. Do I have a choice?"

Father Paulo placed his hand on my head as though giving a blessing. "I would not force anyone into something that they do not wish to do. I only hope your conscience will lead you to continue to help those who are so much less fortunate."

## Chapter 25

After agreeing to be Paulo's courier, a three-week deluge kept me confined to the house. No amount of pacing before rain streaked windows or fidgeting during interminable family meals had the least effect on the lowering skies. As so often in the past, reading became my refuge. The previously ignored science of philosophy filled my days while I kept an eye trained on the weather. I initially chose Voltaire and Rousseau because theirs were the only unread books remaining on the shelves devoted to French writers. How ironic that the Oliveira library contained works condemning the very way of life that made possible the purchase of those gold embossed leather bound volumes. Enlightenment philosophy expanded my belief in the rights of all humanity, but cast a shadow over the cherished memories of my parents and grandparents who had lived in relative comfort on the backs of their slaves. I did not excuse myself from accusations of perpetuating the evil institution because through marriage, I had come full circle, back to the world of privilege that survived on slavery. Contemplation and shame left me even more determined to become involved in Paulo's activities. My mood deepened with each consecutive day of unrelenting precipitation until my in-laws complained of an unbecoming gloominess in my disposition. Just when I despaired of ever having the opportunity to retrieve and deliver the messages on which Paulo's group depended, the sun made a watery, but determined appearance.

The lamps remained unlit and the tall windows framed patches of blue blossoming between scudding clouds when we entered the dining room for breakfast. Gus ate quickly and left to attend to work that had piled up during the bad weather, but I was still at the table when Marguerite and Eduardo appeared. My coffee cup clattered as it settled into its saucer. Tension radiated from my every pore.

"Good morning, Father Oliveira, Mother Marguerite."

"I see you are wearing your riding costume. Where are you going?" My father-in-law's interrogative tone stretched my taut nerves even farther.

"I'm just going to take the air by riding in the hills around the *fazenda* and then to the village for a few minutes of prayer and contemplation in the church."

"The roads are still knee deep in mud. I don't see why you can't pray here at home unless, of course, we aren't pious enough for you."

Eduardo's frequent use of sarcasm was beginning to wear very thin, but too much depended on my not bringing undue attention to my plans. I gave my father-in-law my brightest and, I hoped, my most endearing smile.

"We've been cooped up in the house for so long and it looks like it's going to be a beautiful day. An hour's ride can't hurt anything, surely."

Eduardo lifted an eyebrow as he studied me, but then he sighed. As with most subjects, Eduardo's enthusiasm was already waning. "Oh, well, go if you must, but take one of the boys with you. We've heard reports that the unrest in the north is spreading."

"Thank you, but I would rather ride alone."

"Are you deaf or just willful?"

"I will ride only around *Fazenda Oliveira*. I'm sure I'll be safe."

"Why my son chose you is beyond understanding. Since you won't see reason, you will not leave the house."

I couldn't stop myself. The man just made my blood boil. "Am I to understand that I am a prisoner in my own home?"

Eduardo's eyes bulged slightly as he thundered, "Your home? Insolent chit! You will do as you're told."

Marguerite glanced at her husband and placed her hand on his arm. "Maria, we are just concerned for you. No one is wishing to restrict your movements."

"You now believe yourself to be in charge, Marguerite? She has no business traipsing about the countryside like a peasant. Mother says that whether we like it or not, she is an Oliveira, and as such, she is held to a higher standard."

If Eduardo had bothered to look at his wife, he would have seen her fighting back tears even as she forced her lips to curve upward into a smile. "Surely Constancia doesn't expect her to stay indoors forever. Getting out into the fresh air will be good for her, as long as she is careful. You will take care not to venture too far from the safety of the house, won't you Maria?"

"Of course."

"Eduardo, she will use good judgment. Let's not quarrel, please." Even my oaf of a father-in-law couldn't have missed the tired edge in Marguerite's voice. Since he detested being around illness, he avoided contributing to one of her headaches at all costs.

"Oh, very well. Ride wherever you want. I suppose I am really being rather short sighted. An encounter with ruffians might prove fortuitous." Eduardo smiled as though he had made a joke, but the humor did not reach his eyes, which glittered with an unrelenting hardness. It always struck me how different Eduardo could be when his mother was not present. He assumed her imperiousness and I often wondered what his life might have been like had she not been around. As it was, he alternated between alcohol induced indolence and authoritarian domination of others. My sympathy for Marguerite increased steadily.

A guilty conscience accompanied me on my first ride. I owed my mother-in-law better than lies. Marguerite understood the difficulties of marrying into the Oliveira family. Once the initial shock of Gus's choice of a bride passed, she made an effort to be kind, and when able, she deflected the harsh criticism directed at me. I justified my deceitfulness with the importance of my cause.

The path behind the house led up into the hills and I followed it as promised, but instead of turning back and staying well within *Fazenda Oliveira's* boundary, I crossed over onto a single track that separated our property from the neighboring plantation. Deep ruts filled with muddy rainwater passed between row upon row of coffee trees until they played out into uncultivated forest where the terrain began to rise. After several minutes slogging uphill, the trees became thinner until the track gained the crest of the highest point for miles around. An open meadow surrounded on three sides by forest ended at a precipice with a view out over *Fazenda Oliveira* and the village of Terra Oliveira beyond. Near the edge of the overlook, the huge trunk of an ancient tree supported a broad canopy under which the casual rider might stop to admire the scenery below.

After scanning the area to ensure I was alone, I urged my mare forward through tall wet grass. Within a few paces, we were completely hidden from view behind the tree. I glanced over my shoulder once more, and then without dismounting, placed my gloved hand into the hollow Paulo had described. My fingers folded around something too regular in shape to have been a product of nature. When I withdrew the object, I held a small leather pouch. Inside was a scrap of cheap paper with markings on it that looked more like drawings than writing. I couldn't make heads or tails of the thing and decided it must be some sort of secret code. Following Paulo's instructions again, I tucked the message into the glove on my left hand and returned the envelope to its hiding place.

The ride to Terra Oliveira was not as long as I had feared because of a track leading around the rear of the *fazenda*, a shortcut of which I had been unaware until Paulo described it.

Market day's low roar greeted me when I rode into the village. Chickens squawked and lambs bleated amongst stalls offering an array of fruits and vegetables. I spied Adriana across the square haggling with the pot and pan man over a new wash pot. As much as I loved my adopted mother, I hoped to avoid her. The less she knew, the better for everyone. Putting herself in danger by helping Paulo with his secret project didn't give her the slightest pause, but she would shout until the rafters rang if she even suspected that I was involved. She must have seen me as soon as I entered the village because she appeared at my side while I tied my mare to a post.

"Have you enjoyed your ride? Your skirt is splashed with mud." Her voice indicated this was not a casual inquiry.

"It was very pleasant."

"This would be a good time to say a quick prayer of thanks for all the good luck that has come your way. I'll go with you and pray for a child to be added to your good fortune."

She took my elbow and practically shoved me up the church steps. When we were inside and she saw we were alone, she spoke again.

"Why the sudden interest in riding over the countryside? Do you live in such regal isolation that you have not heard the rumors of violence against travelers?"

"Since I am no longer allowed to work with the poor, I need some occupation that gets me out of the house. I don't see what harm riding around the *fazenda* once a week can do."

"That's the problem! You don't see the danger."

"Really, Adriana! No one in the area would dare defy Constancia, so I'm perfectly safe."

"And how can you be so sure? No one can predict what desperate people will do."

"I ride near the house. What harm can possibly come from that?" Appallingly, lies and deceit now tripped from my tongue as easily as casual conversation. "I have come to place a donation in the poor box as well as to pray. Will you join me?"

An imperious tone designed to quell dissent was a conversational ploy learned from Constancia. The guilt I felt in using it with Adriana was all my own. She put her arms around me and hugged me close.

"*Meu Caraco*, you must be careful. I couldn't bear losing another child."

Silently, I wondered if Adriana's words had a double meaning. Aloud I replied, "I love you too and I promise to be with you forever. You are the only mother I have after all."

She hugged me hard one more time and headed toward the outer door. The fingers of my right hand were inching toward the slip of paper inside my left glove when Adriana stopped and turned back. Backlit by light pouring through the open door, her face was completely obscured. For several seconds she neither spoke nor moved.

When I could no longer bear the silence or her scrutiny, I called out, "I'll see you Sunday afternoon. And don't worry. No one will bother me on the *fazenda*."

She stood in silence for another second or two, then turned away again and departed. An uncontrollable shiver, the kind Bess used say was someone stepping on your grave, swept over me from head to toe. For the second time, I wondered just how much Adriana knew or suspected about my involvement in Paulo's scheme. As I considered the possibilities, I slipped the secret message from my glove and a coin from the pocket of my skirt, dropping both into the locked box to which only Paulo had the key. I sighed in relief. My first mission was completed.

Once my rides settled into a pattern, I heard no more complaints for some time. The rumors of marauding runaways died down until Gus returned from a business trip. I was alone in our sitting room when he burst through the door.

"I have great news! I found the perfect bull. He's strong and virile. His calves are heavier at birth, grow faster, and are stronger than those by our present bull. The seller is driving him and a few heifers overland. They'll arrive within two or three weeks. What do you think of your husband?"

Gustavo was so eager, so in need of praise it made my heart ache. The possibility of being cut from Constancia's will was very real to Gus, even though I doubted she would be so foolhardy just to punish him for marrying without her stamp of approval. I put my arms around him and hugged him tightly.

"You're wonderful!" I looked up into his eyes and brushed his forelock back. "And I'm sure your bull is as well!"

"He certainly has the equipment to get the job done. You should see his . . ." Gus grinned leeringly and said, "On second thought, I have something of my own I'd rather you see right now."

He swept me from the floor and twirled us into the adjoining bedroom. We spent a wonderful afternoon exploring one another's bodies, a pastime that brought both of us immense pleasure.

As we were dressing for dinner that evening, Gus returned to the subject of his buying expedition.

"The seller was somewhat reluctant to make the trip here. Said I should bring drovers and fetch the cattle myself. I had to remind him rather forcefully that our agreement was cash on delivery."

"What was his reason?"

"Apparently there's been a good bit of trouble along the route he must take. Travelers attacked and robbed. Houses broken into. He says the violence is moving south. You must confine your rides to the paddocks behind the stables until the situation is dealt with."

"Do you really think it will come this far?"

"No, but we should be careful all the same. And to ensure that nothing untoward happens, I want you to carry this with you whenever you leave the house." He placed a tiny over and under double-barreled derringer on the table beside me. "Keep it in your reticule or skirt pocket. No one will know you have it. And take no senseless chances."

"I promise I won't."

Although pangs of guilt accompanied every prevarication, I had no intention of keeping within the paddocks because the work I was doing was important. And besides, playing spy was exciting.

As we entered the season of drier weather, I started riding every day. Sometimes I stayed within sight of the stables. Anyone wanting to observe my movements could easily see me from the house's second floor back windows. Other days, I rode to the edges of our property, which was really quite a distance since *Fazenda Oliveira* covered 10,000 acres of prime coffee growing and grazing land. Sandwiched among these innocent excursions were my weekly trips to the message tree and then to the church for confession or devotion, whichever was on offer when I arrived. Paulo never told me anything about the messages' contents or anything about the people who benefited from them, but I didn't need that. I knew I was doing something important and it was enough.

Late one morning about a month after Gus bought the cattle, I paused in the reception hall on my way in from the stables. My husband's voice floating from the other side of the library door brought a smile and a small pang of heartache. His tone was one that had been ever present when I first knew him, but its frequency had diminished with each of Constancia's threats to disinherit him. As Gus's voice rose and fell, I caught a few words. He waxed profound on a subject at which he felt expert. I enjoyed listening to him when he talked like that. He became a different version of himself, one who was confident and certain he knew exactly what needed to be done.

In response to what Gus was saying, a softer voice that I didn't recognize drifted from among the volumes. Curious, I crossed the hall to join Gus and welcome our guest, but when I stood at the door, my hand froze before it touched the knob. I looked around the hall to make sure I was alone and then pressed my ear to the door. It was not the voice that caused my reaction, but its accent, its cadence. It echoed to me from the past, flowing like heavy molasses on a winter morning. I hadn't heard anyone speak like that since leaving Little Georgia and Nathan.

As I listened, I heard my husband say in heavily accented English, "Luncheon will be served shortly. Won't you at least join us for a meal before starting your return trip?"

"Why, that would be mighty welcome. And thank you for the offer of a bed, but my missus wants me home what with her being in the family way. Her time is coming soon and this is our first. She was none too pleased that I took off when I did, but I reminded her that selling the bull was going to buy her a cradle she has her heart set on, so she got quiet real fast." A hearty laugh exploded after the flood of information.

I fled upstairs to our apartment. I knew the voice did not belong to Nathan. It had been illogical for me to think first of him, but there were others I had reason to fear. Gus had not been very specific about where he found the bull, just that it was in the vicinity of Santa Barbara. It never occurred to me the seller might be someone from my past. What puzzled me was why my husband had failed to mention the novelty of dealing with a Confederado. He usually told me everything, or at least I thought he did. As I paced before the sitting room fireplace, Gus entered the room.

"There you are. I heard you come in from your ride, but you disappeared. We have guests for luncheon. You'll want to change."

"Of course." I turned quickly toward my dressing room door, hoping he wouldn't detect the state of my nerves.

Gus pulled me to him with an arm about my waist and peered down quizzically. "Aren't you even curious about who they are?"

"Is it anyone we know?"

"Not particularly. The men with the cattle arrived this morning. I thought you might have noticed my bull and the heifers in the back pasture when you rode in."

"I returned from the other direction. It is my day for confession."

"For someone who was a heretic only a few years ago, you have certainly taken confession to heart. What could you possibly be doing to warrant weekly penance? Are they sins of commission or omission?" The speculative expression in Gus's eyes sparked a twinge of fear.

I mustered my most coy smile. With my fingers gently tracing his handsome jaw, I answered, "Oh, commission, definitely. Sins of the flesh primarily. I enjoy married life far more than a proper lady is supposed to and it occupies far too much of my time and thoughts."

Gus laughed and settled his hands around my bottom, pulling me close enough to give his next words full meaning. "That is none of the church's or my cousin's business. If that is your sin, then we're both destined for hell!"

What I told him was actually true as far as my thoughts and desires, it just wasn't what Paulo and I talked about. In fact, confession had fallen completely by the wayside.

With the luncheon bell about to sound at any moment, I kissed Gus and pushed him away. I discarded my riding attire in favor of my second best day dress and soon afterward, we closed the apartment's outer door. As we crossed the second floor ballroom, I thought about the men from Santa Barbara. Would they be anyone I had once known in Rio or on the boat to Igaupe? If they were former acquaintances, would they recognize in me the little girl who had once hidden beneath furniture and so desperately feared being left behind? The answer waited at the foot of the grand staircase.

I drew a slow breath, looked down at our visitors, and was instantly transported into the past. Once again I raced around the *Alyssa Jane's* deck trying hard to conjure good luck and to avoid the teasing of two adolescent boys who wore their Scots-Irish heritage like signs around their necks with their sandy red hair and Celtic blue eyes. I wondered if those around me could see that my heart was trying to pound its way free of my ribcage. Thoughts of fleeing raced through my mind until a quizzical glance from Gus brought me back to reality. My fingernails were actually digging into his arm. He placed his free hand over mine and we began our descent. Since there was no escape, I put on my brightest smile and braced myself.

"Gentlemen, my wife, Senhora Maria Oliveira. My dear, the Stuart brothers." Our visitors each bent slightly from the waist after taking my extended hand.

"I believe you are from Santa Barbara?"

"Well, not Santa Barbara proper, Ma'am. Our place is about thirty miles southwest of the railway depot at Vila dos Americanos."

A thrill of fear coursed through my veins. "Yes, we are envious of your area's access to the new railhead."

"It certainly makes getting crops and livestock to market much easier, especially with the troubles people are having going overland."

After we joined the family in the dining room and the remaining introductions were made, Gus picked up the topic again. "We hoped a rail line would be built to Terra Oliveira, but with the mountains and rivers between us and Igaupe it isn't possible yet, at least that is what we're told. Have you gentlemen traveled to Igaupe?"

"No, never had the pleasure. Knew some people once who were headed there, though. Families that we met in Rio at Government House where Dom Pedro put us up when we first got to Brazil. Folks from Texas. They left pretty soon after we arrived, so didn't get to know them too well."

Constancia, who thus far had observed the conversation in silence, cleared her throat. "Our local priest was attached to the monsignor's office in Rio when the emperor began encouraging immigration from North America. He assisted some of your people. Perhaps you met Father Paulo?"

"Well, Ma'am, to be honest, we're Baptist. We didn't rub shoulders much with the Catholic folks."

"I see. May I ask where you lived before you immigrated?"

"Alabama, just north of Mobile. It is . . . it was beautiful country. Between the big plantation mansions and the grand houses in town, Mobile County contained some of the finest architecture in the South. This house reminds me of some of the places back home."

The conversation progressed from the architecture of Sao Paulo state and Mobile County to agricultural comparisons between the two areas. When those topics were exhausted, a conversational lull ensued. I remained as quiet as politely possible because it felt as though every word of English I spoke betrayed my origins no matter how much I tried to alter my pronunciation and cadence. I suppose he was just being polite, but the younger visitor suddenly turned to me and asked a question that took my breath away.

"Ma'am I can't help noticing your accent. Georgia, right? Did you ever get to Mobile before you came here?"

Six pairs of eyes were trained on me awaiting my answer. Dismay darkened Gus and Marguerite's. Speculation glittered in Eduardo and Constancia's. I never once considered myself an even mediocre actress, but the spirits of all the great playwrights I had read over the years must have had their hands over me when I drew breath to answer because my accent no longer dripped syrup.

"I'm afraid you're mistaken. I came here from a British possession, the Falkland Islands."

The young man's face flamed and his voice sounded flustered. "Please forgive my presumption. I'm obviously mistaken." As he spoke, he looked earnestly at each member of the luncheon party and then at me. When our eyes met again, I was horrified to see the sign of recognition in his.

## Chapter 26

Luncheon crawled on without further mention of Confederados or their places of origin, but eating became like trying to force down sawdust. Constancia's speculative gaze haunted my conversation, stretching my nerves to the breaking point. When we finally rose from the table, the energy created by relief sent my chair scraping back far too hard. Again, all eyes were trained on me.

"I guess I don't know my own strength." Only our visitors laughed at my feeble attempt at humor. Under Constancia's glacial stare, I offered a revision. "Please excuse the disturbance."

Turning to the Stuarts, she said in her most commanding tone, "As you are wishing to travel some distance before nightfall, we must not detain you further. Cook has prepared a food parcel for the road. Is there anything else we may provide?"

"No, Ma'am. Y'all've been mighty kind already."

At the front door, the men bent over Constancia and Marguerite's hands and again murmured words of gratitude for the hospitality.

When the younger man took my hand, he paused awkwardly before saying, "I understand that you're a fairly recent bride. I hope you'll accept our sincere best wishes for your future happiness."

His grip was unsuitably firm for an acquaintance of such a brief period, and when he spoke of happiness, it became almost painful, but his unspoken message felt like the sun dawning after a stormy night.

As soon as the front door closed, I turned to make a hasty retreat, but Eduardo caught my arm. "Not so fast, my girl. Mother and I will have a word with you. Gustavo, join us in the library."

My father-in-law led us to a front window where there were only two chairs, one sitting in a pool of sunlight. He released my arm only after he shoved me into the brilliantly lit seat. His bulky frame loomed so near that his stale breath made the little wispy curls around my face flutter. Constancia took the opposite chair, leaving Gus and his mother hovering at Eduardo's elbow.

"Marguerite, your presence is not required. Please go to your apartment."

I looked pleadingly at my mother-in-law.

"I think I should stay. Maria will feel more comfortable with me here."

"Maria's feelings are completely inconsequential. Leave as you were told." Marguerite avoided looking at me as she turned and left. This was a battle she apparently wasn't willing to fight. I sought my husband's face, but his father blocked my view of most of the room. I craned to see around Eduardo, but all I got was a glimpse of Gus's back. He seemed to be removing himself from the situation as much as he could without physically leaving the room.

"Now, tell us Maria . . ."

"Step aside, Eduardo. I will handle this," Constancia cut in. "We have taken you into our home and given you our name. You owe us the courtesy of an honest answer. Who are you?"

"I am Ricardo and Adriana Dias's great-niece, as you know."

"Don't be insulting! The younger Stuart is right. In unguarded moments, you speak English as they do. I ask you again. Who are you?"

"I am Maria Dias Oliveira."

"I see." Constancia turned away from me. "Gustavo, you will agree to an annulment or leave this house under pain of disinheritance. Those are your choices. This time we will go directly to the monsignor."

"No."

"What do you mean, 'no'? You will do as you are told."

"Let's see if I have this right. You will disinherit me and give my birthright to the priest who married us without your knowledge and who refused to help with an annulment of that marriage. Does that really make sense?"

"Don't be stupid. Why would I leave anything to Paulo? As his grandmother, I feel a certain affection for him, but he has never been nor will he ever be acknowledged, especially not through inheritance."

"If not Paulo, then what will happen to *Fazenda Oliveira* if you don't leave it to me?" Gus's voice held a note of uncertainty.

"You should consider your parents' situation. I doubt the church would welcome their continued occupation when it takes possession. You may not care so much about your father, but I assume you have some affection for your mother?"

"You wouldn't do that! You couldn't!" I was unable to see my husband's face, but his voice told me all I needed to know.

"I can and I will, unless you comply with my wishes. Now go to your apartment and take your paramour with you."

Gus nearly jerked my arm from its socket. He neither spoke nor looked at me until our sitting room door was closed and locked.

"Maria, I don't think I have a choice. Barring a miracle, I'll have to do as she says." Gus placed a hand on each of my shoulders. "I guess we were a mistake. I just refused to see it. I was blinded by love."

"Is this how you define love? You love only where it doesn't cost anything or only when the going is easy? What of the vows we took?"

"Those can be overturned with the right contacts and influence. My grandmother has both. And speaking of those vows, did you believe you were honoring me as you promised by lying about yourself? At least do me the courtesy of telling me who you really are."

"I am your wife!"

"Ah, yes, a wife who hides her true identity from her husband. I have long suspected you hid something. And from the moment I encountered the Stuart brothers, I knew you were not who you claimed. I heard your secret in their voices. I chose to say nothing, hoping you would tell me the truth on your own, but you didn't trust me enough. Why, Maria? Is that even your real name?"

As hurt as I was, a part of me understood Gus's anger. He believed I had betrayed him and he was right. I had lied to him about more than my identity and now the bill for all of my dishonesty was coming due.

"Gus, it may be difficult for you to understand, but keeping my secret had nothing to do with what I feel for you. I love you with all my heart." I took his hands in mine and led him to the settee. "My story is a long one that starts with a war."

For the next half hour, I told my husband my true history. I left out nothing. When I finished, he was silent for a moment and then asked, "Do you know what has become of your uncle? Half of that farm belongs to you."

"I can't go back there. He would find a way to murder me without anyone knowing like he did my father."

Gus put his finger under my chin and lifted until we looked into one another's eyes. "You know, I do love you and I might have been able to protect you if you had been honest."

"Gus, can't you understand why I've been afraid to tell anyone, even you? I was only fourteen, still a child really, when I fled Nathan. Adriana and Ricardo helped me create a new identity because they were protecting me from the man who was going to force me into a marriage I didn't want. Even they don't know that the man was really my uncle. I couldn't let anyone know I had a relative in Brazil. Once the story was told and I was accepted into the community as their great-niece, there was no going back. I didn't set out to deceive you."

"But you did and the deception hurts more than you know."

"I never meant to be a source of pain. For that, I'm truly sorry. But consider this, you intend to abandon me for land and wealth."

"No, for my home and birthright. Grandmamma means precisely what she says. It would not be beyond her to ensure my parents and I are turned from the house. Can't you see I have no choice?"

Tears flowed unabated down my cheeks. I simply couldn't take any more. I fled to our bedroom and locked the door.

Gus pounded. "Maria, let me in. Don't be like this. At least we can be together for a little while longer."

"Do you really think I will sleep with you and then be lightly put aside when I am no longer convenient?"

"I love you, Maria, I truly do, but *Fazenda Oliveira* is more important than two people. Oh lord, please believe me. Even when I knew you had secrets, I never thought it would come to this."

"How can you say that? I tried to warn you, everyone tried to warn you, but you were so sure you could handle Constancia and your parents."

"Maria, please! Maybe I can think of something that will change Grandmamma's mind."

There was nothing else to say so I remained silent. For some time afterward, I could hear Gus pacing in the sitting room, then the outer door slammed and all was quiet. Dropping down onto our bed, I sobbed until there were no more tears to shed. When the racking gasps ceased, I began to think about my situation. Gus and I had been so wrong about so much. Did we even know how to love authentically?

Stubborn pride was a trait we certainly shared. We both naively thought we could flaunt the rules of family and society without suffering the consequences. Adriana had warned me, but I had been too infatuated and too flattered to really listen. In all honesty, I was probably a little in love with Gus from the very first sighting in the church. His looks, position, wealth, and attention were more than sufficient reasons for any girl to be attracted to Gustavo Oliveira. But why had he pursued me with such vigor?

He had returned from Europe resentful of having been shipped off and of having been unjustly blamed for his father's illegitimate child. Since Eduardo and earlier Oliveira men had taken their pleasure whenever and with whomever they pleased, it must have been particularly galling to Gus that his grandmother held him to so different a standard. It seemed she hoped to break the Oliveira tradition with him, as she had been unable to do with her own son and even her daughter. Eduardo's indifference to anyone's desires but his own and his impotence where Constancia was concerned must have sealed Gus's fate. For a moment, I wondered why Marguerite had not come to Gus's aid until I remembered that he thought he was protecting his mother from the truth. No doubt Gus had made it seem he was happy to take the grand tour.

At this point, I felt sure Constancia wished Gus had taken me as his mistress rather than his wife. And when I looked back over our whirlwind courtship, I wondered why he had been so intent on marriage. Could I have been his rebellion against the stranglehold his grandmother had on the family? And what about my own part in this tale of heartache? Would I have fallen for him if he had been an average looking peasant? As the questions whirled, I felt as though my head would explode. I fell into an exhausted sleep from which I did not awaken until there was a loud knock at the bedroom door. The room was in complete darkness and I stumbled as I went to rejoin the verbal battle with my husband.

"Go away. I don't want to talk to you."

"It is not your husband. He is enjoying a good dinner with the family. I have brought food for you. Cook thought you should have something to eat." Celina's voice made me groan inwardly. I knew she was gloating.

"Put the tray on the table by the fireplace and leave."

"As you wish." A soft chuckle floated from the other side of the door.

I ate, but mental turmoil reduced the food's flavor to that of straw. Options bounced around my tormented mind like popcorn exploding over a blazing fire. I could try to convince Gus that his grandmother was bluffing. He might be persuaded, but I felt sure the day would come when he would resent me no matter the outcome. His class and his pride ensured it. I could accept Constancia Oliveira as a woman unlike any I had ever known, a woman sufficiently in control that her wishes were never thwarted, even if it meant they harmed those closest to her. And what of Gustavo? I had lied to him, the man I loved and whom I had vowed to honor and obey. What did I owe him? What was best for me? The answer presented itself in a flash of blinding clarity.

A small tapestry valise lay in the bottom of my chifferobe, and into this, I placed as many practical garments as would fit. Next, I cast off the delicate day garment in favor my riding costume. Returning to Ricardo and Adriana seemed like the best first step in rectifying many mistakes. I would take my mare and some clothing, but everything else that had come with my marriage would be left behind. In removing myself from the *fazenda*, I hoped to free Gus to make decisions unencumbered by the fire that burned between us. For me, remaining within walls as the center of so much strife was no longer tolerable.

The hall was dim with only occasional sconces lit, as was the custom when only the family was in residence. I crossed the grand ballroom to the servant's stairs because they provided the quickest route to the stables. When I reached the kitchen, there was no one around, which was odd since the kitchen staff should have been busy cleaning up after dinner, but it was a relief to leave unobserved and unremarked. My resolve might have disappeared if Celina and her giggling cronies had been present to roll their eyes and grin behind their hands. Cook would have scolded the maids, but it would still have been humiliating. I hurried through the outer door and slipped onto the veranda.

The well and plantings in the courtyard glowed pale blue in the light of a full moon. Nothing moved in the still cool air of the evening. I took advantage of the perfect moment for escape and started toward the back gate.

As I approached the well, a shiny flicker caught my attention. It came from the shadows of the far wall. Something wasn't right. I couldn't see it, but I could feel it. The hair at the nape of my neck rose like a dog's hackles. I quickened my pace and would have been out of the gate in a second but for the form that dashed to my side and grabbed my arm.

"And just where do you think you're going, *puta pequena*? Get back inside with the others. On second thought, it just might be more fun to cut you right here."

A man I had never seen before pulled me back toward the house. One hand held my arm so hard that it tingled. The other hand held a large knife. Hanging from his side, the handle of a pistol flashed in the moonlight. He dragged me along at such a pace that I stumbled on the courtyard cobblestones and fell. He yanked me to my feet and brought his blade to rest along my jaw line.

"It'd be ashamed to carve up your pretty face too soon, but I could manage it real good if you don't do what you're told. Keep up."

Within minutes, we were standing in the library with the entire family. Gathered behind the family, the white faces of Cook, Celina, and the other housemaids peered at us with wide frightened eyes. The members of the household were either kneeling or standing around Constancia who was seated in a chair placed oddly in the center of the floor. My eyes swept the edges of the room. Shadows took shape and became human. Three men whom I had never seen before glared at me with an animosity I hadn't experienced since leaving Little Georgia.

"Take your hands off my wife!" Gus was on my captor with the ferocity of an *onca*.

They fell to the floor, dragging me with them. As they rolled and struggled, the stranger finally had no choice but to release me. Gus was shorter than my attacker, but he was younger and much stronger. He straddled the intruder and pummeled his face with both fists. With each contact, blood flew. The stranger tried to fend off the blows, but they rained down like hail before an impending tornado. Gus knocked his opponent unconscious and was attempting to rise when a second intruder grabbed his hair, put a knee in his spine, and yanked his head backward. With lightning speed, a blade slid across his throat, sending blood spewing over the wall, the floor, and me. The man then pushed Gus away into my outstretched arms. He tried to speak, but his windpipe was cut through. No sound came other than gurgling from air passing over gushing blood. His lips formed the words I love you. He died in my arms. He died without hearing how much I loved him. He died without seeing my heart shatter into tiny pieces. He died while trying to save me. He answered my questions about his love, but at a price beyond endurance.

Shrieking filled the library. Marguerite covered her face with her hands and crumpled to the floor. Everyone else appeared frozen in place. I placed my husband's body on the floor and flew at the knife-wielding intruder in a mindless fury of grief and pain. I clawed at his throat and pummeled his chest. He was so surprised that he dropped his weapon in order to grasp my wrists before spinning me around and jerking my arm upward until I could feel my shoulder separating.

When I screamed in pain, he asked, "Are you ready to do as you are told?"

The pain shocked me into conscience thought and I nodded. It would do no one any good for him to break my arm or worse. He pushed me so hard I landed in a heap on the floor beside Marguerite.

"Old man, like I asked you before. Where do you keep it?"

"And as I told you, we do not keep gold on the *fazenda*. I have money. I will gladly get it for you. There are many things of value here. Take anything. Just please don't hurt anyone else."

"You lie. We were told gold is hidden in this house. Bring it to me." The intruder strode over to Marguerite and pulled her to her feet. He placed the blade against her throat. "Now!"

"I can't get what doesn't exist, but I'll get the cash."

Eduardo went to the shelves that were in the most distant corner of the room. He pushed on a book's spine and a small section of shelving swung open. From the cavity in the wall, he withdrew a metal lockbox. He handed a small stack of paper money to our captor. The stranger released Marguerite and counted, a snarl distorting his unpleasant features.

"We were told there would thousands in gold and all you offer is this? Get us the gold right now or we will slit your throats one by one until someone does." To emphasize his point, the stranger pulled Marguerite to his chest and flicked the point of his knife. A small trickle of blood traced a path down her pale throat onto the white collar of her gown. When Eduardo didn't respond, the man pushed the point deeper and sliced a small v shaped gash. Marguerite screamed in pain and fear.

She looked beseechingly at Eduardo, but my father-in-law was frozen in place. He was ghostly white and he seemed powerless to stop his wife's murder. Constancia's face was gray and her lips had an unnatural blue cast. She clutched at her chest as though she was in considerable pain. It became clear we were all going to die in one manner or another unless drastic action was taken immediately. I knew I was no match in strength for the criminals, but perhaps there was a way to persuade them to let us live. It was gold they wanted. We had no gold to give them, but I knew someone who did.

"Please, please don't hurt her anymore. I can tell you where to get as much gold as you can carry."

"Why didn't you say so before now?"

"Because it isn't here on the *fazenda*. It's on a farm on the *Ribeira Juquia*. The man who owns the farm found a large gold deposit on his land."

"And who is this man?"

"He is a Confederado named Nathan Jordan. His farm is downstream from the Terra Oliveira landing."

"Why should we believe you?"

"Do you know the rivers in this area?"

"I've traveled them some."

"Then you may have seen his farm called Little Georgia. He completed a large house not many years ago. His gold find paid for the house and the expensive furnishings that fill it. If you go there, I promise you will find what you want."

"How do we know you are telling the truth? Why would you tell us this?"

"Because the man is my uncle and I hate him. He murdered my father and left me to starve. When that didn't kill me, he then tried to marry me off to an old man with twelve boys in exchange for cash. You would be doing me a service if you paid him a visit."

Marguerite's eyes grew large, but she said nothing. The intruder pushed her to the floor again. I had his full and focused attention.

"I don't believe you."

I found an unexpected ally in Gus's murderer. He had regained his senses and sat up, rubbing his bruised jaw. "I know the farm. Saw the house being built going to Iguape two or three years ago. I also heard about a girl who ran away from her uncle when I stopped in a little place called McMullanville downriver from the farm. This has got to be the same girl."

"I am. What I'm telling you is the truth. Take our money and whatever else you want. Then go to Little Georgia where the real treasure is."

"And what will you offer as insurance for our success? Ah, I know. We will take you with us. Then if we find you are lying, we can kill you on the spot." He grinned at his accomplices as though this was the height of good humor.

A new voice came from the shadows. "No, she'll only slow us down. Two of us will stay here to guard the others."

It was evident the true leader of this band of criminals preferred not to show himself. I stared into the darkness from whence the voice had come.

"My uncle's farm is well protected. You will need more than two men."

"Leave me here. I think that *filho da puta* broke a couple of my ribs before his gullet was split."

The leader was quiet for a moment and then answered,

"Stay here then. But if you let anyone escape, I'll finish what the young man started when we return." He looked at Eduardo. "We still need an insurance policy."

The leader and the fourth as yet unseen man came out of the shadows. The band of criminals was a mixed lot made up of three white Brazilians, one of whom may have had Indian heritage. The fourth man was as dark as midnight, but the thing that burned him into my memory was the amulet he wore. A shiny carved wooden *onca* in chains dangled from a leather thong around his neck. Paulo once told me that every sort of evil preyed upon runaway slaves and they sometimes fell in with criminals simply to survive. A puzzled expression filled his eyes. I believe he understood that I recognized the symbol and was trying to decide how this could be.

The criminals' second in command bound Eduardo's hands while the leader took the cash and a sterling vase from the fireplace mantle. They then hustled Eduardo across the room half dragging him when he stumbled and lost his footing.

"Keep up old man or we'll carve you up where you stand. And that would make it difficult for the girl," The leader growled.

"Take her. She's nothing to me."

"Now is that any way for a gentleman to talk?" The second in command waved his pistol under Eduardo's nose.

"Enough of your playing. Let's go. I want to get to the farm while it's still dark," the leader growled.

At the library door, the runaway stopped and turned back so that we looked directly at one another. His *onca* rose and fell with his heavy breathing and I wondered if he was possibly as frightened as we were. The leader tapped the black's shoulder and then they were all gone as quietly as they had come.

## Chapter 27

"Well, ladies, it's just us now. How about we have a little fun?" Our jailor rose from the floor and slithered over to where we huddled around Constancia's chair. His pistol pointed at one then another of us as though he was playing a child's choosing game. Eventually, it oscillated only between Celina and me.

"Lady or peasant? Which one'll be the most entertaining?" He moved closer. The pistol barrel tipped Celina's face up and then side-to-side. Then he repeated the performance with me. "Ice on the outside and fire inside or all fire and earth? Didn't know a thief could be a poet, did you? Both of you step over by the lamp."

As I rose from the floor, gentle bumping against my thigh made my breath catch. The terror of the previous hour had overridden all other sensations completely obscuring memory of the lethal little weapon nestled deep within my riding skirt's pocket.

Our captor's eyes stared at my chest and then wandered down my body as though he was removing each piece of clothing one by one. When he reached my boots, he made the return trip until he gazed into my eyes. "You look as good in your riding outfit off the horse as you did in the saddle under that tree. Bet you'll look better without it though. Get undressed, but go slow. I like a good show before I get down to business."

"I will not." Horror at the realization that these criminals may have been drawn to the *fazenda* by my secret activities for Paulo made my stomach roll and I feared I would be physically sick.

In a flash, he had Marguerite by the wrist and his pistol against her temple. "Have it your way. I'll kill each one and have my way with you in the end anyhow. Actually, it might make you more interesting. Fear and sobbing make some women more attractive, or at least more compliant. What about you?"

It might have been a mistake to refuse, but I couldn't risk undressing. We would lose the small advantage my hidden weapon afforded us. I could feel panic rising. Although I had come close before, I had never stared death in the face like this. What I saw chilled me to the core. After this man finished taking his pleasure, we were all dead anyway, so taking a chance, if it failed, could make little difference.

I had to find a way to get him closer to me while I still wore my skirt. The farther from the target, the less accurate my little derringer would be. It was strictly for close range protection. A desperate plan formed with no time to evaluate it. Its success depended on my acting ability.

"No, no. You misunderstand. I need help with the tight buttons on my bodice. Would you like to undo them?" The coy seductiveness in my voice nauseated me and clearly shocked the other women.

Suspicion and lust played across the intruder's face. Lust won out. Within a heartbeat, he was standing before me gripping the tiny top button on my blouse. While his spatulate fingers struggled with the ivory ball, my hand slipped into my skirt pocket. He managed to get the top button free and started work on the second as my fingers wrapped around the derringer's pearl handle and found the trigger. I could feel his frustration with the small buttons mounting in the way his fingers jerked and I could hear it in his grunts and exasperated sighs. Suddenly he grasped each side of the blouse front. My opportunity would be gone in a flash if I didn't act. The derringer rose inside my pocket accompanied by the sound of ripping fabric and buttons bouncing on the parquet. Pretending that his tugging had pulled me off balance, I fell into his chest while bringing my weapon up against his midsection. I squeezed the trigger releasing both shots and prayed their trajectory propelled them into a vital organ or would at least incapacitate him enough for us to wrest control of the situation.

My captor put his hands on my shoulders and pushed back, his eyes wide with surprise and pain. As scarlet spread over his shirtfront, he grasped the two weeping holes in his gut. In a moment he dropped to his knees and then crumpled over onto his side.

"*Puta*! You've killed me!"

"Time will tell. If you cooperate, we may try to ease your pain. Cook, get rope and bind his hands and feet. Celina, go to the stables and send riders to bring the militia."

With one eye on the intruder, I went to Marguerite and knelt beside her. "Please let me see your injury." I tore a length of fabric from my underskirt and covered the little gaping wound in her throat. "That should stop the blood for now. I'll send one of the boys for Adriana."

It was three days before the provincial militia arrived. In that time, we buried Gus and the intruder, Father Paulo moved into the house temporarily, and Constancia remained uncharacteristically quiet. I went through the motions of what was required in a haze of tears and pent up grief. By the time Captain Branco's boots rang in the reception hall, the realization that life would never be the same had begun to sink in with everyone living on the *fazenda*.

"Senhora, I was enraged at hearing all you have endured at the hands of such criminals. I promise my men and I will bring them to justice." The captain bent forward with a ceremonial flourish and planted his dust-covered lips on Constancia's pristine hand, which was immediately snatched from his grasp. The man had never learned the subtly of the implied kiss. "Please gather the household at once so we may obtain a clear picture of these miscreants and then we will be off in pursuit."

"Let us remove to the library where there are sufficient chairs available. Maria, summon the staff and Father Paulo, but leave Senhora Marguerite."

"But, Senhora, it is my understanding your daughter-in-law is a witness."

"Yes, it is so, but she has been confined to her bed since the unfortunate events. Her health is delicate and her nerves will not permit her to return to the scene of so much horror so soon. I'm sure, as a gentleman, you can understand this."

What Constancia said was true. I had slept in Marguerite's room and cared for her for the last three days and nights, so stricken was she by her injury and terrible loss. That my own heart was in shreds seemed not to have occurred to anyone. Because my mother-in-law was so ill, I had hardly left her room. I succumbed to my own tears when she fell into her fitful episodes of sporadic sleep. Only then could I stuff my fist into my mouth and cover my howling with a pillow. The pain was different from what I had experienced when Mama and Papa died. With Mama's loss, it had been Nathan's words that impaled my soul on twin pikes of blame and guilt. With Gus's death, it was my own inner turmoil that did the deed.

After leaving the library, I managed to round up all household staff that had been present during the ordeal, save one. Celina, dratted girl, was nowhere to be found. In something of a temper, I returned to the library. When I opened the door, the scene before me was eerily similar to the one on the day Gus had been murdered. Everyone was again gathered around a centrally placed chair upon which Constancia sat, only this time a second chair was occupied by Captain Branco.

"Is this the girl?"

"It is."

"But I was given to understand she is your granddaughter-in-law, Senhor Gustavo's wife."

"Unfortunately, that is the case. None the less, she is guilty."

All eyes bore into me as I tried to comprehend what was happening. I sought out Paulo standing behind his grandmother. His expression was grave and he seemed to be trying to speak to me with his eyes, but I couldn't grasp what he was communicating.

"Are you sure, Senhora? While I respect your opinion explicitly, I would not want to take serious action without a little more evidence."

"Celina, did you bring it with you?"

"*Sim*, Senhora." My nemesis stepped from behind Cook and held out her hand. On her palm lay my *onca* amulet. I thought I had lost it in the move to the *fazenda*. Clearly, a thief had been through my possessions soon after my arrival.

"Explain to the captain where you found this object."

"It was among her things in her dressing room." The girl moved closer and pointed at me. "It is the same as the one worn by the black intruder." Celina's smile was hard with malice.

The captain's eyes widened. "Senhora Maria, how did you come by this?"

Partial truths had served me well in the past and seemed the best choice now. "It was given to me by my uncle's slave."

"And why would a slave give such a thing to his mistress?"

I silently prayed the captain didn't know the amulet's true meaning. "He said it was for luck."

"Sadly, I think you are lying. This is the symbol used by runaway slaves to identify themselves to one another. Only recently, we learned of its existence and meaning. I assure you the slave who gave us the information told the truth."

Constancia took charge of the interrogation. "Is this how you repay us? By consorting with criminals?"

I didn't know what to say that would not jeopardize Paulo's organization and lead to his destruction. I had already caused enough harm.

"My uncle's slave gave it to me when I ran away. He told me to use it to move among his people safely."

"My God! You have been in league with these criminals all along!"

"Senhora, I promise I have not. I had never seen any of those men until the night they broke into this house. I would not cause such pain to those I love."

"That is not what the one you killed said. Apparently you have been meeting him under some nearby tree since he seemed so familiar with your riding costume."

I had forgotten my attacker's words until it was too late. "He must have spied on me while I rode around the *fazenda*. There is a tree on a hilltop from which there is a beautiful view. He must have been hiding in the forest when I stopped. It is the only possible explanation!"

"I know the tree. It is on the adjoining *fazenda* where you promised you would not go. Captain, she condemns herself with her own words."

"I fear you are correct, Senhora Constancia. Sergeant, take charge of the young senhora. You will take her to Sao Paulo to await trial while the remainder of the unit continues pursuit."

Within a heartbeat, I was in chains and tied to my mare's saddle. As the gravel on the front driveway crunched beneath the horses' hooves, I glanced back over my shoulder at the grand mansion I had so briefly called home. A figure stood in Marguerite's bedroom window, leaning against the glass.

I tried to see what she was feeling, but she turned away the moment our eyes met.

I was completely alone for the second time in my life. Adriana and Ricardo had no idea I had been arrested and would be powerless when they found out. My only ally in the big house, my mother-in-law, had abandoned me as she had promised to do if I failed her son. Even Paulo seemed withdrawn and distant. He probably feared any defense of me or even continued association would endanger too many other people. My fate was sealed because Constancia would see to it that I hanged.

## Chapter 28

The sergeant led me away from Fazenda Oliveira under lowering skies, but the weather was the least of my concerns. My despair was the greatest I had ever known. Not only had the love of my life died in my arms, but I was also accused of complicity in his murder. Adding to the horror was the guilt I felt over my part in his death, albeit unwitting. If I had not become involved with Paulo's organization, those men would not have followed me and Gus would still be alive. That knowledge was a burden almost beyond endurance. The priest's desertion when I most needed help filled me with fury and compounded my feelings of isolation. My powerful in-laws were sure to be the instruments of my destruction for no one would speak in my defense when I was put on trial in Sao Paulo. If Eduardo did not survive his kidnapping, then that too would be laid at my door since the real murderers could easily melt back into the peasantry and never be found. Even Bess's words echoing to me from so long ago failed to comfort or encourage. For the first time in memory, I lost the thing that had always kept me going in the face of seemingly insurmountable odds. I lost hope and any vision of a better tomorrow.

As evening approached on the first day, the skies opened and torrential rain poured down, turning the cart path we followed into a rutted wallow. The mud sucked at my little mare's hooves as she gingerly picked her way behind the sergeant's big plodding gelding. By the time we made camp in the lee of a stone outcropping, I was covered in mud and soaked to the skin.

My jailor tied the horses to sturdy saplings and then secured a tarpaulin among the trees, settling his bedroll under its center. Next he threw together a campfire of wet wood and fanned reluctant flames until a feeble glow sent smoke drifting from under the tarp. Only then did he finally untie the rope binding my hands to the saddle.

"Get down and sit under this tree where I can keep an eye on you while I cook something to eat." He turned his back and began plundering in his saddlebags then stopped and looked over his shoulder. "You're the girl who ran away from her uncle, aren't you? Well, I'm not going to lose you."

Instead of removing food from his bag, he got a rope and pushed me down until I sat on the wet ground with my back against the tree's trunk. He wound the rope around the tree until only my feet were capable of movement and these he tied together until I was completely immobile. Although the tarp covered most of me, water dripped off the tree's bark onto my head and then ran down my back. Uncontrolled shivering made me wonder if death from exposure might cheat the hangman.

The aroma of frying bacon soon mingled with wood smoke under the makeshift shelter, but instead of enticing appetite, it nauseated. I hadn't really eaten a full meal since Gus's death because I couldn't choke down what little I put in my mouth, so it made no difference to me that the sergeant wolfed down the food without offering me any.

As he licked bacon grease from his fingers, he glanced at me. "It's your turn."

He shoved a piece of grease slathered hardtack into my mouth and held a cup of scalding coffee for me to wash it down with. He checked the rope bindings and then rolled himself up in his bedroll by the fire.

At least the coffee reduced my shivering so that for a while I drifted in and out of a fitful sleep. The position in which I sat and the cold so restricted blood flow to my arms and legs that they soon lost feeling. It seemed probable that by morning I would be unable to stand, much less sit a horse.

I'm not sure how long I had been dozing when my head jerked upright sending pain shooting through my shoulders and neck. My head must have lolled at an unnatural angle for some time to produce such knots. Days and nights of horror and grief had left me exhausted and I awoke with a feeling of being suspended somewhere between worlds, as though my mind and my body had become separate entities, still aware of their relationship, but somehow no longer united. I tried to draw a long cleansing breath to clear my head, but the rope binding my upper body felt as though it had shrunk and was now trying to slowly suffocate me. When I heard a voice whisper my name, I groaned outwardly because I knew I was hallucinating.

A hand slipped over my mouth and pressed down while warm breath stirred the hair around my ear. "Quiet."

The tugging increased until the rope went slack and dropped to my lap. Ricardo moved around to my side and sawed at the rope binding my feet. When I tried to stand, my muscles refused to support my weight.

Ricardo caught me when I stumbled forward. "Lean on me, little one."

We were edging away from the camp when movement by the fire and a shout made us freeze in our tracks.

"Where do you think you're going?" The sergeant aimed his pistol at my heart. "Come over here. This is all I need. Two prisoners to haul all the way to Sao Paulo."

We moved toward the fire, but there was a loud crack and the sergeant suddenly looked very surprised then crumpled to the ground. In his place, Paulo stood with a large branch in his hand. "He'll have a sore head and a long walk in the morning." He crossed himself and continued, "Father, forgive the violence I have committed against one of your creatures. Let him awake without permanent injury, but not until we are well away from here." He grinned and motioned for us to follow him.

When we reached the horses, I leaned on Paulo's arm while Ricardo prepared my mare.

"Hold on tight. We'll get those wrist shackles off soon." Paulo then lifted me up into the saddle and we were away, heading east into the rising sun.

Paulo led the sergeant's horse and Ricardo led mine. We traveled some miles in this fashion until we slowed to cross a small stream.

I gripped the saddle and leaned forward. "Where are we going?"

"To safety," Ricardo half turned and replied over his shoulder.

"But exactly where is that?"

"You will see when the time comes."

We rode all day, stopping only long enough to saw off my wrist shackles and eat a cold meal, then took off again, riding until it was too dark to see the path. When we stopped to make camp for the night, I was determined to have an answer.

"Paulo, Ricardo, I want to know where you are taking me. Will Adriana be there?"

Ricardo dropped his eyes and turned his head away, leaving Paulo to respond.

"You are going to Igaupe. There, you will board any vessel bound for the United States. It is no longer safe for you in Brazil. It's time for you to go home, Maria."

"But Brazil is my home. Adriana and Ricardo are my family. I can't leave them."

"You must. My grandmother will never rest until you are found and hanged. It's the only way."

"But what about Adriana? Will I see her again?"

"I'm afraid not. We can't risk going back to Terra Oliveira and it would create too much suspicion if both she and Ricardo were to disappear when your escape becomes known. And it will become known, Maria. If we are lucky, you will make it into Igaupe undetected and be at sea without anyone ever being the wiser." Sympathy softened his eyes as he placed his hand on my shoulder. "Please understand. It is the only way."

It was more than I could bear. I turned to Ricardo and collapsed against him while sobs broke the silence of the damp night air.

The following morning, we ate a cold breakfast of *charque,* the Brazilian version of jerky, and set off at dawn in an unrelenting drizzle. We reached the river at nightfall and made camp in the shelter of an abandoned shack. I was essentially back where my life in Brazil began–on the river in a drafty palm thatched hut wondering how life could have gone so terribly wrong. That night, I dreamt of Mama, Papa, and Bess. They were in a place that looked like our home in Georgia, but was incredibly part of the Brazilian countryside. They seemed unaware that I was struggling against an unseen adversary, trying to reach them. Every time I got within shouting distance, some force pulled me away. I awoke feeling exhausted, as though I had fought for my life the entire night. Paulo and Ricardo were already dousing the campfire and breaking camp when I came out of the hut into the clear light of the rising sun.

"This is where I leave you, Maria. Ricardo will take you on from here. Words are inadequate to express how sorry I am that things have turned out as they have. Please believe me. Those men who attacked the *fazenda* will pay for their treachery. They will no longer hide among my people. I will pray for your safety and future happiness. You deserve better than you have received at the hands of the Oliveiras." He placed his hand on my head in blessing, made the sign of the cross, and rode away leading the other three horses without looking back.

"Come. We have no time to lose." Ricardo gripped my elbow and pulled me along toward the water. "A dugout has been provided. We should be in Igaupe in three days if luck is with us. Father Paulo has made arrangements for you to stay with friends there until passage can be found."

I was so numb with grief it never occurred to me to ask who had provided the canoe.

We had been on the river for a couple of hours when the scenery began to look familiar. Mountains in the near distance, the river banked by forested rocky outcroppings, creeks flowing into the river, water rushing over and around boulders—all of this I had seen before. Soon the river smoothed out as a valley appeared on our right. My breath caught in my throat when Little Georgia's dock came into sight. Even after years of absence, I recognized it immediately.

I strained forward for a glimpse of my former home. I longed to stop and say a prayer beside papa's grave, but it didn't seem possible even though I had as much right to be on the land as Nathan. My heart beat ever faster the closer we drew to the mouth of Little Georgia's creek and the houses beside it. They were both still out of sight, the little dogtrot cabin and Nathan's grand mansion built with blood money. When we rounded the final bend, I involuntarily rose to my knees in the canoe's bow and gaped at the scene.

Where Nathan's mansion should have been, nothing but a smoldering shell stood open to the sky with charred timbers sticking up haphazardly like so many pick-up sticks in a child's game. Amazingly, the cabin was unscathed. In fact, improvements had been made. The once open-air dogtrot was now enclosed with timber frame walls. A central front door bore a coat of black paint and someone had started on the exterior walls with whitewash.

"Ricardo! Pull in at the dock! I've got to know what happened!"

"What happened here should not concern you. Time is not on our side."

"You don't understand. This is . . ."

Ricardo cut in. "I know what this place is. There is nothing for you here but unhappiness."

"Please stop. Just for a few minutes. I can't just sail past without knowing. And there are things here that are very precious to me."

"Maria, those things won't have survived the fire. This is foolishness."

"They will be where I hid them. I've got to get them! And I must see Nathan. It's the only way I'll ever have any peace. He murdered Papa!"

Rage and grief blended together until I could no longer distinguish one from the other. If Ricardo had refused to do as I asked, I would have jumped into the river and swum to the dock. I never thought I would have the opportunity to retrieve my talismans and now I couldn't leave Brazil without them. Images of confronting Nathan with his crimes raced through my mind. Visions of revenge surged scorching hot like lava pouring down a volcano's sides. It briefly occurred to me that I might be going mad, but I didn't care.

I scrambled to my feet the minute the dugout bumped against the dock. It was as if I had never left. All of the emotions attached to little Georgia came flooding back. Most were filled with heartache, but there were a few happy memories as well—my garden, the steppingstones across the creek, the jungle of flowering plants that created an Eden in the wilderness. As I marched toward the cabin, I began constructing mental scenes depicting my showdown with Nathan.

First, I would go to the door and demand admittance. Nathan would be so caught off guard he would allow me into the house. I would introduce myself to his wife as an acquaintance from the past, the daughter of deceased friends on her way to McMullanville. Nathan would be leery of rousing his wife's curiosity. I was sure she knew nothing of the niece who owned half of their property. When the wife went to the kitchen for refreshments, for Nathan would surely want to maintain the deception of a social call, I would accomplish what I came for.

Knocking echoed from the front door through the now enclosed dogtrot, but there was no other sound. Ricardo joined me on the porch as I rapped again, this time much louder, but still there was no answer.

"They may have gone to stay with friends. We should go."

"No! I haven't come this far to slink away now. I will see my uncle!"

"Then you will have a long wait, Mistress Mary Catherine," called a male voice from the corner of the house.

Shock made me forget to ask how he knew who I was. It was as though I was fourteen again. "Henrique! What happened here? Where are Nathan and his wife? Are Fatima and the children okay?" I was so startled by his sudden appearance that the questions poured out without leaving him space to answer.

When I paused for breath, he replied, "Come into the parlor. I will call Fatima and the children in from the garden." He propped a hoe against the porch and ascended the steps. When he opened the door, he held his arm out in an expansive gesture that reminded me for all the world of how Papa had once ushered guests into our home in Georgia.

While Ricardo and I waited, I took in the changes to my former bedroom. Gone were the corner bed and simple handmade chairs. In their places stood an upholstered settee and matching armchairs placed upon a prettily patterned rug. Whitewash covered the log walls, brightening the room considerably. This was clearly used only as a reception area now and with all of the improvements, I wondered if my hiding hole in the chimney had been discovered and repaired.

I couldn't bear not knowing. I gripped the stone and yanked, but it was stuck solid.

"The tintype and handkerchief are safe with several other things you will want. We hoped to send them to you when the time was right." Henrique stood in the doorway.

I stepped away from the chimney, embarrassed and puzzled. It felt as though Henrique, not Nathan, was our host. Fatima and the children, who peeked shyly from behind their mother's skirt, followed him into the room. She placed a tray on the table before the settee. It bore the blue and white china tea set Nathan had brought back from one of his trips as a gift for Ida and me. Life at Little Georgia seemed to have turned upside down.

"Let's sit and have tea, shall we?"

Henrique's formality puzzled me. He had always possessed an unshakable dignity beyond anything his soul crushing condition of servitude would have produced in others, but this was something new, different. And Fatima, who had been so affectionate when we parted, was now stiff and standoffish. It struck me they were acting like they were afraid and I wanted to know why without the pretense that this was polite social call.

"Henrique, what's wrong? You're acting like we hardly know each other. And where is Nathan? I have a score to settle with him."

"I suppose you will not rest until you know. Come, then." He gestured that Fatima and the children should not follow. When Ricardo did not move toward the door with us, I looked back and beckoned, but he shook his head. I began to suspect he knew more than he had told me.

Henrique strode to the back porch and on to the garden gate. I understood then where he was leading me. When we reached the little enclosure where Papa was buried, clods of freshly turned earth covered two new mounds beside him.

"Did they die in the fire?"

"No, thieves slit their throats before setting fire to the house. Your uncle refused to give them gold. He was the second to die. They took special care with him trying to extract the information. With his last breath, he told the thieves they had taken everything that really mattered to him so he would be damned if he would pay them for their work."

"What happened to Eduardo Oliveira, the gentleman they kidnapped? Did they take him away with them again?"

"There was no gentleman. There were only two white ruffians and a runaway slave." He looked at me imploringly. "Why did you send those men here, Mary Catherine?"

"I'll answer your question when you tell me how you managed to escape with your life!" I was enraged by his question, but also filled with confusion and fear. Eduardo was probably dead, which gave me an even greater reason for leaving Brazil.

Henrique's mouth became a thin hard line. We glared at one another in a contest of wills. I blamed him for surviving the slaughter so that he could accuse me of . . . What? Purposefully sending the criminals to kill my uncle? He had said nothing of the sort and yet I felt guilty of the crime. Perhaps it was what I had unconsciously intended all along. An inappropriate worm of satisfaction had crawled through me upon hearing of Nathan's end. What had I become that I could revel in another person's pain, even if he was a hated enemy? I was only twenty-one years old and yet I had contributed to the deaths of three members of my family and killed a man outright. Who was I? Did I even want to know?

I was saved from seeking the answer when Henrique broke our strained silence. "I gave those criminals what they came for. I knew where your uncle kept his hoard and I gave it to them. Then they set fire to the house and left."

"But why did they let you live?" I shouted at Henrique as though he was at fault for surviving.

"Because we wear the same amulet! They are part of us. For that, I am heartily ashamed."

The genuine anguish in his voice opened my own emotional floodgates. My anger flowed away and in its place feelings of remorse and sorrow settled.

"You must understand. I sent them here to save my husband's family."

"Is this the same family who wants you hanged?"

Henrique clearly knew at least some of my story. I could no longer meet his eyes. I dropped my head and nodded. "No matter what I did for them or how much I tried to fit in, they never accepted me."

"We were sorry to hear of your husband's death. News travels fast among our people, especially about those who risk much to help us. Father Paulo sent word to be on guard, but it did not reach me in time."

"I promise I never meant for it to come to this. I acted on the spur of the moment and under tremendous stress. I really believed Nathan would give them the gold. He was never very brave. I'm sorry for what happened here." But was I? I didn't really know. I had hated my uncle for so many years. Dreams of revenge had been part of me for so long, but I had never envisioned causing his death. At least it's what I kept telling myself.

"As that may be, it still does not solve the problems your in-laws have created for you. Fatima has saved some things of your family that you will want to take when you leave and that should be without delay."

By the time we returned to the parlor, two large carpetbags were waiting.

Fatima spoke for the first time since I arrived. "We kept everything for you, all of it. The clothes you left behind and your uncle's books are in these."

I went to her and placed my arms around her. "Thank you. You have been a good friend."

Next, Henrique pressed a small linen bag into my hand. "This is for your trip. You will need money."

"I'm humbled by your kindness, but I can't take it. You have a family to care for and I will never be able to repay you."

"Actually, there are two things you can do for us, if you are willing. We are still slaves as far as the outside world is concerned. Sign a paper declaring us free."

"Gladly. And the second thing?"

"The gold in that bag belongs to me. I found it and hid it from your uncle. I want to pay you for this land. Will you sign over ownership?"

His request caught me completely off guard. I had been so weighed down by grief that such details had never occurred to me.

When I didn't answer immediately, Henrique continued, "It isn't what the land is worth, but it is all I have. The land will be of no use to you."

An idea formed. Though I was in no position to make demands, perhaps I could help those who had helped me. "I'll sign over my land under one condition."

"And that would be?"

"Divide the land fairly and equally with my adoptive parents, Ricardo and Adriana Dias."

Ricardo's head snapped toward me. "Maria, you can't ask that of him. They have done enough for you. You cannot expect more."

"And where will you and Adriana be when I leave? Do you really think Constancia will let you quietly continue your lives in Terra Oliveira as though nothing has happened? Since she won't be able to get to me, she will take her anger out on you. The bonds formed with Adriana so long ago won't save you this time. Please. Do this for me. I can't leave without knowing the two of you are safe and beyond her reach."

Ricardo tilted his head slightly and glanced at Henrique who said, "I doubt even Father Paulo can influence your fate if you stay in Terra Oliveira. I will do as Mary Catherine asks. This farm can support two families."

"My wife and I are alone. When we die, the land will go to your children. That is the condition under which I accept your offer."

"Then it's done."

It was decided that Henrique, acting as my slave, would accompany Miss Mary Catherine MacDonald on the river trip to Igaupe while Ricardo went back for Adriana. My adoptive father hugged me hard and then departed in the opposite direction from the one I was to take. I watched him until he was gone from sight. It seemed I was destined to lose, in one way or another, everyone I ever loved.

I left Little Georgia with a small bag of gold nuggets and two large carpetbags containing dresses, Nathan's journals, and the Jordan family Bible—the sum total of my life. I left having no idea of what the future held or how I would make my way in it.

Just before the bend in the river that hid the house from upstream travelers, I turned back for a final look. Fatima and the children stood on the dock watching us as though they might never see Henrique again. I lifted a hand and forced my mouth into a broad smile. Little Mary Catherine's dark face and solemn eyes followed me as though she understood the special connection that existed between us. When she raised her hand in response, it came to me that my little namesake might be the only proof I ever lived in Brazil. A door in my life was closing, one that I knew could never be opened again.

## Chapter 29

After the harrowing days following Gus's murder, the trip from Little Georgia to Igaupe was bizarrely uneventful. Henrique and I retraced the miles that had first brought Papa, Nathan, and me inland to the wilderness of the McMullan land grant. Our original trip had taken six days. The trip out again took half the time, unencumbered as we were by excessive baggage, furniture, and farm implements. Traveling downriver eliminated the need to use the poles for anything other than steering. We only stopped long enough to rest for a few hours each night, leaving the water after dusk and returning to it before daylight. Luck was with us, for other than portaging at the same white water as before, we sped along without incident. The nearer we drew to the coast, the smoother Ribeira de Igaupe became.

Late on the afternoon of our third day, a familiar sight came into view and we soon passed the dock from which the rusty old tub *Esperanca* had departed with us aboard headed for our new inland home. Eleven very formative years had passed since I last stood on that dock in an early morning fog praying life would improve and that Papa forgave my terrible mistake. Had the situation permitted, I might have crumbled under the weight of all the memories rushing to meet me. As it was, I had no time for such self-indulgent luxuries.

Henrique guided our canoe through town to the main Igaupe docks. Like the other harbor areas of my experience, Igaupe's was seedy and utilitarian. Warehouses looked out onto the river while dilapidated shanties lined the streets leading away from the harbor. It was in a particularly shabby area that we eventually tied off and climbed up onto a rickety pier in the fading light of what had been the first truly hot day of early summer. Christmas would be here before we knew it, but where I would be was anyone's guess. I had no idea how long it would take to find passage to Savannah or Mobile or where I would stay hidden until that time. Fear does not begin to describe what I felt.

"Why are we just waiting here?"

"For a friend." Henrique, never loquacious, was being positively, irritatingly taciturn.

"I guessed that much. Why here in the open where anyone can see us?"

"He needs to know we have arrived."

"What if the militia comes or someone reports us?"

"That will not happen."

"How can you be so sure? They may have followed us to Little Georgia. They may be hunting us in Iguape right now!"

"They are not."

"How do you know? We shouldn't wait any longer. We should hide and find a ship in the morning." Words tumbled from my mouth with ever-increasing speed. "What if no one comes? We should exchange the gold for cash. We should go to a hotel like respectable people. We should . . ."

Henrique gripped my elbow as though to steady me. "If you continue to shout it is very likely someone will report us. Be calm. Our friend will arrive shortly."

And he did. He refused to speak, led us through back alleys, and left us in a squalid hut somewhere uphill from the docks. I spent the night lying on the dirt floor with my head on a carpetbag since there was no furniture, but between the sounds of animals scurrying and insects buzzing, slumber came only in fits and starts. The morning dawned warm and humid with no water to drink or wash in. When the sun was still on the horizon, footsteps hurrying toward our hideout made my heart race.

"Do not be afraid," said Henrique. "This will be your guide approaching."

"What do you mean, my guide? What about you?"

"At this point, I am no longer of use to you. We must depend on others to complete your journey."

"How can you say that? Please don't leave me with strangers! How do I know I can trust these people?"

He never answered because the hut's door creaked open and a small, wizened figure dressed stepped inside. She greeted Henrique with a nod of recognition then her black eyes darted to me and grew wide with surprise.

"A white woman? What on earth have you brought me? How do we know she can be trusted?"

"Father Paulo sends his regards and asks that you give this white girl particular care. She is not only his cousin, but she is one of us. It is because of her work with us that she is now in need of our help."

The new arrival didn't respond immediately. Instead, she looked me up and down as though she was inspecting a side of meat. After grabbing my arm and turning me this way and that, she harrumphed once and said, "She's filthy. Are these the only clothes she has?"

"There are fine garments in the carpetbags. They were purchased in Rio's best shops."

"I suppose we could pass her off as a rich woman traveling to meet relatives." She turned to me and asked, "Did you bring enough money for the ticket?"

When I didn't answer, she continued, "Well, girl. Don't just stand there gaping at me. Where is the money?"

I looked inquiringly at Henrique. "Show her. It will be all right."

I removed the little linen bag from my skirt pocket and loosen the drawstrings.

My guide peered into the bag. "And what am I supposed to do with this?"

"The priest will make the exchange. Give it to him and he will take care of it."

"But, Henrique, that's all of value I have. I can't give the gold to a complete stranger!"

"Do you trust me?"

I nodded.

"Then do as she tells you."

The woman glared at me and took the linen bag. "You, my girl, are quickly becoming more trouble than you are worth."

"Remember Father Paulo's request. It will go hard on anyone who mistreats this girl." Henrique turned to me and held out his hand. "Mary Catherine, I must be away from Iguape before the day advances. This woman will help you on the next part of your journey."

Everything was changing so fast I could hardly take it in. "I'll never see any of you again, will I?" Henrique shook his head. "Will you promise not to forget me?"

"You will be in our hearts always. After all, we have a constant reminder in your namesake."

I instinctively put my arms around him and hugged hard. After his initial surprise, he returned my embrace and then held me at arm's length. "You survived your uncle. You will survive the journey into the unknown."

Henrique turned and left the hut without looking back. I was now truly on my own.

I looked at the woman who literally could mean the difference between life and death for me and asked, "May I know your name? I am Maria Oliv— Mary Catherine MacDonald."

"We do not exchange names. It is safer. Follow me and keep your eyes down. If anyone approaches us, do not speak. I will take you to the church by the longer, but less traveled path."

"What church? The cathedral on the main square?"

"Are you deaf? Do not speak! Your accent will cause too much comment in this neighborhood."

I could not retrace the maze of back streets and alleys we took if my life depended on it, but after about a half hour, we passed under a small door's lintel in the side of a tall stone wall. Once we were on the other side of the door, I saw that we had entered a dimly lit passage. My guide scurried ahead without turning to see whether I followed. Another minute, another door, and we stepped into a small nave.

"Go into the confessional box. Next to the priest's partition is a rope. Pull it." When I didn't move immediately, she hissed, "Go!"

When I turned to speak, the space where she had stood was empty and echoing footsteps scurried along the hallway's stone floor. Sun coming through small dust clouded windows high up in the walls cast a paltry light over pews in need of a good polish, otherwise, the building was dark. I crept between the wooden seats toward the far wall where my guide had pointed.

The confessional box with its threadbare privacy curtains appeared out of the gloom. Slipping behind tattered velvet that felt like it might come apart in my hand, I groped around until I found a low chair. A rope hung in the corner beside the priest's partition. I gave it a jerk. Silence. I yanked harder and listened intently. Somewhere deep within the building a bell tinkled. With nothing to do but wait, I dropped down on the chair and leaned against the opposite corner. The church was really quite stuffy and since I had neither eaten an actual meal nor slept well in days, I felt weak and lightheaded. If my physical needs had not been so great, fear might have been all consuming, but I was beyond thoughts of anything other than getting through the next hour. The slightly cooler wooden surface provided some relief from the cloying atmosphere of the confessional, filled as it was with a deep mustiness and the stale fragrance of many years' incense. As the minutes ticked by, bone weary exhaustion extinguished all conscience thought.

"Daughter, you wish to make your confession?" The priest's pleasant baritone startled me and set my heart pounding. My eyes flew open, and for a second, I forgot where I was.

"You have nothing to fear. We offer solace to all."

"Father Paulo in Terra Oliveira sent me."

"We have been expecting you. We will wait ten minutes and then you will kneel at the altar rail and say the Hail Mary and Our Father until I send for you. Everything must seem as ordinary as possible."

I found a rosary waiting at the rail and began the repetitions. The beads made a complete circuit before a woman tapped my shoulder and beckoned me to follow her to a side door.

We crossed a small, unadorned courtyard and passed through a door opposite the church, ending our short journey in what must have been the rectory kitchen. A table in the center of the room was laid for four and the aroma of cooking made my stomach growl. Instead of stopping, though, the woman increased her pace until she reached a door in the opposite wall. This she opened and indicated that I should pass through. Once we were on the other side of the door, she closed it and went to the far wall of what was clearly the larder. Shelves stacked with staples and jars lined three walls. I was on the verge of asking why we were there, when the woman pushed aside a large sack and the entire back wall swung open revealing a small alcove lit by a single window high up in the wall.

"Stay in here and do not make any noise. I will bring water for you to wash and food. When you have bathed and eaten, try to rest. There is much to be done before we can move you."

Within minutes a pitcher of warm water, soap, towels, and a tray with soup and coffee sat on a table beside the only other piece of furniture in the room, a single bed made up with snowy sheets and a plump pillow. She turned to go, but I placed a hand on her arm. "Please. Tell me how long I'll be shut up in here."

"As long as it takes. Sleep. It will pass the time."

After washing and eating, I lay back and stared at the small window high above my head. White clouds drifted in an intensely blue sky, the kind I had come to expect during early summer in Brazil. Eventually, I drifted off, but it was neither restful nor peaceful because I dreamed the dream for the first time.

In the half-world of sleep, I floated in nondescript surroundings that could have been anywhere. Nothing pinned them to a particular place or time. Sometimes hazy insubstantial walls appeared only to evaporate, leaving me to drift in a dark void. But wherever the dream took me, I wasn't alone for long. They came to me as though no time at all had passed since we last saw one another. Bess and Adriana smiled and held out their arms. For brief moments, I was enveloped by love. They were so real that the pressure of their embraces lingered after their faces faded. When Mama appeared, an ethereal quality made her too insubstantial to embrace. Her eyes held a rather vague expression, as though she seemed uncertain and sad. When Papa appeared, he pulled me to him at first, but then pushed me away at arm's length and stared into my eyes as though he searched for the answer to an unspoken question. I desperately wanted to ask him what was wrong, but words refused to form leaving me mute and frustrated. So far, there had been no sound. No one spoke and the environment contained no noise. That changed when Nathan attacked Papa from behind, spinning him around and shouting. His words were unclear, but his tone left little doubt about his meaning. The two men rolled and tumbled until Papa began to blur around the edges. I strained to go to Papa's aid, but my body was leaden, my feet rooted in place. With each assault, Papa became less distinct until he finally faded away entirely, then Nathan turned to face me, but he was not alone. Incongruously, Gus stood beside him. Red stains spread from their throats down their shirtfronts and across their chests. Nathan's face convulsed with hatred, but Gus wore an expression of infinite sadness. My dead love stretched out his hand and implored, "Why, Maria? Why?" My vile uncle shouted, "You killed my sister and now you have murdered me!" From somewhere out of sight, Constancia added her voice to the cacophony. "She must hang for her crimes! Hang, hang, hang . . ."

Racking sobs and rough shaking brought me back to reality. "Be quiet and get ready to leave!"

"How long have I been here?" Other than the single candle carried by my keeper, the tiny sanctuary was completely dark.

"It's early morning. You must get to the dock by eight o'clock. The ship sails at ten. Dress for travel and don't dawdle." She placed the candlestick on the table and disappeared as the wall clicked shut behind her.

I hadn't even looked inside the carpetbags, but I knew they could not contain what was needed for the long sea voyage ahead. I hoisted both onto the bed and unbuckled their clasps. The first contained underthings and Nathan's books. The second held the dresses that Nathan had bought. I was fourteen the last time I tried on those garments. I stopped growing in height at about that time, but my body had filled out in other ways since then. After shaking out each garment, I chose the larger of the two and folded the other for repacking. When I bent over the bag, a familiar scrap of delicate lawn fabric peeping out from the edge of a rough covering stilled my hand. I opened the canvas bag and gently lifted tissue light material to my cheek.

That a faint whiff of Mama's favorite scent still lingered in her handkerchief after so many years was amazing, but that it was almost pristine was nothing short of a miracle. Tears welled up as I realized I would never be able to thank Fatima for preserving it for me. I felt hard edges within the little bag and withdrew my second talisman. A young handsome Papa in his captain's gray stared up from astride his war stallion. It would have been a luxury to give in, to lie prostrate across the bed and to howl my sorrow, but a strong sense of self-preservation demanded that grief be packed away.

Dashing away my tears, I placed my soiled riding costume in the carpetbag's bottom, replaced the other items, and buckled the clasps. Riding boots would make a strange complement for the green and pink rosebud sprigged muslin day dress, but it couldn't be helped. The soft cream colored leather slippers that completed the ensemble were unsuitable for walking Igaupe's dirty cobblestone streets. I tugged the dress on, praying its buttons would fasten. As predicted, its full skirt dropped to the appropriate length, barely brushing the floor. The long sleeves trimmed with velvet ribbon ended at my wrists just beyond the little round bump of bone. The real test would be the bust. I sucked in and hunched my shoulders to make the buttons meet their corresponding holes across my chest. The bodice was uncomfortable, but this dress would have to do since my only other choices were my filthy riding habit or a dress that would be obscenely tight. Thus adorned, I sat on the bed's edge waiting for the next phase of my life to begin.

## Chapter 30

I didn't have a long wait, for a new guide appeared shortly. Her brown and white habit announced her vocation as a Carmelite nun. From the open wall, she beckoned silently.

Now that the time to depart Brazil had actually arrived, trepidation grew into sharp reluctance. For the second time in my life, I was on the verge of leaving behind all that was familiar, all that was home. At this point, I had spent more years in Brazil than America. I felt Brazilian. I thought and dreamt in Portuguese. When I closed my eyes, I could no longer visualize America in anything other than vague impressions.

"Are you taking me to the ship now, Sister?"

"Daughter, it would be best if we did not converse. When it is appropriate for you to speak, I will guide you. Please understand it is for the best."

As kind as her tone was, the nun's words did nothing to calm my singing nerves. With each step we took away from the church in its squalid slum, the tighter the muscles at the base of my skull became. By the time we passed the lovely public gardens I recognized from my first trip through the city almost twelve years ago, I feared I might have to excuse myself behind some obliging shrubbery in order to be sick.

Before the day was done, I would be required to pack away my Brazilian self forever. It would be as if Maria Dias Oliveira never existed. Although she was an alias invented out necessity, she felt most like my true identity because she was my adult self. In many respects, I became Maria the night I fled Little Georgia and took control of my future. Mary Catherine MacDonald existed only in the distant past of childhood. She had become like a relative who seldom visits, a person whom I was supposed to know, but whom I was having trouble remembering.

As we left the street and stepped onto the expansive wooden docks, a flurry of activity around one particular steamship drew my attention. Longshoremen shouted and cursed while they hauled on ropes hoisting aloft nets filled with bags labeled *cafe* and *acucar*—coffee and sugar, Brazil's chief exports. At the gangway, two gentlemen in light summer suits and straw boaters waited. They appeared to be chatting animatedly and when the nearer one turned to point at something on the docks behind us, his eyes swept over me twice and he tipped his hat before he continued his conversation. He was youngish and reasonably nice looking, but he might not have existed for all I cared. The furthest thing from my mind was male attention. From his hand hung a satchel like the one Gus brought back from France for transporting important papers.

The steamship's ironclad hull dwarfed the humans on the dock below, and her smokestacks and masts soared so far into the blue morning sky I had to crane my neck to see their tops. She was a new type of ship. Instead of paddlewheels or masts alone, submerged metal blades fitted to the stern propelled her. Gus had traveled on just such a ship when returning from his European exile. He had called the apparatus a screw because it turned round in that fashion.

A steamship's propeller and a leather satchel—two unrelated utilitarian items, but merely thinking about them brought tears to my eyes. Connections with Gus had unexpectedly appeared in the most ordinary things, catching me off guard and sending knives through my heart. Since his murder, I had kept my grief locked away in a strongbox created by the demands of self-preservation, but with safety now in sight, grief slipped its bonds. Perhaps it was well that I faced a long sea voyage among strangers.

My escort hurried across the long dock's massive wooden planks toward the gangway, but before we were half the distance, she glanced at my left hand and whispered, "Remove your wedding ring."

My shock must have shown, because she continued, "It made buying a ticket for an unaccompanied female simpler if you travel as an unmarried woman."

Pretending a misstep, I turned my back to the ship and ran my fingers under my skirt. As I placed the ring in the top of my boot for safekeeping, a feeling of desolation descended. Removing the ring from my finger was another betrayal of Gus and I knew it would not be the last. In denying I was his widow, I was erasing him from my life.

The bursar greeted us as we approached the gangway and the nun produced my travel contract. "Sister, you aren't traveling with us?"

"Only my young charge is going to enjoy an adventure."

He glanced at the document and then looked at me in some curiosity. "You have family in New York?"

"Yes. She is going to her uncle and aunt."

It was well the nun answered for me because I was beyond coherent speech. Until that moment, I had assumed I was being sent back to Georgia via Savannah or Mobile and thus home to Oconee. The hope of seeing Bess and my aunts again had kept complete despair at bay.

"It must be difficult for her parents to send her so far away."

"It would be, but sadly, she is orphaned."

"The contract lists her as unmarried American?"

"May I ask why my charge's personal details are of such interest to you, young man?" The nun's raised eyebrow should have been sufficient warning, but the bursar's gaze was still on my travel document.

"Ship's regulations, Sister. I assure you I meant nothing improper." He glanced up as he folded the papers and returned them.

"Perhaps I should speak with your captain? My charge's safety is of the utmost importance to her relatives and to an important Church official who happens to be her cousin." The nun fixed the poor bursar with the time honored glare employed by mothers, schoolmarms, and mother superiors the world over.

The young man's face flamed as he stammered, "That is completely unnecessary. Welcome aboard the *New Amsterdam*, Miss MacDonald. Sister, please listen for the all ashore."

I could feel the bursar's curious gaze following us up the gangway. Leaning close to the nun, I whispered, "He doesn't believe you. What if he reports us to his captain, or worse, the militia?"

"He will do no such thing. He may not believe everything I said, but he will not contradict me. After all, I have God on my side." When she looked back, I saw humor dancing in her eyes. "Come, child, you are safe now. No one will look for you here."

I heaved my bags along without further comment. We reached the main deck and were directed below to my berth in a cramped dark cabin that contained two beds built into the wall, one above the other. The two men who boarded the ship before us were, so far as I knew, the only other passengers and I prayed I would have the cabin to myself. I understood how a wounded animal must feel when injury drives it to creep away and hide in isolation until either healing or death over takes it.

"It's Spartan, but this is the only ship leaving for the United States this week. We're fortunate this is a cargo ship that takes only the occasional passenger. The chances of encountering someone who might recognize you are greatly reduced. After your ticket was purchased, there was very little money left. You must use it wisely." The nun pulled a small reticule that had seen better days from her voluminous habit and pressed it into my hand.

Within the folds of the worn velvet lay ten large silver coins and an envelope addressed to Father James Boyce, Church of Saint Teresa, 141 Henry St.

"When you arrive in New York, go directly to the church. The parish assists immigrants. Perhaps they can help you find work and lodging. I know it's not much, but it was the best we could do under the circumstances."

A voice called the all ashore and the nun grasped the doorknob, but she turned back when I placed a hand on her arm. "Sister, thank you for everything you've done. You all have risked a lot for me. I don't deserve your kindness, but I will be forever grateful. Please let the others know."

She smiled and took my hand in both of hers. "My child, I can't imagine why you feel undeserving. You're surely too young to have sinned so greatly that you are removed from God's love. Go in peace. My sisters and I will pray for your safe arrival." She squeezed my hand then the door clicked softly closed.

Tears again. If she only knew my crimes, the sister might not be so compassionate. For the present and probably years to come, I knew I would grapple with the choices I had made and their consequences. Finally alone, their full force roared down in an avalanche of bitterness and regret. It felt right to take hold of the horror and examine it. Summarizing my crimes would be splendid torture, so I made a mental list. My beautiful, young husband had died because I was bored and wanted to play the lady bountiful with his family's position and wealth. Because of my deceit, his throat was slit and his father was kidnapped. My despised uncle and his innocent wife, a woman I had never met, died because I sent murderers to find them and then felt an illicit joy when I learned their fate. Of course, I told myself I acted in defense of Gus's family, a family that repaid my protection with accusations of complicity in my husband's murder and father-in-law's abduction. Even though I had killed a man in their defense, the Oliveiras had abandoned me to be tried and hanged. A cycle of never ending betrayals—enough for several lifetimes.

I buried my face in the rough cotton covering of the bunk's pillow and howled. I stuffed my fist into my mouth to block the sound's escape and bit down hard to inflict pain. I deserved punishment, needed it. Without it, I knew I would go mad. Time became of no consequence.

"Miss MacDonald." A male voice accompanied rapping at the cabin door. "Captain Van Der Beck sends his compliments and wishes to know if you will be joining the other passengers for dinner."

The setting sun, reflected from Atlantic waves, danced in odd patterns on the wall opposite the cabin's single porthole. I sat up and glanced at my reflection in the small mirror above the washstand across from the bunk. A frightful looking girl with red rimmed eyes and wildly disheveled hair greeted me.

Additional knocking. "Miss, is everything all right?"

"When is dinner served?"

"The others have already gathered in the mess. I was sent to escort you."

"I've been resting. Please give me a moment to tidy up."

Quickly, I removed the ridiculous riding boots, but a ping on the floor sent me prostrate. I caught my ring just before it disappeared into a separation in the floorboards. I hugged the ring to me as if it were an endangered child instead of a thin gold trinket. Shaken by the prospect of losing the only tangible proof that Gus had lived, I untied my chemise's ribbons and slipped them through my ring. From now on, it would be tied over my heart until I could afford a chain on which to wear it.

Next, I dug Mama's handkerchief and Papa's tintype from the bottom of their carpetbag. I felt like a foolish child clinging to scraps of metal and linen for comfort, but infantile actions were preferable if they kept complete despair at bay. I wrapped the portrait in the linen, returned them to the little bag Fatima had made, and tied it to the waist of my pantaloons. The secret attachments bumped reassuringly against my skin as I removed the delicate leather slippers from their hiding place in the carpetbag.

I was dragging a brush through the mass of dark auburn curls, when the man in the hall spoke again. "Miss, we really must not keep the others waiting any longer. Captain doesn't abide cold food. Please, Miss."

With no time to put my hair up, I left it trailing down my back, dashed some cold water on my face, and took a last look in the mirror. A wild haired girl, one at least five years younger than my real age, stared back at me with wide, sad eyes.

Conversation ceased as five men rose from the mess table when I entered the room—the captain, his first officer, the bursar, and the two passengers.

"Please see you do not keep us waiting in the future, young lady," the captain directed in flawless Portuguese. Captain Van Der Beck, from his gray-flecked mutton chop whiskers to his navy uniform with its shiny brass buttons, was so much the expected image it was like greeting Commodore Perry in the flesh.

"*Eu desculpo-me.*" I dropped my eyes to hide my embarrassment and took the chair pulled out for me by the steward.

After making cursory introductions, the captain nodded and the steward served each of us from several dishes. The excellent meal of fresh fish in a lemon butter sauce, fruit, and salad progressed to the tones of polite dinner conversation conducted solely in English. I don't think the gentlemen intended rudeness, but they had resumed their discussion of the import/export business and I'm sure they assumed I would have nothing to contribute. For my part, I was relieved to be left alone to let my thoughts drift.

"Are you distressed to be leaving Brazil, Miss MacDonald? It's such a beautiful country to call home."

The question caught me off guard. My gaze darted from my plate to the speaker. It was the younger of the passengers. His deep blue eyes looked into mine with a friendly curiosity. My tongue froze.

"I'm not sure the young lady understands, Mr. Atwell. Perhaps you should repeat your question in Portuguese."

"Alas, Captain, my Portuguese is nonexistent. I assumed with her name, she would surely speak English."

"That would depend on how long her family was in Brazil. Most of these Confederados cling to their native customs, including language, but a few have abandoned everything related to their former nation. They've made themselves foreigners either way."

"Do you think that an undesirable state, being a foreigner?"

"Not as long as they stay where they belong. New York's overrun with 'em, breeding like rabbits and more pouring in every day. I'm glad to deal mainly with cargo, I can tell you."

"But surely we were all immigrants at some point in our ancestries. Why should others be denied our opportunities?"

"When did you last travel through the Lower Eastside, sir? The stench in summer alone is enough to make decent folk ill. Disease, filth, depravity, vice, and a veritable Tower of Babel to boot. It's a disgrace, a blight upon our fair city."

"Poverty does have its disadvantages, that's for certain."

Mr. Atwell's words were shocking and I considered giving him a piece of my mind, but the glint of anger in his eyes and the trace of irony in his slightly raised brow kept me quiet. As I studied him, I noticed for the first time the fine cut of his suit and the expensive gold watch fob and chain hanging from his waistcoat. His age was difficult to judge, not young exactly, but not particularly old either. There was no gray in his Anglo-Saxon straw blond hair, but crow's feet featured prominently about his eyes. He must have felt my gaze on him, for he glanced at me and smiled. I averted my eyes at once.

The subject turned to news of the war between Russia and the Ottoman Empire, but Mr. Atwell continued to glance in my direction from time to time. When the meal ended, I made my excuses in Portuguese.

Mr. Atwell bowed slightly as I placed my hand on his outstretched palm. "Miss MacDonald, I look forward to your charming company during this long, and it is hoped, uneventful voyage." When he looked up, I believe he saw signs of comprehension because he smiled conspiratorially.

Someone had lit the two small oil sconce lamps in my cabin, suffusing it with a golden glow that didn't quite chase the shadows from the corners. I slumped down on my bunk and wondered how on earth I would fill my time during the three weeks at sea. I had no work or anyone to talk with. Opportunities for exercise would be limited to strolling the open decks in good weather and walking the few halls where passengers were allowed when it turned inclement. The only saving grace I had seen so far was in the officers' mess. Tucked into a corner next to a window was a small grouping of armchairs in front of bookshelves crammed end-to-end with volumes of varying heights and thicknesses. I doubted the reading material would contain much in the way of entertainment, but their use would surely enrich my education.

Despite my exhaustion, going to bed straight away was unappealing. I sighed heavily and decided that unpacking my few possessions and trying to clean my filthy riding habit might be the best use of time. The carpetbags felt familiarly heavy as I dragged them over by the bed. It was some comfort that I wouldn't have to carry them everywhere for a while. I opened the nearer bag and removed my undergarments.

All thoughts of clothing care disappeared, for under the chemises and pantaloons lay answers to my quest for occupation and perhaps to questions that had plagued me for years. Why I hadn't thought of this before now was a puzzle. I pulled the volume from the bottom of the stack and opened its cracked leather cover.

## Chapter 31

"I see you have found absorbing reading material. Is it from among the volumes in the officers' mess?" Mr. Atwell took the deck chair beside mine and opened a mighty tome of his own. The captain had made a small shaded upper deck available for his passengers' use, but I usually had it to myself during the heat of the day.

"This? No, it's something I brought with me."

"I knew it! You do speak English. If I may ask, why the deception?"

"I didn't intend to deceive. I was exhausted when we first set sail and took the path of least resistance."

"A path you have managed to maintain with skill and aplomb for over a week now. May I let the others in on the secret?"

"Do as you wish. It is of no consequence to me. Now if you will excuse me . . ."

I was appalled at my rudeness. The man was simply making polite conversation, even if he was a little too inquisitive for my liking. Although I was now completely alone in the world, I found I wanted as little contact with other people as possible. That is why I sat in the heat when others sought the cooler interiors with their cross breezes drawn through open portholes and iced drinks offered by the captain's steward. Once we crossed the equator, midday temperatures were quite intense. I tried to ignore my deck companion by concentrating on my reading material.

Nathan's journals were filled with golden nuggets of information interspersed with long passages of the truly mundane, but I read every word as though it was manna for the starving. There were two passages that burned themselves into my memory almost by rote because I poured over them countless times, scouring them for additional meaning and insight with each reading.

The first was toward the end of the earliest journal and shed light on events that greatly impacted my uncle's disposition and outlook.

*June 15, 1853*

*India has thrown me over. I cannot believe it! And all because her little nigger bitch purposefully spilled coffee on me. She knew I wouldn't have her in the house once India and I married, not with her clubfoot thumping on the floorboards and embarrassing guests. The thrashing I gave her was her just desserts for the burns on my thigh and ruining my second best breeches. She planned it and then tried to make it seem an accident and India believed her. Believed her and took her side! Oh, Lord, my heart is broken on account of a worthless slave!*

Although I would never have the chance to meet Papa's first cousin, India MacDonald, as she had died in an influenza outbreak before I was born, I knew from this paragraph alone that I would have liked her immensely. How like my uncle to blame his misery on one who couldn't fight back. How fortunate for Cousin India that she saw him for what he was before they married.

I found the second significant entry in the final pages of the last journal. After that passage, the writing became infrequent and the dates farther apart until they finally petered out altogether. Why Nathan stopped recording his thoughts was unclear. Perhaps his marriage brought about the peace he had sought, but not found, through his writing.

*December 1869*

*Jonathan has gotten himself drowned and I have come to regret not helping him for I am now saddled with his brat. Brother Williams was implacable and advertised my promise to Mary Elizabeth where others from the colony could hear. I can barely tolerate looking at that wretched girl, much less caring for her. She killed my sister with her willful disobedience and everyday her appearance becomes a greater reproach from the past. She looks so much like India I can hardly stand the sight of her. If I were allowed to go back in time, I would pull Jonathan from the river when he lost his footing during our last argument, but all I could think of at the time was protecting what was mine. At least I will not have to share the gold now. How he found out about it is a mystery.*

So now I had the answer. Nathan hadn't acted overtly, but he had contributed to Papa's death as surely as if his hand had held Papa under the water. Each of us, my uncle and I, had inflicted great harm on the other. A wave of guilt washed over me as I thought about how my actions had led to Mama's illness and death, but the actions of a nine year old were in no way comparable to those of a grown man. I truly saved Gus's mother and grandmother from the intruders, but at a terrible price for my uncle and his innocent wife. Part of me still rejoiced at the thought of Nathan's suffering and my part in it and it appalled me.

I finished the final page of the last journal as Nassau's roofs appeared over the *New Amsterdam's* bow. The little library in the corner of officers' mess with its comfortable leather club chairs would probably be deserted for the majority of the day and I planned to take advantage of its shelves while others roamed about the Bahamian capital. I had just settled myself with a selected volume when the outer door opened.

"Not going ashore, Miss MacDonald? It's a beautiful day for an excursion." Robert Atwell's pleasant features appeared as he doffed a handsome Panama hat. "Perhaps you are in need of an escort?"

"I thought reading might prove more entertaining and instructive."

"But surely a young lady would prefer luncheon in a charming seaside establishment to reading a dull . . . What's that you've got there?"

"Dumas. *Count of Monte Cristo,* which I assure you is anything but dull."

"And in the French, no less. Miss MacDonald, you are certainly a woman of accomplishments. But please, won't you allow me to show you about and give you lunch?"

Rebuffing his quiet, persistent attention was becoming burdensome. I really didn't want to seem rude, but my broken heart did not want or need male companionship, even of the kindly platonic sort. I gazed up prepared to refuse his company once again, but found such an imploring expression in his eyes that I hesitated.

The tops of his ears turned red as he continued, "Please forgive me. You want time to yourself and I am being a nuisance. I hope you will forgive my intrusion."

As he turned to go, he looked so forlorn I found I couldn't let him leave thinking so poorly of himself. "Mr. Atwell, you are the kindest of gentlemen. It's just that I am recently bereaved and I'm finding social demands difficult at present. Please, I hope you can understand."

He stopped at the door and turned back. "I may understand more than you realize. If I may?" He took the chair next to mine. "I became a widower last winter and the loneliness is sometimes more than I can bear. This trip was ostensibly for business, but my partner also hoped it would take my mind off my grief. In some ways, it has worked wonders. You remind me of my dear wife. Your quiet grace and coloring are hers. I hope it is not insulting that I find a little peace just being in your presence."

My mouth opened and then closed. For the first time in quite a while I considered that someone else might be in pain and in need of consolation. Perhaps taking advantage of the opportunity to focus on troubles not my own might be good for me. Finally, I replied, "I'm honored to be so favorably compared. She must have been a wonderful woman to command such devotion. Thank you for the invitation. Will you wait for me to change into shoes more suitable for walking out?"

Surprise, then pleasure, suffused my companion's face. When I returned in my riding skirt, blouse, and boots, we departed for the markets and shops of Nassau. We took luncheon in a little shop run by a British lady who had done her best to recreate her little corner of Cornwall in the tropical climate. Robert ordered and presently our hostess placed a savory pie before us accompanied by salad and fresh fruit. The pie was unlike any I had ever seen. Protruding from the crust were shrimp heads, eyes, whiskers, and all.

Robert grinned at my surprise. "Don't be put off by the heads. I promise it's delicious. This Caribbean version of stargazy pie is considered quite a delicacy among the local British. Well, perhaps I exaggerate, but tuck in without fear!"

And it was surprisingly good, so much so, I forgot my manners and inhaled my portion. Catching Robert's amused gaze on me, warmth rose from my throat up to my cheeks.

"I'm glad you are enjoying your lunch. And I hope you will permit me to purchase a remembrance of today's adventure as a gift in gratitude for your delightful company. I intend to have one for myself."

"Thank you for everything, but I couldn't possibly accept a gift from a gentleman of such a brief acquaintance. I really couldn't. You've spent far too much already." It felt as though I was babbling, unable to find a sensible end to my reply.

When I stumbled to a verbal halt, Robert picked up his theme again. "That's the thing about the islands. Nothing really costs very much, so the money is a trifle." He paused and looked out over the azure sea. "You know, Miss MacDonald, Mary Catherine if I may, I rather hoped we had become more than just casual acquaintances these weeks. I hoped we might have become friends."

I was taken aback by what sounded like real sadness in his voice and I felt a small regret that I could not offer him encouragement. "I'm sorry. I didn't mean to be harsh or sound so prudish. Of course we're friends."

"Then you must allow your friend to buy you a small token."

We spent the rest of the excursion strolling among the stalls along the harbor. It was from one of those vendors that Robert bought a beautiful little flower basket constructed entirely from local shells woven together with wire. The delicate pink and white creation was unlike anything I had never seen. The seller wrapped it with great care and placed it lovingly in my hands.

"Your wife, she gonna be likin' de basket for a long time. I made it real good."

I could feel my face glowing hot as Robert laughed and replied, "Yes, I'm sure you're right."

For the remainder of the voyage, Robert continued to pay me quiet, respectful attention, never pressing nor presuming, but always present. I must admit the morning we steamed toward our final destination, I felt a small regret that I would never see Mr. Atwell again. It would be for the best, however, because our situations were so far removed from one another—he was a wealthy merchant banker from an old patrician New England family and I was . . . well, that was the problem. I wasn't really sure who I was, much less how I was to make my way in a strange world where women were not allowed to earn their keep by honest means other than going into service. Without references, I knew I had little chance of securing a position as even a scullery maid. As I stood on the main deck watching seamen lower the *New Amsterdam's* gangway onto the pier, real terror gripped me heart and soul.

"Are your aunt and uncle meeting you?" Robert's silent appearance at my elbow made me jump.

"Yes. They sent word that I'm to wait for them at the Emigration Depot. They've been delayed."

"I see." He leaned on the railing and observed the docking of a large passenger steamer whose decks were filled with people, many of whom were clearly immigrants. He remained quiet for several minutes and then said rather wistfully, "You know, Mary Catherine, there's no need for you to hang about Castle Garden alone among all those strangers. My driver's waiting for me now. As soon as you've cleared entry, I can deliver you directly to your relatives' home."

"That's very kind, Robert, but I'm afraid I must decline. My uncle was adamant that they would only be delayed for a short while. I can't let them come down here and think me missing. They'd be very upset."

"Of course. I didn't think of that."

He looked truly crestfallen. I felt guilty for the lies and for rebuffing his kindness. He lingered with me at the rail until his business partner came bustling toward us waving a scrap of paper.

"Atwell, we can't stand around all day socializing! I've had the most urgent message from the bank." He paused long enough to tip his hat. "Pardon my intrusion, Miss MacDonald. Get your things, man. We must be on our way." His final words were flung back over his shoulder as he whirled away toward the gangplank.

Looking slightly embarrassed, Robert turned to me. "I'm afraid he's something of a tyrant when it comes to business matters, but I don't know what I would have done without him this past year. Mary Catherine, may I call upon you once you're settled? If you'll be so kind as to give me your relatives' address, I promise not to make a pest of myself."

"I'm sorry, but I'm not sure of their exact address." Feeling somewhat panicky made my words blunt and curt.

Reaching into his pocket, Robert produced a calling card on the back of which he wrote two addresses, one for the bank and the other presumably for his home. "I hope you will accept my card. If ever you're in need, no matter the reason, I hope you will call upon me. It would be an honor to be of service."

"Thank you, Robert. You're very kind. I wish you well. Now if you'll excuse me, I must see to my baggage."

I simply had to escape before more lies were necessary. Robert Atwell was a nice, kind man, but he would be horrified if he knew the truth. Although I had no experience of patrician New Englanders, I knew enough about the wealthy to realize he would abandon any association with me once he learned my history. What he believed he saw in me was merely an illusion of his own making.

After disembarking, I joined the long line of immigrants from the other ship as they shuffled toward Castle Garden's huge glass domed reception hall. Once we were inside, we were herded into groups waiting before one of six or so desks behind which sat men charged with examining our travel documents. When my turn came, I found myself standing before a plump New York State immigration commissioner with a bad cough and a runny nose that he mopped frequently with a dirty handkerchief.

"You ain't been through quarantine! How'd that happen?" The commissioner thumbed through my travel documents with ill grace.

"I'm really not sure. I came to this building straight from the ship. There was no mention of quarantine."

"*New Amsterdam,* huh? Hell, that's a cargo ship ain't it? Why we allow 'em to bring in passengers is beyond me. Happens every time."

"I believe my documents are in order. I assure you I am in good health. Won't you please let me pass through?"

"You ain't going nowhere without a health inspection. Go sit on that bench until I can get a doctor to look you over."

And so I waited. The sun was even with the rooftops when the man finally waved me back to his table.

"Should have told me you was by yourself. Medical exam'll be a waste of time. New York don't admit unaccompanied single females. There's a boat sailing for Rio de Janeiro next week. You can stay here until it goes."

"But I'm an American. Surely you have to let me into my own country."

"You may have an American name, but you don't sound like one. Got any proof of nationality? Thought not."

This was an eventuality I had never considered. It was true that my English, once so syrupy, had lost some of its drawl and had become tinted by Brazilian Portuguese.

I sat alone on my bench and pondered my plight. Just how does one go about proving one's identity without any actual documents? It occurred to me that Nathan's journals might offer the needed evidence, but when I opened the carpetbag containing his handwritten volumes a better possibility presented itself. I had completely forgotten I carried the Jordan family Bible. I hadn't even looked beneath its cover in all the weeks since I fled Little Georgia with the militia at my back.

The cracked leather bindings were tooled with an ornate gold filigree pattern, suitable ornamentation for the sacred text within. Surely within the first pages of this huge edition would be a family tree in keeping with the tradition of such Bibles. These books had served generations of families as a written record of important events. The question would be whether the locations of those events were included.

Under the flyleaf, I found what I was looking for. Page after page of Jordan relatives were entered in flowing script, beginning with an ancestor who arrived at Williamsburg, Virginia in 1700 and ending with Nathan's marriage. The keepers of this official family history had been meticulous in their recordkeeping, for each entry contained not only dates and the full names of all involved, but also annotations of other pertinent information. Anxiously I flipped back a page and there it was at the end of a long list of grandparents, great-grandparents, uncles, aunts, and cousins: Mary Catherine MacDonald, born to Jonathan Alexander MacDonald and Mary Elizabeth Jordan MacDonald, January 1, 1857, MacDonald farm, Washington County, Georgia.

"And how do I know this is you?" My interrogator was not going to be forestalled in his quest to follow the letter of New York state emigration statute.

In desperation, I took a risk. "Open it anywhere and ask me something about one of the people listed." I prayed all of the family history imparted over the years would come back to me.

After several questions, he closed the Bible and said, "Looks like you may be who you claim, but I cain't make the decision. You'll have to wait 'til the chief returns."

"And how long will that be?"

"Not sure. He left two days ago to attend a funeral. May be back by the end of the week."

My heart sank to my boots. It was Tuesday and my little hoard of silver dollars had already been reduced by the need to purchase food and toiletry items. While there were no beds available at the Garden, large waiting areas, segregated by gender, with washrooms at their ends provided a chance to clean oneself and try to nap sitting upright with one's back against a wall or to lie across one of the numerous benches if there weren't too many others experiencing delayed entry. I was grateful for the large potbellied stove that poured out anthracite-fired heat in the center of the room. I had left Brazil at the height of summer, which of course was in December. Fatima had been thoughtful enough to pack a heavy cloak under the light day dresses. It was another kindness that I would never be able to return.

Friday morning dawned bitter with lowering clouds promising snow. Despite the considerable efforts of the building's stoves, cold winds howled about the Garden and crept in under the doors and around the windows. I pulled my cloak tightly about my shoulders and sat on the floor as close to the heat as I dared. About noon, a uniformed emigration official appeared at the door of the women's hall and called my name.

He escorted me to an office where a uniformed gentleman sat behind an expansive oak desk. "Miss MacDonald? May I examine your Bible?"

I lifted it from its bag and slide it across the desk. "The page you wish is the next to last in the family history. You'll find my birth at the bottom of the page."

He didn't speak or look up. After what felt like an eternity, he asked, "Who was Eliana Jordan?"

I had no idea. Based on her name alone, I made a guess. "She was my mother's eldest brother's wife. Uncle Nathan didn't marry until fairly late in life. He met her after we went to Brazil."

He looked up, frowning. "Just why did you go to Brazil?"

I wasn't sure what to say, so I told him the truth.

"So, your father didn't want to live under Reconstruction. Guess he never took the loyalty oath then?"

"I don't really know. Is it important?"

"Without it, his citizenship was never restored. Did you become citizens of Brazil?"

"I don't think so. I'm not sure what the rules are, but we never got any papers saying anything about it."

"Well, my dear, it looks like you may be a person without a country."

"But I was born in Georgia." My voice sounded feeble and uncertain.

"As that may be, I can't let you cross into New York without this being cleared up. We don't admit single, unaccompanied females."

Heart in my throat, I stumbled back into the women's waiting room and slumped down on a bench close to the stove. The temperature outside was dropping by the minute. The doors did little to keep the gusts from whirling into the room. As much as the fire within it roared, the stove was unequal to its task. I spent the rest of that day and all of the night shivering and trying to decide what I would do if I weren't allowed into the country. Nothing came to me. I began to deeply regret not accepting Robert's help, but there was no way to get a message to him. I would simply have to wait and pray that my citizenship would be established.

After two more days of waiting and worrying, a commissioner approached and said without preamble or explanation, "You've been cleared for entry, Miss. If I were you, I'd get wherever you're going fast. Snow's begun falling and it has the looks of a blizzard in the making."

He escorted me to the heavily fortified front doors that had once secured the building when it had been a military fort. Opening a small people sized portal, he placed a city map in my hand and then waved me out into the elements.

"You mind what I said about the weather, Miss." The door closed with a solid thud and I found myself alone in an unfathomably strange city where white flakes had begun to swirl.

## Chapter 32

I stood on the corner of an intersection completely befuddled and shivering violently. I had no understanding of the city at all. I would have no choice but to spend a portion of my meager funds to hire a hansom to deliver me to Saint Teresa's door or risk freezing to death in the unaccustomed temperature that dropped by the minute. The city was unlike anything I had ever experienced. The buildings were so close together that the only way to see the sky was to look straight up. Their hulking forms hovered over the streets below them, looking down on all who passed with grim eyes that seemed to miss nothing, evaluating everyone and everything and finding all wanting. And every street looked the same. It was just one long line of multi-storied structures after another with little to distinguish each from its neighbors. I knew how to follow a woodland track and had paddled a canoe into unknown waters, but the sheer masses of wood and stone piled one upon the other for as far as the eye could see in all directions left me confused and disoriented. I hailed the first hansom cab to appear in several minutes and scrambled into its dark leather-bound interior.

Once enclosed in the relative safety of the cab, I watched the city unfold around me as we advanced north through teaming tenement slums that looked as if they might fall in on one another at any moment. I could have sworn that some of the buildings actually swayed as the wind blasted them from one direction and then another. Someone had forgotten their laundry, frozen stiff in the mixture of sleet and snow that was now coming down in earnest. It hung out over the street on a line strung from building to building, looking like the signal flags on ships. Refuse piled on curbs would have sent up a mighty stench, if not for the cold.

Presently, the cab pulled to a stop. The street signs declared we were at the intersection of Henry and Rutgers. On the eastern corner stood a beautiful gray stone Gothic style church, complete with bell tower and clock. I paid the cabbie, who stubbornly remained on his box, refusing to help with my bags. A sudden gust of wind threatened to send me sprawling and I hurried up the church steps into the welcome warmth of the narthex. For the first time in what seemed like years, I felt safe. I had no idea what my future held, but at least I could lose myself in the city. I was just another anonymous immigrant, coming to seek her fortune and to forget. Brazilian or American? It didn't matter which was my true identity. Brazil was another life, another world, one whose grip on my mind and heart I hoped would quickly fade.

Only two events after my arrival at Saint Teresa's bear importance in this accounting, for they were again life changing. After weeks of seeking employment and finding none, I found myself without a home or friends to whom I could turn. The church could do no more for me. There were too many in need to allow one person to depend on it forever. It was then that I drew Robert Atwell's card from my pocket and tapped it against my palm as I tried to decide what to do. The tearoom in which I sat was becoming crowded with noon customers and the manager lost patience with my penny purchases of tea.

"You've been here all morning. Either buy food or leave. Other customers want this table."

"At least may I finish this last cup? I promise I won't be long."

"Make it fast and bus the table before you go." The man glared once more before turning away. I could hear him muttering as he headed back to his counter and the line of customers waiting there. "Don't know why I tolerate these confounded foreigners . . ."

I peeked into the pot and saw about half a cup of tea. Because I hadn't eaten since breakfast the day before, I poured out the dregs into my cup, followed by as much sugar as I thought I could stand and then topped it to the rim with milk. Not much of a meal, but it would have to do. I couldn't afford anything else. The intensely sweet milky liquid provided the last warmth I could expect until I was able to find shelter in a library or train station—any place where I could be anonymous and left alone. Before rising from the table, I glanced again at Robert's card. I had passed his bank several times since leaving Castle Garden. Once in fear and despair, I had placed my hand on its brass embossed front door, but the doorman demanded to know my business and I couldn't bring myself to admit that I was there to beg. Now I put pride into the darkest recess of my being, closed the door, and locked it tight.

A fifteen-minute walk brought me again to the bank's front entrance. This time when the doorman demanded that I state my business, I produced Robert's card and asked to be shown to his office. The doorman looked at it then turned it over. It must have been the handwritten addresses on the back that finally convinced him to allow me admittance. I was conducted up a marble staircase to the third floor where executive offices lined a central hall. A plush carpet runner stretched along highly polished mahogany floors, softening the footsteps of visitors. Robert's office was at the end of the hall on the north side. His double mahogany doors bore a simple inscription in elaborate gold leaf: Robert G. Atwell, President. I paused and checked my image in a large mirror hung over an ornate Louis VX commode. I had done the best I could to make myself neat and clean, but my riding costume was the worse for constant wear and my hair needed more pins. A newspaper lay on the chest and I tore a half sheet from its underside, which I applied vigorously to the toes of my now shabby boots.

Robert's clerk looked up in curiosity when I entered. His eyes swept over me from head to toe. He couldn't hide his distaste.

"Have you become lost? If you will return to the grand staircase and go back down to the lobby, someone there will direct you."

"I am here to see Mr. Atwell."

"That will not be possible. Mr. Atwell is a very busy man. Please return to the lobby."

"Please. Show him this card and tell him Mary Catherine MacDonald has come to take him up on his offer."

The clerk looked at the smudged, dog-eared little cream rectangle and turned it over. His head snapped up, his eyes wide as he looked at me with new respect. He clearly recognized his employer's handwriting. He disappeared behind the door marked Mr. Atwell and returned within a few seconds.

"This way, miss."

Robert rose and came around his desk, holding out both of his hands in greeting. "Mary Catherine! It's wonderful to see you. Please sit. Can I offer you anything? I was just about to send my clerk for sandwiches. May I order for you as well? Or perhaps you would prefer to go to a restaurant?"

"Thank you, Robert. Sandwiches here would be most welcome."

As hard as he tried to hide his surprise, I could see the change in my situation had not escaped his notice. After the clerk left with the luncheon orders, Robert asked, "I am delighted to see you, Mary Catherine. May I ask to what I owe the pleasure?"

"Robert, I need a job."

And he gave me one, just like that. It had been so easy. As unconventional as it was, I became a translator in the bank's international business department. After a year, I advanced to become Robert's personal assistant, much to the disgust of the other employees, all male except for the cleaning women who came at night after everyone else left. It was unheard of for a woman to do such work and I became an object of great curiosity and discussion.

One late afternoon about two years after Robert first gave me a job, he gathered up the papers we had been working on and placed them into his satchel. When I turned to leave the office, he placed his hand on my arm. "Please have dinner with me. I've booked a table at Delmonico's. It's just a short walk and it looks to be lovely out."

And it was. We walked the few blocks to the restaurant in the glow of a beautiful spring evening. There was just a hint of warmth on the light breeze that rustled through the tulips and irises in the little park we traversed on our way. I sensed Robert had something on his mind when he took my hand and rather absentmindedly tucked it into the crook of his arm. Although we had walked out together on other occasions, he had never acted with such possessiveness.

He had ordered an excellent meal of lobster Newberg and salad, followed by an extraordinary concoction of ice cream surrounded by sponge cake covered in a lightly browned meringue. When the coffee was served, Robert suddenly fell quiet. His countenance became quite serious as he placed a small box on the table.

"I've had this for a while now. I've just been waiting for the right time. Open it."

The little blue leather box was one that any New Yorker would recognize. Inside, nestled in plush velvet, was a three-carat diamond solitaire, the famous Tiffany setting, so desired by princes and paupers alike. I was speechless.

"Please put it on and say you will become my wife."

It would be disingenuous to say that I was completely taken by surprise. Robert had been showing me more than an employer's interest for a while, but we had spent little time together outside of the bank. I had never even been to his house nor he to the home where I rented a room from the chief teller and his wife.

"Robert, your offer is generous and you are a wonderful man, but please understand I can't give you an answer now. There are things you must know about me. When you do, you may change your mind." I needed time to think. I had married Gus in haste, against my better judgment, and in defiance of society. I had loved him fiercely, passionately, deeply, and I wasn't sure I would be capable of that kind of love again. Robert deserved better. He didn't even know my true story.

And so I told him everything. As unjust as it might seem, it was a sort of test for both of us. I needed to see his reaction to my past. I needed to know if he believed me guilty of killing the people whom I had loved and the one I had hated. The adult part of myself knew that a young child shouldn't be blamed for making an infantile mistake. The grown woman wouldn't have blamed another little girl for wanting to hold a beautiful doll, but the child that I had been couldn't forgive herself for her tragic error. I attached even greater culpability to the adolescent girl who had ignored the needs and desires of her husband and family, who had lied and deceived, all in the cause of wanting to feel important and to lessen her boredom. Whenever the guilt over Gus's murder gripped me, Adriana's warnings and her belief that my activities were at the root of my barrenness came with it. I would regret for the rest of my life that I had brought such evil down upon by beautiful, innocent Gustavo. And I didn't even have a child as a testament that our love had ever existed.

My guilt over Nathan, however, was in some ways the worst. He had been horrible to me, but he had never overtly tried to kill me. I now knew he hadn't murdered Papa either, but had simply committed an act of omission. I still couldn't deal with the fact that part of me had probably intended for him to die. What kind of woman sends criminals to a close relative's home, knowing they had already committed murder? Would Robert be able to live with such a person? Killing the intruder left to guard us was so far removed from the other situations I hardly gave it any thought. The man had richly deserved what I had given him. But women weren't supposed to have such feelings or to commit such acts. They were supposed to be the innocent victims waiting to be saved by noble knights on blazing white chargers. Could Robert come to grips with my past and accept me as I really was? Would he want to live with such a woman for the rest of his life?

When I finished my tale, Robert was silent for some time. Finally, he took my hand and raised it to his lips. "My poor darling. That you should have suffered so much at such a tender age is unforgivable. If your uncle were still living, I would feel the need to seek satisfaction on your behalf. The man was simply evil. As to your husband's death, there is absolutely no way you could have anticipated what happened. Even if you had stayed in the house and never gone out, those men would still have come. Even if you had simply ridden for pleasure, they would still have broken in. It was not your fault. That you killed a criminal who was harming your family is admirable. It shows you are a woman of principle and courage. I would be proud to call such a woman my wife. Please say yes."

And ultimately I did. We were married some months later in a small private ceremony at Robert's church, Trinity Episcopal. As a wedding gift, Robert unusually took me to Savannah because he understood I had to know what had become of Bess and Papa's sisters. They were all the family I had left. It was a wonderful honeymoon filled with gentle loving and considerable passion.

I rediscovered the city I had visited only once before the war. Its quiet garden squares with their magnolias, azaleas, and camellias, and the beautiful townhouses that surrounded them had almost recovered from Sherman's assault. We spent only two nights in the city and then boarded the Atlanta Special. It made stops all along the way. One of them was at Oconee.

When we got off the train, the stationmaster directed us to a boarding house not far from the depot. Even though evening was closing in, I couldn't wait.

"Robert, I'm sure I can find the house. It's on the main street just before you get to the village square. It can't be far. Oconee isn't very big."

"My love, you don't even know if they're still here. Wouldn't it be better to wait until tomorrow when you are fresh and rested? After all, we really don't know what you will find."

"I've waited for years. I can't wait any longer. Please, Robert."

Against his better judgment, Robert hired a carriage from the nearby livery stable and drove me up Main Street. Some things looked different, but within minutes, a familiar little clapboard house with a white picket fence appeared. I recognized it instantly. With a trembling hand, I lifted the brass doorknocker and let it fall. There was no answer.

I lifted it twice more before a voice called out, "Keep your shirt on. I'ma comin'!"

The door opened and there she was. She had aged, of course. Her hair was now completely gray and her once firm skin sagged into ponderous jowls, but I would have known her anywhere.

"Now what kin I do for you white folks? Let me guess. You bin sent to try and buy my house, ain't you? Well, it ain't gonna work. The Miss MacDonalds, they left it to me in they will and it don't matter who don't like it." Bess crossed her arms and glared.

"Bess, don't you know me?"

"No I . . ." But she stopped mid-sentence. Puzzlement crossed her face and she squinted hard. "Well I'll be. If I didn't know no better, I'd say Miss India MacDonald done come back to life. Who are you girl?"

"It's me, Bess. It's Mary Catherine. Don't you remember me?"

She backed away two steps and screamed. Her hand flew to her chest and she sagged against the wall. Robert rushed to catch her before she fell and eased her into a chair in the front hall. I knelt beside her.

When she had recovered somewhat, she searched my face. "You cain't be. My baby girl died in that godforsaken Brazil where her Papa took her and my Miss Mary Elizabeth. But you do have the look of the MacDonalds about you. That's for sure."

"Bess it's me, Mary Catherine. I promise I didn't die. Ask me anything you want about our life on the farm. Do you remember when I picked off all of Mama's prized rose buds before they even had a chance to break color? Remember the spanking Papa gave me and how I cried in your arms until I went to sleep? You were still holding me when I woke up the next morning."

She stared at me for several moments and then her arms flew around me, crushing me against her ample bosom. "My baby, you done come home. We thought you was dead. Praise God, my baby's alive!"

We cried together, Bess and I, for some time. We sobbed and held each other. We pulled back and let our eyes devour the other's features. After we had calmed enough to make sensible conversation, Bess insisted we remove ourselves from the boarding house. Her baby girl wasn't going to stay with strangers when her Bess had plenty of room, no sir!

Over the course of our week in Oconee, I learned what had happened after we left Georgia. The aunts had kept up correspondence with Papa until his responses suddenly stopped coming. They then wrote letters to Nathan pleading with him to tell them what had become of their beloved brother and niece. Eventually he replied with the news that both Papa and I had drowned in an unfortunate accident. The aunts had never liked my mother's brother and had been suspicious, but they didn't know where to turn. They were much older than Papa, had little education, and had never been particularly strong. When an influenza epidemic struck, they became ill very quickly, dying within a day of one another. They died believing they were the last of their family.

Toward the end of that week, I broached a subject with Bess that Robert and I had already discussed.

"Come to New York and live with us. You took care of me when I was little and I want to take care of you now that you're getting older. It'll be wonderful for everyone!"

"And what if I don't want to go up north? I never been outside Washington County. I cain't just up and leave my home. I ain't so young anymore, you know."

"But you said the white people here have already tried to take this house away from you. With the federal troops gone now, you don't know what's going to happen. It may not be safe. Please, Bess, you're the only family I have left. I can't stand the thought of leaving without you. Robert, talk to her. Make her see sense."

"What Mary Catherine says is true, Bess. There have been reports of lynchings and mob violence against colored people for several years now. It's only a matter of time before that sort of thing happens here in Oconee. I have big house in a good neighborhood in New York. You will have comfort, security, and servants to wait on you for a change. It would be foolish in the extreme to refuse us the pleasure of caring for family, especially someone who is so beloved. Please reconsider and come with us."

I am sad it happened this way, but news of a lynching one county over drove home our point with Bess. She reluctantly packed bags for travel while Robert arranged for the shipment of the furniture she wanted to keep. The house and everything else were put up for sale. A buyer came forward immediately and Robert negotiated a fair price. For the first time in her life, Bess had money of her own and insisted on paying for her own ticket to New York. Together, the three of us went home.

## Chapter 33

My memoir is finished at last. Our sons may not understand why Robert and I decided long ago to tell them only the barest details of my life in Georgia and Brazil. It seemed best at the time. Bess instead filled their heads with tales of their great grandfather's beautiful plantation, the lavish balls he hosted, and of a gallant grandfather riding away to war on his gray stallion. They hated the idea of slavery, but were thrilled that my Papa had been a captain of infantry. They loved looking at his tintype. Even then, a veil of romanticism was being draped over the lost Confederacy, one that it did not deserve. When Bess died in her sleep at age one hundred one, it was like losing Mama and Papa all over again. She was my second mother and the last vestige of my early, happy childhood.

And how exactly do I feel now that I've poured over Nathan's journals again, pressed Mama's handkerchief against my cheek, traced Papa's handsome face with my finger once more, and picked apart my Confederado youth? My sleep has become peaceful. The voices are quiet. I haven't dreamt the dream, not once, since beginning this paper odyssey.

I now understand that a little girl shouldn't have been blamed for her mother's death. It pains me to acknowledge it, but Papa should have given me support instead of sinking into his own misery. He should have gone out on his own the moment Nathan urged him to abandon me. It is what parents are supposed to do, how they are supposed to act. Papa should have taken my side instead of leaving me begging forgiveness for killing Mama and wondering when I would be left alone to fend for myself. I was a child. I didn't bring about the consumption in Kingston and I didn't intentionally get lost. My only crime was in disobeying for a matter of minutes.

And Gus? I will always think of Gus with sadness and regret, but he is now just a faraway memory. After examining the evidence, I believe the intruders would have come with or without my missions for Paulo. They were roaming the vicinity and *Fazenda Oliveira* was well known as the wealthiest plantation for many miles. Even without the tragedy, Gus and I might not have remained happy. Given the culture and his family history, it seems likely we would have settled into the same pattern as his parents. Of course I will never know for sure and I did love him so.

But then there was Robert. I am the most fortunate of women. I have had a wonderful life with a truly good man who gave me two fine sons, both of whom work in their father's bank. I have delightful grandchildren who have brought me incredible joy in my old age. I have had wealth, friends, and position in a city that doesn't easily accept foreigners into its most exalted circles. I have been truly blessed. When Robert passed away last year, Trinity Church wasn't large enough to hold all of the mourners.

As for Nathan? I have come to grips with the fact that I knew he would probably die protecting his treasure. I have returned to the true religion seeking comfort in its familiar traditions and liturgy. I go to confession each week and pray that God will forgive me. Father Joe tells me that I couldn't have known for sure, that Nathan could have chosen to give up his gold, that I was trying to save innocent women. But *I* know. And I will live for whatever time remains with the knowledge that I committed at least this one great sin. I have accepted that I must forgive Nathan if I am to receive forgiveness. It is difficult even now, but each day my hatred of him feels smaller.

And my South American relations? Father Joe is trying to help me trace Paulo through the monsignor's office in Rio. There is a small chance he still lives. He would be over ninety, so I don't hold out much hope. If he is found, I will seek answers to questions that have plagued me since fleeing Brazil. I need to know what became of my father-in-law and Marguerite. I pray that contact can be established with Henry and Fatima's children or grandchildren. Bess encouraged me to write to them, but I never had a reply. I don't know if they even received the letters. Since Adriana and Ricardo were illiterate, Henry was my only hope of getting word to them that I was safe and for me to know that they were beyond Constancia's grasp. I wonder sometimes what has become of *Fazenda Oliveira*. I suspect it is now in the Church's possession.

A muffled plopping against the darkened windows tells me snow has begun falling again. The grandchildren will be delighted. My feet are like ice and I won't hear the end of it if my son and daughter-in-law find out that I turned off the heat and sat all evening with only a thin wool shawl draped over my nightgown. But I would rather be cold than suffocated by confounded mechanical heat. I've never gotten completely accustomed to these winters or to the drying effects coming from that infernal contraption under the front window. Flames flickering gently in an open fireplace and a mantle clock softly chiming the hours are much more pleasing to my way of thinking. Robert's little shell basket now sits under a glass dome on my bedroom mantle. It decorates a blocked up, useless fireplace. Modern times. More's the pity.

The news from Europe on the radio tonight was frightening and it occurs to me that time is running out for more persons than just myself. It's hard to believe the Hun is rampaging across the continent for the second time in a generation. But that jumped-up, jackleg, vulgar little German with the silly mustache seems determined to bring his neighbors to their knees. His obscene ranting is surely that of a madman, but one who has captured the minds and hearts of an entire nation. How the culture of Bach, Beethoven, and Goethe could have fallen so low is beyond my understanding.

The sound of my bedroom door banging open startles me, but the sight of the two tousle-headed moppets tumbling through the opening fills me with unexcelled joy. I shall gather my grandbabies in my arms and hold them tight for they now are the loves of my life and expectations of my future.

Check out this other book from Linda Bennett Pennell:

Excerpt from *Al Capone at the Blanche Hotel*

CHAPTER ONE
*Saturday
June 14, 1930
O'Leno, Florida*

Jack jammed a finger into each ear and swallowed hard. Any other time, he wouldn't even notice the stupid sound. The river always sorta slurped just before it pulled stuff underground.

His stomach heaved again. Maybe he shouldn't look either, but he couldn't tear his eyes away from the circling current. When the head slipped under the water, the toe end lifted up. Slowly the tarpaulin wrapped body, at least that's what it sure looked like, went completely vertical. It bobbed around a few times and finally gurgled its way down the sinkhole. Then everything went quiet.... peaceful.... crazily normal. Crickets sawed away again. An ole granddaddy bullfrog croaked his lonesomeness into the sultry midnight air.

Crouched in the shelter of a large palmetto clump, Jack's muscles quivered and sweat rolled into his eyes, but he remained stock-still. His heart hammered like he had just finished the fifty yard dash, but that was nothing to what Zeke was probably feeling. He was still just a little kid in lots of ways.

When creeping damp warmed the soles of Jack's bare feet, he grimaced and glanced sideways. Zeke looked back with eyes the size of saucers and mouthed the words I'm sorry. Jack shook his head then wrinkled his nose as the odor of ammonia and damp earth drifted up. He'd always heard that fear produced its own peculiar odor, but nobody ever said how close you had to be to actually smell it. He prayed it was real close; otherwise, he and Zeke were in big trouble.

The stranger standing on the riverbank stared out over the water for so long Jack wondered if the man thought the body might suddenly come flying up out of the sinkhole and float back upriver against the current. Funny, the things that popped into your head when you were scared witless.

The man removed a rag from his pocket and mopped his face. He paused, looked upstream, then turned and stared into the surrounding forest. As his gaze swept over their hiding place, Jack held his breath and prayed, but he could feel Zeke's chest rising and falling in ragged jerks so he slipped his hand onto Zeke's arm. Under the gentle pressure of Jack's fingers, Zeke's muscles trembled and jumped beneath his soft ebony skin. When Zeke licked his lips and parted them like he was about to yell out, Jack clapped a hand over the open mouth and wrapped his other arm around Zeke's upper body, pulling him close and holding him tight. Zeke's heart pounded against the bib of his overalls like it might jump clean out of his chest.

With one final look round at the river and forest, the stranger strode to the hand crank of a Model T. The engine caught momentarily, then spluttered and died. A stream of profanity split the quiet night. The crank handle jerked from its shaft and slammed back into place. More grinding and more swearing followed until the thing finally coughed to life for good and a car door slammed. Only then did Jack relax his hold on Zeke.

"I want outta here. I wanna go home," Zeke whispered hoarsely.

Lucky Zeke. Before Meg left home to move into town, Jack would have felt the same way. Now he didn't care if he ever went home.

Jack cocked an ear in the Ford's direction. "Hush so I can listen. I think he's gone, but we're gonna belly crawl in the opposite direction just to be sure we ain't seen."

"Through that briar patch? I ain't got on no shoes or shirt."

"Me neither. Come on. Don't be such a baby."

"I ain't no baby," Zeke hissed as he scrambled after Jack.

When the pine forest thinned out, Jack raised up on his knees for a look around. Without a word, Zeke jumped to his feet and started toward the road. Jack grabbed a strap on Zeke's overalls and snatched him back onto his bottom.

"You taken complete leave of your senses?" Wiping sweat out of his eyes, Jack pushed his shaggy blonde hair to one side. "Check it out before you go bustin' into the open."

"Why you so bossy all the time? I ain't stupid, ya know. Just cause you turned twelve don't make you all growed up."

Zeke's lower lip stuck out, trembling a little. Whether it was from fear or anger, Jack wasn't sure. Probably both. Peering into the night, he strained for the flash of headlights. Nothing but bright moonlight illuminated the road's deep white sand. Finally confident that no vehicles were abroad, he grabbed Zeke's hand and pulled him to his feet. With one final glance left, then right, they leapt onto the single lane track and ran like the devil was on their tails.

## CHAPTER TWO

*August 15, 2011*
*Gainesville, Florida*


Liz Reams glanced at the caller ID and grimaced. She didn't have time for this, but guilt wouldn't let her put the conversation off any longer. Sighing, she pressed the talk button and prepared to listen with forbearance and humility.

"Hello, Roberta. I'm so glad to hear your voice. I was beginning to think we were going to play phone tag forever." Internally, Liz squirmed. Her conscience yelled, *liar, you returned calls when you figured you'd get her voicemail.*

Roberta's reply made Liz cringe. While she endured the diatribe pouring through her cell phone, Liz eyed her purse, book bag, and laptop case huddled together on the sofa. She couldn't afford to be late today of all days. Her eyes narrowed as her gaze paused on her laptop. She had paid more than a month's rent for the thing, but as much as she loved its power and speed, it was also a constant reminder of her dereliction. It only compounded her guilt that everything Roberta said was true.

"I'm really, really sorry. I know I said you would have it by now, but I've been in the process of moving. You know what that's like."

Several expletives burned through Liz's earpiece and then there was ominous silence.

"Look, I know how lucky I am to have a career practically dropped into my lap. You've been wonderfully patient and I've let you down. I feel so bad. I promise, no later than October...." Glancing at the calendar, Liz paused. "I mean November 1. I just need to get the first couple months of teaching behind me, then I can focus on the novel."

An angry question barked through the ether.

Liz tried to keep her voice cheerful and her tone even. "Of course I'm still seeing Jonathan. You know he's the reason I moved to Florida. You'll have something by November 1. I promise. I've really got to go."

The call ended with Roberta's appeal to conscience ringing in Liz's ears, leaving her feeling like an ungrateful, spoiled child. Poor Roberta. She deserved better. Several years ago while on semester break and bored out of her mind, Liz dashed off a few ideas and half a manuscript. On a whim, she sent Roberta, a friend of a friend, a query letter for a series of mystery novels and the sample chapters. She'd been amazed by the response. Roberta had been more than enthusiastic. She believed Liz could be the next Mary Higgins Clark. Liz was thrilled and flattered, but alas, her attention to her fiction had been stop-start at best. Now with the move to Florida, she had a terrible inkling her new situation wouldn't allow time to finish her long overdue first novel.

While her first allegiance had to be to her professional responsibilities, after one of Roberta's talks, Liz would be unsettled for days. She feared her editor might be right: that a lucrative career was hers for the taking, that academia paid squat, and that Liz would live to regret neglecting her fiction for dusty research libraries, unwashed college students, and writing articles for esoteric journals that nobody read. As to the new deadline, Liz snatched November 1 out of thin air, but crossing that bridge could wait. Giving herself a last once over in the living room mirror, she slammed her apartment door and dashed to her Prius for the twenty-minute trip to campus. This job was a fabulous last minute save and Liz had no intentions of blowing it.

The security guard in the building's reception area checked his list and gave Liz a set of keys, two of fairly recent vintage, one battered and old fashioned. He then directed her to the third floor wing housing the University of Florida history department's administrative suite. According to Maria, the departmental secretary, Liz's office was finally cleared of the previous occupant's possessions. After winding through the old building's maze of hallways, she stood before a door that could have used a fresh coat of varnish. She considered the set of keys and selected the one that looked as old and tarnished as the door's heavy Yale lock. Inserting and turning it, she heard the click of the lock's tumblers. She flung the door wide and peered into the sanctum from which she would now conduct her professional life.

*My lord, girl, what you're willing to do for love.*

*Al Capone at the Blanche Hotel* now available on Amazon: http://tinyurl.com/mzknxdz

# Book Club Discussion Questions

*Confederado do Norte*

1. What do you see as the themes running through Confederado?

2. Does Mary Catherine's story change in any way how you define family?

3. Why did Bess love Mary Elizabeth and Mary Catherine despite being in bondage to their family?

4. How would you evaluate Mary Catherine's father?

5. Was Mary Catherine's work for Father Paulo wise or foolish? Was it motivated by a desire to do good or by willful selfishness? Did her actions bring the thieves to the *fazenda*?

6. What defines citizenship? Was Mary Catherine American? Brazilian?

7. What within Mary Catherine created her feelings of guilt and the belief that she had killed four people? Could the society into which she was born have played a part?

8. Did Mary Catherine love Gus or was it more lust that prompted her to marry him against her better judgment?

9. Did she love Robert when she married him? How were her feelings for her two husbands alike? How were they different?

10. Do you believe that Mary Catherine sent the intruders to Nathan believing they would kill him or was it simply an act of desperation during a crisis? Is her late in life admission accurate or another example of her taking on undeserved guilt?

11. How would you define Mary Catherine's actions and choices?

# Biography

Linda has been in love with the past for as long as she can remember. Anything with a history, whether shabby or majestic, recent or ancient, instantly draws her in. This love probably comes from being part of a large extended family that spanned several generations. Long summer afternoons on Grandmama Bennett's porch or winter evenings gathered around her fireplace were filled with stories both entertaining and poignant. Of course being set in the South, those stories were also peopled by some very interesting characters, some of whom have found their way into Linda's work.

As for her venture in writing, it has allowed Linda to reinvent herself. She has this to say about reinvention: "We humans are truly multifaceted creatures, but unfortunately we tend to sort and categorize each other into neat, easily understood packages that rarely reveal the whole person. Perhaps you, too, want to step out of the box in which you find yourself. I encourage you to look at the possibilities and imagine. Be filled with childlike wonder in your mental wanderings. Envision what might be, not simply what is. Let us never forget, all good fiction begins when someone says to her or himself, "Let's pretend."

CPSIA information can be obtained
at www.ICGtesting.com
Printed in the USA
FFOW04n1953050218
44816788-44963FF